THE TWO EMILYS

Sophia Lee (1750-1824)
Engraving by William Ridley after a drawing by Sir Thomas Lawrence
Originally published in *The Monthly Mirror* (August 1797)

VALANCOURT CLASSICS

THE TWO EMILYS

by

Sophia Lee

Edited with an introduction and notes by
Julie Shaffer

𝕶𝖆𝖓𝖘𝖆𝖘 𝕮𝖎𝖙𝖞:
VALANCOURT BOOKS
2009

The Two Emilys by Sophia Lee
Originally published as Volume II of *The Canterbury Tales*
(London: G. G. & J. Robinson, 1798)
First Valancourt Books edition 2009

Introduction and notes © 2009 by Julie Shaffer
This edition © 2009 by Valancourt Books

All rights reserved. The use of any part of this publication reproduced, transmitted in any form or by any means, electronic, mechanical, photocopying, recording, or otherwise, or stored in a retrieval system, without prior written consent of the publisher, constitutes an infringement of the copyright law.

Library of Congress Cataloging-in-Publication Data

Lee, Sophia, 1750-1824.
 The two Emilys / by Sophia Lee ; edited with an introduction and notes by Julie Shaffer. – 1st Valancourt Books ed.
   p. cm. – (Valancourt classics)
 Originally published as volume II of The Canterbury tales under title: The young lady's tale (The two Emilys), 1798.
   ISBN 1-934555-53-3 (alk. paper)
 1. Mistaken identity–Fiction. 2. Good and evil–Fiction. I. Shaffer, Julie A., 1955- II. Lee, Sophia, 1750-1824. Canterbury tales. III. Title.
   PR3541.L2T86 2009
   823'.6–dc22
                                              2009007416

Design and typography by James D. Jenkins
Published by Valancourt Books
Kansas City, Missouri
http://www.valancourtbooks.com

CONTENTS

Introduction	vii
Sophia Lee: A Brief Chronology	xli
Acknowledgements	xliii
Note on the Text	xliv
Reproduction of the First Edition's Title Page	xlv
Genealogical Table of the Characters in *The Two Emilys*	xlvi
The Two Emilys	1
Notes	200
Appendix A: Contemporary Reviews of *The Two Emilys* and Biographical Sketches of Sophia Lee	212
Appendix B: Literary Correspondences	213
Daniel Defoe, *Moll Flanders*	223
Hannah Cowley, *The Belle's Stratagem*	229
Charlotte Smith, *Montalbert*	241
Homer, *The Odyssey*	252
Appendix C: Accounts of the 1783 Calabrian-Sicilian Earthquake	257
Bibliography	273

INTRODUCTION

GIVEN Sophia Lee's prominence as an author in the late eighteenth and early nineteenth centuries, it is in some ways mystifying that she is not well known today even to most scholars of British women writers of the period. She was successful as a playwright; her 1780 comedy, *A Chapter of Accidents*, played on the London stage about one hundred times in the two decades after it was written and well into the early decades of the nineteenth century as well as being translated into numerous languages, and she received praise for her 1796 tragedy, *Almeyda, Queen of Granada*, which was performed with the title role played by Sarah Siddons, perhaps the most celebrated actress of the period.[1] One of her works of fiction, *The Recess* (1783, 1785), considered to be the first historical or gothic-historical novel, was highly admired by contemporaries and influential on authors such as Ann Radcliffe and Sir Walter Scott. According to one critic, it in fact led to her being "one of the best-known novelists of her day."[2] She also, with her sisters, ran perhaps the most respected girls' school in Bath in the late eighteenth century, Belvidere House. Yet few readers know about her now, and of those, fewer will have heard of *The Two Emilys*.

Here is what we do know about her:[3] She was christened Sophia Priscilla Lee by her parents, actors John and Anna Sophia Lee, on May 13, 1750, in London, where she was probably also born. Siblings that

---

[1] For reasons not entirely clear, however, it had a very short run: initially, four nights. On expostulation, it was played on the last night of the season at Drury Lane Theatre, where it was supposed to be performed the following season. That proved to be the last night on which it was performed, however. Despite critical approval, it thus played only five nights total. On its performance history, see April Alliston, Introduction, *The Recess*, Lexington: University Press of Kentucky, 2000, xxxiii-xxxiv.

[2] James R. Foster, "The Abbé Prévost and the English Novel," *PMLA* 42.4(1927): 455.

[3] Most of what we currently know about Sophia Lee is based on April Alliston's extensive research, which is presented in the "Introduction" and "Chronology of Events in Sophia Lee's Life" in Alliston's edition of *The Recess* and in entries written by her in the *Oxford Dictionary of National Biography* (H. C. G. Matthew and Brian Howard Harrison, eds, Oxford: Oxford University Press, 2004. 60 vols. 33: 120-121). These and other sources will be cited where pertinent in this account.

lived to adulthood included Charlotte, born around 1748; Harriet, born in 1757; Anna, born around 1760; and George Augustus, born in 1761. Another brother survived into his twenty-first year, but on him there is little information (Allison, Introduction xxv). Sophia Lee did not grow up solely in London, however; the family moved around quite a bit, not only in England but in Scotland and Ireland as well. Anna Sophia Lee worked in Dublin from 1751-52, and it is reasonable to assume that the couple's two daughters, aged three and one, accompanied her there. John Lee followed, but the family moved to Edinburgh for the 1752-56 theater seasons. They thereafter returned to Dublin and then traveled back and forth between London and Bath, ending up in the latter in 1777. During this time, John Lee also spent time in debtor's prison, and he was accompanied there in 1772 by his daughter Sophia, who was then twenty-two. It is there, ostensibly, that she derived the plan for her first publication, *The Chapter of Accidents*, which was inspired in part by Jean-François Marmontel's "Lauretta" and included at least one character derived from Denis Diderot's *Le Père de Famille*.[1] The play was first produced and published in 1780, and as this was also the year in which her father fell ill, it is reasonable to assume that Lee wrote and had her play performed and published to earn money that she and her sisters would need if her father were to die soon.[2] With money she earned from

---

[1] "Lauretta" was first published in the third and last volume of Marmontel's *Contes Moraux*, originally published in French in 1761 but translated into English as *Moral Tales* as early as 1764. *Le Père de Famille* was first published in 1758. Lee asserts that she did not read Diderot's play until after she completed early versions of her own and that any further resemblance is purely coincidental (*Chapter of Accidents* iii). Few seem to take her assertion seriously, the *Dictionary of National Biography*, for instance, claiming that it is based on Diderot's play (Edited by Leslie Stephen and Sidney Lee, London: Smith, 1908-09, 22 vols., 11: 821). Similar claims are made by James Boaden (*Memoirs of Mrs. Siddons*, Philadelphia: Carey, 1827, p. 102), and Edward A. Bloom and Lillian D. Bloom (*The Piozzi Letters: Correspondence of Hester Lynch Piozzi, 1784-1821*, Newark: University of Delaware Press, 1989-2002. 6 vols., 6: 175 n.6).

[2] Susan Sibbald mistakes the situation and work in question when she claims that Sophia Lee "wrote a play called 'The Recess,' which was so much admired, that she got nearly enough to release her Father, and some other work entirely paid his debts" (Francis Paget Hett, ed., *The Memoirs of Susan Sibbald (1783-1812)*, New York: Minton, 1926, p. 36.) Given that John Lee was in debtor's prison in 1772, Sophia Lee's 1783-85 publication of *The Recess* (discussed below) could

INTRODUCTION   ix

this play, she opened a school in Bath with her sisters in December of that year, not a bit too early, as their father died in February 1781. Lee continued to write and publish regularly, if not prolifically, for the next two decades. In February 1783 Lee published the first volume of the novel for which she is principally known today, *The Recess*, about the fictitious twin daughters of Mary, Queen of Scots; the second and third volumes of this three-volume novel were published in 1785. She is sometimes credited with translating François Thomas de Baculard d'Arnaud's *Varbek*, in English called *Warbeck: A Pathetic Tale*.[1] In 1787, she published *The Hermit's Tale*, a 156-stanza poem, and probably by late in 1793, she completed *Almeyda, Queen of Granada*, which was acted, after many postponements, in 1796. Her next two pieces of fiction were part of her collaboration with her sister Harriet in a series of tales, modeled on Chaucer's, called *The Canterbury Tales*. This collection was composed of five volumes published from 1797 to 1805. Most of the tales were written by Harriet, who had begun her own career as an author in 1786. Sophia's contributions to *The Canterbury Tales* were the general introduction in volume one, in 1797; a tale that constitutes the whole second volume in 1798; a shorter tale in the third volume, in 1799; and a paragraph conclusion following that tale, which presents those three volumes as the authors' daydreams. All the tales in the final two volumes are Harriet's. Sophia Lee's next publication came in 1804; this was the six-volume *The Life of a Lover*, a work Lee claims to have written much earlier in life. Her next and last work offered to the public was

---

hardly have helped him in that case. He had, in any event, died two years before the novel's publication. Even *The Chapter of Accidents* itself was not produced and published until eight years after his release from debtor's prison.

It is unclear whether Anna Sophia Lee was still living at this time. Philip H. Highfill, Jr., Kalman A. Burnim, and Edward A. Langhans provide 1770 as the year of her death ("Lee, Mrs. John, Anna Sophia." *A Biographical Dictionary of Actors, Actresses, Musicians, Dancers, Managers, & Other Stage Personnel in London, 1660-1800*. 16 vols. Carbondale: Southern Illinois University Press, 1973- ca. 1984, 9: 210. Alliston, however, provides evidence to suggest she was alive in 1776 (Introduction xxvi, xli-xlii) but no information is available on when Anna Sophia Lee did then die.

[1] *Warbeck: A Pathetic Tale*. 2 vols. London: Lane, 1786. Antonia Forster, for instance, attributes this translation to Lee, in her *Index to Book Reviews in England 1775-1800* (London: British Library, 1997, 246), as does Janet Todd (*Dictionary of British Women Writers*, London: Routledge, 1989, 406).

a play, *The Assignation*, which failed at Drury Lane Theatre in 1807 because erroneously reputed to be libelous. It was never published.

Some biographers represent Lee as having started her career to make the money she needed for what they considered to be the more respectable purpose of running a school and so forming young ladies, but Lee's publication record belies such a representation of her life.[1] If such claims were true, she would have ceased publishing once her school became successful. It is true, however, that money she earned from *The Chapter of Accidents* enabled her to open her school in 1780, and it was probably in part because of the success of *The Recess* that the sisters, with Sophia at the helm, were able to move their school to Belvidere House in 1786. It is also true that much of her time was absorbed by overseeing this school, which the sisters ran until 1803, and we could surmise that Lee may have written more if she had had more time. As it is, however, she was publishing regularly throughout this period.

Their school was no doubt a time-demanding enterprise. April Alliston writes that, "In 1797 there were seventy-two students there, of which fifty-two were boarders" (Introduction xxx), the latter of which were housed in "ten good bed chambers;"[2] these pupils, Alliston notes, ranged in age from five to nineteen. The Lees themselves did not teach; for that, there were "two governesses and

---

[1] One obituary notice states, "the correct judgment and singular prudence of Miss Lee early induced her to prefer a permanent situation and active duties [of running her school] to the dazzling, but precarious, reputation of a popular author." This obituary notes, however, that Sophia Lee was able "at intervals [... to find] relaxation in the indulgence of her genius" ("The Late Miss Sophia Lee," *Blackwood's Edinburgh Magazine* 15 [1824], 476). Another biographical notice asserts the reverse, saying that it was only after she got her school running that she was able to "[give] way to her literary propensities, and employed the luxury of her leisure in the exercise of her pen," even presenting Lee as having written *The Chapter of Accidents after* she started her school, although it was her earnings from that play that enabled her to open her school ("Biographical Sketch," *The Monthly Mirror* 4 [1797], 8). As Alliston points out, this biographical notice likewise treats running a school as superior to being an author; it stresses that "personal diligence and professional employment are [preferable to] the precarious honour and profit of writing for a theatre, or of any other visionary scheme of life" (*Blackwoods* 476, quoted in Alliston, Introduction xxix). For these articles, see Appendix A.

[2] George James, quoted in Bloom and Bloom (1: 249-250 n.7).

three female teachers in residence" along with masters who were brought in to teach subjects the resident teachers did not (Alliston Introduction xxx);[1] subjects the pupils learned included grammar, geography, French (which the girls had to speak during school hours), writing, arithmetic, music, drawing and dancing (Hett 41, 44). The Lees' school was so popular that girls frequently had to wait to join the ranks of such pupils as Sarah Siddons's daughter Cecilia. When one prospective pupil, Susan Mien, later Sibbald, was interested in going to school, a family friend advised her to enroll at Belvidere House, saying that it was "the best school she knew of," but adding that "the Misses Lee [...] were so well known, and respected, and their School so highly thought of, that application had to be made some time before for the admission of pupils"; she suggested, in fact, that applicants were so numerous that the Misses Lee "might double the number [of their boarders], if they had accommodation." Mien was able to enroll in the following term only because one girl fell sick and after vacation "was too ill to return." (Hett 34, 32). Pupils sincerely admired Lee.

Charlotte married and left the school in late 1792 or early 1793. Sophia, Harriet, and Anna closed the school in 1803 and moved to South Lyncombe, outside of Bath. Anna committed suicide there in 1805, and Sophia and Harriet, understandably, did not want to remain where this happened, so they left to stay with their brother, George Augustus, in Manchester. They then moved near Tintern Abbey, in Wales, and later, to Clifton, close to Bristol. Sophia died there in 1824 and was buried in the churchyard of St. Andrews, which was destroyed in World War II.[2] Harriet died twenty-seven years later, in 1851.

Neither woman ever married, although a courtship between Harriet and the Italian marquis Lorenzo Trotti was forwarded in 1791 by her friends Penelope Sophia Pennington and Hester Lynch Piozzi, the latter of whom was still hoping in 1793 that the match would proceed.[3] This relationship did not lead to a proposal because,

---

[1] Susan Sibbald claimed that there were three governesses when she attended, starting in 1795 (38).
[2] April Alliston, "Lee, Sophia Priscilla," *Oxford Dictionary of National Biography*. 61 vols. New York: Oxford University Press, 2004. 33: 121.
[3] On Harriet Lee's relationship with Trotti, see Alliston (Introduction xxxiii) and various letters in Bloom and Bloom, especially those from 28 July, 1791, to 20 November, 1791 (1: 355-377). On 4 November, 1793, Piozzi wrote to Pennington that

as Trotti told Hester Piozzi's husband, "if he married a Woman of inferior Birth, such were his *peculiar* Circumstances, that exactly one half of his Estate would be forfeited" (Bloom and Bloom I: 372). Harriet did receive a proposal from William Godwin, however, in June, 1798, less than a year after the death of his wife, Mary Wollstonecraft in September 1797;[1] interestingly, Godwin wanted to meet Harriet after reading some of her contributions to *The Canterbury Tales*, just as he wanted to meet Mary Wollstonecraft after reading her *Letters Written During a Short Residence in Sweden, Norway, and Denmark* (1796).[2] Harriet turned down Godwin's proposal, however, because he showed inadequate respect for her intellect and religious beliefs. Sophia Lee enlarged her family in about 1793, when she adopted Elizabeth Tickell, daughter of the brother-in-law of playwright Richard Brinsley Sheridan, to whom she also dedicated *The Hermit's Tale*. The sisters had an active social life, but their main relationship seems to have been the one they shared with one another, which provided each with a lifelong companionship that by all signs sustained them both.

The Literary Output

As I suggested at the beginning of this Introduction, it is hard to understand why Sophia Lee is fairly unknown today, even among scholars. Her varied output demonstrates her versatility as an author: she wrote comedies and tragedies for the stage, an epistolary historical gothic novel set in the sixteenth century, an extended verse narrative set in the thirteenth century, and a short story and a novel-length tale set in her present. And the highly successful reception of some of these works, along with the influence *The Recess* had on

---

Trotti was to return from a trip on the continent and that he was sure to return to Harriet, saying, "I told you he had the arrow fast in his heart. I *told* you *so*" (quoted in Oswald G. Knapp, ed. *The Intimate Letters of Hester Piozzi and Penelope Pennington, 1788-1821*. London: Lane, 1914, 100). She was, of course, wrong.

[1] On Harriet Lee's relationship with Godwin, see Alliston (Introduction xxxiv).

[2] Alliston asserts that the "Lee" in his memoranda of people he wanted to meet listed much earlier, in 1786, was probably in fact Sophia (Introduction xlii-xliv, n.108).

later authors, should have prolonged interest in her work. There are various reasons why interest in it has lapsed.

First, she was in many ways dwarfed by her larger-than-life father, even if she had gained, as Alliston asserts, "a name to rival her father's in the theatrical world" (Introduction xxvii). In some biographical notices and obituaries ostensibly about her, much of the content—in one case nearly all the content—focuses on John Lee, who supposedly rivaled actor David Garrick and was notorious for his difficulties with theater management.[1] For the most part, plays, no matter how well respected at the time, and regardless of the cast originally performing them, seem to have the shortest shelf life of genres of literature in most readers' tastes. In the case of her fiction, while Sophia Lee is justly admired for *The Recess*, her achievement is again dwarfed, this time by the reputation of those she influenced most: Ann Radcliffe, called "the mother of the gothic," and Sir Walter Scott, mistakenly considered the originator of the historical novel. *The Life of a Lover*, at six volumes, is, as contemporary reviewers noted, simply too drawn out and, as a result, tedious.

The fiction she contributed to *The Canterbury Tales* had its own problems in attracting positive attention when it was first published. One is, quite simply, that it appears only as a part of a set of short stories with its own title. This is especially unfortunate in the case of *The Two Emilys*, which makes up the whole of the second volume of this five volume work, where it is titled "The Young Lady's Tale. The Two Emilys." Given its length, it could have been published as a free-standing novel, as it indeed was at least twice before this edition,[2] and had it been thus published originally, it might have fared better with the critics, increasing its chances of remaining in readers' attention in the decades and centuries that followed. Instead, it was criticized as being unrealistic in terms of its very presentation. Very

---

[1] Excerpts focusing on Sophia Lee can be found in Appendix A. The full text of these reviews, including information on John Lee, can be found on Lee's author page on *Corvey Women Writers on the Web*, <http://www2.shu.ac.uk/corvey/cw3/AuthorPage.cfm?Author=SL2>.

[2] The story was published as a stand-alone novel in 1798, as *The Two Emily's* [sic] (Dublin: Moore) and shortly after Lee's death, in 1827, as *The Two Emilys* (London, n.p.). Because it is printed here as a novel, I have dropped the introductory part of the title—"The Young Lady's Tale"—as well as the quotation marks, and I have italicized the title.

roughly following the model provided by Chaucer's *Canterbury Tales*, the Lees' work as a whole was introduced as a series of tales told by travelers who in this case become snowbound in Canterbury while on their way elsewhere; one traveler suggests to the others that they pass time by amusing each other with stories. A tale that takes up 564 pages clearly is not one that a single character would tell in such a situation. Had the tale been presented as a novel, the reception may have been different. As it was, the story received only brief notice in some presses as having appeared; simply as worthy the pens of the two sisters; unrealistic; or flawed stylistically. In Appendix A, I provide the only substantive reviews of this tale.[1]

To situate Lee's achievement in *The Two Emilys* in terms of the rest of her literary output, a brief summary of her other work may prove useful, especially in terms of commonality of themes and strategies.[2] The commonality I will stress here—there are others, of course—is the protagonists' illegitimacy or perceived illegitimacy, or their marginality in their communities. In the first work she presented to the public, *The Chapter of Accidents*,[3] a young woman from the country, Cecilia, has sexual relations with the male protagonist, Frank Woodville, son of Lord Glenmore; they do so due not to depravity but to momentary weakness. Cecilia remains an outsider in part by virtue of the fact that her rank cannot be established—she is, to the best of our knowledge, simply the ward of a Welsh clergyman, Grey. Frank wants to make her the reparation of marriage, but he also knows his father would disapprove of his marrying a woman beneath him in rank; Glenmore also wants Frank to marry Sophia, Glenmore's ward. What equally makes Cecilia objectionable as a wife for Frank, in the eyes of his family, is that his maternal uncle, Governor Harcourt, wants Frank to marry his own daughter, whom he left at an early age with a country clergyman in Wales in the belief that keeping her out of London society would ensure that she

---

[1] Recent critics do not consider Lee's work in *The Canterbury Tales* particularly good, preferring her sister's. Janet Todd, for instance, says that "H[arriet] L[ee]'s contributions [are] far more arresting than her sister's" (406). The *Dictionary of National Biography* entry on Lee asserts that "Sophia's work is far inferior to Harriet's" (11: 821).

[2] The one available text I do not discuss here is Lee's *The Life of a Lover*; I do, however, discuss it in a later section.

[3] *The Chapter of Accidents*, London: Cadell, 1780.

remained pure.[1] Of course this daughter and clergyman turn out to be Cecilia and Grey, as we discover at the play's *dénouement*. Before then, Cecilia's sexual lapse also marginalizes her, placing her outside of the ranks of the marriageable. It does so in her mind, at least; she says that marrying him "was, when [she] was innocent, so far above [her] hopes, as it is now beyond [her] wishes [...] love cannot subsist without esteem; and how should [she] possess [his] when [she has] lost even [her] own?" (22). Her marginality based on her lack of social rank becomes erased when the truth of her birth is revealed, and, interestingly, her marginality based on her lack of chastity is erased because she regrets her fall; Grey declares her "purified and forgiven" and tells her, "you are now most truly entitled to esteem; since it requires a far greater exertion to stop your course down the hill of vice, than to toil slowly up toward virtue" (98).

Almeyda, Queen of Granada,[2] deals with marginality in a different way, based on the female protagonist's both belonging to and not belonging to two cultures at war. She is a Moorish princess who was given up as a hostage as a child to Ramirez, King of Castile, when he won Granada. The play starts when her uncle, Abdallah, pays a ransom that gives him back both Almeyda and Granada. She resists being relinquished to the Moors because, as Ramirez's daughter Victoria points out, Almeyda has been raised to be as much a Castilian as a Moor: she "ever knew to blend / Th'eccentric, noble wildness of the Moor, / With ev'ry polish'd grace of our Castile" (10). Furthermore, she and Alonzo are in love, while Abdallah wants her to marry his son, Orasmyn, and so solidify his family's right to the throne. All here ends in tragedy; Almeyda believes that Alonzo, who has come to seek her, has been killed; she temporarily loses her mind and ends up poisoned by Abdallah, who then poisons himself, leaving only Alonzo and Orasmyn to join in mourning Almeyda's end.

---

[1] This same notion drives much of the plot of William Wycherley's *The Country Wife* (1676). There, one character, Pinchwife, believes that by marrying a country girl, he will be safer from being cuckolded, and it is possible that he would have been right, had he not brought his wife to London and inadvertently made her wish to experience the pleasures it offered. Cecilia is not, however, the simpleton that Pinchwife's wife Marjory is. An adaptation of this play has been attributed to John Lee (*The Country Wife* [...] *Altered from Wycherley*, London: Lowndes, 1786).

[2] *Almeyda, Queen of Granada*, Dublin: Wogan, Byrne, Brown, and Folingsby, 1796.

The Hermit's Tale also revolves around marginality, based in part on the permeable borders between nations at war and individuals at odds with one another when they ought to be united. It tells the story of Edmund, a young shepherd, who has been raised by his mother Emma in the borderlands between England and Scotland, near the Cheviot Hills. Emma's husband denied his marriage to Emma and abandoned her while she was pregnant with Edmund. Edmund loses his mother when he pursues Scots who have come to steal their herds. He triumphs against the sheep thieves but returns to find that his village has been destroyed, its inhabitants killed. "Turn[ing his] sheep-hook to a sword" (7), he sets up towers and raises troops to keep out the Scots. He ultimately discovers that he belongs nowhere at the same time as he discovers the truth of his origins. He falls in love with a young woman, Ethelinda, who is caught by his sentinels crossing the border. At her request, he escorts her back to her father, Lord Ethel, on the shores of the Severn, a river that itself is of no one country, flowing through both England and Wales; it remains unclear whether her father's home is in England or Wales, making her own nationality unclear, adding to the sense of the permeability or even irrelevance of borders. When Lord Ethel then offers Ethelinda to a baron, Lord Albert, she makes it clear that she wants to marry Edmund. Her unlicensed lover ultimately triumphs in a duel he instigates with Lord Albert in a chapel, placing Edmund outside of any law recognizing the sanctity of such a location. Lord Albert confesses on his deathbed that he married and abandoned a woman named Emma near the Cheviot Hills. The man Edmund battled for the rights to a woman, in other words, and over whom he triumphed, is his father. Discovering his father thus proves the boy's legitimacy at the same time as it makes him an Oedipean patricide. Meanwhile, Ethelinda, thinking she is going to be forced to marry Lord Albert, takes poison, guaranteeing her death at the moment when she could become united with the man she loves; their fates are thus the same as Almeyda's and Alonzo's.

 The second story Sophia Lee contributed to *The Canterbury Tales*, "The Clergyman's Tale,"[1] similarly deals with rifts within families and nations and with attempts by the marginalized to find their positions within their culture. Here, a Welsh toddler who speaks

---

[1] *The Canterbury Tales*, Vol. 3 (1799), 195-521.

no English is in effect kidnapped by an Englishman, Pembroke. Pembroke has wanted a son in part to counter his wife's spoiling their daughter Caroline. He names the boy Henry, has him taught English, and then treats him as his own son, telling his wife that Henry is his illegitimate child by a girl who seduced him at a country inn. He sedulously keeps Henry's fictional and true origins secret from Henry himself. Henry's situation becomes untenable when he learns the version of the truth that Pembroke has told his wife; he decides that only he can be responsible for his own name's having any value, and that he can ensure that it does only by making his own way, as a soldier. He is the more driven to do so because his role within his family is doubly impossible: he feels romantic love for Caroline, a form of love clearly not appropriate for blood siblings, at least, to feel for one another.

We discover that his true parents' story is equally problematic. His true father, Hubert Powis, fell in love with Agnes, daughter of the local clergyman, Aubrey; Hubert knew that his father, Sir Hubert, would not accept a marriage between Hubert and Agnes because she was so beneath them in rank. She agreed to marry him only if her own parents gave permission, and he tricked them into doing so by suggesting that he seduced her and wanted only to make reparations, as Woodville wanted to do in *The Chapter of Accidents*. Hubert and Agnes then wed, after which he told her parents that she was in truth pure. He was coerced, however, into accepting a commission that took him out of the country, ultimately to America. Sir Hubert would not recognize his son's and Agnes's marriage, and she apparently drowned herself and her son, whose body was of course never found. Her father surmised that her suicide resulted from shame that she was believed not to have been married, to have borne Henry—or Edmund, as he was named by Agnes, after his paternal grandfather—out of wedlock. The living characters are brought together and their stories revealed because in America, Hubert, under the pseudonym "Cary," unwittingly befriends his own son and returns with him to Great Britain—to Wales, as it turns out, where Pembroke is visiting the home of Lady Trevallyn, who turns out to be Caroline. In America, Cary has been father and no father; Pembroke both is and isn't Edmund's father; Agnes is thought to be no wife, and Henry is thought to be illegitimate and English, whereas he isn't even "Henry." Nearly everyone lives with double identities and no true identities, cast off, not belonging to, or wrested from their parents and countries of origin.

The very conceit of *The Recess*[1] makes it fairly obvious that its protagonists, Matilda and Ellinor, are marginalized, being the (fictive) daughters of the clandestinely-married Duke of Norfolk and Mary, Queen of Scots, the latter of whom is already Queen Elizabeth's prisoner when the novel begins; they too are thus Elizabeth's enemies—in theory, at least, and in fact, once she learns their lineage. As it turns out, Matilda and Ellinor are the more marginalized by being the product of an inadvertantly bigamous marriage; Mary did not realize, when she married Norfolk and became pregnant with these twin daughters, that her husband Bothwell was still alive. Their status is every way marginal and contradictory. While they may be legitimate claimants to the throne as Mary's daughters, they are illegitimate as a result of Mary's inadvertent bigamy, nullifying their entitlement to the throne. Yet in their eyes—and in those of supporters of the Stuarts—their claim to the throne may nonetheless be more justified than Elizabeth's.[2]

Politically and socially marginal by birth, the sisters' marginality is also physical or spatial in that they are raised in the recess of the title, a subterranean abode near St. Vincent's Abbey, well out of Elizabeth's reach. They are raised by Mrs. Marlow, a woman of illegitimate birth herself who has sequestered herself in the recess after discovering that the man she married, who was also conceived out of wedlock, is her brother. Ellinor and Matilda's status becomes no less marginal when they emerge into the world beyond the recess, as their stories subsequently demonstrate: when they first venture out, they are discovered by Lord Leicester, who is fleeing Queen Elizabeth's wrath; Matilda shortly thereafter marries him and he bears her and her sister to Kenilworth Castle. He presents them as his brother's daughters by Lady Jane Grey (81), a story the queen does not believe, although she does not yet have any inkling of the truth of their birth. His position too then becomes precarious under the fickle Elizabeth,

---

[1] *The Recess*, London: T. Cadell, 1783-85; I refer, however, to the edition recently edited by April Alliston (Lexington: University Press of Kentucky, 2000).

[2] For a discussion of the sisters' contradictory status—or as she says, their liminal status—see Anne H. Stevens, "Sophia Lee's Illegitimate History," *The Eighteenth-Century Novel*, 3 (2003), 263-291.

especially once Matilda becomes pregnant. He escapes with her to France and is assassinated there; she is bound prisoner and taken to Jamaica, where, after a series of misadventures, she is imprisoned by the governor for the first several years of her daughter Mary's life; when the governor dies, Matilda is aided by Anana, his mistress of African descent, and returns to England. The life of Matilda's daughter Mary is equally tragic; she falls in love with the Earl of Somerset, a married man, and, after other problems, is poisoned by his wife.

Ellinor, meanwhile, falls in love with Lord Essex, but Elizabeth discovers that she is Mary Stuart's daughter and forces her to sign a paper saying that she and her sister are not Mary's daughters, threatening otherwise to execute Mary; Elizabeth also coerces Ellinor to marry a man Ellinor does not love. As history has of course shown, Elizabeth had Mary executed in any event—to Ellinor's horror, with the acquiescence of their brother James, who becomes king of Scotland on Mary's death. From the aggregate of misery with which Ellinor is afflicted, she loses her wits intermittently, ends up wounded in a scuffle between her husband and Essex, becomes imprisoned by her husband's heirs once he dies, escapes by faking her own death, follows Essex to Ireland disguised as a male, ends up the captive of the Irish chief Tyrone, escapes only to fall for a time under the power of a Scottish laird, and is liberated only to find Essex "tried—sentenced—condemned" (256), leading to the final alienation of her intellects.

There is no legitimate place in England for these two daughters of Mary's secret marriage. Various plots to legitimate them and thereby challenge Elizabeth's (or James's) reign simply by presenting them as Mary's offspring lead only to exile and imprisonments. There is equally no legitimate place for them in Scotland, where James has done so little to protect their mother that he is unlikely to prove anything other than traitorous as a brother. They cannot unify Scotland and England under one (female) monarch; their and other characters' hope that they might do so is as illusory as they are fictional.[1] There is, finally, no place at all for Matilda and Ellinor in history.[2]

---

[1] Mary's son, James VI of Scotland, succeeded Elizabeth as James I of England (and Ireland). Scotland and England were not finally unified, however, until the 1707 Act of Union, under Queen Anne.

[2] See Stevens, however, for a discussion of Lee's using these characters in her "illegitimate history" to suggest that a different form of history may offer more truths than more conventional history.

What links all these stories is a concern with dislocation and dispossession, characters' (in)ability to fill their roles as one might predict, whether these roles be political, national, or familial. Lee explores these issues in part through her treatment of characters' national origins, the extent to which nationality defines the individual; to differing degrees, her doing so can be seen as political, as asking her readers to consider the state of those making up the British nation. Her exploration of these issues is perhaps least obvious in *The Hermit's Tale*, where Scottish invasions of northern English territory and the English Edmund's desire to marry a woman from the borderlands between England and Wales might be seen as suggesting primarily the instability of the family, given that the major plot revelation is Edmund's discovery of his father, hence his own identity, at the moment that he kills his father. The war within the family in this case can be seen as writ large by the war between different parts of the kingdom—northern England and Scotland, England and perhaps Wales. To the extent to which this is true, Lee might be considered as asking her original readers to think about the divisions in their own nation, which should then have made her a more controversial author than she was in her time. Seeing her as thus controversial or political here however is countered by the extent to which Edmund's attempts to keep the border impermeable can be seen as personal, psychological. His attempts to do so can be seen as an effort to find identity through eliminating what one is not, especially in the case where the lack of a father means no one can confer legitimacy on the son. This being the case, readers need not have considered whether the story was particularly about the state of their own nation.

While Lee's treatment of dispossession and dislocation as bound up with national identity is not in the foreground of *The Hermit's Tale*, the opposite is true in *Almeyda*, where characters love and identify with their enemies but may not marry them. Such is most obviously the case with Almeyda, given her feeling herself more Castilian than Moorish. Here, while Lee politicizes warfare between nations and shows its impingement on the personal, she again avoids doing so to ask British readers to consider the state of their own nation because she places the action in the south, in Spain—southern Spain, in fact—and in the past: too distant in space and time, perhaps, to seem to be about their own nation to Lee's original readers.

In *The Recess*, Lee obviously foregrounds the issue of war between countries that make up one nation—or struggles within that nation for control of the throne. By setting it in Britain's fairly recent past, she might be considered as asking her readers to recognize the damage that is done by internecine warfare such as she explores there, and to see it as applicable to their own time. In "The Clergyman's Tale," Lee brings home the issue of disparities in power and indeed respect between the different parts of the nation in part by setting the tale in her own readers' time. She does so as well by the way that Pembroke sees the Welsh—as nearly savage—and by the fact that he feels little compunction about stealing a Welsh child. That the child is Welsh indeed makes his kidnapping safer, because, speaking no English at the time he is kidnapped, the child can tell no one with whom he shortly thereafter comes into contact that he *has* been kidnapped; by the time he has learned English, he has forgotten his origins. Yet the state of the Welsh, and their identity as Britons, is not foregrounded here, which again might allay concern among readers about Lee's politics. As we shall see, Lee treats the issue of marginalized Britons more overtly in *The Two Emilys*, where one character is killed in the Jacobite invasion of England in 1745 and another is viewed as uncivilized because of her Irish origins.

Lee's own experience growing up and moving around in all parts of the nation—not only in England and Scotland, but in England's colony, Ireland—might make her particularly sensitive to the dispossession or lack of power one might experience by being born or spending much of one's life at or outside of England's borders. Witnessing the lives of Scots and the Irish might have made her more sensitive to these people's experiences—their experiences as second-class citizens, so to speak; one might therefore conclude that she was suggesting that her readers might want to ameliorate such marginalization.

One can take this in another direction as well, however, and consider the ways identity itself is susceptible to incursions and fragmentation. By depicting characters' identities as fractured, split by their split allegiances or marginalization, Lee in part calls into question the continuity or coherence of identity altogether, sharing, then, a view of identity promulgated in Lee's own century by David

Hume.[1] In the case of the first-person narratives—*The Hermit's Tale* and *The Recess*, which is made up of Matilda, Ellinor, and their friends' letters—we can see the characters using writing to try to ascertain, establish, or indeed create their identity—to find the moment that makes identity coherent, or to legitimize themselves and their place in their culture and history. As Heather Lobban-Viravong asserts, however, Matilda and Ellinor's very attempts to do so are counterproductive because autobiographies are of necessity constitutive fictions, if only because they must be incomplete and because memory is selective. And inserting such a fiction—especially when the autobiographist is a fictional character—within an account of actual history, as Lee does in *The Recess*, at least, can lead to readerly objection, as was the case with some reviewers of *The Recess*. Lee's combining fiction with history, the unbelievable with the plausible, was in fact consistently a problem in the eyes of some of Lee's reviewers, who objected to the more fantastic elements of her fiction in particular.[2]

The Two Emilys

In *The Two Emilys*, marginality and attempts to establish an accurate, cohesive identity drive the story and dog its characters. Before I discuss what Lee gets out of these issues in *The Two Emilys*, however, I would like to comment on the novel's opening pages, which otherwise seem fairly irrelevant to the plot.

The main story of *The Two Emilys* is that which concerns Emily Arden and her relationship both with her arch-nemesis, Emily Fitzallen, and her cousin, the Marquis of Lenox. In the original 564 pages of this novel-story, however, it takes Lee 49 pages to get to these characters. We start instead with an apparently superfluous outline of the political allegiances of the ancestors of Emily Arden and the Marquis. In part to help readers keep track of these characters and their relations, I have supplied a family tree facing the begin-

---

[1] Heather Lobban-Viravong develops this point in "Bastard Heirs: The Dream of Legitimacy in Sophia Lee's *The Recess; or, A Tale of Other Times*," *Prose Studies* 29 (August 2007): 204-219.

[2] See, for instance, the reviews in *The Critical Review* and *The Monthly Review*, which are included in Appendix A (pp. 212-216).

ning of the text. We start, then, with two Irish siblings: Sir Edward Arden and Lady Lettingham. Sir Edward marries a Scottish woman, never named, who "ranked kings among her ancestors" (1); perhaps because of his wife's ancestors, he is a Jacobite, siding with the exiled Stuart family. After his wife dies, he takes his son, Edward, and daughter, whom we know only as "Miss Arden," to his sister. He then goes off to support the Jacobite invasion under the leadership of Bonnie Prince Charlie. He is killed at Culloden, however, in the decisive battle that crushed all chances of the Stuarts' return to the throne. Lady Lettingham, who did not share her brother's political views, has her nephew, the new Sir Edward, given a commission by the Duke of Cumberland, the very man who had vanquished the Jacobites at Culloden.[1] She raises both her nephew and niece with what might be considered fairly shallow values, teaching Sir Edward the values of pleasing that Lord Chesterfield famously provided his illegitimate son Philip Stanhope, and teaching his niece artificial means to shine as a polished lady who might gain a husband by external appeal, the only personal appeal she has.

Sir Edward's values improve, however, and he falls in love with an entirely deserving Irish heiress, Emily Fitzallen. Miss Arden, meanwhile, has passed from being the belle of the season to being last year's fashion. To avoid becoming a spinster, she marries Governor Selwyn, a man who has made his money in India. When he then almost immediately dies and she realizes his show of wealth was a pretense, she quickly gains the eye of the bashful, gauche Duke of Aberdeen and weds him. Sir Edward's wife and sister become pregnant at the same time, and it is their offspring who are two of the main characters with whom we are primarily concerned during the balance of the novel. Sir Edward's wife bears a daughter, whom her parents name Emily Arden; the mother then dies, and Sir Edward leaves his daughter to be raised by her maternal grandmother, the Countess of Bellarney. The Duchess of Aberdeen bears a son, the Marquis of Lenox, and while she, unlike Sir Edward's wife, does not die immediately thereafter, she does by the time Emily Arden and the Marquis of Lenox's story gets going. We are left, then, with Sir Edward and his daughter Emily Arden, along with the Duke of

---

[1] When Lady Lettingham's brother, Sir Edward, dies, the title passes to his son, Edward. From this point on, the first Sir Edward is unimportant to the plot.

Aberdeen and his son the Marquis. We add to this Emily Arden's enemy, Emily Fitzallen, a girl of uncertain origins who is raised alongside Emily Arden by the Countess, as the Countess's ward and goddaughter.

Why, given that we are involved primarily with the young Emily Arden and the Marquis of Lenox, do we need to know their grandparents' histories and views? What does it matter that the first Sir Edward is a Jacobite and that his sister is not? It arguably matters that Lady Lettingham and the first Sir Edward were born in Ireland, because, as we shall see, it is important for the story that the female protagonist, Emily Arden, be raised in Ireland, and it is on a trip to the estate that the younger Sir Edward inherits from his father—in Ireland, of course—that he meets the woman he weds; it makes sense that the second Sir Edward remains there once married and that when his wife dies, he leaves his daughter in Ireland with her grandmother. It seems to make less sense that we need to know that Sir Edward's father, the previous Sir Edward, is a Jacobite.

I am not ready to argue that Lee supports the Stuart cause—though her sympathy in *The Recess* towards the fictive daughters of Mary Stuart would make it seem that she might—nor that she questions Hanoverian reign. Given her treatment of the Welsh Edmund/Henry, it might make sense that she is sympathetic to the plight of the Welsh or, indeed, of the Irish, as her treatment of Emily Arden suggests. It is impossible, however, to ascertain her political views on the basis of her novels. By focusing on the history of Emily Arden's grandfather, though, Lee asks us to think of issues she raises in *The Recess*, especially, but also in her other work: the issue of lineage and succession, something that proves to be quite central to *The Two Emilys*. Furthermore, focusing on that history prepares us to see the story's characters as outsiders and asks us to think about where to locate the correct seat of power, even when power is not defined solely in terms of politics or might. The history of the Arden family invites us, in other words, to rethink the margins and the center and to imagine an alternate form of power to that which the characters (and Lee's readers) inherit. Such an idea might explain why the novel is not set in England at all, taking place instead in Ireland, Scotland, and, later, Italy. To develop these ideas any further, however, requires my giving away surprising plot twists and turns, so readers who want the pleasure of discovering such surprises while reading the novel should stop reading this introduction here.

Warning: Spoiler Ahead!

Much of the story is driven by the fact that Emily Arden and the Marquis's parents decide, when their children are born, that the two should wed when of age. While the main problem twenty-first-century readers may see here is that we believe first cousins should not marry, such was not considered to be a problem at the time. It was not considered incest for people (or characters) to do so, and in a lot of literature, and some of life, first cousins do (or did) indeed do so.[1] Perhaps the best known literary example is Fanny Price and Edmund Bertram, in Jane Austen's *Mansfield Park*. Their marriage in fact seems necessary to bring proper values back into (seats of) inherited power. In *The Two Emilys*, then, there are two quite different problems that make this match undesirable, at least in the mind of the Marquis of Lenox. One is that he resents having his hand thus bestowed without his consent; the other is that because his cousin Emily has been raised in Ireland, he believes she must be a countrified rustic, not at all suitable as wife for an urbane young man such as himself. He has been told, after all, that he "might chuse, and reject, [a woman] in any house in England" (19); he need not resort for a wife to someone raised in Ireland, a colony of England's, and not, in English views, a thoroughly civilized one. But he is wrong in the way he imagines Emily; Ireland is not presented as backward, and, raised as a Countess's potential heiress, Emily Arden is as genteel a young woman as he could hope to meet. We might want him also to consider that as a Scot, even one who will inherit a title and estate, he is hardly central to English culture himself; his title and estate, after all, are Scottish.

While in disguise at a masquerade party, she learns his opinion of her, or the way he imagines her to be, and is mortified. Having been raised to think of him as her future husband and liking what she sees at this masquerade party, however, she simply sets out to

---

[1] On these issues, see Glenda Hudson, *Sibling Love and Incest in Jane Austen's Fiction* (New York: St. Martin's, 1992); see also *In-Laws and Outlaws: Kinship and Marriage in England* (New York: St. Martin's, 1987), especially p. 21.

court him in another disguise, since he won't court (or even meet) her as herself. She passes herself off as Marian, the ostensible daughter of a farmer on his father's estate. He falls in love with her, proposes, and is accepted. Ironically, then, she gains his love in the form under which he originally rejected her—as a rustic. He then sets off with her father on the Grand Tour of Europe—a tour titled young men made to enable them best to fill their future roles as legislators. Emily foolishly does not reveal her true identity to him before he leaves.

Emily Fitzallen is able to turn Emily Arden's use of disguise to her own benefit. This Emily had hoped to gain the Countess's fortune, but due to a momentary lapse in her plotting, fails at her purpose. When the Countess dies, Emily Arden inherits her wealth and Emily Fitzallen is left penniless. Emily Fitzallen then swears to seek revenge on Emily Arden and does so by meeting the Marquis on the Grand Tour, representing herself as Emily Arden, and marrying him. Taking Emily Arden's identity and the man she wanted to marry certainly offers a promising start to her revenge.

The Marquis is saved from being bound in marriage to the wrong Emily—of even consummating that marriage—by one of the most absurd and unbelievable occurrences in any fiction I have read: an earthquake that throws him into the sea and, as far as he knows, swallows up his bride—an earthquake that, curiously enough, actually occurred, and with the devastating results that Lee depicts.[1] The apparently widowed Marquis is then able to unite himself with the right Emily when he finally meets her. Emily Fitzallen, however, is not dead after all and returns to assert that as she is his legitimate wife, Sir Edward's now-pregnant daughter is no wife at all. Emily Fitzallen is not the only character to return from the dead; when Sir Edward discovers that his daughter's marriage is invalid, he shoots the Marquis and leaves him for dead, but the Marquis returns in the guise of a statue of a faun. Emily Arden fakes her own death, the two become "Mr. and Mrs. Irwin," and they head off to live unmolested by Emily Fitzallen or Sir Edward. When Emily Arden catches

---

[1] For a different use of this earthquake in literature, see below (xxxix-xl). For accounts of this earthquake by eyewitnesses and other contemporary commentators, see Appendix C.

and is disfigured by smallpox, they return to Bellarney and live there incognito, as tenants on the estate that is rightfully hers.

I provide this plot summary to highlight the different ways that characters become marginalized, ejected from their own legitimate lives and identities. The novel makes heavy use of masquerade, after all, not just in Emily Arden's and Emily Fitzallen's courtship of the Marquis, but in the Marquis's return to Emily Arden ostensibly from the dead; in their passing as the Irwins; and in her own disfigurement, which effectively masks who she is to everyone but her husband and one servant, who saw her both before she caught smallpox and after she was transfigured by it. For characters to take their rightful positions—the positions the good characters and we readers want them to take—various forms of self-alienation are required. Emily Arden cannot even meet the Marquis without misrepresenting herself; Emily Fitzallen can best gain revenge by doing so as well; and finally, neither Emily Arden nor the Marquis can find happiness after Emily Fitzallen's return except by passing as other than they are, even giving up the rank to which they were born.[1] It seems unlikely, until near the novel's end, that they can retrieve that rank. Furthermore, it is not until the final *dénouement* that we know for certain that their marriage is even legitimate; until then, they simply decide it is because they want it to be. Yet they know that Emily Fitzallen has a wedding certificate that both the Marquis and Sir Edward recognize as regular and legitimate, officiated over by a priest and signed by witnesses and the parties involved.

Emily Arden, then, goes from being a colonial heiress to being a Scottish peasant, a bride, a mistress and mother of an illegitimate child, an Irish peasant on her own estate, to, finally, head of that estate. That estate, however, is Irish, meaning that she remains a

---

[1] This was a point that Hester Piozzi saw as one of the novel's least believable points; in a letter of 1 August 1798 to Penelope Sophia Pennington, she writes, "Sophia's charming Pen leads one to read on and to perswade oneself for a moment, from line to line, that a Woman made completely ugly should be able to inspire the tenderest Passsion, and have Power beside to keep a Man from enjoyment of all those Pleasures his rank, and that of their Children entitles him to. *This may be so*, but Lothayre's Story of the Skeleton is nearer to my *Credence*" (Bloom and Bloom 2: 513). "Lothayre's Story of the Skeleton" is Harriet Lee's tale, "The Old Woman's Tale. Lothaire," in the first volume of *The Canterbury Tales* (1797), 331-396.

colonial. As such, however, Lee is able to represent that estate and relations on it as something other than readers might immediately call to mind were the estate English (though they might have similar views about it to those the Marquis originally has). The estate, interestingly, passes to Emily Arden through the maternal line; it comes to her from her maternal grandmother. And it remains under female reign.[1] After the convoluted series of events that brings us up to the Marquis's return in the form of a faun, the Marquis recognizes that it was his reticence to meet Emily Arden in the first place, along with his mishandling of his affair with Emily Fitzallen, that was at fault for all of Emily Arden's and his own suffering; he therefore gives over control of their destiny to her, "solemnly vowing, that, whatever line of conduct would give most ease to her mind, should be that he would implicitly abide by, as the only atonement he could make her" (122) and adding, "no duty can come in competition with that I owe the angel my love has unhappily humbled, but could never elevate" (123). It is she who decides, then, the mode by which they should live thereafter,[2] and, given the way the novel ends, with all the good characters reconciled and living together, it is clear that she is the center of power there, albeit not a power that functions by force; she is the lodestone that keeps the family and wider community close:

> Virtue and sweetness, personified in Emily, formed the centre of a wide circle—their mingled beams diffusing a glowing happiness over her own immediate family—a warm interest towards her friends,—and an affecting benevolence among her dependants; while supplying, in her regulated mind, now an example to her father and husband, and now to her children, she had the rare felicity of seeing not one of the many was ever tempted, through

---

[1] Megan Lynn Isaac stresses the bonds of female lineage and family, in a loose sense, that another of Lee's works, *The Recess*, suggests are important; see her "Sophia Lee and the Gothic of Female Community," *Studies in the Novel* 28.2 (Summer 1996): 200-218.

[2] As this summary makes clear, Emily Arden is very active in this novel, in courting the Marquis and then in directing how they should live, including coming up with and executing the idea of faking her own death. I thus differ from Todd, who calls Emily Arden "a morally forceful but inactive heroine" (406).

the course of her long life, to diverge from the sphere of so dear an attraction. (199)

It is worth noting that the notion of the woman as the moral center of the household—as any center of the household—was not prevalent when Sophia Lee wrote *The Two Emilys*; it really only developed during the nineteenth century. For Lee to suggest that a woman should be the decision maker in the home, the one with the better knowledge to make decisions regarding the family's domestic welfare and comfort, was fairly daring. This novel therefore participates in a shift that increasingly presented women as the moral center of the domestic sphere, one that becomes fairly well established by the 1840s, when writers such as Sarah Stickney Ellis wrote books about women's role in the home such as *The Women of England* (1839), *The Wives of England* (1843), and *The Mothers of England* (1844), and that becomes further solidified in such works as Coventry Patmore's *Angel in the House* (1854-56) and John Ruskin's "Of Queen's Gardens," in his *Sesame and Lilies* (1864).

One might argue, in fact, that it is necessary for Lee to put her characters through such dislocations in order to create these new roles and to prepare her characters for them. Only by starting with politically marginal characters such as Jacobites, and such topographically marginal characters as her Scottish and Irish protagonists, can Lee suggest that the traditional center—London and English polite society—will not be the one she will advocate. Only by alienating characters from their identities, delegitimating some and relegitimating some, can new identities be formed for them. And one could argue that to form such a different value system, wherein women are the decision makers and valued as such, requires painful dislocations. Lee thereby suggests that the paradigm shift she advocates cannot come easily.

Doubles, Desire, and Masquerade (warning: spoiler continued!)

As the discussion of Sophia Lee's work in the preceding two sections makes clear, there are certain character types and plot sequences to which Lee returns repeatedly; there are also certain character types and plot sequences that evoke the work of other authors. One of the devices she uses, for instance, both in works before *The Two Emilys* and in that story, is the doubling of the female protagonist. In *The Recess*, that was Matilda and Ellinor; in *The Two Emilys*, it is, as the doubling of the name suggests, the two Emilys to which the title most likely refers: Emily Arden and Emily Fitzallen. Whereas in *The Recess* the doubles are on the same side, here, the two doubled characters are in competition. Predictably, the good Emily—Emily Arden—is light-haired, a Snow White-type heroine, while the bad Emily is dark-haired. In *The Recess*, the doubling of Mary's daughters gives us primarily a reiteration of the same tragic story, though the characters try to make their way in their world in different ways. Matilda marries Leicester, which ultimately leads to his exile from the kingdom and his assassination; Ellinor refuses Essex at key moments, urging him to serve his name (and his country). These different strategies come to naught; both women end up hopeless outsiders, punished for their very attempts at legitimation, and the men they love fare no better. What is startling about *The Two Emilys* is that while rivals, both Emilys act in very similar ways, complicating the extent to which we can see one as good, the other bad. Most notably, they both engage in masquerade to gain the Marquis in marriage.

That they do so is problematic for a number of reasons. First, women were not supposed to initiate or pursue romantic relationships; they were supposed to be open only to loving the man sanctioned for them.[1] That the two Emilys nonetheless pursue the Marquis is in line, in many ways, with Lee's treatment of female desire elsewhere.[2] In *The Chapter of Accidents*, it is Cecilia's desire for Woodville that makes her susceptible to engaging in sexual relations

---

[1] As Samuel Richardson explains, "That a young lady should be in love, and the love of the young gentleman undeclared, is an heterodoxy which prudence, and even policy, must not allow. But [...] applied to [on behalf of her lover by her approving parents], she [if 'inclination opposes not' their choice] is all resignation to her parents" (*Rambler* 97, 1751). Ruth Bernard Yeazell also discusses this point in her *Fictions of Modesty* (Chicago: University of Chicago Press, 1984), 41-42.

[2] As the following discussion makes clear, I differ from Alliston; she asserts that after "'rigid moralists'" judged *The Chapter of Accidents* harshly because of Lee's lenient treatment of Cecilia, "Lee had learned her lesson, and everything she presented to the public after it [...] conformed more strictly to the codes of late eighteenth-century feminine virtue" (Introduction xiv).

with him. She may be responding to his desire for her, but she is not sanctioned to do so; neither of them are sanctioned by parents to pursue the match, even had they been willing to postpone consummating it until after a wedding. Some critics in fact objected to the play on the grounds that it did not adequately punish Cecilia, in their minds, for her fall, and Lee responded to this in the preface to the published version of her play, saying that she wanted to "introduc[e] into the Drama a female heart, capable of frailty, yet shuddering at vice, and perhaps sufficiently punished in her own feelings," matched with "a lover, whose error was likewise in his heart, not head; and [... suffering the] chastisement in the agony of losing her" (ii), and was then surprised that "in adopting a religious tenet, I could ever be accused of offending morality" (ii).[1]

In *Almeyda* and *The Hermit's Tale*, the main female characters also desire and love where they should not. Almeyda, after all, loves Alonzo, the son of the Moors' enemy, Ramirez. Both his father and her uncle disapprove of this match to such an extent that her uncle, at least, tries to have him—and her—killed. She is so intractable in her desires that she cannot accept the wooing of Abdallah's son, Orasmyn, even though Orasmyn is obviously an excellent man, one who is willing to wait until she chooses him and who saves his main competitor, Alonzo.[2] Her desires for a politically inappropriate mate finally lead to her death and to the disruption of a people who are, after all, left without the queen they expected to lead them. Ethelinda, in *The Hermit's Tale*, has a similar situation; it is because

---

[1] Catherine B. Burroughs stresses the eroticism implicit in this play in her "British Women Playwrights and the Staging of Female Sexual Initiation: Sophia Lee's *The Chapter of Accidents* (1780)," *European Romantic Review* 44 (2003): 7-16. She also notes that, "Katharine Rogers has suggested that portions of Sophia Lee's writing (especially her novel, *The Recess*) are shaped by an erotic imagination" (8). Megan Lynn Isaac agrees, saying that in *The Recess*, "the knowledge of female passion and desire is just one of the hidden secrets Lee wishes to announce [...] Lee openly admits [...] that women experience sexual desire" (207).

[2] Audiences and readers recognized Orasmyn's valor, despite his being a Moor, a character to which Lee's audience could have responded with reservation. In a letter written on 17 August, 1796, for instance, Hester Piozzi wrote to Penelope Sophia Pennington, "Like yourself I was all for *Orasmyn*." (Bloom and Bloom 369).

she loves Edmund that she rejects Lord Albert, the man her father has chosen for her, leading to a battle between her father's men and the soldiers accompanying Edmund, then leading finally to her own and Lord Albert's death and Edmund's becoming a patricide and choosing to become a hermit. One could argue that by killing off these female figures, so to speak, Lee is punishing them for their improper desires, but the two are made too sympathetic, too much the victims of others' plotting, to be seen thus.

We then get similar situations in Lee's *The Life of a Lover*,[1] although it may not at first be evident. This novel is about the travails of a young woman, Cecilia, who must work for a living and spends some time teaching, primarily as a governess.[2] Cecilia falls in love with Lord Westbury, the married father of the children for whom she has been hired to be a governess; most of the novel is about her relationship with him. She remains chaste but is believed to have fallen and she suffers for it, corroborating her view that "Reputation may be endangered even when integrity yields not" (1: 272). We recognize that had she yielded, her situation would be even worse; as it is, however, readers might see her woes as deserved based on the fact that she is attracted to and even writes to her married lover. Another female character, Lady Killarney, has sexual relations with numerous men, and she is exposed and judged harshly; her story too, then, shows that a woman who falls will suffer.

But Lee also includes an otherwise virtuous female character, Miss Fermor, who is drugged and raped by her married cousin (3: 50-51), as Clarissa is by Lovelace in Samuel Richardson's *Clarissa* (1747-48); like Clarissa, Miss Fermor has foolishly eloped with the man to whom she is attracted, leading to her rape. Miss Fermor retreats to a convent on the continent, but when her seducer dies, Cecilia suggests she should return. Cecilia asserts that because he did not expose Miss Fermor, she should therefore "banish from [her] own mind circumstances which now exist only in that," thereby mini-

---

[1] *The Life of a Lover*, London: Robinson, 1804.
[2] Boaden says, "It has been said, that much of Miss Lee's personal history may be discovered in *The Life of a Lover*. Cecilia, like herself, is engaged in the work of tuition, for which I have always understood the fair author to have been singularly accomplished" (103). No one who reads the book could consider it as in any way containing Lee's experiences, however.

mizing her culpability in her fall. While we might see Miss Fermor as no party to her sexual fall, raped characters in literature of the time rarely survive, their dying signaling that women who have sex outside of marriage, whether willing parties to it or not, cannot be recuperated into their society. We may see Miss Fermor as guiltless, in other words, but Lee's readers might be less likely to do so. By this point, Lord Westbury's wife dies and he marries Cecilia, who adds here that he "participates the delight of his wife in becoming the means of restoring you to society" (4: 293). Amelia Fermor, however, rejects this view, but not because she believes Cecilia is wrong; she does so because she still loves her seducer/rapist. Her story then adds, perhaps, to the view that those who fall, or even desire, deserve to suffer. But Miss Fermor does not dwell on herself as fallen and she does not receive the harsh judgment that Lady Killarney and even Cecilia receive; the novel does not therefore offer any reason to think that Cecilia is wrong.

Lee complicates the issue by including another character whose pre-marital fall is excused. Sally, the maid of Cecilia's friend Sophia, has gotten pregnant by her lover, Joseph; she had "by a confidence too common among rustic lovers, and a little excusable from her having no mother to advise or guard her—trusted the peace of her life to Mr. Joseph's honour" (4: 140-141). They were plighted to one another, however, but when her father died and turned out to have his affairs in disrepair, Joseph's father forbade the match. The community knew they were virtually married and that "nothing but the ceremony was wanting." Sophia gave Joseph's father the money he thought should come to him as father of the groom and the two "rustic lovers" wed; Sophia avers that "the defect in our [...] bride's shape was hardly thought to be a blemish now she was made an honest woman of" (4: 142). It is true that people of Sally and Joseph's class held themselves to less strict rules on marriage, believing that being plighted to one another was as good as a church wedding at showing their community that they were, in effect, husband and wife. It is nonetheless surprising that someone of Sophia and Cecilia's class goes along with this view, showing an awareness and acceptance of female desire and sexuality.

In *The Two Emilys*, Lee makes it clear that Emily Arden's admiration of the Marquis before he shows that he likes her, as well as her attempts to gain him, are improper, a view Lee highlights as generally held when she writes that, "accustomed to consider the husband elected for her as the being on earth she would have chosen for herself, the gentle Emily knew not the revolting spirit that man often thinks virtue" (21).[1] She is, however, sanctioned in this match by her father and uncle. Her father, after all, has spoken all her life about his hopes that she would marry the Marquis, meaning that the Marquis is, in Sir Edward's eyes, a sanctioned lover. When she disguises herself as Marian, she does so with the knowledge and encouragement of both Sir Edward and the Duke of Aberdeen, the Marquis's father. Nonetheless, she does pursue a man before she knows that he has chosen *her*, and by eighteenth-century literary convention, at least, doing so is immodest and improper. Furthermore, she is puzzled when the Marquis balks at consummating their marriage. Because Emily Fitzallen has appeared at his wedding to Emily Arden, he thinks she might return to claim her previous right to him and puts off doing anything that would compromise Emily Arden. It is only when he (erroneously) believes that Emily Fitzallen, who has disappeared again, has disappeared for good that he has sex with Emily Arden. That the novel spends time on her puzzlement about this—her expectation, indeed hopes, that they will have sexual relations—appears fairly forward in literature of this period.

In some ways, the impropriety of a woman's pursuing a man is highlighted by the fashion in which Emily Fitzallen gains the Marquis. Rather than simply presenting herself as Emily Arden, she disguises herself as Hypolito—a young man—and gets hired as a drawing tutor by Sir Edward and the Marquis while they are on the Grand Tour. She wins not only the Marquis's friendship but, finally, his desire. In a key scene, the Marquis returns tipsy from a party, admires Hypolito, whose shirt is slightly undone, and we get this:

> "'For your own credit and mine,' cried the Marquis, gaily seizing his young favourite by the shoulder, 'row, ride, drive, dig—do something to get rid of this white skin, and those delicate hands; for I cannot long stand the raillery I have encountered for this month past; and you must make up your mind to be considered as a woman in future, unless you contrive to get something more the look of a man.'" (48)

---

[1] "Revolting spirit" here meaning reticence.

Hypolito reveals that s/he is in fact a woman and only then takes advantage of the Marquis's not knowing what Emily Arden looks like to claim to be her, at which point they wed. What may be considered particularly troubling—or particularly interesting—about Emily Fitzallen's winning the Marquis while disguised as a male is that the Marquis *does* desire Hypolito before he knows that this youth is no youth at all, but rather a young woman. As far as he knows, he feels same-sex desire. Her disguise calls into question, then, the stability of his heterosexuality.[1]

To some extent, the different disguises these two Emilys adopt differentiate between them. Masquerade balls were enormously popular during the eighteenth century but also enormously controversial. It was considered problematic that people presented themselves as who they were not; appearance was supposed to provide a seamless portrait of who one was on the inside, as though the trappings of rank and position defined the self. These balls were also notorious for permitting illicit sexual activity; married men and women could have sex with people other than their spouses with relative impunity, because, being in disguise, their true identities were not necessarily obvious. These balls likewise provided a relatively safe space for homosexual men to find partners and have sex with them, something that otherwise was highly dangerous, given prevailing attitudes about homosexuality.[2]

While masquerade was troubling to eighteenth century Britons, there were certain rules that made it less inexcusable than it otherwise might be. One could dress in a way that revealed a truth about oneself that otherwise might not be evident, for instance, or one

---

[1] I focus on the implications of the Marquis's feeling attracted to the cross-dressed Emily Fitzallen at greater length in "Sophia Lee's 'The Two Emilys': When She Was Good, She Was Very, Very Good ... or Was She?" in *Women's Writing* 14.3 (December 2007): 399-418; I focus on the issue of a similar situation in "Cross-Dressing and the Nature of Gender in Mary Robinson's *Walsingham* [1797]," in *Presenting Gender*, edited by Chris Mounsey (Lewisburg, PA: Bucknell University Press, 2001): 136-167.

[2] For additional discussion of the implications of masquerade, see Terry Castle, *Masquerade and Civilization* (Stanford: Stanford University Press, 1986). For a lengthier discussion of masquerade as it relates to this novel, see my "Sophia Lee's 'The Two Emilys'" (402-405).

could dress in a way that revealed who one was by opposition. We might see Emily Arden's disguise as Marian as working thus. It reveals her to be a non-English peasant, which is how the Marquis views his cousin, so it reveals a sort of truth to him, or truth about his attitudes toward her. It also functions by opposition, because she is in no way a simple peasant. This disguise is also fairly excusable because she places herself in an unprivileged, fairly powerless position—as a peasant, a subordinate to men of any rank.

More troubling was masquerade that enabled one to fill a position above one's own, and Emily Fitzallen's functions thus. Passing as a male, she leaves behind the subordination and powerlessness that was considered appropriate for women. In some cases, real women who dressed as males were treated as acceptable or even praiseworthy for doing so, trying to become better than they were thought to be, for instance in the Great Chain of Being, in which males were closer to God than females, who were closer to animals. Sometimes they did so primarily to travel safely, as does Ellinor in *The Recess* (218-252). Otherwise, women who dressed as males—especially to form relationships with other females—were greeted with outrage and were liable to punishment by law.[1] By the rules of masquerade, Emily Arden is thus more excusable than Emily Fitzallen, but given the large body of work against masquerade of any sort, the two may be seen to be alike in choosing to engage in questionable behavior, the more so in that they do so to pursue a man.

In doing so, they both adopt male prerogative, something that Lee foregrounds by having Emily Fitzallen literally dress as a male. And by giving Emily Arden power within the home—by having the Marquis yield to her on important decisions regarding who they will be and where and how they will live—Lee suggests that some women, at least, *should* be granted power more typically males'; she thus advocates masculinization for some women—granting them greater power—and feminization for men—having them give up some of their power. The difference, one might say, is the intention be-

---

[1] Although there were sumptuary laws so that cross-dressing women might have been charged for so doing, women were generally charged for cross-dressing only when they did so to pass for men in relationships with (other) women; they were then typically only for "lewdness" and fraud. I cover this issue at greater length in my "Cross-dressing and the Nature of Gender," especially pp. 140-142.

hind their actions: Emily Arden does what she does for love, whereas Emily Fitzallen does it for revenge. By having the two female characters function as doubles in this regard, Lee is able to define more clearly reasons why women—but only some women—should be granted power.

Interestingly, there is more than just the doubling comprised in Emily Arden and Emily Fitzallen, if names themselves signal doubling; Emily Arden's mother and grandmother are both also named Emily—Emily Fitzallen, in fact, though Emily Arden's mother then becomes the first Emily Arden—and the female protagonist, Emily Arden, names her first child Emily as well; there are, then, five Emilys. Emily Arden's father, Sir Edward, is, similarly, not the novel's first Sir Edward; that would be his father. And he is godfather to the Marquis, whose first name is also Edward, as is Emily Arden and the Marquis's first son; there are then four Edwards. Lee's re-use of characters' names—Edmund and Cecilia in her other works, for instance—might suggest she just had a paucity of imagination and was incapable of coming up with names, but such a plethora of Emilys and Edwards suggests instead a compulsion to repeat and repeat, from generation to generation, until the characters get it right.

Literary and Other Influences

The Two Emilys draws on or points to work of other authors as well as to other work of Lee's own. In early scenes, the first Miss Arden's courtships with Governor Selwyn, her first husband, and the Duke of Aberdeen, her second, draw on similar scenes in Daniel Defoe's *Moll Flanders* (1722); these scenes can be found in Appendix B, on literary correspondences. In depicting Emily Arden as presenting herself to the Marquis as a peasant in order to win his love and his hand, Lee recalls Hannah Cowley's *The Belle's Stratagem* (1782), a play in which the female protagonist, Letitia Hardy, is similarly happy to marry the man her father wishes her to marry, Doricourt, who, like the Marquis, is less interested in the match himself. While the Marquis thinks an Irish woman can be no appropriate match for an urbane man such as himself, Doricourt believes English women to be less attractive than their continental counterparts, saying that the woman he would marry must have "spirit! fire! *l'air enjoué*! that something, that nothing, which every body feels, and which no body can describe, in the resistless charmers of Italy and France" (1.1; p. 233, below). Letitia does not take a disguise of the sort Emily Arden does, when she appears as Marian; Letitia simply presents herself as though she's a countrified ignoramus and then attracts him at a masquerade, where she presents herself as she truly is (albeit while wearing a mask). He then finds himself "charm'd" by this masked woman, by her "English beauty—French vivacity—wit—[and] elegance" (4.1, p. 234, below). Both men have to change their views towards women of the nationality of their intended betrotheds. Excerpts of *The Belle's Strategem* can be found in Appendix B.[1]

In giving her female protagonist the last name of Arden, Sophia Lee draws attention to a potential link between her story and Shakespeare's *As You Like It*, in which the good characters have to retreat to the forest of Arden, where problems in the outside world get solved. One of these is in regards to Rosalind, who dresses as a male and takes the name Ganymede, in part to travel safely to get to Arden, and Orlando, who is in love with Rosalind. He does not know that Ganymede is Rosalind. Ganymede convinces Orlando to pretend that she is Rosalind and to woo her as such, and she thereby trains him in the proper way to treat her. By the end of the play her father, whose kingdom has been usurped, regains that kingdom, Rosalind (as Ganymede) gets her father to sanction her marriage to Orlando, and she then returns to her gender-appropriate dress. This echo of Shakespeare might reiterate to readers that Emily Arden's disguise is necessary to put a world in disarray to rights. *The Two Emilys* also draws on other Shakespeare plays, specifically *A Winter's Tale* and *Much Ado About Nothing*, in both of which a main female character finds her reputation unfairly besmirched and so fakes her death, returning only when the whole of her community, and particularly the man she loves, recognizes her innate purity.

Interestingly, *Much Ado About Nothing* is set in Messina, on Sicily,

---

[1] Oliver Goldsmith's *She Stoops to Conquer* (1773) similarly uses class-crossing masquerade. There, the female protagonist, Kate Hardcastle, learns that the man she is supposed to marry, Charles Marlow, is overly shy around women of his own class. He has already been misled by Kate's brother to believe that he is at an inn while at the Hardcastles' house, however, and Kate takes advantage of this misconception to woo him in the guise of a barmaid.

where key action of *The Two Emilys* takes place. Another novel that is in part set there is Charlotte Smith's *Montalbert* (1795). It too incorporates marital separation and discord due to the earthquake that Lee also includes in *The Two Emilys*. The earthquake in both novels is based on a series of earthquakes and tsunamis that began in February, 1783, in Calabria, in southern Italy, and off the coast of Sicily. These seismic events were devastating and, as I noted above, people were said to have experienced fates similar to those experienced by the Marquis and, supposedly, by Hypolito. Many were flung into the sea or swept into it by tsunamis; others were said to have been nearly swallowed by the earth. In all, over 32,000 were reported to have died from the tsunamis, and countless others from woes derived from the disruption of the water and food supplies and from exposure.[1] Europeans and Americans were very interested in people's experiences in the earthquake, and I have compiled excerpts from reports on it, included in Appendix C, for comparison with Lee's treatment of the event.

Also in the appendices is an excerpt from *Montalbert*, containing Smith's treatment of the earthquake. In her introduction to her recent edition of *Montalbert*,[2] Adriana Craciun suggests that the earthquake functions in Smith's novel in part to highlight the differences between the female and male protagonists. Female protagonist Rosalie, who has become a mother while in Messina, is driven primarily by "maternal love," Craciun notes, which Smith presents as "the strongest passion that the female breast can feel, [and which ...] sustained the timid and delicate Rosalie amidst the real miseries' of the disaster." Rosalie's husband, however—Montalbert—is driven by other passions; rather than search for his wife and son, he first follows the man he believes to have debauched his wife, because for him, "the desire of vengeance was even stronger than parental affection" (quoted in Craciun xi-xii). According to Craciun, his shortcomings—indeed such differences between husbands and wives—are inscribed in "sexual relations and especially the institution of marriage" as they existed in Smith's, and by extension Lee's,

---

[1] For the range in the number of victims given at the time, see Appendix C, p. 257 n.2.
[2] *Montalbert. Works of Charlotte Smith*. 14 vols. London: Pickering and Chatto, 2005-2007. Vol. 8. 2006.

time (vii). While the earthquake highlights the protagonists' differences in *Montalbert* without giving Rosalie any way out, or even suggesting that she wants out, the earthquake functions differently in *The Two Emilys*. Here, it might be seen not only as a comic *deus ex machina* that saves the Marquis from consummating his marriage to the wrong woman—a disruption that ends what Lee's audience would generally have seen as a perversion that should not occur, given both the gender and sexual confusion with which it plays and Emily Fitzallen's iniquitous motivations; it can be seen as symbolically signaling just how wrong things are in the world of her characters and functioning as the extreme rupture that must occur before more beneficial relations within the home can develop.

But such relations do develop and that which is wrong in the world in which Lee's characters move is set right, but to discover exactly how this occurs—with many more plot surprises than I have shared here—readers should now turn to the astounding story that makes up Lee's *The Two Emilys*.

JULIE SHAFFER
Oshkosh, Wisconsin

September 18, 2008

ABOUT THE EDITOR

JULIE SHAFFER is an Associate Professor at the University of Wisconsin Oshkosh, where she teaches courses on the eighteenth- and nineteenth-century British novel and in women's studies. She has edited Mary Robinson's *Walsingham* (Broadview Press) and is currently working on an edition of Robinson's *The False Friend* (Pickering & Chatto). She publishes regularly on British women's novels published in the late eighteenth and early nineteenth centuries and is especially interested in changing constructions of female wickedness and ideal femininity as well as ways these changing constructions arraign men's transgressions.

SOPHIA LEE: A BRIEF CHRONOLOGY

c. 1748	Birth of Charlotte Elizabeth Lee, eldest sister of Sophia Lee
1750	(May 13) Sophia Lee christened in London, in St. Paul's Church, London, by parents John and Anna Sophia Lee
1751-52	Sophia probably in Dublin with her mother
1752-56	The Lees in Edinburgh; John manages his own theater, his wife performing in its company
1756-57	The Lees in Dublin
1757	Birth of Harriet Lee
1757-58	The Lees in London
1758-61	The Lees in Bath
c. 1760	Birth of Anna Lee, youngest sister of Sophia Lee
1761	Birth of George Augustus Lee
1762-68	The Lees in London
1768	Lees move to Bath; John manages Theatre Royal
1772	John sent to King's Bench debtor's prison; Sophia accompanies him there
1772-77	Lees in London
1777-78	Lees in Bath
1780	(Aug. 5) *The Chapter of Accidents* opens at Haymarket Theatre, in London; the play is published later that year
1780	(December) Using the proceeds from *The Chapter of Accidents*, Sophia and her sisters open a girl's school in Bath
1781	(Feb. 19) John Lee dies
	(May 8) *The Chapter of Accidents* first produced at Drury Lane Theatre
1782	(April 23) *The Chapter of Accidents* first produced at Covent Garden Theatre
1783	(February) First volume of *The Recess* published by Cadell
1785	Second and third volumes of *The Recess* published
1786	The Lees move their school to Belvidere House

1787	"A Hermit's Tale" published
1792-93	(Dec. 1792 to Jan. 1793) Charlotte (eldest sister) marries and leaves Belvidere House
1793	Probably the year Sophia adopts Elizabeth Tickell; probably when Sophia finishes *Almeyda, Queen of Granada*
1796	(20 April) *Almeyda* produced in London and also published
1797	First volume of *The Canterbury Tales* published, a collaboration between sisters Sophia and Harriet; Sophia contributes the introduction
1798	"The Young Lady's Tale. The Two Emilys" published, making up the whole of volume two of *The Canterbury Tales*
1799	Third volume of *The Canterbury Tales* published; Sophia contributes one of the volume's two stories, "The Clergyman's Tale." The fourth and fifth volumes of *The Canterbury Tales*, wholly Harriet's, are published in 1801 and 1805
1803	The Lees close Belvidere House school
1804	*The Life of a Lover*, a six-volume epistolary novel written in Sophia's youth, published
1805	(23 October) Anna Lee commits suicide
1807	(28 January) *The Assignation* plays at Drury Lane
1824	(13 March) Sophia Lee dies in Clifton, near Bristol; she is buried on 18 March, in St. Andrew's churchyard

ACKNOWLEDGMENTS

I have many people to thank for their encouragement and their response to my project of getting this novel into print. My first thanks are due to those who encouraged the project, especially the participants in the 2003 NEH Summer Seminar, "Rethinking British Romantic Fiction," led by the immensely generous Stephen Behrendt, as well as the session leaders and audiences of a number of eighteenth-century and Romanticism conferences at which I presented papers setting forth some of the ideas outlined in my introduction. I would also like to thank individuals for information they provided on questions that arose as I prepared textual notes for this edition. I thank Nancy Mayer for the information that a marriage performed and valid in Italy would be valid in Great Britain. For information on the shift in French orthography, I thank members of the eighteenth century listserv, C18-L, especially Gilles Denis, Christophe Paillard, Rudy de Mattos, and Ted Braun. I also want to thank Franca Barricelli for translation help and discussion of works on the 1783 Calabrian earthquake and Chloe Chard for help finding information on a number of different issues that arose as I prepared this edition. I am also grateful to the interlibrary loan and reference librarians for their assistance finding sources and making them accessible to me.

In the spring of 2008, I was fortunate to have the opportunity to teach this novel while I was preparing this edition of it, and I am grateful to the students of that eighteenth century British novel class I taught at the University of Wisconsin Oshkosh. I am indebted to the students of this class for their enthusiasm about the text as well as for their feedback, questions, and suggestions. I am also grateful for their catching typing errors that I missed despite numerous re-readings of the manuscript. I am also indebted to James D. Jenkins for his truly scrupulous attention and help at all stages of the production of this novel. It has been a delight working with him.

Finally, I would like to dedicate this novel to my very favorite Emily, my mother, and to her brother, Irwin. Indeed, it was the coincidence between the name of the novel and the name of my mother that originally sparked my interest in the text, and then encountering the name Irwin within the text was just an additional delight that bolstered my desire to bring this fast paced, always surprising book to my contemporaries, so that they might enjoy it to something near the extent that I do.

NOTE ON THE TEXT

This novel-length tale was originally published as the whole of the second volume of the five-volume *Canterbury Tales* (1797-1805), a collaboration between Sophia Lee and her sister Harriet, who wrote most of the tales in the collection. The collection as a whole was published from 1797 to 1805 in London by G. G. and J. Robinson; the second volume was published in 1798. Here, the story was titled, "The Young Lady's Tale. The Two Emilys." My source text is the first edition of this volume. Because the tale is published in this Valancourt edition as a novel, however, I italicize the title when I refer to it and shorten the title to *The Two Emilys*. I make an exception where I refer to the original publication of the story, however; I then use its original title.

    I have made an effort to remain as close as possible to the original. I have for instance retained Lee's original spelling of words such as "shewed," "risque," and "stopt," extending to her use of different spelling for words such as "surprise" and "surprize." In the case of inconclusive markings in the first edition, such as hyphens in multiple word terms that fall at the ends of lines in the original, I have checked the second edition; where such hyphens remain at ends of lines in both editions, I have chosen to retain them. Where a word such as "a" or "of" or where a punctuation mark seems inadvertently missing in both editions, I have added it in brackets, generally without providing a textual note that I have done so. Where errors have been corrected in the second edition, however, I do provide a textual note.

CANTERBURY TALES.

VOLUME THE SECOND.

BY SOPHIA LEE.

And sure there seem of human kind
Some born to shun the solemn strife?
Some for amusive talks designed
To soothe the certain ills of life?
     SHENSTONE.

LONDON:
PRINTED FOR G. G. AND J. ROBINSON,
PATERNOSTER-ROW.

MDCCXCVIII.

Sophia Lee's *The Two Emilys*

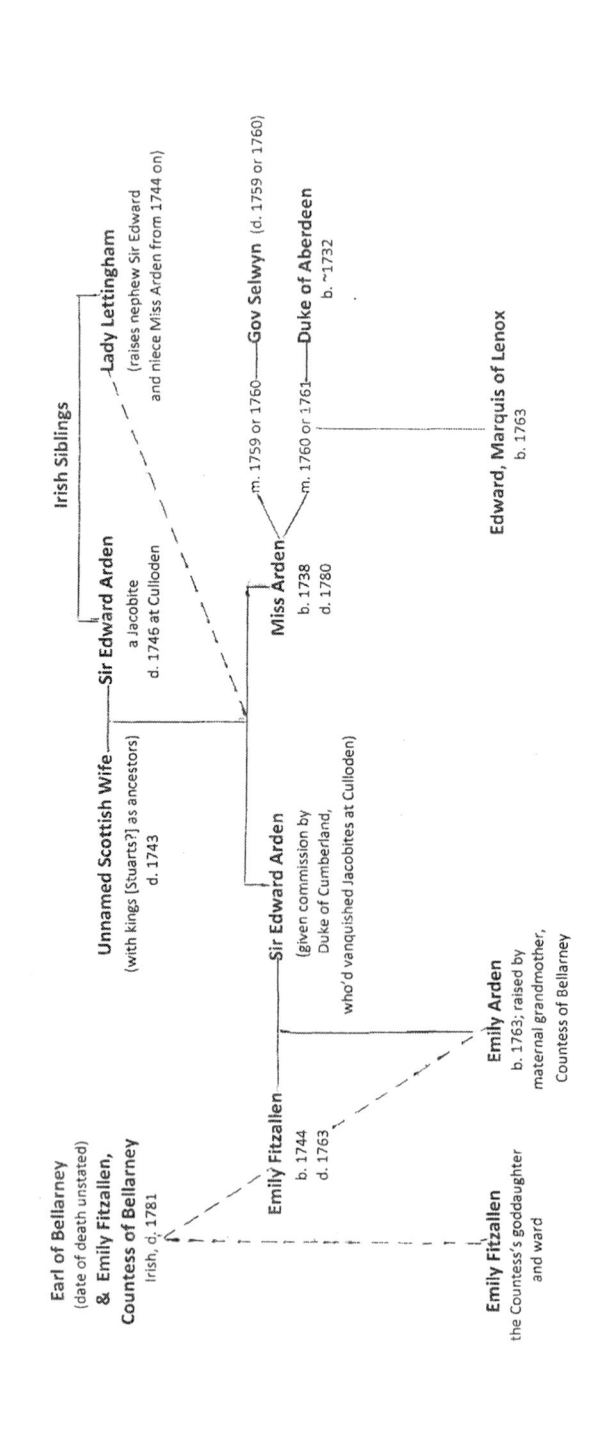

Earl of Bellarney
(date of death unstated)
& Emily Fitzallen,
Countess of Bellarney
Irish, d. 1781

Emily Fitzallen
b. 1744
d. 1763

---- (dashed line to) **Emily Fitzallen**
the Countess's goddaughter and ward

Irish Siblings

Unnamed Scottish Wife ———— **Sir Edward Arden**
(with kings [Stuarts?] as ancestors) a Jacobite
d. 1743   d. 1746 at Culloden

Lady Lettingham
(raises nephew Sir Edward and niece Miss Arden from 1744 on)

Sir Edward Arden
(given commission by Duke of Cumberland, who'd vanquished Jacobites at Culloden)

Miss Arden
b. 1738
d. 1780

m. 1759 or 1760 — **Gov Selwyn** (d. 1759 or 1760)
m. 1760 or 1761 — **Duke of Aberdeen** b. ~1732

Emily Arden
b. 1763; raised by maternal grandmother, Countess of Bellarney

Edward, Marquis of Lenox
b. 1763

THE

YOUNG LADY's TALE.

THE TWO EMILYS.

Unaw'd by piety, who, led by will,
Dares boldly to retaliate ill for ill,
Too late, in bitterness of soul, shall own,
Judgment, and vengeance, are with God alone.*

SIR EDWARD ARDEN was the chief surviving branch of an Irish family of that name, lineally distinguished for birth, and for many generations very highly allied.* He had early married a Scots lady, who ranked kings among her ancestors; and her prejudices had confirmed his own, in favour of the rights of the expelled house of Stuart.* Perhaps in this opinion he only indirectly flattered the pride that told him his children might hope much, did a monarch reign to whom they could claim affinity. Pride has been justly ranked among the first of human foibles; but it has one advantage over the rest—it is generally single in the mind. A proud man demands so much of himself, that if his heart is not the seat of virtue, it must be from his reckoning among his wants, understanding. Sir Edward Arden had no other failing than pride: with bounded means he often contrived to be munificent; and with many immediate claims on his feelings, he had yet a stock of sympathy ever ready for the unfortunate. Not doubting that he should meet a counterpart in his sister, Lady Lettingham, whom he had not seen for many years, he set out for England in the year 1744, with two children the preceding one had left motherless; resolving to commit these treasures to the care of his sister, and follow the fortunes of Charles Stuart.

Lady Lettingham was not without her brother's failing: though pride in her took not the rich colouring of virtue. Distinguished for beauty, she had early married advantageously, and passed her whole life within the chilling circle of a court. The great satisfaction she expressed at seeing her little nephew and niece were exquisitely handsome, was soon lost when she found from their father they were to become her charge, and that he was going to embark in a desperate scheme; the event of which the courtiers prognosticated,* while the prospect filled them all with horror. The arguments used by Lady Lettingham to detain her brother, were so ill calculated to act on a high and generous spirit, that he only lamented he had exposed himself to hearing them; or sought for his children a guardian so worldly and narrow-minded. The two so dear to him were yet, however, but children; and he thought he should certainly return soon enough to prevent their being contaminated greatly, either by their aunt's precepts or example. Finding every effort to change Sir Edward's resolution ineffectual, Lady Lettingham exacted one compliance, even her brother thought not unwise—to assume the family name of his wife, in taking up arms, that his own might be saved from disgrace, if he failed. Having acceded to this, Sir Edward took a long leave of all dear to him,—for he was among the butchered prisoners, after the battle of Culloden.*

Lady Lettingham consoled herself with thinking the evil ended there. She wore no mourning, paid her devoirs to the triumphant duke, and ere long got her young nephew recommended to his protection; whose innocent little hand took, from that stained with the blood of his father, a commission.* Her beauty yet gave Lady Lettingham influence; and a nobleman, distinguished for his wit, politeness, and general acceptation, undertook to give the young Sir Edward Arden some of those diabolical worldly precepts, he perpetuated in his letters to his son, since published.*

Lady Lettingham having thus, to her own admiration, acquitted herself of her promise to her brother, in taking care of his son, now turned her attention towards his daughter. Nature had been lavish to the young lady of the dangerous grace of beauty; and her aunt well knew if the mind could be turned in a certain manner, that might procure the possessor every other advantage. She had once been near supplanting the Countess of Yarmouth herself;* and there would be more kings, as well as more favourites. Anxiously did she practise on a most delicate complexion, by delicate cosmetics: anxiously form to every fantastic twist of fashion, Miss Arden's rich profusion of auburn hair: now would she sodden, by chicken gloves,* to an insipid whiteness, those white hands teinted within, by the bounty of nature, with the hues of the rose, and the hyacinth; and now check the agile grace of youth, that the drawing-room step, and haughty bend, might early become habit, and a due consideration of the rank of the person spoken to, be always taken into view in the civilities of salutation. All this was done to Lady Lettingham's great satisfaction; and Miss Arden, at the age of fifteen, was as cold hearted, supercilious, and ignorant, as even her aunt herself. But she had beauty, manner, fashion; and, in the glow of intoxication universal admiration excites, sunk on her admirers all her inward deficiencies.

Thus to have formed her niece could alone console Lady Lettingham for the misery her nephew brought on her. He had, most unluckily, his father's failing, pride; therefore knew not how to accept a favour, far less to sue for one. He had another failing, equally incompatible with success in life,—sincerity. He had been known to treat Lord C's opinion with contempt; and even to mention openly many other noblemen as knaves or fools. To add to his aunt's affliction, he had warm passions, and gave a boundless loose to them. Hardly less lovely in person than his sister, he was surrounded with rich young women, among whom he might have commanded his own fortune, had he not been for ever raving over a dice-box,* or masquerading with some kept mistress. Want of money, which makes so many men villains, alone made Sir Edward rational, or good. The generous spirit of his father would then revive in him; and he disdained to be lavish at the expence of other people.

The beauty of Miss Arden soon drew to her aunt's house the amorous, the gay, the dissipated. Lady Lettingham played well, and high: nay, it was thought she thus half supported her splendid establishment. Those who knew this, chose to purchase the honour of flirting with the beautiful Miss Arden, by a sacrifice of their superfluous cash; while spendthrifts, new to life, imputed those immense losses to love, they should rather have ascribed to ignorance.

The race of life, however, in the higher circles, is soon run: bounded minds, like sickly appetites, are subject to satiety; and it is not so necessary the object, or the dish, should be superior to the former, as new. Miss Arden with astonishment saw one train of lovers disappear; but another succeeded, and her astonishment was forgotten. Lady Lettingham found such a harvest in the attraction of her niece, that she was in no hurry to marry her; and it was not till Miss Arden was a deposed toast, that she ever guessed her sovereignty was doubted. Disappointment embittered a mind not without pride, though without any power to turn that to a generous use. In this frightful conjuncture she cast her eyes upon the few admirers who had not yet deserted, to see if among them she could chuse a husband that might save her vanity—her heart she had never thought it necessary to consult. But now, her condescension was not less fatal to her views than her insolence had been. The man who understood the proud beauty meant at last to marry him, found so many reasons to avoid the chain, that Miss Arden soon saw herself without a lover. To be a departed beauty at twenty-one, was beyond all endurance;—she arraigned her aunt for bringing her out a mere child—the men for liking the mere children better that had come out since, and the whole world for not doing justice to her charms. Taste still was hers; and that, happily displayed, might have the effect of novelty. Milliners were worn out; mantua-makers' brains racked; but, however singular—however elegant—the Arden robe, the Arden bonnet, no more became the rage; and miss Arden was obliged to be overlooked, or to follow the whim of some other miss, who had no advantage over her but that of not having yet palled the public eye.

Her mother's prayer-book continually reminded Miss Arden she was only twenty-four, when, in the world of beauty and fashion, she saw too clearly she was a dead letter. If a young country baronet presumed at an assembly to use his own eyes, and cry out, there was not a woman so handsome as Miss Arden present, the opera-glass of *ton* was instantly levelled—"Ah, Miss Arden! poor Miss Arden! yes, she *has* been handsome;—I *remember* her a toast." The stranger stood corrected, and often was ashamed to have given a judgment no man of his own age joined in.

Life is not life on terms like these to an acknowledged beauty; and Miss Arden was considering how to change to advantage her sphere of action, when the death of Lady Lettingham ascertained her fate. The high style of that lady's establishment made her debts exceed all she left behind; and the beautiful Miss Arden suddenly found herself without a lover, a friend, a fortune, or a home.

Sir Edward Arden, on whom, in the helplessness of an unformed mind, his sister threw herself, felt now, even to the extent, the evils of thoughtlessness and self-indulgence. The little fortune he had inherited was already gone—the beauty he eminently possessed already faded—the friends mere kindness might have secured to him, offended by his excesses, or chilled by his neglect, were all withdrawn; and he had now to support and guard a young woman, spoiled by the idolatry of that world by which she was already forgotten; and without one resource in her own mind against its insults, or its evils.

It is among the advantages men possess over women, that they may, if they will, know themselves; and perhaps to that alone may be ascribed their superiority of judgment in all the great contingencies of life. Women breathe, as it were, in an artificial atmosphere; and what hot-house rose can bear without shrinking even the genial gales that bring the garden plants to perfection? Yet, let not the men, therefore, impute to themselves the power of escaping the universal charm of flattery:—on the contrary, from its very novelty, it has on them, in some instances, such a wonderful effect, that a well-imagined, or well-timed compliment, from a fair lady, has, perhaps, ere now, deposed a king, or made one.

During a country visit to a lady Sir Edward Arden prevailed on to invite his sister, while she mourned for her aunt, it occurred to them all, that India was a soil rich in wealth, and as yet unpeopled with beauties: where a young woman, with merely a tolerable person and reputable introduction, seldom failed to make her fortune.* What might not the highly born, highly bred, beautiful Miss Arden, promise herself? The Governor, who was soon to depart for that country, was among those *bon vivants* Sir Edward termed his *friends.* He had already brought home an immense fortune from the East, and was now to return in a high style. Several ladies availed themselves of his patronage and protection, and were to partake his accommodations; but to Miss Arden all gave way: and Governor Selwyn always presenting her his hand, and the first place, she found, even in her humiliating voyage, a consequence, that gratified a mind at once arrogant and weak.

Governor Selwyn was one not less favoured by fortune, than slighted by nature. He was more than ordinary,—disgusting. Courage and cunning had, at his outset in life, supplied the place of virtue and fortitude: he therefore had brought back to England rank, wealth, reputation. He lived for some years magnificently; not because he was generous, but luxurious; and he speculated in the Alley,* only to multiply those riches that already were more than he ought to have possessed, or knew how to enjoy. The consequence is obvious. A single error undid him. His substantial wealth vanished, but the shadow still remained; and, to impose on his own circle, he even increased that high style of living he had no just means of maintaining. But Governor Selwyn had already lived long enough to know, that the only way to get money is not to appear to want it. He now assured his circle, all things in the East were going to rack and ruin for want of him; and that he could no longer resist the kind urgency, and splendid offers of his friends, to take once more upon him the irksome office he thought he had given up for life. A word was sufficient to make the first tradesmen in London wait on him for orders; and the Governor embarked in all the pomp of Eastern luxury, and surrounded with fair Europeans.

Miss Arden was so naturally beautiful and elegant, and so anxious ever to appear to advantage, that the Governor, having trifled in secret with two or three pretty light coquets,* who laughed at his ugly face, and his superannuated gallantry, now resolved to devote himself to this lofty charmer. He already knew she had no other aim than the other misses; to make her fortune; and that she would value him but as she thought that might be ascertained: yet still he devoted himself to her. He was certain she was ignorant of the change in his circumstances; and he had cheated his own sex so often, that it appeared a mere amusement to cheat a woman. Miss Arden listened to his gallantry like a well-bred lady, who knew exactly how to estimate it. He soon saw, a rich or handsome rival might step in, and at least puzzle her choice. He therefore became more passionate, more importunate: and that no doubt, on the score of fortune, might make her hesitate, he offered to sign a deed, obliging himself to settle the whole of his, on her and her heirs. Miss Arden paused. This was the best offer she had for a length of time had. The Governor might always interfere with her views, if rejected. She could have no more than *all* of any man's fortune. She forgot he was old and ugly, in the remembrance that he was rich: and having allowed him to make a will, as the most secure and simple method of ensuring to her his property, Miss Arden yielded; and the ship's chaplain married her to Governor Selwyn. Each suppressing their motives in the match, love and reason could hardly have given to matrimony more apparent happiness: but, alas! all our enjoyments are uncertain, and this was fugitive.* Governor Selwyn died almost immediately on landing. His disconsolate relict* forgot neither the forms of her situation, nor its rights: but judge of her mortification and amazement, when she found herself little richer than at her embarkation. She however adroitly availed herself of the example by which she had been duped. The fame of possessing a large fortune is almost equal to the possession of it, if the feelings are not nice.* Governor Selwyn was embalmed in great state; and his lovely widow again set sail for England, with all his train of black slaves, Indian canopies, gold services, and magnificent china.

Sir Edward Arden had procured his widowed sister a sumptuous dwelling; and she celebrated the obsequies of her "dear, dear generous Governor" with a grandeur that drew all eyes upon her.—"Good God! how lovely is Mrs. Selwyn in her weeds!"* cried those who knew not Miss Arden, in her simple mourning for Lady Lettingham. Her doors were besieged, and when it became her to open them, lovely, lovely Mrs. Selwyn was again the *ton*. Again her name appeared in the newspaper—again her face was at every print-shop: and all the world was at the feet of the rich widow.

But Mrs. Selwyn now knew the world in all its ways; and had no time to lose in fixing some man of rank and fortune, yet unversed in them.* In her parties sometimes was to be seen the young Duke of Aberdeen.* Through the avarice and partiality of his father, he had lived till near eight-and-twenty with little more information or acceptation than his steward; when a surfeit, taken at a public feast, carried both his father and elder brother out of the world, leaving him sole master of a large fortune, and distinguished by high rank. He rolled up to London immediately, with that prodigal splendour incidental to suddenly enriched persons; and then had good sense enough to perceive he wanted every thing but money to qualify him for superior society. The elegant manners of Sir Edward Arden struck him. The beauty of his sister seized on his heart. Hardly able from *mauvaise honte** to reply to her graceful address to him, the Duke yet adored her for the very ease he wanted: and Mrs. Selwyn was in possession of the Duke of Aberdeen's heart, ere the younger coquettes had woven the light chains by which they meant to enthrall it. Mrs. Selwyn soon saw in the constant visits of the Duke, and the increasing aukwardness of his address, her power: but in the great advantages of such a match, she was easily led to overlook the little defects of his mien.

Time, however, shewed her, that this unformed Duke had not only strong passions, but strong sense; and, however easy it might be to bias the first to her purpose, to act on the last required most refined address. She now grew more reserved in her conversation, though more impassioned in her manner. Whenever marriage was hinted at, she sunk into a tender rêverie; and sometimes, on her raising her eyes, the Duke saw those fine eyes flooded with tears. The indistinct alarm such a conduct caused, increased his affection. He importuned her to confide to him the care that preyed on her heart, and blighted the happiness she allowed him to hope for. Having wrung from her a promise of revealing the secret, she appointed him to come to her house the next evening, when the door should be closed on all but himself. The Duke saw, in this flattering distinction, a full assurance of success, and past the interval in revolving every possible cause for the distress of his beautiful widow, without once dreaming of the real one.

Mrs. Selwyn saw her fortune now at the point of a moment; and omitted no art of the toilette to improve her natural beauty. Her apartment was scented with the rich odours of the East; gauze shades softened every light; a gold muslin robe was girt to her graceful waist with a purple sash, and fell in the luxurious drapery of a Circassian slave:* while her heart, throbbing now with hope, and now with fear, gave to her character what it naturally most wanted—sensibility and interest. The Duke of Aberdeen, unused to the world, and to women, felt a strange and exquisite delight, when mysteriously conducted to such a Mahometan paradise.* No sooner were they alone, than, falling at her feet, he implored her full, her promised confidence. She now entreated his pardon for having given him reason to expect it, but found herself so utterly unable to avow a circumstance that might rob her for ever of him, that she in vain resolved to be sincere. The anxious lover now found fear wrought up to agony: his conjectures over-did, as she meant they should, the reality: in fine, in learning that Mrs. Selwyn had nothing to give him but her heart and her hand, the Duke felt a transport so great, that all the factitious part of her conduct and character was at once forgotten.* A special licence was obtained the next day; and Sir Edward Arden was called upon to give the hand of his sister to the Duke of Aberdeen. She had influence enough over her husband to prevail on him to keep her secret; and his fortune was too ample to render the payment of her debts a matter of any consequence.

Elevated almost beyond hope, the Duchess of Aberdeen had now only one wish to gratify; it was to mortify by her magnificence, overbear by her rank, and humble by her beauty, the whole circle with whom she had once mixed. But the Duke had no taste for this kind of gratification; and to indulge the passion she had inspired, entreated her to retire to his seat in Scotland, in terms so strong, that she knew not how to avoid complying. Her brother took occasion to point out to her the necessity of shewing her gratitude and affection to the Duke, by other means than a perpetual self-indulgence. To rid herself of a Mentor, and weary her husband of his own plan, the Duchess at length consented to set out, with a magnificent suite, for her banishment. That her spleen* might have an object, when it overpowered her resolutions, the Duchess, however, carried with her an humble cousin, of the name of Archer, who was thrown by family derangements on the bounty of Sir Edward and his sister. Miss Archer had had the singular advantage of engaging the regard of all who ever knew her; and for a very simple reason—neither nature, nor fortune, permitted her to rival any body. Her features had every disadvantage of ugliness, but that of being remarkable; her figure was small, her articulation imperfect. Accomplishments would have been unnoticed in Miss Archer, and she had good sense enough to forbear displaying those she indulged herself in acquiring. She had, however, a mind strong by nature, and improved by literature; a just and refined taste, and a sweetness of temper few women can boast. These advantages are of so little estimation in polished society, that Miss Archer had reached five and twenty without having it in her power to gratify any passion, in either accepting, or rejecting, a single lover. She had the additional vexation of being always a selected person to assist at the nuptials of her young friends; and the universal confidante of other people's love affairs and griefs, because she had none of her own to burden them with in return, and [showed]* patient sweetness in hearing, as well as advising. Such a friend might have been the first of blessings to the Duchess of Aberdeen, had she sought by rational means rational happiness: but no sooner was that lady convinced that the Duke's magnificent domains contained not one person worth either charming or fretting, than she sunk into *ennui.** Even her beauty no longer was her care; and when the Duke insinuated any displeasure at her utter neglect of herself, and him, she petulantly asked him, if he would have her dress for the owls and the daws; and that if he meant to see her what she used to be, he must let her mix again with those she was used to mix with. Miss Archer's advice she treated with superlative contempt; and the Duke of Aberdeen felt his heart was already thrown back on his hands.

In the friendship of Sir Edward Arden, both yet found a solid good, and an equal satisfaction. The generous assistance of the Duke had enabled the Baronet to visit his native country, and pay off a mortgage on his patrimony, without which it would have been added to the estates of the Bellarney family.* The Earl being lately dead, his vast fortunes were just vested in his only child and heiress, Lady Emily Fitzallen; who was now first brought out at the Castle,* and the beauty of the day. Sir Edward Arden saw her there, and was not himself unseen. Beauty, symmetry, polished manners, and a most winning address, made him a universal favourite among the ladies; and the gentle Lady Emily amply repaid him for the admiration he gave her. The old Countess of Bellarney was unwilling to give up a mortgage so very advantageous, as that of Sir Edward's estate. Many conferences ensued, at which Lady Emily was sometimes obliged to be present; at length the Countess, to her infinite surprise, far from keeping Sir Edward's estate, understood Lady Emily was ready to bestow on him all those she inherited. The old lady's consent was unwillingly wrung from her; and Sir Edward suddenly found himself possessed of a most lovely and tender bride, with half a principality as her fortune. Time had corrected his love of dissipation, and every other foible, bounded fortunes, and boundless wishes, had produced in him, during the early period of youth:

and his high spirit, glowing heart, and refined character, so completely endeared him in a few months to Lady Bellarney, as well as to her daughter, that his will became no less a law with one than the other. Sir Edward constantly corresponded with the Duke; and, in the description of his domestic felicity, sharpened the pang of disappointment in his brother-in-law's heart. Yet in the hope of an heir the Duke found his affection revive; and as Lady Emily gave Sir Edward the same hope, it was gaily agreed between the husbands, that the lady who was first enough recovered to travel, should come to the other. The delicacy of Lady Emily's habit made her a severe sufferer for some months, when she became the mother of a sweet little girl. Great was the delight of Lady Emily; but, alas! brief. A cold taken by quitting her room too early, to visit her mother who was seriously indisposed, brought on a fever, so delicate a subject could not struggle through; and the distracted Sir Edward lost at nineteen the idol of his soul. So acute was his grief, that his health severely suffered. The scene of a happiness so dear became odious to him; he assisted with the old Countess at the baptism of his daughter, called her by the beloved name of Emily, and bathing her with tears, he committed her, with all her vast fortune (for by the will of Lord Bellarney it was so to descend) to the charge of her grandmother, and resolved to seek, in the society of his sister and the Duke, for the peace he despaired even with them to find.

And well might he despair; for peace was already wholly banished from the seat of the Duke of Aberdeen. Born to love and hate with vehemence, that nobleman no sooner found his wife took no pleasure in exciting the first passion, than she exposed herself to become the object of the last. Yet the impassioned heart will have some object, and none was within reach of the Duke but Miss Archer. She had no attraction save mind; yet, in the tyranny of a beauty, that was first brought to light. The Duke soon studied her convenience, soothed her wounded pride, found her necessary to his happiness, and well knew how to make himself so to hers. Exquisitely susceptible of gratitude, Miss Archer perceived not the danger of indulging its emotions, nor how fine that fibre of the human heart is by which the passions communicate. Hers were all awakened by the Duke, who better knew how to calculate his own influence than she did. Honour, feeling, every right principle, bade him spare the young woman who had no other good than that he might rob her of; but she loved him, she alone loved him; and, in giving her up, he destined himself to know only a chilling existence. He ventured, in a moment of loneliness, a mark of partiality; and surprised at a novelty like that of being beloved, a fearful kind of pleasure caused an exclamation from Miss Archer, but ill calculated to check a lover: the Duke felt his power, and soon won her. The bitterness of her remorse even in yielding, the excess of her tenderness, the reproaches she lavished on herself, and the anxiety with which she sought to keep alive in his heart even the passion she arraigned, all acted upon a strong character like the Duke's, and bound him wholly to her.

Tired of the constraint both were under in the house with the Duchess, the Duke often importuned Miss Archer to quit it, for a hunting lodge he had at a little distance, which was accordingly elegantly fitted up for her; but the boundless passion she had for him, made her rather endure all the humours of his wife, than lose that portion of his society she must, were she to accept this disgraceful, though safe, home. Yet the situation she soon found herself in, shewed that was a measure she must ere long yield to.

The pregnancy of the Duchess caused a public joy, and that of Miss Archer a secret one, to her lover. He passionately desired a son; and therefore, as far as possible, indulged the whims of the Duchess, while soothing more tenderly her guilty rival. A delicacy of mind Miss Archer still cherished, made her anxiously conceal her situation; nor had the Duchess any suspicion of it, when one day, the dessert being on the table, both cast a longing look on a peach of singular beauty and size. Both at one moment reached out a hand to take it; but the Duchess, as the nearest, succeeded. Miss Archer struggled for a little while with her sense of disappointment, when, after changing colour many times, she fainted away. The exclamation of the Duke, his suddenly starting from his chair, his manner of caressing the guilty insensible, together with her person, on which the Duchess fixed her eyes, in one moment unfolded to that weak and furious woman the whole truth. The frenzy of her passion could not be controuled; she exhausted herself in reproaching her husband; and, seeing her wretched cousin beginning to revive, reviled her in the most opprobrious terms. The only effect of this ill-judged rage was to make the Duke throw aside all regard to decorum: he avowed the guilt she charged him with, but bade her find in herself his excuse; and soothing the unfortunate and silent Miss Archer, admonished his wife to imitate at least that part of her cousin's conduct. The Duchess, exasperated beyond all speech, threw herself into violent fits; and the Duke, ordering the servants to convey her to her own apartment, led Miss Archer to hers himself; and leaving at the door several servants, he charged them, at their peril, neither to admit the Duchess beyond that threshold, nor any of the domestics peculiarly hers. He now went to visit his wife, who refused to see him; and having given orders to her attendants no less carefully to guard her, he withdrew.

The weak and guilty Miss Archer, who had against her better judgment sacrificed her virtue, recovered from insensibility only to sink into despair. The Duke found her in its extremity, and spared no effort to reconcile her to herself, and those indignities and sufferings from which he could not save her. He solemnly vowed, as soon as the Duchess should have given him an heir, he would separate for ever from her; and that her own safety should be assured by her going immediately to the lodge, already prepared for her reception, whither he meant to retire, till his wife came to reason. The physician he had sent for now arrived, and finding Miss Archer had strong symptoms of premature labour, ordered her not to be removed. The Duke having re-inforced his injunctions concerning her being unmolested, to the servants in charge, mounted his horse, and rode to the lodge, to meditate more at leisure.

The Duchess of Aberdeen, having no complaint of the heart, was not long a sufferer. She no sooner understood that the Duke had quitted the house, than, notwithstanding her situation, she flew to Miss Archer's apartment, to thunder in her ears the flaming indignation she was yet bursting with. The servants posted at the door resolutely opposed her entrance; and after threats and prayers, she was obliged to retreat, and study a revenge proportioned to such insults. The suffering Miss Archer sent many humble letters, and messages, expressed in the most penitent and moving terms, to her cousin; but these only added fuel to the fire. The Duchess exhausted language to compose her answers, without finding any words bitter enough to express her feelings.

It was at this trying crisis the melancholy widower, Sir Edward Arden, landed from an Irish bark on the shores of Scotland, and rather chose to be his own harbinger, than have notice given of his approach. Confused and astonished at sight of a guest so unexpected, the servants, by their eyes, referred Sir Edward from one to another, when he inquired for the Duke. Wholly occupied with his late loss, and his own sufferings, he now took up the idea that his sister had ended her days in the same miserable manner with his Emily, when he suddenly heard her voice in not a very harmonious key. He flew to her arms, and remained long there (for he fondly loved her) lost in affliction and tears: those she shed, he for some time imputed only to sympathy for his loss; but observing, at length, that they redoubled when he named the Duke, and that her cheeks burnt with anger, he considered what had past more dispassionately. He saw in her disordered dress, indignant features, and, when he named her Lord, broken accents, some grief beyond a common occasion; and he fondly entreated her to confide her soul's inmost care to a brother who adored her. The haughty imprudent Duchess gave way at once to all the frenzy of her jealousy; she related the past scene with every aggravation her fancy suggested; while all the faulty part of her own conduct was unmentioned.

Having shewn Miss Archer in a light sufficiently odious to exasperate even Sir Edward, the Duchess implored him to assert an authority she had not; and first turning the Duke's servants from the door of Miss Archer, then employ his own to expel her from the mansion, into which she had first brought guilt and misery; declaring this the only satisfaction he could give her. Sir Edward felt even to the utmost the unworthy conduct of the Duke, and the representations of his sister; but his generous nature revolted at the idea of thus dismissing* a wretched woman, who might be more unfortunate, than culpable; nor would he promise to be guilty of inhumanity, however worthless the object. After pausing, he required of his sister a little time to prepare his mind and regulate his conduct; then pressing her hand, fondly assured her, she might safely entrust her cause to his care, since he would either restore or revenge her.

Sir Edward walked out to ruminate on this strange *éclaircissement*,* and form an eligible plan for removing Miss Archer, as the primary step to reconciling the married people. By the account of the Duchess he in fact believed his cousin the sole aggressor, and of course the just object of punishment.—The bark that brought him over was yet moored in a little creek; it was manned by some Irish fishermen, whom an extraordinary payment would easily persuade to go to France; and his valet might by the same means be won to take charge of Miss Archer, and lodge her in a convent, where his interest, and liberality, he was sure, would confine her.—This appeared a safe and eligible plan, if he could get the imprisoned lady to adopt it voluntarily. Yet he could hope to win her compliance only by one method—the idea that it was the wish of the Duke; who chose this way, that he might avoid further exasperating his wife, or endangering her own safety.

Sir Edward had received many letters from the Duke, and he past part of the night in counterfeiting his hand: at length he thought himself sufficiently successful to write a billet to Miss Archer.—He informed her, that, learning Sir Edward Arden was arrived, he was doubly unhappy about her safety; he advised her to escape, ere his imperious sister should have enraged him by her story, adding, that, to secure her from pursuit, he had sent a small vessel with a woman to attend her.—She had only to steal in the dusk of the evening alone to the garden gate, nearest the beach, where she would find that woman and a mariner waiting to guard her to the bark. Early in the morning Sir Edward confided his plan to his valet, who readily undertook to execute it; and having charged him to fix on some woman capable of assisting Miss Archer, should the pains of childbirth seize her, and provided with every accommodation a person in expectation of them required, Sir Edward thought he had thus acquitted himself of the duties of humanity, as well as of his promise to his sister.

The frail Miss Archer had a little recovered from her pains, when the news of Sir Edward's arrival almost caused her to relapse. The quiet that succeeded lulled her into a false security; and his letter, which was delivered to her in great secrecy, as from the Duke, seemed a comfort sent her from heaven itself. Without once reflecting on the improbability of the Duke's being awed by the arrival of any one into a mysterious underhand proceeding in his own house, Miss Archer waited impatiently for the appointed hour that was to enfranchise her. When that approached, she desired to pass the servants directed to guard, but who had no authority to imprison her; and stealing through the garden, blessed the moment that put her into the power of those she found waiting for her. Sir Edward's valet sent him the glad news of her having voluntarily, and unobserved, embarked, at the moment the vessel set sail. Sir Edward hastened to inform his sister, without speaking of his arrangements, that she had for ever got rid of her troublesome and formidable rival: when the Duchess, subject to extremes, in a transport of gratified revenge, fell into labour, and soon gave birth to a fine boy. This event caused in the family a jubilee: the servants vied who should fly first with the news to the Duke, and Miss Archer was in a single hour forgotten.

In the time he had been obliged to spend in solitude, the Duke had reviewed his past conduct; and, even giving all the weight self-love could to the faults of his wife, he had not been able to acquit his own heart. Miss Archer, however tender her claim to compassion, escaped not her share of blame; and not all his understanding could reconcile interests so opposite, or fix on the point of morality, without sacrificing feeling and honour. He had half resolved to abide by his duty, even though he should for ever renounce Miss Archer, when he was informed of Sir Edward's unforeseen and unwished arrival. In the expectation of a challenge, the Duke relinquished all idea of conceding to his wife; and he found, with astonishment, a whole day passed away, without either brother or sister taking any step in which he was a party. This moderation on the part of Sir Edward the Duke considered a favourable omen; when the amazing news that Miss Archer had by her own choice quitted his house, and that the Duchess had brought him an heir, at one moment reached him. Convinced that no force could have removed Miss Archer, the Duke imputed her withdrawing only to the good offices of his brother-in-law, and called for his horses, impatient to return home. He was, however, met on the way by Sir Edward, whose face conveyed to the Duke the tenor of the conversation he wished to hold with him. The servants retiring, Sir Edward haughtily inquired if the Duke was returning to atone for the wrongs he had done his helpless wife. The Duke replied, he considered the question as a challenge, and demanded his pistol. A word must have made them friends or foes, and to be the latter was thus their choice. They passed behind a thicket, and dismounting, the Duke stood the fire of Sir Edward; then gallantly and firmly returned it. Sir Edward's second ball grazed the shoulder of his antagonist, who, throwing down the remaining pistol undischarged, cried out, "You have had your revenge, Sir Edward; and now, without attaching to myself an odious imputation, I may own I have erred. Forget that error, and let this embrace renew a friendship, that will, I hope, end only with our lives."

Who could resist so generous an enemy?—Sir Edward embraced the Duke, and felt his sister must have been wrong, though he knew not how. The servants saw them return unhurt, and arm in arm, with a joy they dared not express, and knew not how to dissemble. Sir Edward desired permission to hasten on, and prepare his sister to receive her husband. With infinite tenderness he imparted to her the whole proceeding; assuring her, if he had the least knowledge of the human heart, gentleness and affection would for ever bind the Duke's. If, therefore, she prized her present or future happiness, she would never recall the idea of Miss Archer for one moment to his mind; but, by cherishing his tenderness towards herself and [her]* child, strive to make that unfortunate woman forgotten.

The Duchess's present situation had subdued some of her turbulent passions. She thanked her brother affectionately for his counsel, which she promised to follow. Sir Edward now conducted the Duke to her bed-side, and left them together. The Duchess never looked more lovely than in the maternal character, and she was quite the mother. She held out one hand to her husband, and, with the other, pointed to the fine babe who lay sleeping beside her. A thousand tender and hitherto unknown sensations rushed through the frame of the Duke. He sunk on his knees, and now kissing the hand of his wife, and now the infant, entreated her to pardon, and rely on him. Tears were the general conciliators; and, from this time, the Duke and Duchess of Aberdeen began mutually to concede, and live well together. Sir Edward enjoyed the happiness he had made, and gave his own name to the young Marquis of Lenox,* whose baptism was celebrated with princely magnificence.

The Duke, from time to time, vainly hoped Sir Edward would unfold to him the fate of Miss Archer; but, as her name never escaped his brother's lips, the Duke determined to rely on his honour, in having properly provided for her, and to shew his sense of the generosity by silence. Sir Edward himself was not so easy. The time that had elapsed ought to have brought back his valet, yet he came not. He wrote to France—Miss Archer had not been heard of:—he then enquired for the fishermen, and their bark, at Bellarney; but, alas! they had never returned: and Sir Edward, after many vain enquiries, was obliged to conclude that the unfortunate woman, whose fate he had ventured to decide, had found in the ocean a premature grave, together with the infant she was on the point of bringing into the world. Melancholy was so much the habit of his life since the death of Lady Emily, that even this gloomy impression added little to it. Time—the good consequences resulting from the sending away Miss Archer—and other contingencies, at length wore from Sir Edward's mind the painful recollection of her sad, and untimely fate.

The limited understanding, and advanced age of Lady Bellarney, together with the infancy of his daughter, made Ireland a melancholy, and unpleasant residence to Sir Edward. Both the Duke and his sister delighted in his society; and, save those periodical visits to his little Emily, the tender remembrance of her mother exacted from Sir Edward, he passed many years with relatives so beloved. The little Marquis, growing thus under the eye of his uncle, became his dearest care, and almost the sole object of his affection. Delighting to instruct the lovely boy, Sir Edward made the office of preceptor almost a sinecure to the gentleman entrusted with it. Nor was his fondness for his nephew to be termed partiality. The Marquis of Lenox joined to a beauty not less striking than his mother's, a manly grace and mental energy, together with insinuating address, and polished manners. When Sir Edward left this beloved youth, to visit the blossom blowing in the wilds of Ireland, how would his soul melt over the gentle image of his heart's dear Emily. Miss Arden already blended enchanting softness of manners with a frankness in which her father delighted. It was much, though vainly, his wish to educate her in England, and insensibly lead her heart towards that of the youth he fondly thought he could at any time lead towards her. This project by degrees took possession of his whole soul. He suggested it to the Duke and Duchess, who, seeing in Miss Arden the sole heiress of two great families, and an immense property, adopted the idea with all the facility her father could desire. The gentle Emily heard so much of her accomplished, her beautiful cousin, that all the vague indistinct attachment her early feelings allowed, followed the bent of her father's; who, triumphing in the soft blush the name of the Marquis now always called into her cheek, saw, in the ardour of his soul, its darling project already realized. Sir Edward had not calculated all the prejudices he might have to contend with. The Marquis of Lenox, born to a title of the first rank, an immense estate, great natural, and, in time, acquired advantages, felt a haughty independence of mind neither of his parents ventured to over-rule. He had from his birth been such a general concern—so inexpressibly dear—that to find himself irremediably bestowed in the most important of all points, shocked and offended him. That constraint at which all young minds revolt, appeared to him a peculiar hardship, and the little rustic in the wilds of Ireland a most unsuitable wife for a nobleman, who, all the family flatterers declared, might chuse, and reject, in any house in England. His mistaken parents, and fond uncle, increased his disgust, by reckoning on his prepossession; and the health of his little wife was at length a matter of ridicule to himself and his young companions. As time ripened his judgment, he recollected this *little wife*, this *early betrothed*, was the daughter of Sir Edward—that uncle, whose indulgence for him knew no bounds: still she was a mere rustic, and a bride imposed on him. Therefore, to avoid seeing her, and break this tie, involuntary on his part, was the sole object of all his plans. Miss Arden and her cousin now were eighteen, and Sir Edward made many unsuccessful attempts to carry him over to Ireland. Now he was sick—now engaged in a shooting party—now obliged to appear at court—or, when all other excuses failed, the Marquis had but to assert his influence over his weak mother, and she would declare, her death must be the certain consequence of his leaving her a single month. A little piqued at delays he could no longer misunderstand, Sir Edward departed, at length, without even asking his nephew; having been much pressed to visit Ireland by an anxious, alarming letter from his daughter. On arriving there, he found, a very common effect of dotage, that a young woman, who had been reared and educated by the bounty of Lady Bellarney, and many years the humble companion of Miss Arden, had, through the indulgence of her aged benefactress, assumed to herself an authority and consequence very mortifying to a creature too gentle to check the insolence she suffered by. Emily Fitzallen, for this upstart was Lady Bellarney's god-daughter,* had, by perpetual attention, and mean adulation, almost shut out Miss Arden from the confidence and society of her grandmother, who was persuaded by this cringing assiduous friend, that Miss Arden was wanting in both affection and duty. The concessions Sir Edward recommended to his daughter, as the most likely way to recover her influence, and displace the encroaching favourite, were, by her means, treated as mean and servile in Miss Arden, whose life would have been without hope or happiness, had she not imbibed the fond impression her father had so often sought to give her, of the young Marquis. She languished to visit England, that she might improve the partiality she had been taught to believe mutual, and judge how true the representation made of his charms and graces had been. She had asked for his picture, and her father had brought it to her: but, though the Marquis never demanded hers in return, she was too new to life to see the slight, and contemplated *his* every hour with increasing partiality. Finding how little the old Countess valued her society, Miss Arden sometimes obtained leave of absence to visit her mother's relations; but, even for that, was obliged to humble herself to her former companion.

Miss Emily Fitzallen was not less distinguished for either natural or acquired advantages than Miss Arden. Though of too low a birth to bear to have her origin investigated, she had a graceful and majestic mien, that often made her mistaken for the heiress of Bellarney. Miss Arden had blue eyes, long fair hair, and an air of the most exquisite feminine delicacy: the eyes of Miss Fitzallen were dark, penetrating, and impressive. Her complexion was of the white rose teint; and she strove to blend with a haughtiness of countenance, that sweetness which was foreign to her nature, though the genuine expression of her fair companion's.

In a little excursion Miss Arden was permitted to make, with a neighbouring young lady newly married, it was proposed the party should cross the channel in a pleasure-bark on the estate, and surprize the sister of this lady by an unexpected visit.* Miss Arden alone prevented the execution of this plan: yet who so much desired it? To breathe the same air with this irresistible cousin—to have but a chance of coming across him unknown—romantic thought! what girl of eighteen could reject it? Despairing to obtain Lady Bellarney's permission, which her father had often vainly solicited, Miss Arden suggested, that, by taking another name, it might never be known she was one of the party. The idea charmed them all: they vowed profound secresy, and the anxious Miss Arden thus came at once upon her fate.

This scheme was not quite so unstudied as it appeared. The two sisters had agreed to convene a large party of the young, the gay, and the agreeable; and those who headed it, well knew the two betrothed lovers would come across each other, though the Marquis would not be aware of his own predicament.

In a large party an individual excites little attention; but the consummate, though simple, grace of Miss Arden attracted universal observation. Her young heart beat without ceasing, when she found she was really going to see at last this cousin, on whose perfections she had been taught to dwell; but he, unapprised of the anxious expectation he excited, loitered by the way; and the masquerade, which was to be the last fête, came without the Marquis of Lenox: yet still he was hourly expected. Never had the lovely Emily found it so hard to arrange her dress. In this solitary situation she had little variety, and no resources; but true beauty never appears more conspicuous than when thus thrown upon itself. In the habit of an Italian peasant, her neck and shoulders half covered with her rich profusion of fair hair, a mandoline in her hand, and the light air of a Grace in every step, Miss Arden appeared more captivating than if arrayed in all her mother's jewels. A buzz in the pavilion when she entered, informed her a knot she now first saw were the persons newly arrived, and a glance, that one of the dominos* must be the Marquis. Her heart instantaneously made its election, and "Oh if that should not be my cousin!" sighed Miss Arden. Yet with the anxiety of the moment no mortification was blended. Accustomed to consider the husband elected for her as the being on earth she would have chosen for herself, the gentle Emily knew not the revolting spirit that man often thinks virtue.* Surrounded by a crowd of uninteresting admirers, Miss Arden studied in vain how to attract the notice of the elegant stranger her heart had turned to; and whom she learnt, by the flying whisper of her friend, to be the right person. That very notoriety she shunned, proved in reality the allurement by which the Marquis was drawn. "Who is that graceful Italian peasant, with the redundant locks of fine fair hair?" was his enquiry often repeated, and always in vain. "The fair stranger," was the general reply. *Fair,* indeed, thought he, if her face answers to that light and delicate figure. He hovered near awhile. Emily forgot the crowd that surrounded her. He spoke, and she heard in the whole busy circle only the voice of the Marquis. He lamented his loss in not seeing her face, or rather, he added, he ought to congratulate himself, as his fate would then have been for ever fixed. The timid air with which this interesting stranger answered gallantry so general, something surprized him; but he imputed her embarrassment to being unused to these meetings, and still followed, still flattered her. An irresistible something in the tone of her voice fascinated him: yet all it uttered bespoke a mind so sweetly formed—a soul of such sensibility—that he felt afraid to treat her as a common character. She is no masquerader, cried he to himself; now let me address her more respectfully: and, to convince her no impertinence is meant, I will shew my own face. That beautiful face, so highly expressive of sense and sweetness, caught the eyes of Miss Arden, and impressed itself for ever on her imagination. The fine flush of agitation, hope, and a full room, heightened every glowing charm. His gay and pleasant air, the variety of his manner, in answering such numerous addresses as the freedom of the place authorized, and the delicate way in which he interposed between this unknown charmer, and every light speech made to her, more than delighted, fixed Miss Arden. But dare I hope to gain such a creature? sighed she: or even if I do, dare I think it possible to keep him? They were now in an illuminated walk, leading from the pavilion to the house. The Marquis had distanced her masqued admirers, and the saving her from falling, when she accidentally slipt, left him in possession of the softest whitest hand in the world. He now addressed her at once with more tenderness, and more rationality. The delicacy and justness of her replies enchanted him. This is indeed a creature to share one's life with, thought he; and Miss Arden felt he more passionately grasped the hand she was not prude enough to draw from him. Love insensibly became the subject of their discourse; he found the little white hand tremble: good! thought our young man, I would have it do so—but before he had sufficiently recollected himself, Miss Arden was mistress of her mind: "No my Lord," said she, with a gay raillery, in return to some fond avowal of his partiality, "I will never be a receiver of stolen goods; and when I tell you it has been whispered to me your heart was allotted ere you knew you had one to give, you will not be surprised at my doubts of my own power over you."—Emily now drew her hand from him, and was lost in a brilliant crowd. And who are you, cried the Marquis, pursuing her with his eyes, who know so well the foolish bargain made for me? I must follow and render the knowledge mutual.—In a moment the Marquis was at the side of Emily, with whom he again gaily trifled, till the crowd dissipated.—Never will I part with my fair Italian, cried he, grasping her hand as if he then felt it his own for life, till she does more justice to my sensibility than to suppose I shall ever deign to take a wife chosen by others, and to my taste than to conclude a little unpolished rustic bred in the wilds of Ireland, and my perpetual ridicule, would be that wife.—The Marquis ceased to speak; but how was Miss Arden to reply?—To raise the curtain between human nature and eternity, could hardly astonish a doubting anxious wretch, more than these words did the thunderstruck Emily. "He hates, he despises me!" exclaimed she mentally: "the Marquis of Lenox, my betrothed husband, the man whom of all men I alone can love, loathes the wife imposed on him; and have *I* been so imposed? Oh unfortunate Emily! undone by too much kindness."—Finding the charmer replied not, the Marquis pursued his discourse: "You, whoever you are, who know me so well, need not perhaps be told I have never seen this redoubtable, troublesome, uncouth cousin of mine; need I add that I never intend so to mortify my eyes?"—"Never, never, shall you," sighed to herself the afflicted, yet incensed, Emily. To him she spoke no more; but replying to the indiscriminate compliments of the many who hovered near her, took the first opportunity to quit the masquerade, and hasten to her own apartment. Alone, tearful, mortified, dejected, she threw aside her mandoline, and hastily tearing off the gay paraphernalia assumed for conquest, sat down to quarrel with the lovely face her glass reflected. "Yes, no doubt I have always been flattered: if my father is blinded by my fortune, and his own partiality, well may the mean, and the interested, deceive me. I am, I dare say, the uncouth wild Irish rustic, this insolent irresistible Lenox so frankly calls me; and, but for him, I had never known it. Yet ah! why came I in pursuit of affliction? Why invited I the odious sincerity? Why did I ever see, or, in seeing, why did I not hate in turn, my capricious, charming cousin—the allotted of my early days?—Oh! why, in the erroneous choice of my father, did this weak heart find, or fancy, the most perfect of human beings? I will not, however, be as unjust as himself. *He* is certainly all he would be; and I can only lament the wanting that superiority over my own sex, he so eminently possesses over his."

Emily now cast her eyes on the elegant dishabille, her maid had laid ready for the morning. "What! to appear again before this cousin—repeat the same mortifying scene under the scrutinizing eyes of a large company, many of whom knew both the relationship, and the engagement? No, that I can never, never submit to," sighed Miss Arden:—"to fly home is yet in my power. The Marquis knows not the insult he has offered me; and if he knows, may hate her he now only scorns. The bark is at my command, and I may sail for Ireland with the next tide. There, unnoticed and unknown, let the little rustic wither. Yes, dear Lenox, this way I may shew a generous regard, which will one day ensure me thy esteem. Be from this hour master of thy own resolves; find the happy woman who may give thee happiness; nor ever learn thou hast thus humbled, and afflicted a creature whose dearest hope has long been that of becoming thy choice."

Emily flew to the apartment of her hostess, to impart the strange incident of the evening,—to implore a general secresy as to her name,—and then declared the magnanimous resolution she had formed of quitting the party. But this had no sooner the sanction of her friend's approbation, than a strange kind of regret, a secret ill-humour, made poor Miss Arden know, she had hoped to be entreated to stay. Alas! she might never more see the Marquis, and how was she sure that when he knew, he would disdain her? But *if* he should, that tremendous *if*, ever so conclusive in a delicate and virtuous mind, at once made Emily satisfied to be gone. Orders were sent to the mariners to be ready at sunrise, and Miss Arden retired; to walk about her chamber, meditate, wonder, wish,

———— "resent, regret,
Conceal, disdain, do all things but forget."*

The Marquis of Lenox, in the interim, wholly unconscious of the malice of his stars, was something surprised, and perplexed, at suddenly missing the fair Italian, but naturally imputed her retiring to heat, fatigue, and the lateness of the hour; and having enquired her name, and being told the one she assumed, threw his head on his pillow, to dream of the face that to-morrow morning would present to him in all its beauty.

The sun arose too soon for Miss Arden's wishes; and the sailors had sent notice the tide served at that hour. Impatient to be at home, they came for the trunks, and urged her to hasten to the beach: it was only two hundred yards below the gate of the garden. All was dead silence—the variegated lamps in the walks, late so crowded, were yet burning; but

>"'Gan to pale their ineffectual fires."

So general had been the fatigue, as well as enjoyment, that hardly could the servants of the family open their eyes to unbar the gates for the fair, the early traveller: those gates that were perhaps for ever to shut her from the object of her tenderest contemplations: even at the moment of renouncing him, the sad pleasure of her life—by the most grievous occurrence become so dear, at the very point of time that assured her of his loss. Emily lingered—she sighed—nay, she wept—It is true, she insisted to her maid, that her feet were wounded by the pebbles; for not to herself would she own the wound to be in her heart. Seated, at length, on the deck of the bark, Miss Arden once more wistfully surveyed the hospitable mansion she had perhaps too hastily quitted. The beams of the rising sun burnished all the windows, but the shutters were universally closed; and Emily saw the idol she sought there, only in her heart. "Thank heaven, he knows me not, however," repeated she to herself; and though this grateful exclamation recurred every moment, her own soul told her all it knew of comfort was the recollection, that, if he was *very* inquisitive, many of the company could inform him who it was had excited his curiosity.

The cause of the perpetual delays made by the Marquis, as to visiting Bellarney, was now too clearly explained—too fully understood. "Why, why, my father, would you then dupe me?" sighed Miss Arden: "why studiously bias my heart towards a young man, by whom you knew it slighted—scorned? Yet, alas! my father might, like myself, be deceived, and the dupe of his own wishes["]. To complete her mortification, she then discovered it would be her hard fate to explain to Sir Edward the insult to which he had involuntarily exposed her.

Such were the continual contemplations of the melancholy heiress of Bellarney, as she wandered, spiritless, heartless, through that splendid mansion, the increasing infirmities of her grandmother would soon make entirely her own. The chilling air of Miss Fitzallen, now the chosen and perpetual companion of the old Countess, and the fretful questions of the invalid, made the gentle timid Emily retreat often, as if she felt herself an intruder. In the solitude of the woods of Bellarney she, however, found nothing repelling, though the sound of the "wilds of Ireland" yet rang in her ears; nor could she survey the fair face her glass reflected, without recalling the idea of the "little unpolished rustic." Yet, by one means or another, it is certain she passed almost the whole of her time in thinking of a man, who, it was plain, thought too little of her, either under her own name, or that she had assumed, to cross a safe, and very short passage in pursuit of her.

In this she was, however, mistaken. The Marquis had risen, on the morning of her departure, at an earlier hour than usual. He had been more studiously elegant in his undress than his valet ever knew him, and was pacing in a saloon, where a magnificent breakfast was prepared for the whole party, ere a creature appeared. Convinced his Italian could neither hide her luxuriant fair hair, nor lose her graceful mien, he watched the entry of each lady, till the signal was given for breakfast, without being able to discover, in the gay group, one he could mistake for the charmer. He now ventured a faint enquiry for her. "She sailed for Ireland at break of day," half a dozen ready voices answered.—"Sailed for Ireland!" returned the lover, in a tone of dismay, "while I was stupidly dreaming of her I should have attended! But are you sure she is gone?" The beaux, as in malice, conducted him to a telescope, which shewed him the vessel, though it was hardly visible to the naked eye. Ardour of heart, and impetuosity of temper, characterized our young man; and it was happy for those allied to him, that he had hitherto been too rational greatly to desire many things, for those he did desire he never knew how to deny himself: and, to prevent even his wishes, had been from his infancy the study not only of his parents, but of every one around him. The breakfast, the party, the modes of life, vanished at once from his mind, and he hastened through the garden to the beach, where a group of fishermen sat warming themselves in the sun, and leisurely mending their nets, while their ready boats, now plucked from, and now thrown towards the shore, invited them to try the fortune of the day. The Marquis hastily demanded, if it was possible to reach the vessel which sailed with the tide of the morning. "What, with the pretty young lady?" cried one of the men, with an arch smile, and scratching his head. "You saw her, then?" returned the eager lover. "Saw her! aye, to be sure, we saw her, sure enough; and so might you, if you had opened but half an eye; for she did look back many's the time and often, and examine all the windows of the great house. I warrant she thought somebody would have been stirring with the lark this morning."—"Ah! could it be for me she looked?" thought the Marquis, while a faint blush reproved the vanity—"no—for then she would have staid—at least, a few hours. Hoist your sails, however, my honest fellows, and follow; here is gold to encourage you."

Already was the boat prepared—already the Marquis had leaped into it, and his servants were hastening to embark with his trunks, when a signal was made which stopped the fishermen; and a man on horseback appeared, the domestics of the Marquis knew to be one of the Duke's. He waved to them to stop, and presented to the young Lord letters from his father and uncle, informing him that the Duchess had had a paralytic seizure, so alarming, as to leave her half motionless, and quite without speech. Even in this state, she by signs continually demanded her son, who must hasten to her without delay, or lose the consolation of softening her last moments.

Never was son more fondly, though to weakness, beloved:—never was mother regarded with more affectionate devotion. The power of nature overwhelmed that of passion, and the fair Italian was no longer remembered. Actuated by the same impetuosity, however distinct the occasion, the Marquis mounted the horse which had brought the servant, and flew towards home, leaving his suite to follow, for to overtake him was not possible. The Duchess had still some remains of recollection, when her son took her in his arms; but it seemed as if she had struggled to retain her last sigh only to breathe it on his bosom.

For a considerable time the generous, affectionate heart of the Marquis mourned a loss he felt the more sensibly, from seeing how little impression it made on his father; in whom he soon discovered a coldness never till that period apparent. In truth he had been the first bond of union between his parents, and he had long been the only one. The indulgence of the Duke to him had been merely habit, and diminished daily, as it interfered with that he thought it right to grant to himself. Neither apathy nor sensuality withdrew however from the Marquis the sympathy or indulgence of Sir Edward Arden, who had, though he often greatly blamed, always fondly loved his sister, and now joined with her son in deeply lamenting her. The youth she had a thousand times recommended to his parental care and attention, became doubly dear as her representative; and the Marquis felt his attachment to this generous uncle so augmented by the tears they daily shed together, that when the cherished remembrance of the fair Italian presented itself, he rejoiced he had been prevented from following her; since to have been known to visit Ireland without paying his devoirs to Miss Arden, would have wounded Sir Edward to the soul; nor could the little trip have been concealed, had the boat his father's groom stopt, once put from the shore with him. The Marquis was of an age when the impressions of one week efface those of the last; and he found it a much easier task to give up all thoughts of the fair stranger, than to encounter the formidable heiress to whom he had been so long affianced.

To avoid sealing by word, or deed, the compact, till increase of years, or other circumstances, should make him master of his own resolutions, was now the object with the Marquis; and this he thought might best be effected by making the grand tour.* He daily found it advisable to discover deficiencies in himself, not obvious to any other person; and declared nothing but a more general knowledge of men and manners could qualify him to fill the rank he was born to. The Duke had been too sensible, in his own person through life, of the disadvantage of a contracted mode of education; and nothing but the ill-judged fondness of the Duchess had kept her son so long in his own country. Since her death, the Duke had likewise made another discovery;—that his son was grown a man, while he found himself in some respects yet a boy; and that both the Marquis, and his rational, correct uncle, were terrible drawbacks on the use of that liberty he now began again to enjoy to licentiousness. The choice of the Marquis being applauded by his father, Sir Edward found his opposition would be vain. Yet mortal was the chagrin he felt at seeing this darling nephew, with a heart glowing and unfixed, formed by nature to charm, and disposed to be charmed, ready to plunge into the world, where he might so soon be lost, ere yet his Emily had been allowed the chance of attaching him to whom she was betrothed. Perfectly aware of all the seductions to which an ingenuous open nature exposes a young man, Sir Edward could not, to the one in question, insist on what, by implying weakness of character, often mortally offends self love. Nor did Sir Edward Arden fail to value duly the advantages of his daughter, although he forbore to urge them. He well knew the Marquis, seeing him live within the narrow bounds of a scanty patrimony, could form no judgment of the high style of life his daughter's birth demanded, and her fortune accustomed her to;* yet how, in the calculation of her rights and her merits, could a proud spirit bring forward advantages merely accidental, though often decisive in their effects in the grand computation of human happiness. On mature reflection, the fluctuating father gave up the project of bringing the young people together for the present, and resolved to accompany the Marquis in his tour. The enthusiastic joy of the young man, when informed of his uncle's kindness, well rewarded that uncle.

Due preparations having been made, the Marquis, and Sir Edward, were ready to set out for the Continent, when a courier from Ireland stopped the latter. Miss Arden conjured her father to hasten over, as Lady Bellarney was pronounced beyond all hope, and she had reason to fear she should be unprotected, in case of her death; perhaps insulted by the overbearing Miss Fitzallen; who now assumed rights, which the loss of her patroness would either wholly assure to her, or rob her of. Sir Edward requested the Marquis to delay the tour, till he could fulfil a duty so important; and having vainly waited to hear his nephew offer to accompany him, suppressed as much as possible the bitter chagrin so mortifying a coldness could not but occasion; and, leaving the Marquis in London, hastened to Bellarney, attended only by his valet, and a groom.

It was not without reason that Miss Arden dreaded being in the power of Lady Bellarney's upstart favourite; by whose means she had long been excluded from the fortune, as well as favour, of the Countess. Miss Fitzallen had infinite address: she had in childhood obtained an ascendancy over a weak mind, since subdued by infirmity and age, to imbecility, and by fondness to dotage. The patrimony of Miss Arden was, in right of her mother, secure, and immense; but the old lady had great fortunes she could bestow by will, together with the mansion of Bellarney,—a family honour it ought not to have been in her power to alienate: this, and all in the old Countesses own gift, she had often declared she would bequeath to her *dear girl*, her *tender nurse*, her *young friend*, her *God-daughter*, and *namesake*, Emily Fitzallen. It is true there were some among her neighbours, who would insinuate this young person had a claim beyond those alleged;—that the old lady had been a *gay widow*, and this girl, christened after her, *resembled her very much*. It is certain the Countess never would allow the origin of her protégée to be known; and the haughty Miss Fitzallen latterly always threw at a distance those who presumed to treat her with less distinction than the heiress.

How uncertain are ever the resolutions of a weak mind, and tenacious temper! Lady Bellarney had indeed made a will wholly in Miss Fitzallen's favour, and was in so infirm a state as to make her existence very precarious; when, in a luckless hour, this favourite, against the choice of her benefactress, joined a party going to some races, and who only invited her from knowing the consequence she would shortly have a right to. The peevishness of age, increased by loneliness, aggravated this little selfish indulgence into a heinous fault. The old Countess began bewailing the loss of her own dear Emily, her darling daughter, long laid in the grave. The poor orphan she had left, now came across her mind; but she was cold, inattentive—no matter, she was better than nobody; and Miss Arden, to her great surprise, was summoned to keep her grandmother company. Long the visitor of a moment only, to pay her duty, and superseded in every right of affection, Miss Arden had felt, and appeared a cipher. It was otherwise now. She found no insolent competitor, and soon saw how she could conduce to the personal ease, and mental amusement of Lady Bellarney. Astonished to find such tenderness, skill, and readiness, in a young creature she had been taught to think wholly occupied with herself, the old Countess relaxed at once. During the evening, she confessed to Miss Arden her having given all her possessions to

Miss Fitzallen; and, finally, shewed her a copy of the will. Miss Arden returned it respectfully, and only said, Lady Bellarney could never give her favourite any thing she grudged her like her affection; nor could she live on terms with herself, if she had lost the distinction by any voluntary failure in duty, gratitude, or tenderness. So mild and sweet a reproof had full weight with the capricious Countess; and when Emily knelt, as she nightly did, for her blessing, the invalid, throwing her arms round her, hastily committed to the flames the unjust will, made in a moment of mistaken fondness: vowing, that if she lived to the morning, she would dictate one in favour of her grand-daughter; and if she did not, all would by law devolve to her. This important change in her resolution kept Lady Bellarney awake almost the whole night; and finding herself, of course, weaker and worse, her lawyer was sent for. He, in a summary, but regular manner, assured to Miss Arden all the possessions of her grandmother; who, with an almost equal injustice, left unnamed, and unprovided for, the young woman she had raised so far above her condition; and who had, from childhood, been subjected to all her whims. Till this unlucky hour, she had, indeed, sacrificed every pleasure of youth, and principle of honour, to soothing and working on the weak woman, who had repeatedly assured her of an ample fortune. Miss Arden knew it rested with herself to secure the discarded favourite a competence; but vainly tried to have it done in the properest manner,—as the act of the obliged.—So inflexible are the resentments of age, so fluctuating the determinations of dotage.

The whole family loved Miss Arden too well, to notice to Miss Fitzallen, when she returned, what had been done in her absence; while, to the astonishment of Miss Arden, her grandmother once more yielded to habitual subjection; and in the servile solicitude, and fulsome flattery of her favourite, forgot her sudden sense of affinity, feeling, and regard to herself. It was impossible to guess what might be the *last* will of a woman, who hardly seemed to have any; and when Lady Bellarney expired, poor Emily Arden knew not, but she might be an intruder in the mansion of her fathers.*

Miss Fitzallen, who was ignorant of any will, but that in her own favour, assumed to herself the necessary powers of directing; and lamented with all the dignity of the heiress of Bellarney. Her mourning was made exactly similar to Miss Arden's, and as for a mother.

With civil enquiries for that young lady's health, she requested to know when Sir Edward would arrive, to attend the opening of the will, and the funeral, *if he chose it*; as well as to remove his daughter from *her* house. In the mean while, she had given orders to the servants, to show every *proper attention* to Miss Arden. Hearing that Sir Edward was hourly expected, she convened not the family circle, exulting in the thought, that by having the will read in his presence, she should effectually mortify a high-spirited man, whose keen eye had often rebuked hers.

To be the object of impertinent politeness, from one born in a manner to wait on her, was a great trial of Miss Arden's temper. Yet, as it was possible she might have the power of retribution too amply in her own hands, Emily deigned not to appear offended. On the day appointed for the reading of the will, the two ladies accidentally met in a narrow gallery; and Miss Fitzallen taking Sir Edward's daughter by the hand, assured her, she took her *behaviour very kindly*; then with a haughty conscious air added, that she should *find her account in it*; for though the library, with every thing else, was willed to *her, that* should be her *present* to Miss Arden.

At this extraordinary juncture Sir Edward arrived; and hardly knew whether he should take the horses from his carriage, or deign to set foot in a house he could doubt to be his daughter's. Miss Arden sent to entreat he would shew her grandmother the last respect of following her to the grave. It was the grave of his angelic wife, and Sir Edward yielded. But Miss Arden had a greater difficulty to prevail on him to listen to the reading of the will. The high and peremptory air with which Miss Fitzallen had announced herself to be sole executrix, and heiress, of the old Countess, left no doubt among the remote relations of her being indeed so; and though Sir Edward thought it possible a will was extant in favour of his daughter, he thought it merely possible: so bad was his opinion of the artful Miss Fitzallen. The relations and friends of the family who had attended the funeral were invited to the reading of the will; and the self-named heiress, overwhelmed with modesty, gratitude, and tears, swept her long mourning robes through the whole train of sycophants, to an upper seat in the room.—Miss Arden, distinguished by simplicity, and sweetness, took the place she had always filled in her grandmother's lifetime: and Sir Edward, not deigning to mingle with the set, leaned on his daughter's chair, as ready to lead her out, the very moment any word that offended his ears reached them.—Imagine the confusion of the mean train who had bowed to Miss Fitzallen, when they heard Emily Arden pronounced, both by nature, and choice, sole heiress, and executrix of Emily, Countess of Bellarney.—Miss Fitzallen remained for a few moments speechless—convulsed—in a manner distorted.—She then outrageously discredited the will; called it a forgery—a base fabrication of Sir Edward Arden, who had ever, she said, hated, and insulted her.—But the reign of arrogance ends with the means.—This wretched creature found hers was already over.—No eye now paid her homage.—No ear now heard a word she uttered.—All parties united to overwhelm Miss Arden with gratulations, which, knowing their true cause, she despised: and feeling even for the insolent by whom she had suffered, she alone spoke to Miss Fitzallen.—The latter, in bitter agitation, implored, entreated, to be suffered to look at the will.—"What makes this young woman so troublesome?" was the chilling exclamation of those persons who had an hour ago thought her born to grace her fortune.—Again agitated beyond utterance, Miss Fitzallen sunk into a seat, to which Sir Edward's generous daughter kindly advanced.—"Recollect, my dear Emily," said she, mildly, "how patiently I have borne, during my whole life, my grandmother's partiality for you; nor thus repine that she has at her death duly considered an affectionate, unoffending child.—Let me lighten your affliction, not add to it—I am not yet by law impowered to say *how* I will provide for you; but be assured the proportion of fortune I shall offer you, if I live to be mistress here, shall not disgrace your education, or my own; nor shall you ever have reason to think yourself forgotten by Lady Bellarney, while Emily Arden represents her."—Dashing with superlative insolence the hand of Miss Arden from hers, the disappointed Miss Fitzallen arose from her seat—the natural majesty of her form dilated by passion to an almost fiendlike grandeur—her large dark eyes flashing with supernatural brightness, and all the rage of her heart burning in scarlet teints on her cheeks.—"Who could mislead you so far Miss Arden," cried she, when words came to her assistance, "as to make you believe *I* would ever owe any thing to Sir Edward Arden's daughter? Since he has taught you how to step between me, and the provision long mine by promise, keep it all—

dear to you may one day be the acquisition—your whole fortune could not buy off my hatred, nor could the empire of the world buy off my revenge."—Rushing through the astonished train of gaping relatives, Miss Fitzallen passed the gates of Bellarney, nor once recollected, till they were closed on her, that she had not whereon to lay her head; or one friend in the world anxious to soothe, serve, or receive her. In a neighbouring cabin, gold procured her a temporary home, till her maid could pack up her cloaths, some jewels, and other valuable presents of the old Countess.

On the mind of Sir Edward, the unmatched insolence of Miss Fitzallen had made such an impression, as doubly endeared to him the daughter he found so unlike her. That amiable young lady, at the age of nineteen, mistress of herself, the magnificent seat of her maternal ancestors, and immense wealth, thought so generously, and acted so wisely, that Sir Edward groaned under the secret sense of her cousin's injustice: that cousin she seemed born to make happy! New hopes and plans took possession of his mind. No duty now bound Miss Arden to move in the narrow circle of her maternal connexions; and her father thought it right to carry her to England, with a suite and establishment proper for her birth and fortune: resolving himself to present her at Court; he fondly hoped the Marquis could not know his Emily, without blushing at his own coldness and injustice; and, being led by the lovers she must necessarily attract, to avow his prior claims, and endeavour to win her heart. As it was not possible at once to arrange all Miss Arden's newly devolved fortunes, Sir Edward was obliged to pass some time in acting the guardian, as well as the parent; and often adverted to the brilliant *entrée* she would make under his auspices, in the gay world. Coldness, silence, dejection, always followed, on the part of Emily. "No—she had not the least taste for the world; and would rather, if her father pleased, pass the time of his absence at Bellarney." The vexed father now sighed to himself, *"Both—both* infatuated* alike!—what can be done with them?"

In renewing the leases, and other negotiations with the tenants and dwellers round Bellarney, Sir Edward learned a hundred tales of the selfishness, meanness, and overbearing disposition of Emily Fitzallen, who still remained at the cabin she had at first retired to, languishing in a fit of sickness. To Miss Arden's proposal, of giving her a handsome fortune, Sir Edward refused his concurrence; nor could Emily dispose of aught considerable without his knowledge, after having made him her guardian, as he ever had been trustee. An annuity just sufficient to save this wretched woman from want and ignominy, Sir Edward thought as much as she merited. To this Miss Arden could only add her own jewels, which were indeed a fortune. With these she sent a kind letter, assuring her former companion, that nothing but her inability to act for herself could have made her appear deficient in generosity or feeling. The jewels sent, she would redeem, when of age, of the price of a proper provision for Lady Bellarney's favourite friend; and, if she died in the interim, she entreated Miss Fitzallen to consider them as her own.

Unaltered in mind, though humbled in fortune, Miss Fitzallen returned the bond of annuity, jewels, and letter, with sovereign contempt, and without a line, into the hands of Sir Edward Arden: who considered his daughter's generosity as mere weakness of temper. He soon converted it into an argument in favour of his own plan of carrying her to England. From arguments he came to injunctions; and finally hinted, that, if she remained without a male protector in her own country, she would be carried off by the first fortune-hunter who had half the courage, or assurance, of Emily Fitzallen. This conclusion appeared so unfair and humiliating to Miss Arden, that she burst into tears, and declared her fate very hard. Sir Edward would know, in what it appeared so. "I shall offend—nay, I shall, I fear, pain you," sighed the gentle Emily, "if I am candid." Still Sir Edward insisted on the truth.—"Pardon me, then, my father," resumed she, "if, weak of character, lowly of mind, as you think your daughter, she should have pride and spirit enough to shun for ever the Marquis of Lenox." Sir Edward started angrily, and gazed intently. "Why shun him, Emily?" was all he could utter. "He hates me, my dear father—he ridicules, he despises me." "And who dared tell you this?" returned Sir Edward, in a tone that admitted the truth of what she said, though his eyes struck fire at the indignity. "Alas! I could not doubt, Sir:—it was from his own lips this mortification reached me.—Controul your passion, and learn the whole story. I do not suppose, had he known, my cousin would have insulted me:—we met in masks, nor does the Marquis guess, to this hour, the wound he gave to a heart he might have won. Alas! it has been my misfortune to be imposed on him: had he thought himself unfettered, I might have had a chance of winning him. He is now lost. Under these circumstances, to *force* myself on his notice—insist on the poor advantages I should in turn despise him if he valued me for—would for ever disgust a mind it would be my pride to convince, my pleasure to win. The little merit I possess would be lost, under the pomp and splendor of my rights in life; which he no doubt concludes the family reason for making him wretched. And could a cold compliance with his engagement fail to make me so? No—rather would I waste the rest of my life in this seclusion, bewailing the want of his heart, for whom," faltered the sweet girl with encreasing confusion, "I had wholly, I will confess to my father, reserved my own." Sir Edward hid her ingenuous blushes in his arms, and fondly prayed to Heaven "yet to unite those hearts so equally dear to him."—"I have not told you," resumed Miss Arden, in the same timid tone, "that I even now despair, if you will leave me to execute a plan I have meditated ever since I found myself at liberty to quit my native country. My wayward cousin is, I must first inform you, a stranger to my features; nor knows he that it was Emily Arden he cruelly humbled in the description of herself. Unless you betray me, I may yet appear before him in any character I chuse to assume; and I have a romantic fancy afloat in my brain, that I cannot execute without your concurrence. Return, my dear father, to England, alone: urge, persecute the Marquis, to visit me in Ireland: and, while he, of all human beings, detests this troublesome overbearing heiress, might he not, on some obscure spot of his father's estates, stumble on a simple rustic, with just such a face as mine, and perhaps love her with his whole heart? Dennis, my silver-headed foster-father, may not unaptly personate my real one; and be a protector. Think of the delight we should both feel, if the poor Marian, in a plaid jacket, should step before your rich Emily, covered with diamonds.—If, on the contrary, I make this effort in vain, let it be a last one. To Bellarney let me fly undiscovered: nor ever allow the Marquis to know he has personally slighted the daughter of a man to whom he has been long endeared by a parental affection."

Age had not yet so chilled the heart of Sir Edward, but that he caught in a degree the glow of his daughter's. The romance was simple—was safe;—if he discharged his groom (for he could trust his valet)—practicable.—While Emily had been thus sweetly insinuating wishes and views so consonant with his own, Sir Edward had considered the soft and unassuming grace of her figure, the delicate turn of her beauty, and the artless eloquence of her voice. He now fancied her in a straw hat, with her fair locks playing round her face, and now adorned for a birth-night;* and he plainly perceived that she might lose, could not gain, a charm, by splendor or fashion. Her plan every moment grew upon his imagination. He saw his prudent Emily, even in her romance, had guarded both his pride, and her own. He well knew, he could not brook the having his daughter, as herself, refused, even by this darling nephew; yet he never recollected the mortal coldness, and probably eternal alienation, such a procedure might cause, without a feeling almost amounting to horror.

After a long silence, Sir Edward embraced his apprehensive daughter, and told her, this experiment had not only his sanction, but warmest approbation; nor would he omit calling upon the Duke, to aid the malicious persecution meditated against her lingering lover, the more fully to prepare his heart, by the agitation of dislike, for the reception of a more pleasing passion. The transport expressed by Emily called forth the power of her soul, and the more dignified graces of her mien, till Sir Edward half rejected the scheme, in the firm persuasion that she could not fail to charm, as herself: but having won his consent, Emily bound him to his word.

How pleasing was her employment, while preparing all things for her obscure departure, and instructing Dennis, and her nurse, in the parts they were to act. When the Scottish cot* should be ready, Sir Edward was to inform his daughter; who could then embark from her own estate.

Nor was Sir Edward without his share of delightful hopes and recollections. To know the fate of the two most dear to him on earth, so near a crisis that promised to be happy, gave his heart those sweet pulsations, which have all the charm and softness of passion, without its danger.

And now, what became of the Marquis? Why, he devoutly wished the old Countess "an earthly immortality."* But, finding her soul had made its escape without his permission, he heartily prayed he could make his, ere Sir Edward returned to London: for that he would bring with him this odious Irish heiress, was, he thought, too certain. At the moment Sir Edward's carriage drove to his father's door, he was coming out of it: and, what a relief was visible in his features, when he saw it contained not a female. How cordial were now their greetings! The Duke, however, not having the least objection to Miss Arden's company, enquired why her father had not, at last, brought her. Sir Edward very naturally answered, that he had fully meant to do so; had not some of Miss Arden's romantic female friends in the interim insinuated to her, that it would be a high indecorum in her to seek the Marquis of Lenox; and, from the moment that whim had taken root in her mind, it was impossible to remove it. Fixed as every thing had long been for the tour abroad, he added, that he imagined it would have been irksome to his nephew, had he then proposed the visit to Ireland. A female, of advanced years, and due consideration, had therefore been found to give propriety to Miss Arden's remaining at her own seat, till the tour, which they must now necessarily shorten, should be made; when he hoped the Marquis would be as ready as himself to attend on his bride elect.

The Marquis, finding the evil day of insipid courtship once again deferred, was no longer in such haste to commence his tour; and heard that law affairs must detain his uncle for some time in town, with great satisfaction. This conduct made Sir Edward enjoy, almost to malice, the meditated attack on him, which he meant should shortly come from his father.

In hours of loneliness, Sir Edward recounted to the Duke his daughter's little history of the slight she had borne, and the effort she now meant to make to engage the affections of the Marquis: but the natural delicacy of his mind made him represent the plan as his own, and one to which she had with some difficulty consented;—resolving, if this failed, no longer to sacrifice her claims in society, to an ungrateful relation who despised her. The Duke was a matter-of-fact man, and easily followed the idea presented to him; nor failed to lecture his son on the disrespect shewn to Miss Arden; which was not only calculated to rob him of all hopes of her heart, but to induce her to carry into another family the immense fortune she inherited; while that he was born one day to call his own, was already insufficient for two men, neither of whom was old enough to give up his tastes, or young enough to be controuled in them. It is true, the love, respect, and confidence, the Marquis once had for his father, had declined from the day of his mother's death; but he had not yet learned to act in opposition to his will. Indeed, till this moment, he had not felt it. The important cause was argued, and re-argued; and Sir Edward, by turns, appealed to, as the judge. He had always the address to avoid so odious an office; yet his nephew thought he could perceive it would be easier to work on his mind, than the cold, worldly, selfish one of his father. How grievous to find he had such a father, and to recollect that his mother brought no fortune into the family, and that he had not a claim to a guinea during the life of the Duke!

The arrangements in Scotland were now made for the establishing of Emily; and the feelings of the Marquis wrought up to a high pitch, when the two fathers found out that his signature, ere he went abroad, would be essentially necessary to some family deeds, which must be executed in Scotland. The recollection of the vicinity of the castle to Port Patrick,* made the Marquis very unwilling to go, lest his father should drag him to the feet of Miss Arden; yet he ventured not to hint the idea, as that might lead to the determination.

Sir Edward having no need of an English groom on the Continent, easily parted with the one who had attended him in Ireland: nor was there a single domestic in the suite of the family party, who had ever seen Miss Arden. Arrived within a bowshot of the cot where she had taken up her abode, whole days passed away without Sir Edward's daring to set foot in it, or see his daughter, lest suspicion should follow. He could not persuade himself it was possible she should conceal her birth, of which her deportment was so expressive; or avoid, on seeing the Marquis, the deep confusion that implies design. On full deliberation, Sir Edward resolved to break in upon her by accident; and in taking a morning's ride with his nephew and the Duke, affected to be seized with a vertigo, and almost fell from his horse. The Marquis and grooms lifted him off, and assistance was hastily demanded from the adjacent cot, whence came the silver-headed Dennis; soon outstript by a wood nymph so exquisitely animated and lovely, that, to the astonished Marquis, the Graces seemed all embodied in a rustic of Scotland. The disguised Marian, alarmed with the sudden attack of Sir Edward, forgot the Duke would be a spectator, remembered not the Marquis, even when their looks met; but sensible only to filial anxiety and affection, fixed her dark blue eyes on Sir Edward, and gave to herself the first, and dearest charm in humanity,—the having forgotten she had one. A wicker chair was now brought, and Sir Edward placed in it; the white hands of Marian assiduously sprinkled his forehead with cold water, while drops, more vivifying than art, or nature ever otherwise prepared, fell from her cheek to his. How sweet was this moment to a father so tender; to find love itself was lost in the sense of his imaginary danger. Placed on the humble bed of Dennis, a valet opened a vein in his arm.* Marian, the ready Marian, prepared, and fixed the bandage, administered the cordial, nor was it till all that could be done, was done, that she suddenly found herself standing before those who were to decide her fate; the single object of their attention. In the looks of the Duke she discovered that he knew, and, knowing, approved her. In those of his son she discerned a restrained, but boundless admiration; a something, that passing from his heart to hers, seemed to bind them sweetly together, by an unseen, but indissoluble ligament. Sir Edward cast his eyes from one to the other, and had his full share in a feeling, that made the humble hut of Dennis appear a paradise to every being it contained.

The Duke had sent for his coach to convey the invalid home. The Marquis desired to accompany him; and the carriage was no sooner in motion, than each fell into a rêverie, though in both the same object caused it. The Marquis at length broke silence; and not having yet had experience enough to observe that the thing a person first speaks of, after a long meditation, has generally been its subject, exclaimed, "how beautiful, how redundant, her fair hair! once only"— Sir Edward, not more cautious, cried, "and the softest hand in the world—would it were now bathing these burning temples."—"I can fetch her in a moment, uncle"—said the impetuous youth, attempting to open the coach door, and glad of an excuse of returning. "Not for the world, my dear boy—she is young—not ordinary—I would neither trust your father, nor his dissipated servants:—were I to cause her innocence a risque, I should never forgive myself." The Marquis put up his lip in silence: could Sir Edward think so superior a creature could listen to the servants—or be bought by his father? Sir Edward read this in his face, and saw, in the contempt the Marquis ventured not to avow, the interest Marian had already gained in his heart.

The Marquis now again was in no hurry to commence his tour:—he, therefore, less lamented his uncle's illness, though it kept him almost wholly in his apartment—where he often revolved the means of establishing an interest in the heart of this lovely creature, who alone, of all he had ever seen, reminded him of the fair-haired Grace, who, as an Italian peasant, appeared, as it were, to enchant, and vanished to bewilder him.—After many contemplations on the subject, he put twenty guineas in a purse, and having wandered doubtfully for some hours round the cot of Dennis, faintly rapped at the door.—Marian herself opened it: but Sir Edward being no longer near, to mark, or to divide her attention, so rich a blush mantled on her fair cheek, as might give the most modest of men a hope he had not been unnoticed by her. The Marquis, with a varying complexion, and timid air, enquired for her mother.—The aged dame rose from her spinning wheel, and the silver-headed Dennis from reading the Bible: each depositing a pair of spectacles in the case, remained standing to receive the commands of the young Lord.—To behold thus in the light of subjection his charmer, and the venerable old people, strangely distressed the Marquis.—Had Marian not been there, his rank would have been less oppressive.—With much hesitation, he gave them to understand, that Sir Edward Arden had made him the bearer of his acknowledgments for their benevolence. He then put into the mother's hand the purse, and its glittering contents.—"No, no, my Lord," cried the respectable Dennis, "that can never be.—Wife, give his honour back the purse. Sir Edward sent his own valet yesterday evening with a present of two new guineas, fresh from the mint, for our Marian." The Marquis was dumb at what he thought the meanness of his uncle.—To affront the charmer of his soul, with the paltry gift of two guineas!—sent by his valet too!—He turned to apologize to Marian, but she had disappeared: no wonder, when she heard herself, and two guineas, spoken of together. "Well, my good old friend," said the Marquis, "my uncle might do the odd, mean thing you say, for he has been delirious, and raving often of your assiduous Marian.—But he is now in his senses, and better knows how to respect himself, and your daughter. I have no mind to drive him into a frenzy again, by taking back the little mark of his gratitude." Having thus said, he laid down the purse, and ran out of the cot. Having perceived in a field very near, the plaid dress of Marian, he was at her side in a moment;—spoke of her generous sympathy—the illness of his uncle—the wild beauty of the scenery around,—any thing, every thing, that might prolong the exquisite pleasure he found in being one minute the single object of her attention, the engrosser of her thoughts, and conversation; yet Marian seldom spoke, and always said the least she could; nor did she often raise her dark blue eyes to meet the impassioned glances of the Marquis. Still a sympathetic charm never to be defined told him she was not insensible to his presence—not willing to bid him farewell.

Neither in the sick chamber of Sir Edward, nor in the saloon with the Duke, did this Grace of the woods ever become the subject of discourse; yet both the fathers were well informed, that the Marquis hovered anxiously, early and late, near the cot of Dennis, well rewarded if he obtained but a word, a glance from Marian.—Sir Edward did not find it convenient for him to recover very soon; and never did his nephew think it possible till now, that he should dread seeing him leave his chamber: but to be dragged out of the kingdom ere he had time to win on the affections of her he adored, or to bind her to him by mutual vows, almost distracted him. The Duke easily perceived his distress, and agitation; but as the two fathers had agreed that the fear of losing her would best secure the attachment of the Marquis, by rendering her the perpetual object of his thoughts, they would not consent to her avowing herself.

Nothing but the dread of separation, and the necessity of employing the short time the lovers were able to pass together in conversations respecting the future, could have kept the Marquis in ignorance of the past; for his mind was often filled with a vague idea of something mysterious in the situation of Marian; as well as elevated in her language, and manners.—But who, thinking every look he gives to her he loves may be the last, can press for details of remote occurrences?

Sir Edward was now ready to depart: the happiest of fathers to know his Emily had conquered;—that she reigned in the ardent heart of the young nobleman, who had in secret solemnly affianced himself to the choice of his parents,—the once dreaded, hated Emily Arden.—Often, when she saw him at her feet, the glowing exultation of secret triumph so heightened her beauty, that the delighted lover wondered in vain at its suddenly acquiring so celestial a charm.—It was now the precise moment for tearing him from her; and both fathers again proposing the tour to the Continent, any delay, on the part of the Marquis, would, he easily saw, have led to a discovery of his motive. Every leisure moment he flew to Marian, to lament his untoward fate, and execrate the cold nature of those who thought it possible he should find in the overbearing Irish heiress, a creature who could dispute his heart with Marian.—That name, so humble, so rustic, now was music to the ear of Sir Edward's daughter; for under that she had given, and received, vows, which no time, no circumstance, could ever annul.

Sir Edward now suddenly seemed to recollect how proper it would be for him to make his personal acknowledgments to the daughter of Dennis, and chose to have the company of his nephew. The cottagers received the visit with joy and gratitude. Sir Edward very gravely exhorted them to guard so lovely a creature as Marian from the attacks of the Duke, or the humiliation of marrying one of his servants. The Marquis, and his charming mistress, exchanged souls in a glance, not unseen by the watchful Sir Edward. He concluded this exhortation with informing the old people, that whenever they found a suitable match for their daughter, they might apprize him, and he would portion and patronize her. Ah! uncle, will you really do this when a *suitable* match occurs? said the intelligent eyes of the Marquis.

Sir Edward allowed the cottagers an annuity of twenty pounds a year, and departed overwhelmed with blessings: unable himself to utter one of the many his heart poured on his Emily. The Marquis no sooner saw his uncle again in his own apartment, than he flew back, to reiterate, under a more flattering and tender form, the same cautions to Marian. He made her again promise, vow, solemnly swear, to live for him, and him alone. What laws in return did he not impose on himself! how impossible did it appear to him that he should ever find a charm in another woman; or ever breathe to a second object a vow like that he now blended with his parting kiss, his long farewell. The interesting Marian left on his cheek, the seal of true love, in a tear; and had the resolution to see him depart in the full conviction he spoke only as he thought, and that all their present pains would eventually complete their mutual wish.

"Ah! happy error in the good and just,
Whose upright natures never know distrust:
Distrust, which is itself almost a sin,
And often marks the villain wrote within."

With the embarkation of the Marquis, Miss Arden's disguise ended. She accompanied the Duke of Aberdeen to London, where a lady was already waiting to sanction her living in his house. When presented at court, the admiration she excited, procured her high offers of marriage, though many lovers retreated, her engagement with the Marquis being universally understood. Surrounded with her own friends, and suite of attendants, Miss Arden had no motive for anxiety but the absence of the Marquis; yet as that only could prove the truth and strength of his attachment, which the most impassioned letters daily confirmed, she had very little cause to complain of her fate.

And now the Marquis and his uncle were for the first time in Paris; plunged into that busy vortex, the world, where the virtues are often at once ingulphed; and if they ever rise again, it is in fragments, hardly resembling their first state. Yet such a guard, on a noble nature, is a true and tender passion, that the Marquis found not the love of pleasure lead to licentiousness, nor that of distinction, to corruption of soul. The strongest emotion of vanity he felt, when the object of universal attention, was a faint wish that the charmer of his heart could know the value of it, by seeing how many were willing to dispute it with her. But what an enviable fate was Sir Edward Arden's! enabled, unsuspected, to trace to its inmost recesses the emotions of the heart he best loved; to see all that was generous and amiable in nature point to one object, and that one object his own dear Emily! Not a letter did the trembling hand of the Marquis open from her, that the glow of his cheek, the triumph of his soul, did not announce to his watchful guardian; who, thus satisfied that he was relieved from his charge, gave the young man up to his own pursuits, and followed those himself that were more adapted to his period of life. And if the father thus exulted, how must the lover, who found in those letters of his fair rustic, a delicacy, softness, and refinement, he in vain sought in the rest of her sex: for, however cautiously Miss Arden veiled, in her correspondence, the high polish of her education, the feelings of her heart alone gave them a charm peculiar to herself; while the confiding tenderness they breathed, was the dearest of all claims on the faith of her lover.

Sir Edward, who had ever a turn for study, and the fine arts, introduced his nephew, with himself, into the society of all persons eminent in literature and science.—The Marquis had a taste for drawing, in which Sir Edward excelled. As both proposed taking views of the scenes that most should please them, the young nobleman engaged an eminent master, under whose instruction he made a rapid progress; and, ere long, had almost as much knowledge as might perpetuate to his soul the pleasure that otherwise fades on the eye. The season now was at hand, when Sir Edward and his nephew proposed following the course of the Loire in their travels. The drawing-master, one day, while they were enlarging on the labours they should embark in, suggested how irksome it ever is to fill up the outline we delight to throw off the fancy; and that he had, among his less fortunate pupils, a youth it would be an act of benevolence to employ: that he was an orphan, in narrow circumstances, but of very superior talents; who, having no hope of future provision, but by improving and exerting them, would think himself well rewarded in the protection and patronage of two men of taste, who would allow him to employ part of his time in studying the immortal models they must necessarily visit in Florence and Rome. The Marquis, it is true, loved drawing, but he was of an age to love his ease; and this proposal united things as distinct. He appointed a time to see the youth; whom, in the interval, he proposed to his uncle as an addition to their little suite. Sir Edward agreed, that if his talents equalled the account of them, to take him, would be an act of kindness to themselves, as well as the boy.

When the drawing-master presented the young man by the name of Hypolito (for he was the son of an Italian painter so called), his extreme youth and pallid looks (for he seemed hardly sixteen, and consumptive) struck Sir Edward, who, with unusual abruptness, urged that objection. The modest lad shrunk back. Tears rushed into his eyes, and the wild air of distress was blended, on his languid countenance, with unmerited humiliation. The Marquis took an interest ever in the unfortunate; and, having cheared Hypolito, sat down with him to draw. The youth took the piece the Marquis was finishing; and at once proceeding with rapidity, while he touched all parts with elegance, shewed he was indeed a treasure to travellers, and a master in his art. Sir Edward was now no less charmed than his nephew. "Nor is drawing his only talent," said his introducer, handing to the youth the flute the Marquis played in a capital manner. Hypolito breathed on it, and it seemed to have the charm of the lute of Orpheus,* on all but the person who held it; and he, sinking back in a chair, almost fainted. On reviving, the poor lad with blushes accounted for the illness, by confessing he had not tasted food that day. Immediate succour was given him. The Marquis caressed him like a brother. From that hour he cast off the mean garments of poverty, for some of his younger patron's own cloaths—by care, and good living, recovered his looks, and was the constant companion, in all elegant and scientific pursuits, of the Marquis of Lenox. The world had given him every good but a friend, and that he found in Hypolito.—While Sir Edward saw with delight his nephew filling up his life with so rational a pleasure, many a time did he shiver on the water, or broil on the land, without complaining, when he found their ardent natures bent on perpetuating the scene before them. Sir Edward himself played on the violincello; and seldom did they rest at a town, or village, where they could not add a performer, or two, to the concert, and thus inspirit the evening.

Enchanted with the gay scenery, the romantic pleasures of Italy, the Marquis wanted only his Marian to share the delight; and well could he have been pleased to pass his whole life there. But it had not this charm for Hypolito. From the moment they quitted France, urbanity of manners vanished. In the petty states of Italy, the little souls of the nobles contract into a very narrow circle what they are pleased to call society. Not all the advantages Nature can lavish—not all the acquirements Genius can attain, give acceptation, among that arrogant body, to a man born without a positive rank in life, or at least that affluence which bestows on him the appearance of rank. How, then, can he who supports himself by the exertion of talents hope to be received by those who make it their pride to be without any? Sir Edward and his nephew mixed, as they were every way entitled to do, in the first circles; but a deep sense of the solitary situation of poor Hypolito, who was in that middle state which made it as impossible he should associate with the domestics, as be countenanced by their lords, often drew towards home the heart, and not unfrequently the feet, of the Marquis; for seldom found he a companion he liked so well.—The gratitude and affection of Hypolito induced him to exert every talent and grace, to endear himself to so generous a patron; and, as there is no charm so fascinating to the young mind as that of giving at once distinction and pleasure, the Marquis grew daily more attached to the humble Hypolito. So marked a friendship drew the observation of the young noblemen, who wished not to know more of the merit that caused it; yet every day produced a new banter among the set, who, by rudely staring at the youth, marked a strange doubt of his sex.

Sir Edward began, after passing a year in Italy, to bend his thoughts towards home; and proposed returning to his nephew. The unpleasant recollection of Miss Arden damped the tender one of Marian; and the Marquis found it easier to live without the latter, than to see the former; for to marry her came not within his calculation of things. Till the heiress should have disposed of herself, he knew it would be vain to hope he should prevail on either his father or uncle to approve his humble bride; and he resolved to travel to the Antipodes,* if Miss Arden persisted in waiting his return.

Sicily, the land of fable, was yet unvisited by the travellers. The Count Montalvo, a nobleman of that island, with whom Sir Edward, and his nephew, were in habits of intimacy, offered to ensure their safety, and become their Cicerone* in visiting the many monuments of art and history that celebrated spot abounds in. Hypolito was urgent for the tour, as well to escape the observation of a circle he had no pretension to mix with, as to indulge his natural taste. The Count had a bark of his own, which, shortly after, conveyed him, with a large party of friends, to Messina.* During this little voyage, it was impossible for Hypolito to be wholly invisible; yet the Marquis was hardly less disgusted with his Italian friends, than his *protégé* declared himself. The rude inquisitive eyes, and broken observations, of the ill-bred grandees, made both youths happy to be once more on land. The Marquis had another reason for avoiding the sea; he was always a severe sufferer by the indisposition it very commonly occasions. When, therefore, the party proposed visiting the Lipari isles,* the Marquis excused himself, and remained with Hypolito at the palace of Count Montalvo, who accompanied Sir Edward. The Prince, then Governor of Messina, ordered a splendid entertainment, to which the English strangers were universally invited; nor could the Marquis decline going, though not accustomed to attend these parties, and very unwilling to leave his Hypolito, for whom his attachment had been daily increasing in a manner very surprizing even to himself. They had ridden together in the morning, which proved so sultry, as to have heated the blood of the Marquis, before he went to the palace of the Prince. A very little excess in wine acted powerfully on a constitution already feverish with violent exercise; and he quitted the Governor's party ere the masqued ball, with which the entertainment was to conclude. The day was not closed when he came home; but Hypolito, who was drawing, had already called for lights. As the Marquis entered the magnificent suite of rooms allotted to himself and friends, his eye was led through them all, to the last, where he saw Hypolito deeply engaged with his subject. Shades over the wax-lights softened the glare, and gave the most feminine delicacy to the youth's naturally delicate complexion. His dark locks broke in redundant curls over the fairest forehead in the world, and played upon his throat and neck, the heat having obliged him to throw open his shirt collar. Suddenly he took the piece he was drawing, and, holding it behind the light, to survey it, the Marquis could not avoid observing the whiteness and smallness of his hands. "For your own credit and mine," cried the Marquis, gaily seizing his young favourite by the shoulder, "row, ride, drive, dig—do something to get rid of this white skin, and those delicate hands; for I cannot long stand the raillery I have encountered for this month past; and you must make up your mind to be considered as a woman in future, unless you contrive to get something more the look of a man." It was only by chance the Marquis removed his eye from the landscape he had taken from Hypolito, to raise it to his face; but, dropping the drawing from his hands, it there became in a manner rivetted. That beauty, always too delicate for a man, had now the softest charm of woman, a mantling suffusion, a downcast grace.—The dangerous silence that followed, was at length, in a faltering voice, broken by Sir Edward's nephew. "And what embodied angel, then, are you," cried he, "dropt from the skies only to guide and guard me?"—The Marquis spoke in the most winning voice; yet the charmer replied not; but, sinking on his shoulder, as he knelt at her feet, hid there her blushes, and communicated her tremblings.—Let no one vaunt fidelity, who avoids not danger.—The Marquis, already fevered by wine, found the intoxication now passing into his soul. The fair, the pure image of the distant Marian vanished from his memory; and he saw, heard, thought of, only this nameless, trembling, charmer. That she had followed him by choice, was very obvious;—for his sake had endured inconvenience, indignity, fatigue, and even servile degradation. The entreaties he redoubled to extort her secret, bewildered more and more, every moment, a head and heart already confused and impassioned; nor were the tears she now profusely poured forth, wanting to confirm her influence over the surprized, delighted lover. How, then, were his feelings awakened, when she at length avowed herself the slighted, detested daughter of Sir Edward Arden!—that, hopeless of ever conquering in her own character the inveterate prejudice he had conceived against her, and resolved he should never be master of her hand from any motive but choice, she had quitted Ireland ere her father and the Marquis left England; had assumed this disguise, and sought them at Paris, hardly hoping to escape the keen eye of her father: but convinced, if he should recognize her, his pride would make him conceal what he would never have authorized. Happily, however, he had not lived enough with her to have the same quick recollections other parents have of their children. And, far from being discovered by him, she had found herself so long overlooked by the Marquis, though beset by most of his Italian friends, that it was her full intention, the first safe opportunity, to quit Messina, and give up all thoughts of a man, who, whether as Miss Arden she sought a lover in him, or as Hypolito a friend, knew not how to distinguish or to value her.

But this was a charge she knew her own injustice in making; the eyes of the Marquis now dwelt enamoured on her beauty; his eager ear carried to his heart the comprehensive, though implied tenderness, her words conveyed. Too well he recollected the slights he had shewn Miss Arden; to atone for them, he knelt, implored, repented, vowed; *would* be forgiven: in fine, he was so. In the impassioned conversation that ensued, nothing occurred to enlighten the Marquis: he found this impostor as familiar with his family,—its relations, feelings, secret occurrences, and future prospects, as Miss Arden herself; and, wholly unsuspicious of the possibility of any deception, indulged the ardour of his nature, and urged her to give him, as the pledge of her forgiveness, that very moment, the hand which alone could ensure it to him. To surprize Sir Edward on his return, appeared to his nephew a most happy device: the glowing cheek of the fair one contradicted her words, when she insisted on waiting the consent of her father. "Why, why should we?" cried the eager Marquis; "has he not, from the hour of your birth, bestowed you on the favoured Lenox? Ah! wherefore sacrifice happiness to form? Now, this very moment, give yourself, my Emily, to a husband, who will add the remembrance of this generous condescension to all your virtues and your charms." She urged the indelicacy of being married in her disguise.—It was the only way they could be married at all, the lover insisted; and they were in a place where love wore many a disguise. Once let the priest join their hands, and he pledged his honour to leave her full liberty to give decorum to her situation, by allowing her to assume the habit of her sex. Her denials became every moment fainter; and the Marquis, half inebriated with pleasure, as well as wine, more importunate. In fine, they stole from the palace to the great church, where Emily informed him her confessor officiated; and as he already knew her secret and its motives, from him no painful objection would be made respecting her disguise. The priest was found; two more joined in the secret as witnesses, and the mistaken, impassioned Marquis was solemnly, regularly, married to Emily.—The name of Arden was not mentioned necessarily in the ceremony; and the bridegroom read not the certificate he signed, or he would have seen that of Fitzallen subjoined; for it was, indeed, that fiend in human shape, who had thus accomplished the deep revenge she had so bitterly vowed on Sir Edward and his daughter.*

Never, for one moment, had Emily Fitzallen lost sight of the persons she was determined to persecute. She followed and discovered the little delicate artifice by which Miss Arden sought to win the affections of her betrothed husband. That name, that consequence, the gentle Emily thought it wisdom to give up, the vindictive Emily saw she had the power of assuming: and finding, when his constant companion, that in her own person she might not have influence enough to decide the fate of the Marquis, she resolved to avail herself of the rare advantage of Sir Edward's absence, to borrow his daughter's name: and the unfortunate youth, as if willing to second her views, and destroy his own, had that day allowed his judgment to be weakened, and his constitution inflamed with wine. The priest who performed the marriage ceremony, had been previously prepared to attend at a moment's notice, as well as forewarned to be cautious in rendering it full, authentic, and duly witnessed.

The new-married pair found, on returning to the Count's palace, some of his domestics already arrived, to notify the intended landing of the voyagers that evening. The Marquis felt it a respect due to his bride, to allow her leisure to resume her own dress, as he had promised; and the increased agitation of mind in which she appeared, claimed this consideration from him.

It would have been much more agreeable to the Marquis, as well as the bride, had the return of their friends been a little deferred. However, as that must happen when it would, the lover was anxious to find Sir Edward, ere he reached the palace of the Count Montalvo; as well to apprize him of the recent ceremony, as to prepare him to avow a previous knowledge of his daughter's disguise. Wandering, with this view, through those beautiful groves that on all sides border the shores of Messina, the pure air insensibly calmed the spirits, and sobered the brain, of the Marquis. He half wished he had waited the return of Sir Edward, ere he wrested from him his daughter; and turned towards the walk on the quay; where he anxiously looked out for the bark of the Count. The grandeur and beauty of the view never struck the Marquis so sensibly: behind him arose the magnificent natural semicircle, with the lofty columns of the Palazzata;* before him appeared the celebrated strait, once sung by all the Muses; and the elegant fictions were yet present to his mind. Blending, in an hour and situation so singular, the romance of poetry with that of love, he threw himself on a marble seat by the fountain of Neptune, and repeated, as he gazed, the verses of Homer.* The blue strait, hardly dimpled by a breeze, was half covered with gaudy galleys, and the boats of fishermen; the fires of the light-house were reflected in glowing undulations on the waves; heavy black clouds, tinged with a dun red, seemed to seek support on the rocky mountains of Calabria; and the winds, after a wild concussion, subsided at once into a horrible kind of stillness. The rowers, whose laborious and lively exertions animate the sea they people, now made vain, though more vigorous efforts, to take shelter in the harbour. Suddenly the atmosphere became murky and oppressive; the clouds, yet more swoln and dense, sunk so low, they almost blended with the waters. Not a bird ventured to wing the heavy and unwholesome air; and the exhausted rowers could not catch breath enough to express, by a single cry, the agonizing fear that caused cold dews to burst from every pore. A tremendous sense of impending evil seemed to suspend all vital motion in the crowd late so busy around the Marquis; who impulsively partook that sick terror of soul, to which no name has ever yet been given. This awful intuitive sense of the approaching convulsion of nature was, however, only momentary. A tremendous shock followed; the Marquis felt all the danger, and tried to arise: the earth rocked beneath his feet. The marble fountain, near which he rested, was cloven in twain instantaneously; and hardly could he escape the abyss he saw close over the miserable wretches, who, but a moment before, were standing beside him. Columns of the Palazzata, and other surrounding buildings, fell with a crash, as if the universe were annihilated. The horror yet raged in all its force, when the sudden rise of the earth he stood on, threw the Marquis, and a crowd around him, towards a wall, which must have dashed their brains out, but that, weak as they were, the wall was yet weaker, and fell before them in a cloud of dust. Oh! God, what it was to hear the agonizing shrieks of suffering humanity, blended with the thunders of desolation, and the deep internal groans of disjointed nature! when, to complete the calamities of Messina, the sea, in one moment, burst its bounds; and boiling, as it were, with subterraneous fires, rolled forward, with horrible roarings, a mountainous deluge. As quickly returning, it bore away a train of bruised and helpless wretches; and among them, him who was so lately the gayest of the gay, the happiest of the happy,—the unfortunate Marquis of Lenox.*

Recollection was too fleeting, life too dubious, too fluctuating in the Marquis, when first he found he was yet in the land of the living, for him to connect his ideas, or utter any sound but sighs and groans. He soon perceived that he was in a small, but miserable place, encompassed with faces he had never beheld till that moment, while hoarse voices resounded in his ear, equally unknown to him. Alas! the only eye he could have seen with pleasure, dared not meet his; the only voice he could have found comfort in hearing, uttered not a word, lest the agitation, even of pleasure, should, in so weak a state, be death to him. Yet watching every breath the unfortunate youth drew, ready to echo every groan that burst from him, sat, hid by a curtain, his anxious, his affectionate uncle, Sir Edward Arden: and that the Duke of Aberdeen had yet a son, was rather owing to his natural sensibility, than his immediate affection.

On the memorable evening of the earthquake at Messina, Sir Edward, the Count Montalvo, and two other Sicilian noblemen, were making the harbour; the sailors having predicted foul weather, though no one suspected the immediate and awful danger impending. In one moment the mariners, by expressive cries and gestures, made the noblemen comprehend that a singular and frightful motion of the vessel was not natural. Now, as gravitation were, by a strange inversion, removed to heaven, it was drawn at once back and upward, then thrown impetuously down into the dark abyss of the waters, and again in one moment caught upward, with a reeling, convulsive trembling, as if the timber had a vital sense, and felt the fears of those who would have worked it, had human art availed against the struggles of disjointed nature. Yet, tremendous as was the state of those on the sea, it was safety, compared to the situation of the sufferers on land; which the vessel was often so near, that the horror-struck passengers could see the victims on the beach lift up their hands one moment to heaven for pity, and the next sink into the burning abyss that yawned at their feet. As no power could steady the vessel, or direct its course, the Count and his friends knew not whether they, with the helpless mariners who yet contended hard for life, were to have a watery, or a flaming grave. Nor was the concussion and entanglement, with other vessels in the same tremendous predicament, the least of their danger; though, when thrown out to solitary suffering, that danger appeared yet more horrible. At this fearful moment every evil was increased, by one of the prime sailors falling from the mast he was climbing, into the sea. His comrades, with the bold humanity incident to their profession, made the most strenuous efforts to recover him: and one of the sailors fancying, imperfect as the unnatural light was, that he saw the body, leaped overboard with a rope tied under his arms, and was drawn up, clasping a half-drowned wretch, who, it was soon discovered, was not his lost comrade. Having disengaged this man from the plank he convulsively embraced, and which had, in reality, saved his life, on finding him a mere stranger, they would perhaps have abandoned him to his fate; but that the fineness of his linen, and a rich watch chain, attracted their notice; in a moment they stript and plundered the insensible sufferer; and the surgeon of the vessel alone saved him from perishing by neglect, who had thus wonderfully escaped the wreck of nature. It is true his humanity was quickened by the recollection, that a man of so delicate an appearance, and who had been as delicately drest, might one day well recompense those who preserved his life. Thus, by a strange ordination of things, unknown and unnoticed, in the poor cabin of the surgeon, lay, with hardly a symptom of existence, the Marquis of Lenox; and there, so precarious was his situation, he might perhaps have expired, but that the sailors, who had possessed themselves of his valuables, burnt to convert them into money. Interest is often the last, as well as first principle, in vulgar minds. Hardly had the vessel got out enough to sea to promise safety, or the elements subsided enough for the compass to guide, before a calculation of the plunder was made; and the watch-seals, and other ornaments of the Marquis, handed among the domestics of the noblemen for sale. What was the astonishment and horror of Sir Edward's valet, when he saw to whom they had so lately belonged! Far from guessing the fact, he only concluded the man on whom they were found, to be the murderer of the Marquis, thus overtaken by the justice of heaven. Instantly he rushed into the cabin where Sir Edward, and the noblemen, yet remained, stunned as it were with fear and horror. The earthquake was however forgotten by Sir Edward in his agony for his nephew; and not forming the harsh conclusion of his valet as to the stranger, he demanded to see him, that such care might be taken as would preserve his life, and enable him to give all the account in his power of the unfortunate Marquis of Lenox.—Ah! what tender anguish overwhelmed Sir Edward, when, wounded, wan, insensible, wrapt in coarse and dirty linen, he found the dearest object of all his cares, the sole delight of his remaining life—the darling son of his darling sister!

From the surgeon Sir Edward understood, that, beside a great number of bruises, the Marquis had a contusion on the head, attended with a high fever, nor, if it once flew to his brain, could human art save him. The sense of his own danger yet not over—the dreadful images of the horrors he had witnessed—all, all, was lost in the impression made by the beloved object before Sir Edward.—The Marquis was immediately removed to the best bed the small vessel afforded; every comfort, as well as medicine, anxiously administered: yet many, many, miserable days, and sleepless nights, did Sir Edward pass, before he was sure his own life would be prolonged, much less that of an invalid, in so weak a state.

The fever of the Marquis was at length enough subdued, for Sir Edward to appear by his bedside—faint ideas of affinity, and tenderness, were indistinctly afloat in the aching head of the youth, when his eyes wandered over the features of his uncle, and in a weak inward voice he murmured out "Hypolito."—Sir Edward spoke not, but raising his eyes to heaven, and letting his hand fall, implied by this action, that the youth was no more.—Intense faintings, and convulsions, seized the Marquis. The relapse was so alarming, that he had been many days in a palace at Naples, and attended by the Embassador's* physician, before he was allowed again to behold a face, that might once more confuse those faculties on which it was plain his existence depended.—Yet no sooner did the interesting affectionate eyes of his uncle meet his, than he again sighed out, "Oh, Sir, Hypolito!"—"That we have life ourselves, my dear Lenox," returned Sir Edward, "is little less than a miracle:—to preserve yours, you must be patient, silent, submissive—need I say, you have not a wish I would not anticipate—a feeling I would not spare? Imagine every thing said you would have said—every thing done you would have done."

Alas! of the most generous assiduity the Marquis was well assured, and this it was struck so deep a despair through his heart. The sad history of the affinity the lost Hypolito bore to Sir Edward, was yet in the bosom of her lover; and no other being knew at what an interesting moment the disguised fair one was so awfully inhumed.—In the delirium which attended his fever, Sir Edward had, with great surprize, heard his nephew now call for Hypolito, now for Emily—now for Marian—now urge the disguised fair one to an immediate marriage; and smile at the scruples she made to decide her fate without her father's being present, when "it would make Sir Edward so happy to find her a bride." These vague rhapsodies applied so exactly to the disguise, the passion, and the secret situation of the Marquis with Sir Edward's daughter, that the only conclusion that tender father drew from these complicated wanderings and feelings was, that Emily had, in spite of all her promises, betrayed her own secret to her lover. How sad and dear was the delight of thinking then, that even in delirium she was the only object who existed to that lover.

Time, however, strengthened the intellects, and improved the health, of the Marquis; who soon learnt the melancholy tale of the almost destroyed Messina, by that earthquake, which, throwing him into the sea, had in fact preserved his life. He dared not flatter himself that his bride had alike escaped; for, alas! it was too sure she would have eagerly sought her father and her husband; and how should he be able to disclose the tremendous secret? Should *he* afflict the generous uncle who lived but in his looks, by telling him, that the very moment which accomplished his wishes had snatched away the dearer object of them? Ah! no; better was it that Sir Edward should still suppose Miss Arden living in Ireland, and waiting their return.

The Marquis was at an age, when the spirits make great efforts to rise above the calamities of life. However strong the impression made by the lovely disguised fair one, however tender and sacred the tie that bound her to her lover, the impression was sudden, the tie incomplete. Sir Edward judged it wise to assume a general chearfulness, that might renovate his nephew's spirits; and the attempt insensibly wore off the gloom and horror that for some time hung about the young man. The soft, the soothing remembrance, of the fair, the gentle Marian, aided in reviving him. Marian yet lived—lived too for him: nor would ever know his generous infidelity—an infidelity the grateful affection he felt for his uncle almost sanctified; and which, having swayed him to fulfil a dear and sacred duty (for thus frail mortals daily extenuate to themselves their lapses), no longer obliged him to forego the cherished choice of his heart. During the term of his nephew's sickness and convalescence, Sir Edward had kept back the letters of Marian, which now were delivered to her lover in a packet; and the Marquis drew thence a renovating power, not even the pure air of Naples could afford.

In the long leisure of a sick chamber, the Marquis had often pondered over the extraordinary situation from which he had so miraculously escaped with life; and though there remained not a hope that Hypolito survived (for why, in that case, did he not appear?), an ardent wish lived in the mind of the widower bridegroom once more to re-visit the memorable scene of his marriage—to learn if possible the manner and moment of the death of the disguised fair one—to see at least the priest that had, in an hour teeming with horror and evil, united their hands—to shed with him some tears of generous anguish—and, in the great church of Messina, to consecrate the memory of the unfortunate Emily, by a magnificent monument.

The danger of re-visiting Sicily had now for some time been over; and when Sir Edward found his nephew strenuous in the wish, he no longer opposed, though he chose not to accompany him. A bark was engaged by the melancholy Marquis; who, passing many a scene of desolation, at length sailed into the almost choaked up harbour of Messina; an awful memento of the vain labours of man, and all the little pride of human magnificence.—The half-fallen pier—the tottering Palazzata—the solitary strand,* and the indistinct streets, through which crawled a few mangled wretches who lived only to envy those the earth had wholly swallowed up, made the very soul of the Marquis recoil within him, before he reached the great church, and convent adjoining. An enormous mass of ruins alone marked the spot where they had stood. Of the priest he sought, not a trace remained. The whole brotherhood had vanished, either into a premature grave, or in search of a remote, but safe home. The bare walls of the palace of Count Montalvo, though injured, had not fallen, but it was plundered of the magnificent furniture, nor inhabited by a single domestic. In fine, no being remained in Messina the Marquis had ever seen there, nor was the unhappy stranger he enquired for known, either by description or name. How could an individual be remembered in a place where society was become an echo, and the grandeur of ages annihilated by a single convulsion in nature? The Marquis again slowly, and sadly, ascended his bark, and, casting his eyes over the ravaged glories of Messina, "Ah! why, my Emily," sighed he, "when I have so awful a proof how vain is the busy pride of mortality, should I attempt to raise a monument to thee? The God who at such a moment, and in such a manner, claimed thee, has made Messina thine!" Then turning appalled from the enormous mass of splendid ruins, he hastily cut through the green waves, on which the evening sun still played with undiminished, unaltered beauty.

Again in Naples, the Marquis, though silent and melancholy, was not inconsolable. During his convalescence, he had rather felt, than seen, his boundless influence over his uncle; which it was now his first wish to increase; that, when the day came when he should acknowledge the humble choice his heart had made, he might act on a nature so generous, in favour of his lovely, his interesting Marian. It was the subject of great surprize to him, that Miss Arden's fate was yet a secret to her father: but, as Sir Edward had long forborne to mention her from prudence, and the Marquis always avoided it from choice, this was not a moment to lead to so painful an enquiry, by a single question. Too soon would it be, whenever a father so tender learnt her melancholy fate. It would then become *his* duty and choice alike to sooth and to console his uncle. Perhaps, when the bitterness of grief was assuaged, and Sir Edward learnt the sacred rite which brought them still nearer in affinity than nature had, that generous man might in turn be brought to adopt, and second, the only feeling that could induce him to take another bride.—And why should he prolong his banishment? His own country now contained not the once-dreaded Miss Arden, while in that country lived for him, and him alone, his Marian.

After an apparent weariness, and constraint, the Marquis one day abruptly proposed to his uncle, returning home. The keen, but delighted eye of Sir Edward, seemed to pierce his very soul, yet vainly sought to account for the cloud that immediately succeeded on the brow of the Marquis, or a kind of stifled compassion for himself that followed the proposition. No possible objection to it, however, occurred on the part of the uncle: on the contrary, a gay flow of spirits, extremely embarrassing and distressing to his nephew. He found himself almost unable to keep the dreadful secret; and seeing, in all the gay scenes of Italy, only the grave of Sir Edward's lovely and affectionate daughter, he could not controul his increasing impatience to depart, and urged his weak health, as rendering it necessary he should travel very leisurely, a mode he knew his uncle detested. Having settled his route, and appointed to wait in Switzerland, he left Sir Edward to fulfil some excursive engagements, and set out, attended by only his servants.

Gentle exercise, pure air, the variety of simple scenes, and objects, around him, gradually invigorated, as he went, the health of the Marquis, and made him delight to linger in Switzerland. Ah! who would not delight to linger in Switzerland? Who would not wish the soul now to dilate into grandeur, and now, with sweet compression, to contract into content, as simple or majestic nature takes its turn to act upon it?—In that wild region our traveller found all the fervour of romantic passion rekindled in his soul. He walked till he could walk no longer;—he rested only to gain strength to walk again:—and, if fatigue caused him to sleep, he carried into the torpor necessary to repair exhausted nature, rich and fanciful visions, not less delightful than those he cherished when awake. Nevertheless, a carriage and led horse accompanied our pedestrian; for such had been the orders of his father.—The carriage he was often pleased to fill with tired and rosy vintagers, on whose gratitude he made no demand. His horse often lightened the way to the sun-burnt veteran, who sought,

> "When all his toils were past,
> Still to return, and die at home at last."*

The Marquis, thus generously employing his superfluous advantages, would delight to linger behind; resting under the shadow of some grotesque mountain, and listening to the dashing of some distant waterfall, while his mind now solemnly paused upon the past, now fondly mused, on the uncertain future.

After a day passed in this luxurious manner, night so suddenly surprized the Marquis, at a solitary but beautiful valley, a few miles from Lausanne, that, had not his servants, apprehending him to be too ill, or too much exhausted, to come on, returned with the carriage, he must have slept on the grass. Once seated in his chaise, he indulged the slumber fatigue occasioned, and had been well shaken by his valet, ere he could be sufficiently roused, to understand that his chaise was stopt by another, overturned, and so broken, that the lady and her maid were hopeless of reaching Lausanne, unless some benevolent traveller would either assist to repair the mutilated equipage, or accommodate them with his own. The poor Marquis, still a little cross at having so comfortable a nap interrupted, did not find himself in the humour to alight. Nevertheless, he sent in his own name a polite offer of his carriage, and did not think the stranger too complaisant in immediately accepting it. However, he had no choice but to spring out, and shew his involuntary knight-errantry.* The hills on each side were covered with wood; which, meeting over the road, added darkness to the night. Having got his chaise safely past the broken one, the Marquis with great gallantry handed in two trembling females, who seemed hardly able to thank him; and having given the postillions strict charge of them, returned to survey the shattered chaise: his valet being provided with phosphoric matches, by which he had now lit a taper. After various proposals to tie it together, the Marquis thought its appearance so unsafe, that, tired as he was, he chose to mount a horse, and follow his own carriage, which was not yet out of hearing. He was near enough to the inn when the strangers got out, to have offered his assistance; but, a little disgusted with the want of consideration on their parts; and perceiving, by the lights held at the door, that his hands and cloaths were covered with dust, he thought it a respect due to himself, rather than the stranger, to rectify his appearance. To dress never took the Marquis much time; and to his request to enquire after the lady's health, an immediate permission was accorded. As he had sent in his name, the landlord stood ready with lights to precede *"Milor Anglois"** into the apartment of the stranger. As the Marquis glanced his quick eye forward, he saw, leaning one arm gracefully on a low old-fashioned chimney-piece, and with the other caressing a beautiful Italian greyhound, a female, at once so slight, graceful, and dignified, as to rivet his attention, and give a strange, wild, prophetic pulsation to his heart. This elegant traveller had the air of high rank, affluence, and fashion. She was wrapt in a riding robe of black velvet, lined with white satin, and girt to her waist by a cord of silver. A pale blue velvet hat, with a plume of white feathers, was thrown carelessly on one side, yet tied under her chin by a white and silver handkerchief. Over the black velvet robe fell, in vast profusion, rich curls of fair hair, from which the Marquis, by a kind of intuitive knowledge, seemed to recognize his fair Italian; while the whole graceful figure announced to him his Marian. Nor did he err in either instance; the charmer turned towards him, and he saw,—not the humble daughter of Dennis, though every feature of Marian. Ah! no, this was, and was not, Marian;—an elegant, conscious, high-bred beauty, now stood before him: yet, in the chastened delight her eye surveyed him with, he read the triumph of his own. How new—how tumultuous were his emotions! how exquisite, yet agonizing, the embrace she denied not! That Marian was distinguished, her lover plainly saw,— that she might be infamous, he severely felt. Yet, such is the contrariety of human emotions, that the tears his eyes swam in, sprang more from perceiving she was independant of himself, than a juster cause. The air of this irresistible charmer, however, was not more tender, than it was innocent. She blushed, it is true; but it seemed to be only for the distress she occasioned; for she hardly knew how to interpret the agitation the Marquis attempted not to controul. "I have surprized you, my Lord," faltered she; then, sweetly smiling, added, "and I too have been in turn surprized."—"The meeting with my Marian," replied her lover, again fondly clasping her, "would be a pleasure past all speaking; *but*"—"But what, my Lord?"—"To find her *thus!*"—the Marquis cast his eye over her dress. "Oh! is that all your distress?" cried she, with a glow of triumphant pleasure; "I will not be my own historian, positively, when there is a better at hand: let Sir Edward Arden be summoned to expound the mystery."—"Sir Edward Arden, my angel, is far from hence; and my Marian must, in pity of the heart wholly her own, expound this mystery herself."— "Nay, my Lord," playfully and in exultation returned the charmer, "I may hazard much with *you* in the avowal of my name; but nothing with Sir Edward Arden, by demanding in his arms a welcome for his wandering daughter."

The concussion of nature that swallowed up the impostor Hypolito, could alone equal that which now shook the mental system of the Marquis. Yet a single thought was conclusive; a single impulse conviction. Yes, the gracious, the graceful creature, now bending benignly to raise him from the earth where his misery had laid him, was, could be, only the angel daughter of Sir Edward; the being, formed and finished, "the cunning'st pattern of excelling nature:"* who, whether as a masqued Italian Grace, a rustic maid, or a high-bred beauty, was intuitively adored by him, and claimed in his heart, whatever shape she wore, a rightful sovereignty. But whence then came the arch-fiend he had at Messina plighted his hand to? No doubt, from the hell that opened to swallow her, ere yet the sin was consummated.—How, how, unless endued with supernatural knowledge, could she have discussed with him the many secret domestic occurrences, not more familiar, as it appeared, to his mind, than hers?

And well might this bewilder the ideas of the unhappy Marquis; who had never been enough a party in the little history of Miss Arden, to learn that a creature, like Emily Fitzallen, even existed;—still less that this companion of her youth had ungratefully supplanted her; and then vowed a bitter revenge, she had, alas, too successfully executed.

That delicate pride nature makes one of the first charms of woman, was a little wounded in Emily Arden, on observing a revulsion of soul so strange in the Marquis. Yet it was plain he suffered much; so deadly a paleness lived on his cheek, so melting a sadness marked his voice, that, unintelligible as the cause remained (for he answered not to her fondest entreaties), so tender was her heart, and the lover at her feet so entirely the object of its tenderness, as to make her lose every other care in that of consoling him. Too true was the sympathy for her to attempt it in vain; their hearts were formed for each other, and, without a single vow, united. Hypolito, in a moment so dear, as completely vanished from the thoughts of the Marquis, as if the impostor had never existed. Sir Edward Arden was no longer missed by his daughter; and two whole happy hours past in endearment and protestation, ere Miss Arden remembered she was faint for want of food, or the Marquis that he was dying with fatigue, when they met. But was ever repast more delicious than the humble one they sat down to, when mutual love thus graced, and blest, the board? How playfully did the Marquis arraign the inflexibility of the fair one, who commanded him to recover his good looks by the morning, when from the table she past to a chamber; where the sweet consciousness of rewarded virtue, hallowed the slumbers of the amiable Emily.

Ah! not alike pure and unbroken was the rest of the Marquis; so strange, so singular, was his situation, so inexplicable his recollections, that he found it impossible to calm his spirits. To his distempered fancy the chamber rocked with the earthquake of Sicily one moment, and the next was illuminated with the visible presence of a guardian angel, in the form of his adored Emily: nor were his slumbers more peaceful; marriage and death, by turns, seemed to demand a victim; and glad was he to see that day break, which restored to his eyes and heart the beloved object, who alone could chase away each painful thought.

But what a day of delight arose to Miss Arden! At last to be worshipped! at last to see herself the sole hope of the man who ruled her very fate! Now no longer shunned, dreaded, abhorred, the remembrance that she once had been so, only gave her sweet confirmation of her power, and exalted happiness into triumph. She was told her father was coming to meet her; and though well she knew the share he would take in the transport, she felt it most perfect without him. Safe in her lover's protection, she enjoyed the fond pleasure of solely depending on him.

The Marquis, on the contrary, counted the hours till his uncle should arrive; for from his hand alone could he hope to receive that of Miss Arden: and dear as the heart she gave him was, he felt it to be only part of an invaluable treasure, wholly destined for himself.

A most simple train of circumstances had produced this romantic meeting of the lovers. The awful escape of the Marquis at Messina, left him in a state of such danger, that Sir Edward could not conceal it entirely from the Duke; though he forbore, as long as possible, the communication, in hopes of some favourable turn. The Duke, impetuous as his son in all his feelings, forgot how acutely Miss Arden would sympathize, and almost killed her with the dreadful recital of her father. To fly to the beloved of her heart, to watch over, cherish, soothe, recover, or perish with him, was Emily's first thought, and indeed her only one. The alarm of the Duke left her without a doubt of his setting out on the arrival of the next letter; and hardly could the afflicted Emily breathe till it came. That letter brought better accounts of the Marquis; and the Duke coolly left him to the care of his uncle, and thought, from that moment, once more only of himself and his libertine indulgences. Plunged in grief, shut up from company, yet disgusted with her home, Emily soon was shocked with discovering it to be an improper one. The Duke was either less attentive than usual to the respect due to Miss Arden, or she found her perception quickened by the desire she felt to be gone; but it was impossible for her to misunderstand the terms on which the Duke, and the widow lady engaged to give propriety to Miss Arden's residence in his house, now lived. The disgust and shame of such an affront, however, was soon lost in the recollection, that it authorized Emily to follow her own inclinations, and seek her father. She hinted her dissatisfaction at the conduct of the *lady*, without seeming to include the Duke in the censure; and announced her intention of availing herself of the return of Sir Edward's valet, who might guide herself, and servants, to Italy. The Duke took no pains to investigate, much more over-rule, a resolution which left him peaceful possession of his mistress, and his own mansion, but allowed Miss Arden to stay or go as she should think most eligible. On the most mature deliberation, she found (so fallacious are our reasonings where the heart is impressed) that to run over the Continent in search of her father,—for she never allowed her lover to appear a part of her consideration,—was absolutely an act of discretion, and accordingly took leave of the Duke.

When once on the road, the impatience Miss Arden could not restrain, shewed too plainly the tender motive of her journey. Having agreed to rest in Switzerland, merely till Sir Edward's valet should notify her approach, she had sent him forward only one day, when the breaking down of her chaise prevented her passing, in the dark, the very person she sought.

The delightful rambles of two lovers through that delightful country, may easily be imagined. Sir Edward lost no time, from the moment his valet reached him, in seeking his daughter; wondering much at every town that he saw her not.—But where could it be such happiness to see her, as leaning, with frank affection, on the arm of his nephew, while the glad eyes of both hailed him as the author, the partaker of their felicity? This was, indeed, all of joy a father can know:—to see his Emily, at last, sweetly conscious of absolute power, yet using it only to give delight:—to hear the nephew, he had ever loved with parental fondness, implore absolution from him, for the sins of ingratitude and perverseness, while both, with tender anxious eyes, demanded from his hand each other. Ah! where could three beings be found so much to be envied? Yet, of these three, the father knew, perhaps, the most exquisite happiness; for he had known the most cruel doubts.

The Marquis, impatient in all things, was for being married immediately; but this, Sir Edward urged, was, from a variety of causes, impossible. Miss Arden's fortune would then be too much in the Duke's power; who, perhaps, loved himself well enough, poorly to leave his son, during a life that promised continuance, dependent on his wife. So mortifying an idea silenced the Marquis, but made him alike urgent to set out for England, where all these arrangements could most expeditiously be made. And now the gentle Emily became the objector; she could not, truly, leave unseen the beauties of Italy, nor was troubled with the least fear for her fortune. All necessary points might, she observed, be settled without their presence: in short, her father comprehended that Miss Arden feared, in returning unmarried, she should be exposed to the ridicule of having come abroad to seek a tardy lover; or rather, that she veiled, under this idea, the same determination with the Marquis; and both were alike ready to be united. Sir Edward, therefore, once more dispatched his valet to England, with such proposals to the Duke as he thought eligible; and only required of the lovers to accompany him to Naples, where, on the arrival of the settlements, they could be publicly married in the chapel of the English Embassador; after which Emily might, without impropriety, visit Rome. The Marquis was perfectly easy on every point, but the tedious time which must necessarily elapse: as Sir Edward, however, during the journey, almost always chose to ride his nephew's horse, and give up his seat in the chaise to him, the lovers contrived to pass the interval pleasantly enough.

The reason Sir Edward gave for delaying the marriage was so prudent, that it easily imposed on the Marquis, but not Miss Arden. She had penetrated too deeply into her father's character, not to perceive that pride was his foible; and, by the refinement of his nature, she was become his pride. Sensible he was born to give way to his nephew himself, it was only by holding Miss Arden high, he could render it obvious that she was not elevated by marrying her cousin. In the splendour of the union, the fond father sought to give an addition to happiness;—the hearts of the lovers told them it was not to be given.

The valet, dispatched to England to await the drawing up due settlements under the auspices of the Duke, could not so soon return, but that the party had ample leisure to visit the classical scenes around Naples, in all the intoxication of youth, love, curiosity, and pleasure. Yet fits of absence and gloom, wholly unintelligible to his fair mistress, frequently came over the Marquis; and the name of Hypolito often trembled on his lips, but never passed them. Ah! how should he resolve to debase himself so far, as to tell his adored Emily, that an impostor, infamous for aught he knew, had so successfully assumed her name and character, as to seize on his heart, and decide his fate? or even, if he might venture to rely on her forgiveness, was it possible he should admit to Sir Edward that he had been made so egregious a dupe?

Sir Edward understanding too well one cause of his nephew's melancholy and abstracted air, now apprized his daughter of the history and deplorable fate of Hypolito: whom he spoke of so partially, that Emily wept for the loss the Marquis must long feel of an accomplished, attached associate. Warned by her father, that to appear to know the sorrow of her lover, would be to cherish it, she employed all the charms she well knew how to render successful, to inspirit the Marquis; nor would ever suffer the conversation to turn toward Sicily, or an earthquake. Yet, in the exquisite sense of power and passion, she sometimes envied the lost Hypolito, even in the grave, his influence in the heart where she would exclusively have reigned.

A palace and establishment, suitable to her fortune, having been provided in Naples for Miss Arden, her father, and the Marquis, contented themselves with their former home. The lady of the English Embassador was distantly allied to the Bellarney family, and soon circulated the reason of the obvious difference in Sir Edward's mode of living and his daughter's. She introduced Miss Arden at court, who was thought so irresistible, that hardly had the Marquis a friend, who was not secretly his rival. Sir Edward exulted in the admiration his daughter excited; but she loved too truly not to blush at pleasing any man, except him it was her duty, as well as choice, to please. Often did she sigh at the vain parade of her almost empty palace, when she saw its gates close every evening on her father and her lover; nor had she any consolation for the tedious etiquette she was enslaved by, but that of knowing the arrival of the courier from England would end it.

Sir Edward's valet at length returned, and the Marquis had the gratification of finding his uncle had not been just in the idea he formed of his father. The Duke of Aberdeen very liberally assigned to his son, during his own life, a third of the estates he would wholly inherit; and to Miss Arden made over, with the concurrence of the Marquis, for the term of hers, all her own possessions, settling them on the younger children of the marriage, to be allotted at the joint pleasure of the father and mother. To this the Duke added letters equally kind and polite, with the promise of a splendid set of jewels to the bride, which were now preparing.

There was no longer a cause for delay, and the evening of the next day was fixed for the nuptials, which the English Embassador claimed the honour of witnessing, with his lady, in his own chapel; nor would he excuse the party from supping *al fresco** in his gardens.

The happy day at length arrived; and the Marquis, having ordered a gay *divertissement*,* came to the hotel of Miss Arden to breakfast. The performers were all stopt in the hall, and the lover only admitted to the garden; where, as by magic, had arisen a straw-roofed cottage, in which appeared, in the simple garb of Scotland, the affianced bride; while, by her, in a habit humble as that of Dennis, stood her real father. The repast was in the same plain style; and had not the gaudy tuberose, and flowering orange, scented the air, the delighted Marquis would have thought himself still in his native shades,—those sweet solitudes, where first his heart expanded to love and happiness.

The more brilliant entertainment of music, the lover had prepared, was given afterwards; but, to the masquers, was added the fair-haired Italian peasant, whose light fingers once more swept the mandoline with inimitable grace: that pleasure past, Emily again vanished, but soon to appear in the chaste elegance of her bridal dress. Long robes of white muslin, spangled with silver, were girt to her waist by a zone of purple, clasped with rich diamonds. The redundance of her fair locks was a little confined, by part of them being braided with glowing purple, and strings of pearl, without any other ornament. Several bracelets of Roman pearl encircled her polished and snowy arms, the beauty of which never was so obvious, as while her father holding one hand, and her lover the other, conducted her up through the portico of the Embassador's palace. At the gate, the party were met by the noble owner and his lady, who ushered them through a magnificent gallery to the chapel. It was splendidly illuminated, and so gaily decorated with festoons of roses, as to appear, indeed, the temple of Hymen. Sir Edward Arden, in the fullness of delight, now fixed his eyes on those of his beloved nephew, and now on the downcast lids of his daughter, and saw, in the arrival of this moment, every wish he ever formed, accomplished. The chaplain began the solemn service; and Sir Edward, taking the two hands so dear to him, in the presence of God and man, joined the pair he once thought no time, no chance, would ever unite. In the gardens of the palace, a splendid collation was soon after served, and an invisible concert prolonged the tedious time to the Marquis, who watched the glance of Sir Edward's eye, to lead home his Emily,—his own dear Emily. During the interval, the palace had been universally illuminated, and a great crowd had assembled on the steps of the portico. Emily, distressed at becoming in such a moment the object of attention, stumbled; the bridegroom thought some one had trod on her robe, and turning hastily round to disengage it, fixed his eyes on those of Hypolito.—Yes, the ghastly phantom appeared in the very same boyish habiliments he wore when the Marquis last beheld him: and, oh! fatal memento of their tremendous meeting, and yet more tremendous parting, held up in full view the ring, the fatal ring, with which the Marquis had wedded the fair, the fascinating impostor. It had been one of his mother's, hastily applied, however unsuitable, to this purpose; but it was too remarkable to be mistaken; nor could the wretched gazer doubt its identity. The exquisite vision of love, hope, and happiness, faded at once from the soul of the agonized bridegroom; and he sunk, a corpse in appearance, at the feet of the trembling daughter of Sir Edward Arden.

The portico resounded with the cries of the sorrowful and astonished spectators. The miserable Marquis was carried into the nearest apartment, and a medical gentleman immediately lanced a vein in his arm.—Wan as though arising from the grave, the lover at length opened his eyes, and wildly glancing them around, no longer allowed them to dwell on her so lately their sole object; but, hardly permitting the surgeon time to bind up the orifice, sprang with the strength of a lunatic from those who encircled him, to fly through the arcade—traverse the chapel—the illuminated galleries—from thence, in the desperation of sudden frenzy, he rushed down the steps of the portico—but too certain, at length, that the object of his search was no longer to be seen, he struck his head against a marble pillar with such force, as to stun himself. Sir Edward Arden, hardly less frantic at a misery so wholly unintelligible, directed his servants to lift, while yet insensible, his nephew into his coach, and carry him back to the hotel they both inhabited. A trembling white hand seized the arm of Sir Edward; and the pale face of his Emily anxiously explored his, while repeating, "The Marquis, my father, has now a house of his own—it is your Emily who must henceforward entreat for a home with him."—Conscious of she knew not what violation of decorum in this, she sweetly shrunk from his glance, and blushed: yet in a moment

> "A thousand innocent shames
> In angel whiteness bore away those blushes."*

Pressing his tender Emily to his bosom, Sir Edward dropt on hers, tears of infantine softness and affection. "Sweetest of creatures," cried he, "hardly can this unhappy young man be termed thy husband."—"Have I not even now called on heaven and man, my father, to witness the vow that long, long since, wedded my soul to his? Yes, Edward, beloved Edward," cried she, turning with a gush of tears to the still insensible bridegroom, "I am thine—for ever thine. Sick or well, happy or miserable, thy Emily feels it the dear, sad duty of her life, to watch over, soothe, sustain thee. The grave alone, perhaps not even that, can sever from thine the soul now repeating the fond, unalienable vow, to him who is, alas! no longer able to return it!"

Sir Edward made no further opposition to the wish of his daughter; and the bridal hours were past by the tender, agitated Emily in anxious watchings. A raging fever followed the horrible convulsion of mind the Marquis had undergone: in its paroxysms the affrighted bride a thousand times heard him renounce, abhor, the vow of marriage, "by which he had allied himself to perdition." Starting up with fearful glaring eyes, he would command her to quit his sight—never, never more, to appear before him. The frenzy, then, would be illumined with a ray of reason; he suddenly saw in her a benignant angel, descended to save him from the horrors of his own soul.— He then would, with that tenderness which was ever so successful, implore her *never* to quit his bed-side—*never* once to take from his eyes those charming ones which alone could soften his sufferings; and now pressing her hand to his throbbing temples, and now to his burning bosom, seem to think it quieted each dangerous pulsation, and thus, at intervals, lulled himself into the stupefaction which gave him strength again to struggle. From the imperfect slumbers her fondness sometimes soothed him into, he would again start with convulsive shudderings—insist that the room rocked with an earthquake; that the sun was turned into blood—heap dreadful curses on an Emily, "loathsome to his eyes, and fatal to his honour"—demand in wild transports "the ring, the fatal ring, with which *the fiend had enchained his very soul*"—and, when the agonized daughter of Sir Edward Arden hastily drew her wedding ring off, to present it to him, he would gaze mournfully on that, and mysteriously on her—then cry, "No, no"—wander through faint recollections, and, gently replacing the bond of dear affiance, draw fondly towards him the heart-broken Emily, and deluge her bosom with his tears.

Sacred is the bond of calamity, when thus the visitation comes from heaven. Could Emily in the arms of the Marquis have known so dear a tenderness as that she felt when hovering near his sick-bed, conscious that he existed but by the love that would have made him immortal? Ah! when did any pleasure of sense equal that with which the almost expiring lover took from her eyes, and her hand, the daily portion of prolonged existence?

Sir Edward shared in the assiduities of his daughter, as soon as the Marquis began to recover. Yet a strange apprehension, in spite of his better reason, arose in his mind, that Emily knew not: he saw, or fancied he saw, that as the strength and spirits of the Marquis returned, he found their company an oppression. Alas! the tender father was not mistaken. What tortures of mind succeeded the sufferings of body, from which the miserable Lenox at last escaped! He knew the only good on earth his soul desired, to be his own, yet found himself not the richer. Could he, in the fatal circumstance he stood in, dare to sully the purity of his angel Emily? Too well he knew the ring she wore gave him no claim to her endearing tenderness—would convey no inheritance to her children—nay might, by the malice of a fiend, be taken from her finger. To the fury of fever, and frenzy, now succeeded a sullen, settled, deep despair. If he appeared at all, his eyes were haggard, his hair dishevelled; he hardly sat a moment at the table—forgot he was desired to eat—and, strangely departing from all the civilities of life, no less than its social feelings, would rush from the room, to shut himself up again in his own apartment. Nor was that apartment now accessible to the miserable Emily. Yet hours and hours she waited anxiously in the ante-chamber, while he paced irregularly in the one within. Alas! the sighs and groans that at intervals escaped him, pierced her very soul.

Sir Edward Arden now too sensibly felt, how incompetent we are to judge of that we so boldly demand of heaven as happiness. A thousand times the Marquis had, with the energetic delight of a lover, told him he adored his daughter: he could not but see that she lived in the looks of his nephew. It had been the pride, the pleasure of his life, to give them to each other, yet not one of the three found, in the accomplishment of this only wish, felicity.

Not from his daughter, however, could Sir Edward draw a breath of complaint. It was her wan cheek, when she was no longer permitted to watch over her husband,—it was the faint flutter, and delicate glow, that teinted her complexion, when he appeared,—it was the tears she stifled in his presence, but that flooded her eyes whenever he vanished, that told to her fond father the painful sense she had of so deep an unkindness. A thousand times Sir Edward resolved to enquire into the motives of his nephew's total estrangement—as often the apprehensive Emily left him nothing to complain of, by taking on herself the fault; and insisting that time, and time only, would enable her to recover the shock and fatigue of so long an attendance on so alarming a malady—confess an obligation to the Marquis for returning her kindness, in allowing her to do as she pleased; and finally, with a delicate address conveyed through her father this to her husband. What was her grief and astonishment, to find this information contribute more to tranquillize his mind, than all her cares! The fatal idea, that she had been from the first deceived, and he had married her only for her fortune, then suddenly sunk into her soul: no sooner did the Marquis begin to ride abroad, and resume his usual habits of life, than the deserted Emily shut herself up in her own apartment, and almost died at so marked, so cruel a neglect.

Ah! could she have known the employment—the sole employment of the man she distrusted,—every moment of his absence was spent in searching for that fiend, whom once found, he hoped to soothe, or bribe, to allow of the annulling of a marriage certainly incomplete, but which only her acknowledgment could prove so. That once obtained, he meant to throw himself at the feet of Sir Edward's lovely daughter; and, by confessing the truth, prove, what appeared to be his fault, was in reality his virtue—the daring to shun the bride whose tenderness he returned with adoration.

The search, the enquiries of the hapless husband, availed not: this fearful phantom, at whose presence virtue and happiness at once vanished, having completed that object, seemed ever to sink into the hell that alone could have engendered her. After a thousand struggles to reconcile his feelings with his conscience, the Marquis found, he must still shun his Emily, and, by returning immediately to London have the advice of the civilians there on the possibility of annulling the first marriage, and making the second valid.

But the latter object, it soon seemed probable, the Marquis need not strive so assiduously to attain: it appeared to himself, as well as to the distracted father, a dreadful doubt, whether Emily would live to see England again. A grief, too acute for medicine to cure, had already made deep ravages on the delicate constitution of the Marchioness. Her heart, thrown back upon her hands, chilled the pure bosom it returned to. The hours usually devoted to rest were spent by her in vain conjectures concerning her husband, to whom she naturally imputed some other attachment. Yet still, in company, his eyes were ever fixed on her with a dying fondness, though he sought her not at any other time. Determined to fulfil her duty, even in the extreme, Emily yet exhausted herself to please, or to amuse him. She played, she drew enchantingly. She charmed all who came within her circle, and often saw, in the pride the Marquis felt when she was admired, that fond appropriation of herself, wholly irreconcileable with his painful neglect.

The physician having declared the Marchioness in too delicate a state of health to venture a long journey, proposed her leaving Naples, for a more retired situation. A villa was easily procured; and the afflicted father, unable to endure the inexplicable vexation, made an excursion to Rome, to endeavour to beguile, in the society of the wise and lettered men of that city, the deep chagrin of which he saw no probable end.

He had the little relief of shortly after hearing, from Emily, that the sweet spot she lived in, revived her spirits, and amended her health. Each letter gave him more chearful accounts. Not only his daughter, but the Marquis, at length implored him to return, and both joined in assuring him that his presence, his paternal presence, alone was wanting to their happiness. This assurance had too often reached Sir Edward's ears, while only misery was before his eyes, for him to give much credit to it; but the anxious desire he had, to know whether his daughter's health was really amended, made him at length risque visiting the infatuated pair, whom wedlock, as it seemed, alone could alienate. But they were alienated no longer; every trace of vexation and sickness was so entirely vanished, that it was only by his memory Sir Edward could assure himself either had existed. In perfect harmony with each other, the married lovers diffused over the beautiful spot they inhabited the charms of paradise itself: for what were they but innocence, and love?—Ah! was the Marquis then innocent? fain, fain, would he believe so. The angel Emily, that lived *for*, lived *with* him, and was perhaps too charming always to be withstood. Her image so wholly occupied his soul, that the horrible one of Hypolito became at length faint, indistinct, aërial—it was the interest of the hapless lover to convince himself, that the heart-harrowing form, holding the ring on the steps of the Embassador's palace, was shaped by his fancy merely: and the variety of frightful visions which impressed his brain in the progress of his fever, assumed figures so various and distorted, that well might he doubt, whether fear had not conjured up the formidable phantom which thus shook his nature. So fruitless too had been his after-search, that he fondly flattered himself the object of it no longer existed; and it was not the dead, but the living, the unhappy Marquis was born to dread.

Yet nothing but a favourable judgment from the civilians in England could ultimately relieve the mind of the adoring husband; for while one doubt remained in it, that he might yet bring affliction on his Emily, the dear delight of living with her was imperfect pleasure. Their return home was once again in contemplation, when a new cause of delay occurred to the tender father, bringing with it the dearest hope in human nature.—Sir Edward was suddenly struck with the same delicacy of complexion, and uncertainty of appetite, that had fore-run the birth of his Emily, in herself; and by recalling the beloved remembrance of her mother, the Marchioness was doubly endeared to him.—How exquisite was the pleasure he gave her husband in the hint! Both agreed to leave to the timid Emily the time for disclosing a secret so pleasing to all three; and both with tender studious care promoted her every wish, nay sought in silence to anticipate them all.

Retirement was no longer necessary to the restoration of the Marchioness; but from the delicacy of her nature it now became her choice; and she formed too entirely the happiness of her husband, and father, for them to wish to change the scene.—How indeed, when three informed, and united hearts devoted every power to pleasing each other, could the enlargement of the party improve it?—Sir Edward among his studies pursued that of botany, and Emily delighted in drawing plants, in which she excelled.—It was the favourite employment of her father, and husband, to discover in their rides, and walks, new subjects to amuse her mind, and engross her delicate pencil.—She was engaged one evening in perpetuating a very perishable flower, while the Marquis was walking backwards, and forwards in the saloon, trying on his flute, from whence he drew most melting music, a thousand desultory strains, as they floated through his memory.—One struck Emily; but busied with her pencil, she hastily asked him, without raising her eye, where he had learnt that passage.—The Marquis paused, and, in the fluttered tone that to worldly observers would have announced insincerity, replied, he could not recollect; though too well he remembered it was from Hypolito he learnt—it was with Hypolito he had often played it.— After a period of hesitation, the Marquis ventured in turn to enquire if she had ever heard it before.—"Certainly, my Lord," replied Emily, gaily smiling, and half raising her eyes—"it is a stray of my own; composed when I was a little rustic, wandering in the woods, and wilds of Ireland, and thinking of my obstinate charming cousin:—it seemed something odd thus to hear the echo of my heart from your lips, especially as I never gave the air to more than one human being, and that one was not likely to fall in your way."

A strange cold tremor seized the frame of the Marquis—Ah! God, thought he, who then was that *one human being?*—Yet to discover even the object of our fear, is among the invariable, though painful propensities of human nature.—Almost breathless, he faltered out, at last, an enquiry.—The Marchioness replied, in the same gay, careless tone, "I detest Ireland so thoroughly from its having given you an unfavourable impression of your poor little wife, and Emily Fitzallen so much for having made my paternal mansion a miserable home to me, that I never willingly think of, much less mention, either one or the other."—"And who," said the Marquis in an impressive manner, "is this Emily Fitzallen?"—"Nay," cried his lady, "it is your own fault you do not know; for she has made no small figure in my little history. I wonder my father never told you the extraordinary scene we had, when my grandmother's will was opened, with her upstart, insolent favourite. The proud, passionate wretch, no sooner found herself thrown on my mercy,—though well she knew she might have trusted it,—than the fury appeared at once through the veil of her consummate beauty. I think even now I see, and hear her, solemnly vowing a revenge on me, which happily it will never be in her power to execute; or hardly heaven could save me;—so vindictive do I know her."

The Marquis raised his hands and eyes, in an agony too mighty for expression; and rushed out of the saloon, ere his groans should lead to the mysterious sorrow struggling at his heart, the yet happy Emily. Thrown at his length in the garden, he tore his hair, and gave way to the frenzy of instantaneous, horrible conviction. "Oh! Emily," exclaimed he, "adored, unfortunate Emily, didst thou know how successful this fiend has already been, what but death could follow?—Alas! that is, perhaps, only for a little while delayed, and we shall both become victims. The minute, inexplicable informations of that deliberate destroyer, that smiling Hypolito, are now accounted for: too well do I perceive, the fiend yet walks this earth, and vanishes at intervals, only to seduce me into that exquisite guilt, that shall give her, when she again appears, a yet more exquisite power of torturing. That I should, till the moment I fell into the snare, have been ignorant of the existence of this serpent,—and that I should *now—now* first learn it! Oh! just, yet killing punishment!—blind, arrogant, wilful, I would not obey the voice of duty, or of gratitude. Alas! my heart's dear Emily, had I sought thee, as any other man would have been proud to do, in the house of thy ancestors; had I shewn thee but the common respect due to Sir Edward Arden's daughter, this minister of iniquity would have been known to me; and, never, never could she thus fatally have accomplished the vengeance, which hardly yet has a place in the apprehension of my beloved."

From the moment of this accidental explanation, which made no impression on the mind of the Marchioness, peace and rest fled from her unhappy husband. The sad sense of impending evil, no human care could guard against, the painful consciousness of error, poisoned the dear delight of calling Emily his own, and wore him down to a skeleton.

> "He withers at his heart; and looks as wan,
> As the pale spectre of a murder'd man:
> Nor, mix'd in mirth, in youthful pleasure shares,
> But sighs when songs and instruments he hears,
> Uncomb'd his locks, and careless his attire,
> Unlike the trim of love, or gay desire:
> But full of museful mopings, which presage
> The loss of reason, and conclude in rage."*

Yet impelled by I know not what restlessness, continually to add to the knowledge that killed him, when the Marquis entered into conversation at all, it was to win, indirectly, from either Sir Edward or Emily, more minute informations and recitals, concerning this detested impostor.—The strange singularity of her excelling on the flute was at once accounted for by Emily, who informed him that it had been the peculiar instrument of the master who taught both the ladies at Bellarney; and the bolder genius of Miss Fitzallen, she added, ever pursued what pleased her, without a thought of the proper or improper. Thus had she been accustomed, in playing, always to accompany Emily Arden; and in every accomplishment kept pace with her.

The more the Marquis ruminated on the fatal ceremonial, which was the perpetual subject of his thoughts, the more he saw that, though a sudden resolve on his part, it was not so on that of the seducing Hypolito; nor had been imperfectly solemnized. The witnessing priests, no less than the one who married him, were all men high in consideration; and too well he knew the impostor had secured documents of the fatal rite, which he now plainly perceived no wealth could purchase, no agonies win her to give up. Never did he lift his eyes to the still unsuspicious Marchioness, that they were not ready to overflow upon the lovely wretch, who knew not yet she was so.

The wan cheeks, the wild and haggard looks of the Marquis, could not, however, be equally guarded from the observation of Sir Edward Arden, who saw too plainly some deep-seated sorrow in his soul, that it was his only employment to hide from his Emily,—the beloved of both. In hours of kindness and confidence, when they were alone, Sir Edward often sought to lead his nephew to a disclosure of his grief; but the effort generally produced vague transports, threatening either despair or madness; and glad was the afflicted father to retreat again into ignorance, so that he could soothe to peace pangs wholly unintelligible.

A love thus steeped in tears, is, however, too trying a sight for a father. Sir Edward, now again unable to endure a state of total retirement, hinted to Emily that it might be advisable to return to Naples. She readily consented, from the idea that the melancholy she perceived yet lurking about the Marquis, and now, she feared, infecting her father, might proceed from the sacrifice both made of society for her sake. At Naples she should, at least, feel that they were independent of her; nor would it be necessary for her to mix in its gay circles.

Ah! hapless Emily, couldst thou have known the misery awaiting thee at Naples, to the extremity of the earth wouldst thou have flown to avoid it!—A few days after her return, the Marchioness was persuaded, by her husband and father, to drive, in their company, on the Corso.* Before her was an equipage, which they all perceived to be English. The slow parade of its motion made the servants of the Marquis pass it abruptly; and curiosity, to see who of their own country it contained, caused all the party to lean forward. A lovely face did the same in the other carriage; and with a power, scarce inferior to the fabled one of the Gorgon,* transfixed, in a manner, a trio, who, at that moment, had not a single thought of Miss Fitzallen. It was herself—that fair fiend, gay, triumphant, elegantly attired, and sumptuously attended. Her face was too strongly impressed on Sir Edward's memory, to be mistaken; to his daughter it was familiar as her own; to the Marquis it was a vision of guilt and horror. Ah! had either of his companions instantaneously turned towards him, words would not have been wanting to tell the cause of all his silent struggles, his embittered enjoyments:—his heart died within him, thus to find his worst fear verified.

Emily, suddenly recollecting that to the Marquis this fatal face was unknown, turned to account to him for the astonishment it had excited in herself and her father. She saw him sunk lifeless and low in the carriage; and snatching his hand, found on it the chill of death. Miss Fitzallen was no more remembered; the whole world vanished from the eyes of the tender wife; and prognosticating a second attack of the Marquis's fearful fever, she hastened home to call medical assistance, and use every possible precaution. Happily the common methods for alleviating the diseases of the body, are the only ones that can lessen the anguish of the mind. Loss of blood, abstinence, and solitude, misery requires no less than fever. The last of these prescriptions gave this unfortunate husband the painful privilege of shutting his door on all the world,—even on his adored Emily. Once more alone, he would have regulated his ideas; but thought was chaos. He would perhaps have died, had he not known he must alike kill the wife he adored. Alas! he could only rend his hair and groan, till exhausted nature sunk to stupefaction.

To address with supplication the heart base enough to lead him on to guilt, the Marquis saw, on cooler reflection, would be a vain attempt; and only shew the infamous Miss Fitzallen the extent of power she had acquired. To threaten, might lead her to assert it.—Whence, too, came she? How had she escaped the horrors of the earthquake? how acquired the splendour with which she was surrounded? and under what name and character was she received in society? Ah, where was he to gain self-command and patience enough to pursue these enquiries? Yet, if they should ultimately tend to break the tie so abhorred, and render Emily happy, was it not his duty to sacrifice every feeling to that great one?

Under this impression, the Marquis again resolved to dissemble what was passing in his heart; and, by mixing with the gay nobles of the Neapolitan court, trace out the history of this striking stranger. What was his astonishment, when he returned into that circle, to find that she was no stranger there;—that, while he was vainly seeking her in the character of Hypolito, without any disguise, and in her own name, Miss Fitzallen had appeared in Naples, almost from the day he left it;—that she was considered as a beautiful Irish heiress, enchanting in her manners, and careless in her conduct. A woman who dares affect this character, has all the male sex at once on her side. Not an associate of the Marquis who did not profess himself of her train; yet not one impeached a life, by all considered as very equivocal. To his other cruel chagrins, the Marquis now added that of knowing, if she once dared to assert her marriage, and the laws sanctioned it, she would bring on him, in her own person, indelible infamy; since it was sufficiently obvious she could have no wealth which vice did not procure. Yet so well are disgraceful secrets usually kept, that it might be for ever out of his power to prove the guilt he in a manner witnessed.—But was it for him to attempt proving guilt on any other human being? Did he not crawl on the earth, the abhorred of his own soul, and endure existence but for the sake of that angel, his adoration alone had sullied? Such was the beginning, such the end, of the daily, nightly meditations, of the Marquis of Lenox.

Time, however, crept on; and no change in the situation of any party occurred. Emily Fitzallen, occupied with herself, her lovers, and her gallantries,* seemed not to mean any further to annoy the Marquis. Sir Edward, and his daughter, knew not they were to fear, and soon became used to see her. Could the miserable Lenox have compounded with his own conscience, he might yet have called his that happiness, which love, friendship, and fortune, in rare union, sometimes lavish on humanity. Oh! most acute of miseries, to remember his own hand could alone have poisoned the cup of felicity!

But it was not the fate of the Marquis long to enjoy even the rest which doubt now gave. The Duke of Aberdeen had at length sent over to his daughter-in-law the splendid jewels promised on her marriage. They were the first set in the manner, since become so fashionable, called transparent. Emily's natural delicacy made her decline appearing at court, as her person now shewed her situation; but these beautiful diamonds were so much the subject of discourse, that the Queen* sent to desire the Marchioness would entrust them to her jeweller, to alter some of her ornaments by. The jewels were committed to his care, and the cause of their not being worn by their owner, thus became public. As any trifle will amuse the great, the jeweller's house was immediately the resort of every lady who had, or thought she had, a right to either jewels or fashion. Nor was Miss Fitzallen wanting to her own consequence on the occasion. What was the state of the Marquis, when, an hour after her visit there, this billet was put into his hands.—"Hypolito is charmed with the jewels; in three days' time they must be sent, or you abide the consequence." The incensed and haughty soul of the Marquis would have abided any consequence, but for the peculiar, the interesting, situation of his Emily. The mere fact, without the least aggravation, would be death to her: but with the colourings this malignant fiend might give it, madness would, perhaps, fore-run some tremendous catastrophe. After the most desperate struggles with himself,—an anguish past all description,—the wretched Lenox tried to unfold a fabricated tale to Emily; and saw, in the alarm that instantly shook her, what the truth would infallibly have produced in so delicate a creature. How sweet was the relief that glowed on her countenance, when she at last wrung from his labouring heart a confession, that he had incurred a debt of honour,* beyond the utmost amount of the money at his immediate command, nor could payment be delayed. "The jewels alone"—Emily suffered him not to conclude the sentence:—"Take them at once, my love; take any, or all my fortune—Oh! that the whole of it could restore colour to those bloodless cheeks, or peace to that beloved bosom! Indeed then would it be employed:

> "For never should'st thou lie by Portia's side,
> With an unquiet soul."*

Who would not have endured a daily martyrdom for such a creature?—Miss Fitzallen had the jewels she demanded. The only one the gentler Emily wished for, the heart of the Marquis, was wholly her own.

It happened, a short time after, that an English nobleman gave a *fête* ere he quitted Naples, to which of course the Marquis, his lady, and Sir Edward, were invited. The Marquis shared not in any pleasure Emily retired from; and she no longer mixed in company. Sir Edward, either from thinking the absence of the whole family would be an affront to their countryman, or a latent taste for gaieties he was not yet too far advanced in life to enjoy, accepted the invitation; though he joined not the party till late. Among the masqued dancers, he suddenly saw one who appeared to him to be adorned with the unworn jewels of the Marchioness. Yet this was so unlikely, that her father drew near—rather to satisfy himself they were not the same, than from the belief that they were. It was not possible to doubt their identity. Neither would the wearer allow hers to be doubted; for, as Sir Edward approached, Miss Fitzallen took off her masque, and, holding it carelessly in her hand, surveyed the incensed father with an exulting malignant smile, as though she bade him drink to the dregs the deadly poison of conviction.

Almost frantic with wrath and indignation, Sir Edward rushed from the ballroom, and in one moment would have rendered the two beings most dear to him miserable for ever, but that their better angel had bade them retire early, and escape the storm.

Though the fever of passion raged all night in Sir Edward's bosom, reason at intervals endeavoured to counteract it. In England, he recollected, it was not unusual for arrogant people to hire, at an extravagant price, additions to their own diamonds, on occasions of parade. The same custom might prevail at Naples; and the queen's jeweller have availed himself of the confidence reposed in him, to make a temporary advantage of ornaments he knew the owner would not be near to recognize. This was possible, and only possible; for Sir Edward hardly could persuade himself, that any jeweller would venture to entrust diamonds so valuable at a masquerade; or that any person would chuse to hire those so singular in their taste, as to prove they could belong only to one lady. There was yet another remote idea came to his relief (for it was death to him to think but for a moment, that her husband had thus plundered and insulted his daughter)—Emily herself might have been acted upon by this artful mean creature, and have given her now a princely fortune in her diamonds. He remembered her having sent Miss Fitzallen, when she so insolently quitted Bellarney, all the jewels she then possessed (for the bounty had been haughtily and ungratefully returned into his own hands): Emily might not, in the fervour of her feelings, have either taken into view the vast difference in the value of the benefaction, nor the disgrace which must result either to herself, or her lord, in allowing a woman of a character at the best dubious, publicly to appear in ornaments prepared for, and only suitable to, a Duchess.

Morning, however, at length came; and though prudence had imposed present silence on Sir Edward, he was not the less determined to trace to its source this extraordinary incident. When an hour of loneliness gave him opportunity to try how far his daughter was concerned, he turned, as if accidentally, the conversation on the jewels. Emily blushed, sighed, and strove, by beginning on another subject, to wave that. Though this too plainly proved that the jewels were gone, yet, in the painful state of the father's mind, he was obliged rather to wish the egregious folly of giving them away might be proved on his daughter, than a cruel doubt remain, that her husband had been guilty of ingratitude and baseness. Sir Edward was on the point of reproving Emily for thus unworthily bestowing the magnificent present of the Duke of Aberdeen, when his native pride prevailed; and, not deigning to utter the name of Miss Fitzallen, his alarmed daughter understood all he applied to that base woman as referring to the Marquis (for it never occurred to her, that she could be suspected, by a human being, of having given to any creature but her husband such valuables). She betrayed, without designing it, how she had disposed of them; but, shocked at the change in Sir Edward's face, extorted a promise of secresy from him, by the offer of unreserved confidence. That promise was so necessary to his learning the whole she could tell him, that her father did not hesitate to comply. She then imparted the specious tale of the Marquis's loss at the gaming-table, and expressed the sweet relief her heart found in taking from his the disgraceful weight of a debt of honour. To smooth the furrows on her father's brow, Emily ventured to vouch for this debt being single in its kind, and generously called on Sir Edward to rejoice that the first went to such an extent, as would, in a rational mind, prevent a folly from becoming a habit. Sir Edward, though perhaps not more satisfied than at the beginning of the explanation, saw such merit and softness in Emily's conduct, that he yielded to her entreaties, and promised never to mention either the jewels, or the debt of honour, to the Marquis. On his own part, he carefully supprest the painful knowledge he had thus accidentally acquired; resolving, by future watchfulness to fathom the heart of the Marquis, if the fault lay so deep, and to admonish him, if it should only influence his conduct.

Time, however, past on; and the tender lovers, inseparable in their pleasures, gave no cause to the most watchful parent for dissatisfaction. Sir Edward had almost forgotten his cause of distrust; when, in a moment of hilarity, it not only was revived, but indelibly impressed. In a meeting of the dissolute Neapolitan nobles, with the gay travellers who wander from England, to disseminate the bad habits of their own country, and bring home those of all they visit,* Sir Edward found Miss Fitzallen was suddenly becoming the subject of very light discourse, which began with her being toasted by an Italian after the Marchioness, and rejected by an Englishman, as not a fit association. The sprightly sallies of gallantry and admiration this creature excited in her defenders, would have been ill borne by Sir Edward, had he not taken a strong interest in her conduct, from the desire he still had to learn the means by which she obtained his Emily's jewels. He now began artfully to unbend; and the company with eagerness listened to authority so indubitable, when Sir Edward recounted all he knew of her history: not concluding without an obvious desire to benefit in turn by their communications, and a marked wonder at the high style of her establishment, when he knew her without any inherited resources. A laugh, that proved he had shewn ignorance where he might have been supposed to have information, embarrassed Sir Edward; who, struggling to conceal his anxiety, redoubled his address, fully to develop the truth he almost trembled to know. Without hesitation, the thoughtless party spoke of a variety of lovers as favoured by Miss Fitzallen, and lavishing their wealth on her: but the most profuse, they all admitted, was Count Montalvo, who *first took her from the Marquis of Lenox.* Sir Edward Arden thought his senses failed him; or rather, that apprehension shaped into words the workings of his fancy. The conversation, however, was pursued. Those who named the Marquis, rather treated him as one who had formerly followed, than who now paid her homage. Sick, sick at heart, the fond father smiled; though on his lips the smile stiffened almost into a convulsion, that still he might hear: and hear he did. The name of Hypolito at length was mentioned; and the start of Sir Edward shewed this, as applied to Miss Fitzallen, to be a discovery. He now was obliged to stand their raillery on his own blindness, and be told, that almost every one around him had discovered this favoured youth to be a woman, who had thus disguised herself to deceive the uncle, and make the nephew happy.

And now, to the jaundiced sight of Sir Edward, the whole horrible truth stood revealed in its most odious colours. In this nephew, so beloved, admired, esteemed, he suddenly beheld a man capable of licentiousness and hypocrisy in the first instance—baseness and ingratitude in the last. He now could recollect, that the features of this feigned Hypolito had from the first struck him as familiar to his eye: still they caused no suspicion; confiding, as he did at that time, in the Marquis, and almost inseparable from both. Seeing in the impostor the talents, mien, and manners, of a youth, how was it possible he should surmise her sex? Yet well he remembered, long after the earthquake at Messina, the agony of the Marquis when Hypolito was named; and he bitterly reproached himself for not reflecting, that the feeling of man for man never produced so pungent a pang.

That the Marquis, at Messina, either by the calamity, or her own choice, had lost the worthless wanton, was, to the erroneous judgment of Sir Edward, very plain: that he never bestowed a thought on Emily Arden till that moment, seemed equally obvious. It is true, when he met, he condescended not to hate the gentle creature who lived in his looks: nay, he even deigned to marry her. But no sooner did the beautiful impostor appear, in the new charm of her own shape, than she resumed her full empire over the ungenerous Marquis; and he not only sacrificed to her his fortune and his honour, but feeling, nay even decency. "And such, then, is the husband I have a thousand times implored of heaven for my innocent, my noble-minded Emily!" groaned forth the afflicted father.

Only one hope of happiness remained to them all, in the judgment of Sir Edward, and that was a hope horrible to humanity. A single lover might not be able to attach Miss Fitzallen; a single fortune certainly could not support her; and if once the Marquis discovered the first, her reign would be over. Sir Edward had bound himself to endure the scene before him with patience, and he determined he would do so; though his secret soul misgave him, that the fair fiend, if she ruined not the husband by her extravagance, would sooner or later destroy the wife by her malice.

The favourite and trusted valet of Sir Edward, knew his master too well not to understand something of the cares that preyed on his peace. From that domestic, Sir Edward had the additional vexation of learning, that every servant in the family had, from the first, suspected the sex of the feigned Hypolito; and all concluded that it was a love affair of the young Lord's, his uncle would not see. He, too, confirmed the opinion of his master, that, in the earthquake at Messina, this disguised favourite vanished: and the affliction her lover long shewed, proved he believed her among the victims.

By means of his valet, Sir Edward had a strict watch kept on the wanderings of the melancholy Lenox; but, from these, no conclusion could malice have drawn against him. No being could point out the moment he passed not in lonely misery, save those he beguiled in the society of Emily and her father. Yet the latter no longer sought, still less condescended, to sooth him. Each had his own sad secret to guard; and the Marchioness became soon the only link between two hearts, that once preferred each other to the whole world.

Nor was Emily without a latent fear,—a buried sorrow. Among her insipid Italian female visitants, one had been found capable of shocking her with the information of who now possessed, and displayed, those rich baubles, that seemed to have been sent only to torment her: and though it was possible the winner of the immense debt, that the jewels were appropriated to pay, might gratify Miss Fitzallen with them, it was likewise possible that the Marquis himself might have been the donor. The long absences which he rendered everyday longer, perplexed and afflicted his wife; who, more and more confined from her situation, had ample leisure for conjecture. Had she too set a spy on the Marquis, well would she have known, that the periods when he no longer gladdened her sight, were always spent by him in the deepest shade of some convent* garden, in solitude, penitence, groans, and anguish.

The days that passed rapidly to the fearful Emily, seemed to creep to the Marquis; who expected, with more than a lover's impatience, with more than a father's anxiety, the one which would render her a mother: her recovery would leave him at liberty to hasten to England, and satisfy his mind as to the predicament the laws of that country would place him in.* By those of Italy, he knew himself condemned, unless Miss Fitzallen consented to prove the marriage incomplete. It was an enquiry too delicate to intrust to any human being; nor dared he on paper commit himself. Every day, every hour, he repeated with what impatience he should hasten, when able, to England; and even Sir Edward, not knowing how to reconcile this lively anxiety to return, with the charm he still fancied Italy contained for the Marquis, now gave him credit for reviving virtue, and now despised him for consummate hypocrisy.

Sir Edward foreseeing how little Emily would like to mix in the Neapolitan society, and quite convinced it was necessary, in her condition, to take exercise and amusement, had resolved to surprize her with a useful present. He had, therefore, ere she left the country, employed his grooms to break a set of beautiful Spanish horses; and sent for a light, low, elegant kind of carriage, which ladies often safely drive. The rides round Naples are beautiful, but not contiguous; and thus was the Marchioness to be seduced into exploring them. The sweetly fancied carriage no sooner was seen, than, like her diamonds, it became the object of universal attraction. Miss Fitzallen was among those it captivated;—to admire, and to appropriate, was, with her, the same thing. The success of her first bold demand, ensured her whatever she required of the Marquis; and another peremptory billet from her almost overset his reason. The little equipage in question had not been *his* gift; it had no comparative value; nor could human ingenuity invent a mode of obtaining it from the generous owner, that would not wound her to the heart. Yet, oh! too sure the fiend must have it. A day and night of exquisite torture, on the part of the Marquis, announced to Emily another impending affliction; when her tenderness wrung from his sad soul an insincere confession, that he had, in an hour of accidental inebriation, wantonly staked her little favourite carriage and horses; which having lost, he found, to his unspeakable chagrin, no equivalent would be accepted, nor any thing on earth but the simple stake. The tender Emily listened, but it was no longer with an implicit reliance on his honour and veracity. Neither could she find, in this recital, however agitated his manner, that openness or probability, by which his actions had been heretofore characterized. Yet it was certain, whatever the cause, he greatly desired the beautiful trifle in question; and it was still her duty, as it had always been her pleasure, to comply with every wish of his. She faintly hinted a fear of offending her father; but bade the Marquis honourably acquit himself to his inexorable opponent: nor could she account for the burning drops her cheek the next moment imbibed from that of her husband, as with a long embrace he strained the generous charmer to his heart.

Perhaps rather to please her father than herself, Emily had shewn a singular delight in this little carriage; and he had felt the delicacy of her gratitude. She now continually made excuses for staying at home, which Sir Edward sometimes sought to over-rule; and, after a time, urged her health as his motive. His daughter became chagrined and embarrassed. A secret consciousness that she had not wholly relied on the account of the Marquis, as to the disposal of her father's present, made her hesitate to repeat it. She therefore slightly answered, that the Spanish horses were too spirited. Sir Edward was hastening to talk to the grooms on that subject, when his daughter, with increasing embarrassment, added, that the alarm she had taken, had made her resolve to put it out of her own power to risque so dangerous an indulgence in future, by desiring the Marquis to change the carriage with one of his friends, who was urgent to get such another. The simplicity of this account, though he might have thought his little gift too slightly valued, would, at another time, have entirely satisfied Sir Edward; but, watchful as he was now become, and sweetly ingenuous as Emily had ever been, it was impossible but he must perceive that she veiled the fact, if she was too upright to falsify it.

To accord with her father's wish, as far as was in her power, the Marchioness ordered her coach to be made ready; and, attended by her woman, drove to the Corso. What a spectacle awaited her there! Miss Fitzallen, in all the insolence of exultation, seated in the beautiful carriage, so lately Emily's, was driving the same horses in the English style, to the admiration of a set of Italian nobles, by whom she was surrounded. Hardly could Sir Edward's gentle daughter suppose even Miss Fitzallen capable of an outrage so gross: but her woman could not forbear confirming the fact, by an exclamation of disdain. At that moment the gay, insulting fiend, perceiving by the livery, who was approaching, made her coursers fly as close as she dared to the coach of the Marchioness; who, lifting her tearful eyes to heaven, pressed her white hands on the heart that had betrayed her peace, in adoring, as she believed, a worthless object, and sunk back in a swoon.

The proud career of Miss Fitzallen was something checked, however, by her meeting, in the way to her hotel, Sir Edward Arden on horseback. His indignant eye suddenly fell from herself to the well-known horses: again it was pointedly raised to her face, and again, with contempt and fury, glanced upon the carriage. A look informed him, that the base woman who had, through the Marquis, thus poorly plundered his daughter, had not the decency to expunge from her acquisition, even the arms of Lenox. Sir Edward stopped his horse a moment, as dizzy and stupefied; but recovering himself, turned the animal round, and was presently by the side of Miss Fitzallen; who felt not quite easy at finding he meant to accompany her. She slackened the reins, and summoned all her resolution, when she saw him alight at the same moment she did, and abruptly follow her into her own hotel. Passing into the first apartment, from a something of fear she could not controul, she threw herself into a seat; and, with the dauntless air she usually affected, demanded to know to what extraordinary occasion she was to impute the extraordinary intrusion of Sir Edward Arden. "The intrusion is so extraordinary to himself," returned that gentleman, "when he considers the company he has joined, that he will speak to the point, and spare discussion:—all other feelings are lost in those of the father. I come not, Madam, to *ask* aught. I come to *command* you to efface, from the beautiful bauble you have just quitted, the arms of the Marquis of Lenox. Though he may empower you to destroy the peace of his wife, it remains with her father to guard her honour."—"Have a care, Sir Edward," returned the lady, suffering all the Fury to glare over her fine features,—"have a care how you venture a *command* to me. If ever your daughter carries a point in which I am concerned, it must be by very different means."—"Weak, insolent, wanton woman!" cried Sir Edward, with increasing bitterness, "do you mistake me for the worthless young man, over whom you tyrannize with a power so absolute? Do you think it possible *I* should ever level his mistress with his wife?"—"Address to your own daughter," retorted the lady with a smile of diabolical triumph, "those gross terms, misapplied when lavished on me. *Command her* to efface from her carriage the arms of the Marquis of Lenox. Bid her lay down *my* title; and when you henceforth speak of the mistress of your nephew, think of Emily Arden; when you mention his wife, remember only *me*."

Too powerful was the emotion of Sir Edward's nature at this assertion, incredible as the fact appeared, for him to utter a single syllable.—Miss Fitzallen, after a pause, resumed—"I can easily guess how little weight my claim would have, did it depend only on my own word, or your idolized nephew's honour. But I have full, authentic documents, which prove me the wife of the Marquis, months ere he in idle pageant gave that name to your daughter: and here," cried she, opening a locket which hung at her bosom, and taking from it the witnessed certificate, which she spread before the miserable father's eyes,—"is one irrefragable proof, which will convince even you, that the rite was solemn, regular, and valid."

Sir Edward Arden's quick eye, rendered even more quick by disdain, saw (and seeing recognized) the hand-writing of Padre Anselmo; with whom he had once held a literary correspondence: nor were the names of the witnessing priests unknown to him. Wrung as he was to the last gasp of suffering nature, the dignity of his mind did not desert him. With that lofty obeisance which is rather a respect paid to ourselves, than the object before us, Sir Edward in silence admitted the claim, however insolently made, and hastily withdrew: while in his pallid countenance too plainly appeared the deep, the uncontroulable anguish of his soul.

Nor was it anguish alone the insulted father felt—unconquerable indignation, burning rage, strung every nerve, and the storm burst only with more dreadful violence for his allowing it to collect with a deceiving stillness.—Calmly mounting his horse, he rode home, and there giving it to his groom, returned as usual to his own apartment.—Having taken thence a pair of pistols, he always kept in high order, and ready loaded, he resorted to a convent garden, which his spy had informed him was among the favourite haunts of the lonely, melancholy Marquis.

Sir Edward was too successful in his research.—In the most retired spot of the sacred ground, where a deep shade extended over a sainted oratory, thrown at his length, on a stone seat near the entrance, and lost in sad meditation, was the interesting object of Sir Edward's fury.—There had been a time when so to have seen his darling nephew would have melted Sir Edward to the weakness of childhood.—The waste of his graceful form was never more visible. His wild and hollow eyes now scanned heaven impatiently, and now sunk heavily to the ground.—No sense of pleasure—no flow of youthful vigour, was now to be traced in the unhappy Lenox.—Yet did not his countenance bespeak the perturbation of guilt. A silent, sullen, impenetrable sorrow lived there; which, hoping nothing, demanded nothing: but draining as it were the sap from the tree, left it without life, though it fell not.

Yet who can wonder, that, in the deep sense of present injury and outrage, Sir Edward Arden lost for a moment the acute sensibility, nay even the humanity, of his nature? Fiercely approaching, without deigning a word, he offered to the unfortunate youth, who hastily started up on seeing his uncle, one of the pistols, and waved to him haughtily to take his ground. Dear from any other hand would have been the tendered death the Marquis dared not give himself; but from his uncle!—the father of his Emily!—He gazed in mute misery. Taking with the pistol the hand that held it, in fond agony he kissed, he clasped it: it was the hand that had cherished his infancy—the hand that gave him the sad invaluable blessing he knew not even now how to part with. Sir Edward snatched it from him with a fury that almost threw him backwards. "Coward too are you, as well as villain?" cried he with almost inarticulate passion. "Double your infamous perjury—swear to me that you are not married to Miss Fitzallen—that you did not deliberately dishonour"—his native pride would not allow him to finish the sentence. In a tone even yet more choked, he resumed, waving with his pistol the due distance to the Marquis, "Take your ground, Sir; keep your guard; worthless as you are, I would not be your murderer."

The Marquis had arisen, and a faint flush, at the personal insult of his uncle, gave a wild indignant charm to his natural beauty: but he spoke not—moved not—nor, though he held the pistol, did he lift it. Sir Edward observed him no more; but, conforming to the modes of duels, retreated properly, and turning, impetuously fired,—alas! with but too sure an aim. In one moment he beheld his nephew in the agonies of death. Passion expired—human resentment and injury were at once forgotten—and he who killed the wretched young man, hung lamenting over him, even like a fond father some unforeseen stroke had rendered childless. The Marquis perhaps accelerated his own fate, by a fruitless effort he again made to seize and kiss his uncle's hand. With a dreadful struggle, he at length found voice to cry, "Fly, save yourself.—Oh God! save Emily: leave me to"—life now flitted from him, and Sir Edward remained a monument of horror.

And it is thus we daily arrogate to ourselves the bloody right of adding crime to crime, and call it honour—justice! an impious law, by which proud man lives to himself alone, and defies his maker!

In the Neapolitan government, as well as many other Italian ones, justice is lame as well as blind; and he must be a lagging criminal indeed, who cannot escape so tardy a pursuer. Hot and impetuous spirits have therefore often presumed to right themselves, and personal vengeance is become an almost licensed evil in civil society. The safety of Sir Edward was not endangered, he well knew, by a duel; but the spot on which it had taken place was hallowed: he could not, as a protestant, claim sanctuary with the monks, therefore knew himself liable to be seized for sacrilege. In the situation of Emily this would be consummate ruin; and for her sake only did he think it necessary to guard himself from being stopt in retreating from the garden. The loaded pistol would enable him to command his freedom; and, approaching again the lifeless body of his nephew, he took it from his hand, dropping the fatal one he had himself fired. What cruel pangs seized on his heart, as, kneeling, he fondly gazed on the wan face of the Marquis, and groaned forth the name of his sister! Each feature seemed moulded by death to a yet stricter resemblance of those long buried in the grave.—Again Sir Edward returned; again he wept; again he smote his breast; and willingly would he have laid down his own life, to restore that he had so rashly taken.

It happened, the part of the convent-ground the Marquis had fallen in, was at certain hours open to all visitants; nor did Sir Edward, either at entering or retiring, meet a single being. Not daring to risque one look from his widowed daughter, he retreated to an hotel, and sent for his valet; a rational man, in middle life, on whose conduct and fidelity he could fully rely. Having hastily and imperfectly imparted to this trusty domestic the fatal fact, he bade him think, if possible, how it could be for a time concealed from the unfortunate Emily; and how she could be wrought upon to remove from the terrible scene of her husband's death, ere she knew she had lost him.

Sir Edward's valet, who had long seen some heavy evil brooding in the three bosoms, was less surprized than shocked at the present one. After pausing a moment, he called to Sir Edward's recollection, that in the bay, lay prepared, by the orders of the Marquis, for a little voyage to the neighbouring isles, a small pleasure-bark, that nobleman had purchased. This might in a few hours be ready to put to sea, and was the only way a lady in the condition of the Marchioness could venture to travel, as well as a secure mode of avoiding either following couriers, or accidental intelligence. He would immediately wait on her, and by a partial communication of the truth, prevent her from a more close enquiry. She would easily, he thought, be persuaded to embark, if assured her husband and father had both been engaged in a duel, in consequence of which, though unwounded, they had been obliged to fly. In the interim, he promised to keep so strict a guard at home, that no alarm should reach the ear of the Marchioness, till she was again in her father's protection: but not as easy for his master's safety, as Sir Edward himself was, he exhorted him to mount his horse; and, posting through the Neapolitan dominions, make the utmost speed to gain those of the Pope.

The distracted state of Sir Edward's mind caused him at once to acquiesce in minute arrangements he had hardly power to comprehend, much less make. His horses were soon ready; and, as motion seems always a temporary relief to an overcharged soul, he involuntarily complied with the advice of his faithful domestic, in hastening towards Rome, which he reached without attracting any observation.

The faithful valet of Sir Edward felt all the weight of the charge he had undertaken, when he learnt that the Marchioness had been brought home from the Corso in fits, and was now shut up in her chamber. From her woman, however, he heard not any thing that implied a knowledge of the truth; and, having dispatched orders to the mariners to be ready to sail in two hours, he imparted to the servants Sir Edward's directions to get immediately together whatever might be necessary for their lady's accommodation, when she should be ready to go on board. While this was doing, he underwent the most painful apprehension, lest the body of the unfortunate Marquis should be brought home for interment, with the rude train of an unfeeling mob. The hours, however, passed on, and nothing alarming occurred. In the abrupt and broken manner Sir Edward had spoken of the rencounter, the place where it had happened had not transpired; nor dared the prudent valet risque any enquiry, lest he should shew prior information.

The bark was now ready; and the servants, having made due preparations, Sir Edward's valet desired to be admitted to Emily, whom he found lying on the bed, weak, dejected, and tearful: but she in a moment sprung hastily from it, on being told her husband and father were obliged to fly, and implored her to hasten after them. The sad circumstances she was in, so much to others the object of consideration, as to detain the whole family for months at Naples, vanished at once from the mind of the impassioned wife—the affectionate daughter. Ah! could an unborn child engross a thought, when the life of the father was in question?

The bark of the Marquis was only one of a number the nobles of Naples keep in the bay for parties of pleasure; and those who saw Emily carried into it, annexed no idea to her departure but that of amusement: and indeed the season was so favourable, and the shore so lovely, that this was a very natural conclusion.

The widowed interesting Emily, as yet unconscious of her own misfortune, was no sooner off the shore of Naples, than a sudden lightness seized her heart. Its tormentor was left behind, and surely would not venture to pursue the Marquis, to whom she fondly supposed herself hastening. The duel, she immediately concluded to have been between the Count Montalvo and her husband; the former being known as the favoured lover of Miss Fitzallen, and the latter but too probably as his rival. She questioned the valet of Sir Edward: but he, who really was informed of very little, would not repeat that little, and only insisted, that he knew Sir Edward and the Marquis had been together.

Ah! if they were indeed so, and in harmony with each other, might not this rencounter have the happiest consequences, in removing from the eyes of the Marquis that film an illicit love had spread over them? With what facility does the heart adopt every idea that favours its feelings! The fancy of Emily now sweetly pictured her husband returning to her in confidence and love. She saw his amiable penitence—she heard his vows of future unalienable faith—she enjoyed the fond delight she should find in forgiving his errors, the endeared charm she might obtain in his eyes, by forgetting them. The most balmy slumbers followed contemplations so innocent and affectionate; and, when the Marchioness awoke in the morning, she found herself in better health and spirits than she had known for a long time.

The little voyage was, by the management of Sir Edward's valet, ingeniously prolonged, though the Marchioness knew it not, that his master might have time to prepare for her reception at Frescati,* where Sir Edward had some time since procured a villa, as an occasional residence for himself, to which it had been settled his hapless daughter should be conveyed. When the agreed time had elapsed, the bark put in at Cività Vecchia,* where a litter, with some domestics of Sir Edward's, was in waiting. The interesting Marchioness, supported by the energies of mind, against the weakness of sex and situation, lost not a moment in rest at the port, but hastened to Frescati; impelled by a generous hope she was not permitted to realize, that she should speak peace and consolation to one, or both, of those waiting for her.

Like a worn wretch, who had never known quiet or rest since she saw him last, stood at the gate to receive her Sir Edward Arden: but, dear as he was, her heart demanded one yet dearer; and she cast her eyes anxiously round the saloon into which her father led her, in impatient silence. The swell of pride, grief had a little allayed in her absence, burst out in all its force, when Sir Edward cast his eyes on his dishonoured child, ready to bring into the world a memento of perpetuated ignominy. All other considerations vanished from his mind; and, when Emily, in faltering accents, demanded her husband, the indiscreet indignant father clasped her in his arms, and, in a haughty tone, exclaimed—"Unhappy girl, you have no husband; you never had one; the wretch, who, under that name, dishonoured you, was already married to Miss Fitzallen: but he has expiated his crimes against us both with his life." Emily, who had made a violent effort to sustain herself, lest the truth should not be allowed to reach her ear, at these words with almost supernatural strength, sprang from her father's arms, and, turning on him a look of mute repulsive horror, staggered to a couch, and throwing herself on her face, shut out with recollection, for a time, the deep sense of incurable anguish,—utter despair.

Sir Edward, sensible too late that he had risqued, by this abrupt avowal, incurring a second misfortune, not inferior in magnitude to that he was lamenting, summoned her women to Emily, and warned them to be tender and careful of her. Long, long was it ere they could recall her to life—Ah! what was life to Emily?

> "Why should she strive to catch convulsive breath,
> Why know the pang, and not the peace of death?"

Existence was perhaps only prolonged in her, by the agonizing effort nature obliged her to make to bestow it. After a few hours of acute suffering, the nurses put into the arms of the exhausted widowed mother, a poor little girl.—By what fine working of the human soul is it, that we sometimes extract rapture from agony, and sweetness from shame? The first cry of the infant was a claim on the mother's affections, which time could never weaken; and, under all the sad circumstances attending her birth, Emily was proud to hold in her arms a daughter of the Marquis of Lenox.

Far otherwise were the feelings of Sir Edward; nature made him wish to preserve his daughter; but in the bottom of his wounded heart lived a faint hope that the child of so many sorrows would not survive, a grievous record of them. The joy which the arrival, and promise of continued life in the little stranger, gave to his domestics, shocked and offended him; nor did he less offend or shock all the females of his family, by peremptorily refusing to see the infant, and forbidding them to speak of it, unless an enquiry came from him.

Torn as Sir Edward was by grief and remorse, his pride still prompted him to guard against the persecuting fiend, whose machinations, any more than her rights, might not end with the life of the Marquis. But the passions of powerful minds take so high a tone from the understanding, that it is not easy for common observers to discriminate between their faults and their virtues. Actuated by that dignified pride, which, daring to humble itself to the dust, leaves the mean, or malignant, without any power of humbling it at all, Sir Edward Arden immediately resolved that his daughter should not appropriate aught, any human being had a right to take from her. Calling therefore together her domestics, and his own, he ordered the former to throw off the liveries of the Marquis of Lenox, and expunge his arms from her carriages; concluding with a stern command to the astonished circle, never more to mention the name of his nephew in his hearing, or call his daughter by any other than that he himself bore. His tone shewed he would be obeyed: and he was so.

This grievous effort being made to provide against the future attacks of the infamous Miss Fitzallen, Sir Edward resolved never more, if possible, to see, certainly never more to exchange a syllable with her, whatever steps either to sooth, or exasperate him, or his daughter, she might hereafter take.

The morose humour in which Sir Edward had long been, the solitary life he now affected, co-operated with this singular and severe command, to give the servants an idea that his senses were touched by the death of the Marquis; which the daily, nightly lamentations of the miserable Emily, had circulated in the family. It was whispered, universally, that the unfortunate youth had ended his own days; which, though it occasioned much sorrow among the domestics, gave them little surprize. In fact, they had long apprehended his wasting health, and deep melancholy, would have that termination.

This idea was now no less general at Rome; and Sir Edward found, to his own astonishment, that the tremendous secret of who ended the life of the Marquis, was confined to his own breast, and that of the valet, to whom he had himself confided it.

Cardinal Albertini, a prelate of the first rank and merit at Rome, who had long been in habits of particular friendship with Sir Edward, and who much admired and esteemed the Marquis, now, with sympathetic tenderness, conveyed to the former the regular account of the melancholy fate of his nephew, as transmitted to the holy college by the superior of the convent, where the body had been found. It expressed, without any doubt, that the unknown young man must have been his own executioner, as only one pistol had been found lying by him; and two balls, which were lodged in his side, had been indisputably discharged from that pistol.

Sir Edward now remembered, with mute horror, having taken from the lifeless hand of his nephew the loaded pistol; though, in so doing, he only sought to secure his own departure from the convent, not to veil his guilt.

He resumed the letter. The fathers of the convent were ignorant of English; and all the letters and papers found on the body, were unfortunately in that language. The disgrace of having had their holy precincts stained with blood, made them so cautious who they called in as a translator, that some time past ere they could be sure the miserable victim of his own rashness was identically the Marquis of Lenox. A faithful brother was then dispatched in search of his worthy uncle, Sir Edward Arden; but through a singular and unlucky chance, he was just gone by sea, with his daughter, on a party of pleasure to

Frescati. The melancholy duty of interment admitting, as must be obvious, no delay, the Marquis was buried with the utmost privacy, and the whole as yet kept a secret in Naples. It was now submitted to the Holy Father of the church, to judge of their proceedings; and give such instructions for informing the young nobleman's relations, as he in his piety and wisdom should see fit.

So extraordinary a circumstance as that of having, by mere accident, escaped the odious stigma attending a duel with his nephew, was matter of perpetual astonishment to Sir Edward. But it is not in the secresy of its fault, a noble mind finds any mitigation of suffering: the specious palliations, the extenuating pleas, self-love boldly urges against the censures of the world, an ingenuous nature dares not bring before the secret tribunal of conscience, where man sits sole judge of his own actions on this side of the grave. At that awful tribunal, Sir Edward Arden every day, every hour, pronounced his own condemnation; and the image of his bleeding, dying nephew, fondly striving to clasp the unrelenting hand which had struck at his life, was forever present to his eyes.

Ah! how is it that our deep sense of a past fault, prevents not the commission of a new one? Had compunction operated to amendment, Sir Edward would, with endeared fondness, have soothed the daughter he had widowed, and have kept in his "heart of hearts" the babe he had made fatherless. But his nature was unequal to sorrowing for more than one object; and, while he lamented the dead without ceasing, he shunned, nay almost hated, the innocent causes of his crime.

That Emily should shrink from her father's sight, was, in her weak and melancholy situation, too natural. The little sensibility he had shewn for her, in abruptly disclosing her loss, with its mortifying and calamitous occasion, was never absent from her mind. The harsh and cruel sound of his fine-toned voice, when pronouncing, *"you have no husband—you never had one"*—rang like the knell of death for ever in her ears; nor did her ignorant attendants leave her unacquainted with the humiliating command Sir Edward had given, that she should be called in future Miss Arden only: thus marking with opprobrium the infant that once was to inherit the highest hopes,—superior rank,—immense fortunes. When life had thus lost every charm to the widowed Emily, the recollection, that in the grave she should escape from the authority of this severe father,—that the killing tone of his voice could no more wither there her heart,—that she should, at last, sleep in peace with the Marquis of Lenox,—made that cold retreat, human nature commonly shrinks from, to her a dear and desirable asylum. To the poor infant, when the nurses put it into her arms, Emily would fondly whisper,—"Thou, my beloved innocent, wilt grow up, as thy mother never did, under that severe eye, which will, perhaps, deign to beam tenderness on thee, when I can offend no more. Thou wilt not shudder at the sound of that decisive voice; for the destruction of thy happiness it may never announce: thou art among the few, the very few, to whom the loss of parents is ultimately a blessing."

Feelings and lamentations like these might well, in the reduced state of Sir Edward's daughter, urge on the fate she implored. A slow fever seized her, and first robbed the babe of its natural nourishment; finally leaving the mother hardly power to receive any to recruit her strength. Dr. Dalton began to be alarmed, and apprized Sir Edward of the precarious state he thought the lady in. Her father started, as from a dream, and almost envied the fate she was threatened with. The danger increased; and as Sir Edward was one day gloomily ruminating on its probable termination, he suddenly recollected, that in the singular predicament his daughter was placed in, by this disputable marriage, her child's right to the immense inheritance vested in herself, might one day be contested, perhaps with success, by the remote heirs of the Bellarney family; unless, as Emily was turned of twenty-one, she made a will, clear and unequivocal, in favour of her daughter. To suggest so mortifying, as well as alarming a measure, to a young creature on the verge of the grave, required all the firmness of Sir Edward: but he calculated his own feelings at so high a rate, as to fancy he imposed on himself, in seeing the mother and a child he abhorred, and discussing this odious and painful necessity, a suffering quite equal to that of Emily.

If to see his daughter was an effort to Sir Edward, the receiving his visit was almost death to Emily: she no sooner heard the sound of his feet at the chamber door, than she shrunk into the arms of her attendants, and fell into fainting fits. The horrible remembrance of his last abrupt disclosure, made, however, all he could now say, more trying in the apprehension than reality. It might be too true, that the unhappy child, were her legitimacy undisputed, could not inherit the entailed estates of the Lenox family; Sir Edward himself had only a competence to give. The fortune of Emily alone could be rendered its ample provision; and to prevent future law-suits with her heirs on the maternal side, she must, Sir Edward said, by will secure all her property to the infant.

The tender mother, and obedient daughter, gave no other reply to her father's discourse, than that she submitted to his judgment the right and proper, and should fulfil this last duty to him and to her child, whenever he should command her.

But what a trying duty did it prove to the poor Emily, when the moment came for her to read, in the presence of the necessary witnesses, this legal instrument. Conscious, through the whole term of her existence, only of generous tenderness, of hallowed obedience, of every pure and virtuous feeling, that softens or elevates humanity, the innocent daughter of Sir Edward, the wife of the Marquis of Lenox, was obliged to hear herself ignominiously recorded as Emily Arden; and the fatherless babe at her bosom, not allowed to derive even a name from the noble family of her husband, alike termed Emily Arden, as the only mode of securing it from poverty. Nor was Sir Edward's proud and embittered spirit less overwhelmed; he seemed almost frantic.

The sweet saint, who was the more immediate sufferer, with pale composure desired to be lifted and supported in her bed; and bending solemnly over her child, raised her white hands awhile in earnest, though silent supplication to heaven; then meekly kissed and blessed the smiling cherub—"Dear child of misfortune, memento of misery," sighed she, "become not its sad inheritor. Be the pangs of thy father, the anguish of thy mother, in the sight of God, sweet babe, a merit to thee! and, through his mercy, whatever name the pride of man may give or take from thee, may'st thou ripen into a blessing to all who cherish thy little being, an honour to him who bestowed it!"—Emily then signed the memorable will; and duly delivering it, inclined towards her kneeling father with touching dignity, as bending for his blessing; and finding it in his sobs, turned in silence, and waved thence all the spectators; as though her life had been closed by this act of Christian grace and sad submission.

That lively remembrance of the past, which made Sir Edward Arden's days a burden to him, recurred with additional force after this severe trial of his feelings. He found that he was of no comfort to his unhappy daughter; and he felt she was a caustic to the wound ever bleeding in his heart. He therefore changed the scene awhile, and sought, by mixing in the lettered circles of Rome, to diversify his thoughts which, in solitude, dwelt ever on a single object.

Among the grievous and odious necessities of Sir Edward's situation, had been that of giving information to the Duke of Aberdeen, of his son's early, and dreadful catastrophe.—Unwilling to avow the guilt he was ashamed to conceal, he had forborne addressing the childless duke, till Cardinal Albertini sent to him the simple record of the Neapolitan monks.—A copy of this he could remit, and not implicate himself, and in his own narration he only included the account of the Marquis's fixed attachment to Miss Fitzallen, and the gross insults that followed towards his wife;—the arrogant assertion by that worthless woman of her legal rights, and his carrying from Naples his daughter in consequence of this discovery.—He concluded with, in bitterness of soul, describing the decided manner in which he had obliged his daughter to recede from a disgraceful contest, by laying down the title of the Marquis; and called upon the Duke to bewail with him the birth of a grand-daughter, who could only be a grievous memento to both, of the crime of the father, and the misfortune of the mother.

It is ever in the power of virtuous and enlightened minds to pour balm into the deep wounds of human calamity.—Sir Edward Arden's friends at Rome well knew the heavy visitations in his own family, that shook his character, and preyed upon his peace: all, with unremitting kindness, assimilated themselves in his sorrows, till insensibly their severity abated.—The venerable Cardinal Albertini particularly sympathized with him, and hardly more for his own sake than his nephew's. The sweetness of temper, elegance of manners, and frankness of heart, that always characterized the Marquis of Lenox, caused him to leave an impression on the minds of those to whom he was known, not common for young noblemen of his age to make, when on their travels.—It was therefore sensibility, and not curiosity, which actuated the Cardinal, to learn if possible from Sir Edward, the unknown cause of that deep despair, which had, in the young man, so fatal a termination, as that described by the Neapolitan monks' memorial.

There are moments when the surcharged heart cannot resist the secret workings of unmerited kindness.—In one of these the afflicted father disclosed all of the tale, but the sad truth that his hand had shortened the days of his nephew.—He amplified on the joy he took in the birth of the Marquis—on the love he had ever borne him—described the mortal chagrin his nephew's coldness towards the bride proposed to him, in his own daughter, had often given him; and passing from thence to the history of Emily, described her innocent predilection, her successful little romance, and the peace all were in, when he, and his nephew, quitted England.—Sir Edward now came upon the imposture of Miss Fitzallen, and the fatal success of the diabolical artifice.—But it was not possible for him to trace the infamous means by which she had kept her hold on the Marquis, and urged him to injure, and insult, that amiable creature whose honour she had at last sullied, by claiming the Marquis as her husband, and whose days she would as certainly shorten in having caused so horrible a catastrophe.

Hardly could a stoic have heard a father tell his own sad story thus impressively, without emotion: the venerable Cardinal was all sympathy and sorrow. The affecting pause was at length broken by that prelate's enquiring, in what manner Sir Edward had been assured of the prior marriage? When told, again he paused: Padre Anselmo, of Messina, was not unknown, either as a lettered or a pious man, in Rome; and the Cardinal was struck with chagrin to learn that he had been the officiating priest at the fatal ceremonial. Another long silence followed—again broken by the Cardinal, who, in a more animated manner, enquired of Sir Edward if he was sure that priest survived the earthquake? It was a thought that had never occurred to the passionate father: yet, oh! how comprehensive was the possibility!—the Marquis again lay bleeding at his feet,—killed without cause, perhaps; and his knees knocked together. The Cardinal, seeing in his agitation only anxiety, and wholly unsuspicious of his self-accusation, assured Sir Edward that there were records in the College of all who had perished in the convulsions of nature in Sicily; and he had a wandering recollection of having seen Padre Anselmo numbered among those swallowed up; but he would be assured on this point ere they met again. The wary prelate took the further freedom of advising Sir Edward to be very guarded as to any step he might take respecting his daughter's nuptials, and the consequent claims of the Marquis's child by her; since it appeared to him almost impossible for the base Miss Fitzallen to authenticate her marriage; and nothing but her doing that in the clearest and most unequivocal manner could affect the rights of a lady of the Marquis's own rank in life, regularly united to him in all the rights of his and her own country, in the presence of her father, and with the full sanction of his.

And now, what became of Sir Edward, who saw, that, had he advised with one calm, rational, affectionate friend, he might perhaps have escaped whole years of anguish, and a life of conscious guilt? Now, that he might be able to endure his own existence, he almost wished all enquiry on the painful subject stopt. It was some mitigation of misery and horror to believe the Marquis the first criminal. Ah! what would become of the wretched father, if he should be obliged to know himself the only one?

The beneficent Cardinal knew how to sympathize in sorrows he had never personally felt; and saw, in the fair unfortunate Marchioness of Lenox, a motive that quickened his diligence. The next day he hastened to confirm to Sir Edward the supposition he had formed. Padre Anselmo, with most of the fraternity, *had* been swallowed up with the great church, or buried in its ruins: and, to all human probability, even if the rite of marriage had been regularly performed between the Marquis and Miss Fitzallen, it was now become impossible for her to establish any claim to his name or fortune; nor would the church of Rome recognize or support the assumptions of a worthless woman, only because she called herself a member of it, against honour, justice, and the rights of an infant, born, as it was obvious, either to disgrace, or to all that gives distinction in society.

The wildest frenzy of soul preyed in silence, as his friend spoke, on Sir Edward Arden: he—he himself then had eventually, as it appeared, become but the most decisive implement of Emily Fitzallen's vengeance; and had killed his nephew, and defamed his only child, merely to accomplish those views she never, without the aid of his blind passions, could have accomplished.

He was rouzed from this horrible contemplation on the ruin he had surrounded himself with, by the Cardinal's proposing to visit Frescati, and comfort the youthful mourner with the information that neither she, nor her daughter, need shrink from that world where their rights were yet unquestionable. But here, again, by an error of judgment, Sir Edward interfered. He represented Emily, as she really was, in a very weak state—reconciled to her fate and the will of God, in its present form: but, as the discovery now made carried not conviction till confirmed by cautious enquiry, to awaken a hope, or quicken a pang in her bosom, might only tend to shorten the days his benevolent friend wished to make long, and peaceful. On the contrary, he thought it highly advisable, that they should both remain profoundly silent on the painful but important subject, for the present: while he, who had no use for life but to serve or save his daughter, would immediately embark for Messina; where, by every enquiry ingenuity could devise, both among the monks, and the domestics of Count Montalvo, he would inform himself of such particulars as should ascertain the future rights of Emily and her infant, and prepare him to cope with the vindictive fiend he daily expected again to encounter.

The Cardinal assured him Rome was not the place Miss Fitzallen would be likely to chuse for the scene of another exploit: since the estimation Sir Edward was held in among the first circle of learned men there, and the rank and merit of his unfortunate daughter, would make it more probable that she should be shut up in a dungeon as a licentious woman, than sanctioned in bringing forward any claim to the name or fortune of the Marquis, were she daring enough to announce that intention. The voyage of Sir Edward his venerable friend, however, approved; as well as the reasons he assigned for not communicating to the Marchioness the apparent prospect of her re-assuming rights so dear to herself, so important to her child.—Alas! this was the reasoning of man, and man only would thus have reasoned! The tender heart of woman would have told her, the bleeding one of a lover might break, while cool calculations of the future were thus making.

Sir Edward, on returning to Frescati, found the mourner still invisible from debility—an alien still to comfort. Dr. Dalton, however, assured him, that the symptoms of present danger had disappeared, and it was possible she might recover. This news enabled the anxious father to prepare for his voyage with less reluctance. In the projected enquiry was comprehended a hope soothing to his pride on Emily's account, though killing to his peace on his own. Yet, at whatever cost to himself, he felt it his duty to invest her again, if he had a conviction of no prior claim that could be established, with the title he had so madly robbed her of. That once done, he intended immediately to set out with his whole family for England; where, placing Emily under the Duke of Aberdeen's protection, as the Marquis's widow; and, having seen her child acknowledged as the heiress of both, he fully purposed to leave them; and, returning to Naples, expiate his sin, by mourning eternally on the grave of the Marquis.

The bark that had conveyed the Marchioness to Città Vecchia was still lying there, and soon made ready to sail with Sir Edward Arden to Messina.* Ah! could he have known how ineffectual the enquiries made by his unfortunate nephew on the same occasion had proved, never would he have visited the scene where all his miseries originated.

In sailing near the beautiful shore of Naples, the self-reproaching Sir Edward was strongly tempted to land; and, on the spot where he had left the victim of his wrath, the beloved son of his beloved sister, weltering in his blood, to pour forth vain lamentations—eternal compunction:—but he conquered the impulse, resolving first to fulfil every duty to the living; when his embittered soul told him he should consecrate all his future existence to bewailing the dead.

It seemed as if the air Sir Edward had breathed, had conveyed poison and death to his miserable daughter; for, from the day he quitted Frescati, her fever decreased. Emaciated, and dejected, she still continued; but her complaints no longer threatened to undermine her existence. With the dear increasing fondness of a mother, she watched over the last memorial of a husband she still adored; and the cares necessary for her own preservation, she could only be prevailed upon to take, by its being urged to her, that they were essential to the welfare of her daughter.

The villa she inhabited was not large, but the grounds and gardens belonging to it enclosed variety of natural beauty, together with marble fragments of some vanished but memorable building, once seated on nearly the same spot. These gardens were in a neglected disordered state, but abounded with the rich and beautiful plants natural to the soil, and cherished by the softness of the climate. In this solitary domain Emily suddenly found herself sole sovereign, and explored its limits with a melancholy pleasure the grand contention of glowing nature with majestic yet mouldering art, never fails to produce in a reflecting mind. The myrtles, vigorously emerging between narrow lines of fallen columns, and shedding their uncherished blossoms over the perishing works of man, brought home a thousand sad monumental ideas to the sick heart of Emily, and made it sometimes pause upon its sorrows. Amid this splendid wilderness, those sorrows acquired an influence doubly dangerous, as they now kindled into romance.

In the deepest shades, and by the cooling fountains the gardens abounded with, antique statues, saved from the ruins still scattered around, were fancifully disposed; some of which were invaluable for the design, no less than the execution. There is something in sculpture inconceivably touching to the soul of sensibility, when deeply impressed with sorrow. The almost breathing statue, uniting the chilling effect of death, with all the energetic graces of life, diffuses a fearful holy kind of delight, that, by a charm incomprehensible to ourselves, blends the distinct feelings peculiar to each state, dilates our nature, and lifts the admiring soul beyond the narrow bound of mortal breath, and mere existence.

These saddening contemplations aided the tender workings of Emily's heart, where still the Marquis reigned, though he lived no longer. Fancy, at intervals, almost gave motion to solidity, body to ideal objects. It is only those who have loved, and loved even unto death, that find a freezing pleasure in calling for ever the mouldering tenant of the tomb before them: and when the painfully rational consciousness that he can no more revisit earth will obtrude, it is such only who "turn their eyes inward, and behold him there."—No fear finds place where perfect love has been; and, once more to behold her Edward, was, in the depth of midnight, no less than the blaze of noon, at every hour, and in every place, the wish, the prayer, the sole desire of Emily.

From loathing Italy, and, above all, Frescati, the wild and sublime melancholy that had now seized on Emily, made her partial to both. "Let my father return to England by himself," cried she often to her own heart, while she wandered: "here remains all left of my Edward.

The world has still something for the proud mind of my father; for me it has nothing but the child of my Lenox, and his ashes. Here, then, will I fix my abode, and pass my days in lamenting my love; till, sinking into his grave, I assert a right no one there will dispute with me."

Emily, with her lovely infant, now almost lived in the romantic and shady solitudes of Frescati; here her lonely rêveries at times broke into invocation; and her domestics began to apprehend, that her mind, too highly wrought, was preying on itself, and melancholy was but too near taking the distorted form of madness. Her musical instruments were laid in her way; but that once favourite science she now, with a kind of horror, rejected. Melody was become to her but the echo of annihilated pleasure; creative fancy had, however, supplied her one, not less soothing, in poetry; and to that internal music, Emily began insensibly to adapt the tender effusions of an overcharged heart.

The servants, thus gloomily employed in watching over and commenting upon their lonely lady, found a contagious kind of horror insensibly creep over them. It was not long settling into a fear, which Emily could not but perceive: they dared not, after evening closed, venture over the threshold; and, even in traversing the villa, usually moved in a body. The neighbourhood of Rome is not sufficiently secure for a lady to wander alone, after night falls, in solitary gardens; and as Emily now found the aversion of her domestics to guarding her nocturnal rambles, to be avowed, universal, and unconquerable, she was obliged to retire, when the day closed, to her own apartments; and listening to the wind as it agitated the surrounding foliage, catch, through the breaks, imperfect glances at the ever-varying moon, and address to that the passionate elegies, she past whole nights in composing.

It was soon whispered through the busy train of domestics, and fully credited, that their lady had at midnight a constant visitation from the spirit of the Marquis: and some were so daring as to affirm that they had heard his voice. Credulity is no less the characteristic of the vulgar Italians than Irish, and of these two nations was the household composed. It is true the former added superstition to credulity, and the latter soon resorted to it. Beads and reliques were the reliance of all the servants in their hours of retirement; and liberal potations enabled them to hold out while in society with each other. As they all knew their lady never took either of these modes of keeping up her spirits, they agreed one evening over their cups, that, unless they ingeniously devised some way of diverting her thoughts from the moon and the dead, she would soon be lost to all the purposes of life. They recollected how fond she had formerly been of music; and as she always sat now with her windows open, they resolved magnanimously to venture in a body into the colonnade her apartment was over, to cheer her with a lively strain. Some of the men were tolerable proficients; but the terror they were under, and the ignorance of the rest, made the concert a most hideous performance. Yet their gentle mistress saw so much kindness in an effort, which she knew made the whole train of musicians tremble, that she had not the heart to shew her sense of displeasure, in any other way than by shutting her windows softly, whenever the miserable dissonance began. An intimation so delicate would not, however, have induced the servants to discontinue a practice, that gave them importance with themselves, if not with their lady, when a hint of another kind not only silenced them for ever, but drove them into the house, over each other's backs, to apply to their beads, reliques, and pater-nosters.—A low and heavenly melody one night suddenly issued from a dell in the garden, not very remote, and entranced the listening Emily. The strain was wild as the winds, yet harmonious as the spheres; eccentric, awful; the spot from whence too it appeared to come, was romantic, singular: the ground in that part of the garden sunk, with sudden yet beautiful inequalities, into a deep dell, rich with bold rocks, and shadowed with lofty trees. In its hollow, a translucent fountain sprung playfully up, and fell as playfully again; upon the farther side, on the rise of the velvet margin, was happily placed an antique statue of a Faun,* who seemed surveying himself in the water, as he played on a pipe. The workmanship was exquisite; and the charmed eye almost could believe the graceful figure moved its arms, and gave breath to the pipe its light fingers rested on.

    Eagerly did Emily wait for the morning; when she impatiently issued out to trace, if possible, the nocturnal warbler. From a light Grecian temple on the boldest of the brows overhanging the dell, where Emily often passed whole days, she could with ease survey the whole lovely scene. Her eye, however, found in that no change. The beautiful Faun touched his marble pipe with his usual grace; but from it no sound issued. The fountain still dimpled with a pleasing murmur the pool it formed; but no human foot was imprinted on its margin. All that day, and many a following one, did Emily pass in this favourite temple, without seeing, or hearing a living creature; save the servants, who, with fear and trembling, brought her at noon a light repast. As evening came on, she would take her beloved infant from its downy bed, and retire to her own apartment, there to wait, with reverential awe, for the nocturnal visitation. Nor did it ever fail. Night after night, irregular, but entrancing melody, soothed her sense, and sunk into her soul. The grand enthusiasm of her nature blending the hallowed charm of another world with the wild visions of this, the nursery leaves on every mind, at times almost led her to believe her prayers were heard, and heaven granted to her sorrowful soul this visionary intercourse with him, it no longer permitted her to behold. Yet much she languished to know if mortal sense might not be allowed to discern the aërial harmonist, thus veiled in night.—To venture through the shades alone, was, however, more than she dared do; not that fear with-held her: it was a solemn awe, she thought it impiety to over-rule. Bending from the window, she often fondly exclaimed, as to the spirit of her husband:

> "Oh! vanished only from my sight,
> While fancy hovers near thy urn,
> And midnight stillness reigns, return;
> But no ethereal presence wear:
> In the same form, so long belov'd, appear;
> Each woe-mark'd scene let me retrace,
> And fondly linger o'er each mortal grace:—
> Oh! strike the harp of heav'n, and charm my ear
> With songs, that, worthy angels, angels only hear!"

Yet even thus invoked, no vision floated before that sense she strained to penetrate the thicket leading to the dell. The servants, forming as usual their own premises, and fixing their own conclusions, had, in full assembly, agreed, that this strange music proceeded from the pipe of the Faun; and, for a very good reason, that there certainly was nothing alive in the garden, and the Faun was the only musical performer, even in marble. That he was formed of no better materials, they did not attempt to deny, when their gentle lady urged the conviction; but accounted for their own opinion, by in turn asserting, that the devil reigned, ever since the creation, from midnight to the break of day; and, during that interval, it was plain, animated the marble Faun, notwithstanding all the Aves and Paternosters they were constantly repeating: though, to their own pious diligence in that respect, they imputed his remaining still stationary. That they might for ever continue in the same state of ignorance, as to whether the midnight musician was, or was not, the marble god, at the very first harmonious sound they heard in the dell, as at the stroke of a house-clock announcing the hour of rest, they all, with one consent, hastened to their beds; and tucking their heads under the cloaths,* past there the whole time of the solemn serenade: had the Faun walked into the house, he might have walked over and out of it, without being seen by a single creature, save Emily; who, ever at her window, listening, wondering, and weeping, pondered frequently on exploring this solitude by herself. But, alas! though she knew not how to fear any inhabitant of a better world, this yet contained one she was born to dread;—and Miss Fitzallen, too, excelled on the flute. Ah! if, by indiscreet curiosity, she should put herself into the power of that eternal foe of her peace, and rob her Edward's child of a last parent, (for that was often the only, and ever the predominant consideration with Emily) how, how, should she be acquitted to God and the precious infant?

Yet the servants appeared to their lady to be in the right, in asserting the music not only came from the dell, but from the precise spot where the statue stood. There were moments, however, when she fancied it approached her; and others, when, with sweet languishment, it sunk, as if retiring, into silence.

So deep a hold had this melancholy, visionary delight, taken on Emily, that the days hung heavily with her; and a restless impatience for night became the habit of her mind: which, then, no less eagerly awaited the mysterious indulgence. Its period was as regularly announced by the wan faces, and trembling steps of her domestics, as by her own high-raised fancy and beating heart. One night, of peculiar beauty, when the moon, with a more pure and radiant lustre than usual, sailed through the deep blue of a clear Italian sky,

> "When not a Zephyr rustled thro' the grove,
> And ev'ry care was charm'd but guilt and love,"

Emily, as had long been her custom, was at her window, in fond expectation of the aërial music,—it broke at once upon her ear as very, very near her. She started, turned round, as thinking it in the room; it was not behind her; she leaned over, to seek it in the colonnade; it was not below.—From those vague, grand, and uncertain strains, she had been used to hear, the nocturnal musician wandered into one, dear to her heart, familiar to its beatings. She sprang up, and leaned from the window, with wild and increasing energy,—wrung her white hands, and called upon the invisible power of harmony, to stand revealed before her; for this, she cried,

> "This is no mortal visitation, nor no sound
> That the earth owes."*

Irresistibly impelled to trace the visionary charmer, she snatched the taper, and descending to the saloon, threw open the door, and found herself alone in the colonnade. Glancing her quick eyes around, she saw only the long range of white marble pillars, half shadowed, and half shewn by the trees and the moon. The music became more remote, low, faint, and, to her idea, ethereal; it seemed to retire towards the dell, and woo her thither. "It is, it is the shade of my Edward!" sighed Emily, resting her forehead on her arm, and that against a pillar, to save her from falling. "How often have I called thee from the grave, my love!" cried she: "and shall I fear to follow thee even thither?"—She tottered, her heart beating high, to the winding path, which, breaking the descent, led safely to the hollow glen. Bright as the moon shone, it had hardly power to penetrate the thick foliage of the lofty trees, beneath which the trembling Emily lingered. No step, however, could she hear; no form could even her fluttered imagination fashion; yet still the music, with more melting sweetness, invited, and she fearfully followed. On a point near the depth of the dell, the shade suddenly broke away, and disclosed the fountain, quivering to the moon it sweetly reflected. Faintly, though she knew not why she feared, Emily turned her eyes towards the statue of the Faun. Ah, God! what were her sensations, when she fancied she saw two resembling figures, one half shading the other! A quickened second glance convinced her this was no error of her sense; she tried to save herself from falling, by grasping a tree, but sunk at its root.

From the temporary suspension of her powers, caused by terror, Emily recovered, at the soft sound of a voice, that, to her impassioned mind, "might create a soul under the ribs of death."* The murmuring whisper of known endearment, seemed to her the sweet tone of the Marquis. The arms, that with fond familiar pressure supported her from resting on the damp earth, could, to her apprehension, be only those by which alone she ever wished herself encircled. She dared not unseal her eye-lids, lest the dear, the cherished delusion, should vanish, and some hideous form, either living or dead, again harrow up her nature. Still fondly urged to look up, by many a whispered prayer and soft entreaty, she at length timidly lifted her eyes to—Gracious God! could it be?—her husband?—the Marquis himself! to her the single being in creation! Invigorated in a moment, she sprang up with ethereal lightness, and the enraptured embrace, mutually given and received, repaid these unfortunate lovers for all the miseries that had marked their union. Too mighty was the ecstasy to waste itself in words: again they gazed, again embraced; they could only gaze, sigh, weep, and murmur.

"Lives then my love?" cried Emily, at length: "and has my cruel father, in wanton power, tortured me even to the extremity?"—"That I live, soul of my soul," replied the Marquis, "your father neither knows, nor ever must know. Oh! Emily, *to* you, *for* you alone I live; be gracious then and hear me: allow me at last to pour forth all the secrets of my heart; to you, as to God, will I be sincere, and then shall my beloved decide my fate and her own. But this is a dangerous place for long discourse; the dews of night might prove fatal to so delicate a frame:—my Emily is much changed, since we parted, by sickness and sorrow."—"And you too, Edward"—Emily could not utter—"are not less changed." A gush of tears explained her meaning, and she hid the wan face her nature melted over in her bosom. Recovering herself, she took his hand:—"Come to my apartment, my love, nor fear any eyes, save mine, will observe you; terror, at this hour, closes all others in my house."—"Nor would seeing induce your domestics to follow me," replied her husband; "since, to win you to seek, and oblige them to shun me, was alike my object, in assuming a disguise that might yet, perhaps, startle my Emily, unless she coolly and collectedly surveys it." Emily cast her eyes in fond certainty over his figure, as though in no disguise could it ever shock or startle her; yet owned his tender precaution not unnecessary. He was clothed in a white vest, fitted close to his graceful form, and exactly resembling the Faun; the mask, which covered his whole head, with his flute, painted alike white, he held in his hand. When, at her desire, he put the artificial head-piece on, it was sufficiently clear he might encounter her whole family, and not be known to any one of them for a being of this world.

Conducted by his wife through the saloon to her apartment, the Marquis removed the mask; and Emily, still unsatisfied with gazing, fixed on him again her fond eyes with deep intentness, as even then doubting whether the blessedness of the moment were not a vision, or the dear hand she clasped, might not, while yet she held it, become marble.

During this affecting silence, each lover too visibly perceived what it was to have lost the other. The Marquis, still pale, even to lividness, from the effusion of blood in his duel, was debilitated by the half-healed wound, which obliged him to lean to the right side. Emily soon discovered this new claim to her tenderness; and abhorring the necessary disguise, felt it as a great relief, that she had hoarded, among the treasures sacred to his memory, a part of his wardrobe, often kissed and sprinkled with her tears. She refused to hear a word till she had seen him comfortably arrayed, and resting his aching side on a sopha; then taking the posture he had implored her to allow him to pour forth his soul in, the tender Emily threw herself on her knees by the couch, and filled up the pauses, pain and fatigue occasioned in his narration, by prayers and devout ejaculations to the God who had graciously preserved, and thus miraculously restored him to her.

The Marquis now required not a moment to methodize his recital; he had no past thought to conceal, no wish to leave untold. He began the detail, that sunk into Emily's soul, at the period when the persecuting fiend first gained his pity and protection at Paris. His wife heard the name of Hypolito with comparatively little emotion; for she was fully assured of her own boundless empire over a heart, she ever, till this moment, believed she had divided with that youth and Miss Fitzallen; for only now did she understand that they were one and the same person. He described the talents and tastes of the impostor, so naturally consonant and studiously adapted to his own; and the influence the feigned youth gained in his affections. The ingenuous nature of Emily, made her admit it must be almost an impossibility for any man to escape so secret and near an attack from a lovely woman, unrestrained in the pursuit of her object, by either virtue or feeling. He, in the most natural manner, painted the discovery made of her disguise at Messina; and bewailed the wandering, both of his senses and his reason, by the fever of wine and passion. But, oh! how the gentle Emily started and wept, lamenting, too late, her own innocent romance as the daughter of Dennis; when she learnt that, and that only, could have enabled her ingenious and base enemy to add, to her own dangerous allurements, the assumption of her name, character, and rights in life. How strange appeared it to Emily, to find that the Marquis had married, or meant to marry, her in the person of another. She was lost in horror at the awful catastrophe of the earthquake; and her heart was more lightened than she chose to own, at finding it prevented the Marquis from consummating his mistaken and miserable marriage. The agony he felt at the deplorable fate of the fair impostor; his subsequent and sorrowful researches, for the dear supposed daughter of Sir Edward Arden, all, all appeared natural, touching, and hardly questionable, to the generous spirit he was now appealing to.—Emily's own heart now took up the tale. The moment of their meeting in Switzerland, the gay discovery of herself, she then meditated; and the shock it appeared to give him, to be told she was the daughter of Sir Edward Arden, Emily well remembered. The hours of unalloyed pleasure that followed, till the hapless one arrived that united their hands, she never could forget. The frenzy that then seized him, he fully explained, in representing to her the impressive spectre that extended to him the ring, on the steps of the portico, and annihilated, at once, their bridal happiness. The scene lived with equal force before Emily's eyes, as she read, in the wild glances of his, the eternal impression made on his mind by that horrible moment. Oh! how generous, how noble, how pure, appeared to her informed judgment, the mysterious coldness and constraint, which, at the time, had so shocked,—perhaps offended her. She now would again interrupt him; she would no longer allow him to be the historian; her delicate nature made her anxious to spare him all further mention of Miss Fitzallen; who, hard and self-loving, had, it was obvious, wrung from him, through the medium of his fears, those rich baubles she in the exultation of malice every where displayed—nor doubted the generous Emily, but that her little favourite carriage, was obtained by the same insolent exaction.

But, oh! much yet remained for Emily to feel, when the Marquis, straining to his heart the generous creature who would not allow him to accuse himself, and fondly melting under the sad blessing of her tearful forgiveness, faintly uttered—"Oh! Emily, adored of my soul! had your harsh father thus treated me—I should perhaps in bitterness of spirit have shed at his feet my own blood, and spared him the horror of having poorly satisfied his vengeance with stretching me there."—This was a thought the tender wife had not ventured to trust her own soul with:—the idea spread at first through the family, that in a fit of phrenzy the Marquis had rashly ended his sufferings, soon by means of her woman reached Emily: and, horrible as such a fate must be, it was less so than the faintest apprehension that her father had shortened his days, and she should be for life compelled to implore a blessing from the hand yet crimson with her husband's blood, or claim protection from the heart, hard enough to render her a widow, and her unborn babe fatherless.—The intelligence from Naples, sent by Cardinal Albertini, the valet of Sir Edward officiously circulated in the family; and Emily dared not trust herself to make any minute enquiry on the agonizing subject, nor needed an exact account, to figure to herself all the horrors of his fate.

She in turn described to the Marquis the sudden manner, and the means, by which she had been decoyed, as it were, from Naples—and her memorable meeting with her father at Frescati; when, in the ungoverned state of his feelings, he was incapable of reflexion, and insensible to pity.—She repeated, in all the force in which the words dwelt on her mind—*"You have no husband—you never had one;"* and her convulsive shudder proved too plainly that Sir Edward lost at that moment the affection of his daughter.—The haughtiness with which he had ordered, without her consent, that she should be deprived of the name of the Marquis, lived no less in her memory;

and finally the severe justice by which he had outraged every feeling, in obliging her to provide for her innocent babe in case of her own death, by a will which stigmatized the infant's birth, was too wounding to be unmentioned.—That nice sense of female delicacy, which speaks even in silence, made Emily by intuition convey to her husband's heart a deep resentment at the indignity, while both overlooked the mortifying necessity, nor could allow the father to be an equal, perhaps, as the proudest of the three, the greatest sufferer.—This union of grievances strengthened every other, and the hearts of the only two beings on earth Sir Edward Arden really loved, agreed, while they renewed to each other the sacred vow of eternal tenderness, and faith, in shutting him entirely out, and utterly rejecting him.

After an interval, the Marquis resumed his narration—"Left in the garden of the convent, drowned in my own blood, and to all human appearance dead, or even your incensed father would not so have left me, many hours must have elapsed ere any of the monks wandered that way. I faintly recollect, that it was torch-light when the pain I felt in their lifting me on a mattress, to convey me to the convent, caused me for a moment to open my eyes.—Delirium, and impending death were long, long, my portion, in the lonely cell where the benevolent brotherhood attended me with unremitting care; one of them, who had been an eminent surgeon, dressed my wound with tender skill:—nor, in the intervals of my delirium, when the agony of my mind made that of my body forgotten, did the pious fathers omit all those holy attentions, so comforting to the wretch in this world, so necessary to prepare him for a better.—I easily understood by the tenor of their consolations, that they regarded me as a frantic wretch, who with rash hand had sought to end my own calamities.—I found a sad pride in saving my inhuman uncle from censure, and never gave any other answer to the enquiries the superior ventured, as soon as he saw me likely to recover, than that the fatal catastrophe had been caused by my own despair: and that, unless they meant to drive me to the same extremity a second time, they would conceal from every human being, even my nearest relations, or tenderest friends, that I survived; on this condition, and this condition only, would I promise to endure prolonged existence.

"In the miserable state of my health, and the frantic irritation of my mind, the pious monks held it wise to yield to every request that might conciliate my feelings, or mitigate those complicated sufferings which were perhaps an ample punishment for my sin, great as I own it—and by this indulgence was I won to live on.

"I soon learned Sir Edward had quitted Naples with you, nor doubted, as the monks assured me no enquiries were made for me, that you had been wholly governed by his impression of my conduct, and turned from my very grave with abhorrence. Oh! misery, never to be understood but by the wretch who has like me felt it; to see all the sacred ties reason, fancy, feeling, can form, and choice sanctify, burst with a force that throws you a solitary sufferer to the utmost limit of creation! When I remembered Emily was mine no more—no more wished to be mine—it would have been happiness indeed to die.—My infant too—my dear unborn—the cruel Sir Edward could not teach *that* to shrink from my embrace—to close its little ears to my lamentations. But that too was torn from me; and I stood alone in the universe. My embittered spirit for a time soured me to all soft impressions; the deep gloom of my abode co-operated to lead my thoughts only to monastic seclusion. By annihilating myself in a manner, and yet enduring the sufferings I had brought on my own head, I thought I might in a degree expiate my sin against my Emily and her father, and perhaps obtain the pardon of heaven. But, with the least improvement of my health, silence, solitude, La Trappe, disappeared from my eyes—love, and Emily, still throbbed at my heart, and incurable tenderness was blended there with a grief no less incurable.—Alas! had I not cause to dread a resentment on her part at least equal to that of her inexorable father, though she would not shew it in the same bloody manner? I often felt myself sinking into the grave, under the curses of both. Yet there were moments when her angel form appeared before me with all that softness which renders her sway so absolute.—I sometimes seemed to see her mourning for the very wretch who had marked her days with ignominy and affliction, and clasping to her snowy bosom with increased fondness, because springing from me, the infant inheritor of both. Returning strength (though I was still very weak) impressed with more force this cherished idea. I resolved, the moment I was able, to venture into the country where my adored Emily had fixed her abode, and there meditate on the mode by which I might acknowledge, even to the extent, my offences against her, and make her judge, sole judge, in her own cause.

"I had not patience to wait till my wound was healed; crawling, only half alive, as yet, on the face of the earth, I assumed the habit of a common labourer, and found a neighbouring peasant, with whom I could abide. I told him, my employment was that of a mason, and the hurt in my side was occasioned by the sudden fall of a fragment, as I was hewing marble: that the weakness it brought on threatened a consumption; and, now I was able to get abroad, I had been advised to try whether the pure air of Frescati would not remove the alarming symptoms. I might have added, that if not, here should I end my days. Alas! I had reason to think their termination at hand, when first I had the misery to be told my wife had again taken the name of Miss Arden; and the infant she cherished in her arms, was not allowed to bear that of its father. Yet, oh! that precious infant lived; it was mine, my Emily, no less than yours; I languished to behold you both; and to claim my fond, fond right, in our mutual treasure. Night after night did I pass, in wandering round the consecrated abode of my Emily, and pondering upon the possibility of conveying a letter to her. Yet a single indiscretion might be ruin, even if I moved her compassion. Sir Edward would not, it was true, again strike at my existence in my own person; but, alas! he had it in his power even more effectually to do it, in the person of his daughter. In the cruel predicament I stood in, the right of a father was lost to me: that of a husband I dared not claim. It was only the gentle heart of Emily would grant me either, and to that heart I felt I must appeal, or die. In exploring the limits of the wilderness, I one day found a little aperture; through which, the following night, I made my way, and boldly passed into the garden. My sick soul seemed to revive, when I breathed the same air with my Emily; and these nocturnal rambles became a dear indulgence. To account to my host for such long and late absences, I owned a love affair with one of your domestics, and escaped all suspicion of having any other object in view. Never shall I forget one night venturing so near the house, as to see my uncle walking about in his chamber, and sometimes standing at the window: the lights were behind him, and I plainly discerned his figure—never, never can the strange, the complicated feeling, escape my memory—that form, always so natural to my eyes—once so dear, so very dear to my heart!—A frantic kind of emotion came over me; I felt ready to cry out—to demand—to extort his pity—perhaps to undo myself—and not only lose for ever my Emily, but rob her of the little peace my fatal love had left her.—That I might no more risque so exquisite a temptation, I withdrew to Rome, till Sir Edward should depart.

"In wandering, as I often did, whole days among the colossal fragments of ancient magnificence, a fallen and mutilated statue of a Faun drew my eye, and recalled to my mind the one by the fountain. The strange thought of procuring, under the idea of wearing it at a masquerade, a habit exactly resembling the statue, then occurred to me. I had often apprehended meeting some of your domestics, whom curiosity or love might lead to wander at the same hour in the garden; but, thus hid, I was sure of having it all to myself. This disguise being prepared, I again housed with my peasants; and, such is the energy of even a remote hope, was flattered by them on my improved looks.—Sir Edward Arden was at last gone; and his lovely daughter, whom they touchingly termed the melancholy lady, left alone. Now then, or never, I must obtain the sight of my Emily; and, a month ago, when the moon shone with the same blessed brightness it now does, I assumed my disguise, and hid my own cloaths in the grotto in the wilderness; then, without fear, sought the deep dell, to survey my fellow sylvan. How exquisitely beautiful was the silent scene! The temple, hanging on the rude brow above, had now the windows thrown open. I made no doubt, but that my beloved had been sitting there. I wound through the shady path, and, after listening intently, found all was solitude, and ventured in. Ah! think of the melting softness that seized my heart, on beholding the sopha she had so lately quitted; and on which a basket of her work yet remained! I knelt, and worshipped, as if the fair form I adored were still reposing there. On the ground were scattered flowers, which, as perishing, she had cast from her bosom. I gathered them up, as devout pilgrims do holy reliques, and thrusting them into mine, bade them thus return to Emily!

"An emotion, new—sacred—eternal, yet remained for me to experience, when I cast my eyes on a large wicker basket quilted with down, and covered with a mantle. Softly I raised that covering, as though the jewel were yet enshrined within it. Ah! no! the cradle was empty. Yet, on the pillow, still remained the dear, the soft impression of my infant's tender cheek. That inanimate pillow was wet with the first tears of a father—greeted with his kisses—consecrated by his blessings. I remained rivetted to a spot enriched with such interesting local remembrances. I could not resolve to quit it; and, in that sanctuary of innocence, the basket, resolved to hide, for my Emily's observance, some known memorial of our plighted love; when a sound that suddenly reached me, of "riot, and rude merriment," suggested a better mode of attracting her. I guessed this rustic serenade to be some mode of amusement your servants had found for themselves; and they had repeated the discordant strains several evenings ere I discovered it was meant to entertain you. I then coloured my flute to correspond with my dress; and, in the depth of night, silenced the savages with my lonely pipe. At intervals I paused, to learn whether curiosity had brought too near my retreat, any of my auditory. Not a step could I ever hear: not a whisper reached me.

"Night after night, I pursued my wild symphonies, always apprehending, some one of the domestics, bolder than the rest, would pierce the thicket to descry my haunt: but convinced no second person would ever venture near it. All were, however, equally timorous; and this beautiful solitude, I now feared, would ever belong only to my brother sylvan, and myself. Assured I had put all my vulgar hearers to flight, I soon became bolder, and ventured from behind the marble Faun. Sometimes I could see your shadow in your dressing-room—sometimes knew it could be only you at the window. Yet, one incautious word might have betrayed me; and I almost despaired of wooing you into the garden, when, this evening, I suddenly called to mind that little air your tender heart so feelingly acknowledged. Ah! God! when I saw the effort successful—when the light disappeared from the room above, and faintly began to illumine that under it—when I found that love, stronger than death, could win my Emily to follow even my supposed phantom, my heart no longer feared hers.—Alas! it feared only the alarm it was impossible to spare her, ere she could be encircled in those arms that never, never more, will resign her."

In discourse like this, whole ages might have elapsed, unheeded by the Marquis; but Emily, exquisitely alive to his danger, now saw with affright, that day had unobserved stolen upon them, and it was impossible for him, disguised or otherwise, to return through the garden. The Marquis made light of his stay, or departure; for, if she approved the former, who should object? but, in the soul of Emily, the fear of her father was now incurably impressed: and all their future views were too uncertain, and indistinct to both, for her husband to urge a rash discovery. He therefore permitted her to conduct him through her own, to the apartment of Sir Edward; where, having fastened the door at the extremity, she insisted on his endeavouring to recruit his emaciated frame by needful rest, and, locking the intermediate door, retired to repair her own strength and spirits with a balmy slumber. How different was this day from the last, when, waking, she felt happiness once more possible. The husband she adored, ever faithful, though apparently otherwise, was for life her own. With light elastic footstep, a hundred times in the course of the day did she visit the door that divided them. As often did she softly pace back again, and fearfully shrink from the indulgence of even looking upon him. Once, and once only, did she unlock it, and impatiently wait to see him partake of the refreshments she carried him.

The approaching evening, Emily meant, should afford the Marquis the dear pleasure hardly more desired by him than herself—the sight of their infant. Affecting an alarm, she took it from the charge of the nurse, to place it for that night in her own bed. Let those who have borne a child to an absent husband, tell the soft exultation nature makes powerful enough to compensate the pang which renders them mothers, when they lift the mantle which shelters the sleeping innocent, to shew to the returning father the little features in which each tender parent, by a magic of mind, discerns only the likeness of the other, combined with the pure charm peculiar to infancy!—Sorrow—sickness—the past—the future—all was forgotten by the Marquis and Emily, when, with sweet contention, kneeling together, they blessed and kissed this dear little third in their union.

Who can fail to lament, that a nature so generous and susceptible as Sir Edward Arden's, had lost, by one moment of ill-judged passion, the dear delight of sharing a bliss it had been the single object of his life to ensure to the two so exquisitely endeared to him?—Alas! occupied wholly by gloomy reflections, and a hopeless pursuit, Sir Edward was wandering, without one social bosom to confide a thought to, through the scenes in Sicily most afflicting to his remembrance; nor had he been able to gather any further information concerning the monks, immediately parties in the ceremony of the Marquis's marriage, than that Padre Anselmo certainly perished; but it was doubtful in what quarter of the world the others might now be seeking means to rebuild a part of their convent.

Hours, days, and months, fly swiftly to those who love, and love happily. In the nocturnal interviews which they still mysteriously carried on, the Marquis and Emily had ever so much to say of the past and present, that both, as by tacit agreement, threw as far off as possible the more important and immediate consideration of the future. The full confession, and explanation of the Marquis, had removed every fear of impropriety from the mind of Emily. It was to her sufficiently clear, that nothing but the pride and ungovernable fury of her father prevented the previous ceremony that had been read to the Marquis and Miss Fitzallen (since it was a mere ceremony), from being, when submitted to ecclesiastical discussion, declared, if not informal, certainly invalid; while her own marriage, celebrated in the face of the world, and by every rite of her own church, had the full confirmation of her having borne a child, whom it would be impossible to deprive of legitimacy, when its claims were duly made. It was no new vow, therefore, on the part of Emily, to follow her husband through the world; but she exacted, in consideration of this concession, that he should allow her to do it in her own way.

The Marquis, who had long found his love for his uncle on the wane, now felt all fear of him vanish. He was fully sensible that Sir Edward had no authority over his daughter's person, if once she could be brought to assert a will of her own, and abide by her marriage. He sometimes almost wished accidental circumstances would, by betraying their secret correspondence, oblige her to a decision, he found it a vain attempt to urge her to fix. Nothing, he was assured, would so soon effect this, as the dread of their separation; and were his visits once known, she would have no choice but to fly with him, and thus compel her father to second their views, by annulling in the Romish church the former ceremony. Yet, delicately as Emily was situated—delicately as she ever felt—to *force* her to any thing would be so ungenerous a procedure, that the Marquis suffered time to steal on, without forming any fixed plan for the future.

That time, however, had a consequence so favourable to his views, so gratifying to his heart, that he rejoiced he had never, by word or thought, grieved his Emily. Terrified—pale—dying in a manner with fear—she threw herself one evening into his arms, and whispered, "that the child he was holding to his bosom, was not the only one it would be her misfortune to bring him." To all his soothing endearments, she only cried out in agony—"How, how should she ever face her father? He, who had already, when she was in the same state, killed her with his eye-beam, would now wound her with a sense of shame, even while she was unconscious of guilt, too humiliating to be endured. Never, never, could she again encounter, thus circumstanced, the severity of her father." The Marquis, softened with the occasion of this anguish—shocked at seeing its excess—and ever yielding to her wishes—entreated, conjured her to compose herself; solemnly vowing, that, whatever line of conduct would give most ease to her mind, should be that he would implicitly abide by, as the only atonement he could make her, for having a single moment exposed her, in the most interesting of all situations, to the indignity of her father's looks.

"Never, never, will I again encounter such a hateful feeling, my Edward," cried she with increasing affliction, "while there is either a spot to be discovered on the earth to hide this wretched head in, or a grave to be found beneath it. I have sometimes thought—yet that would be very difficult—imposes on you years,—perhaps a life of seclusion—total annihilation of our rights—shall I, poorly* to save my own feelings, bury with me, while yet living, the heir of high rank, splendid fortunes; with every charm, and talent, that shall make him a grace to his equals, a blessing to his dependants?"

"Emily," returned the Marquis, with a sweetly sad solemnity, "I am yours—as we are circumstanced, yours only: no duty can come in competition with that I owe the angel my love has unhappily humbled, but never could elevate. Imagine my impatience, and tell me all those meaning eyes are full of."

"I have only a few valuables, and no money," continued Emily, as if thinking aloud, rather than speaking to any body.—"Sold, as they must be, to a disadvantage, I could hardly hope they would produce more than three thousand pounds."

"Sell your ornaments, love?" returned the Marquis, in a tone of chagrin, as well as surprise:—"what for?—I have money to the amount you mention."

"Ah! Edward, we shall want that too," cried his wife, surveying him with a mournful steadiness, as doubting whether she had influence to bend the pride of his nature to the humble purpose of her heart.

"And what," cried the Marquis, with some quickness, "can my Emily want so large a sum for?—to endow an hospital?"

"No!" replied she, in a firm voice, and with a dignity of mien that gave her new charms in the eyes fondly fixed on her. "All we can both gather, will be hardly enough, perhaps, to maintain us during the life of my father. You have bound yourself, my Lord:—thus must it be, if I am again yours. Dare you, on these terms, confirm your vows? Dare you take this hand, and swear on it, never, never to risque the little peace we now enjoy, by putting it in my father's power to tear us asunder? Poor man! I am not without pity, any more than you, for his future fate; yet am I only going to take from him what he has shewn me to be without value in his eyes—my wretched self."

"Oh! Emily," returned her husband in tender agitation, "think well, think often, ere you finally determine on a point so important. You will not, in this, accuse me of the indelicacy of considering myself. I am a man, ever retired in my taste, nor expensive in my pleasures. I could easily reconcile myself to the inconveniences of humble life, did I not feel acutely for you; but, born as you are to immense fortunes, bred on the bosom of luxury, yourself the most fragile and tender of nature's productions, can you endure to inhabit an humble home; and perhaps be hardly able, even by severe economy, to keep that? How will you bear to see your little ones, entitled to every advantage, confined to a narrow spot and scanty education?"

"There was a time, my love," returned Emily, bitterly weeping, "when, vainly exulting in the advantages of nature and fortune, we both thought, that among the many modes of being happy, each of us might make a choice. Already that vision has vanished; and all the option that now remains to either, is what kind of suffering we can best bear. It is my fixed determination never to endure that of meeting my father: nor," sobbed she, throwing herself into his arms,—"parting with you."

The Marquis pressed her to his heart, but was not collected enough to reply.—Emily continued:

"And why, Edward, should we think ourselves poor with the sums mentioned? Fear not but that I can descend to minute attentions without murmuring; for I have feelingly learnt that the splendour of an equipage relieves not the repining heart—the gaudy drapery of a dress dries not the tearful eye. In waving, for a time, our claims in life, we neither renounce them for ourselves nor our children. The day will come when the Duke of Aberdeen may recover a son; it is Sir Edward Arden," faltered she, bursting anew into a passion of tears, "who, by lifting his hand against your life, and embittering mine,—it is he who has for ever lost a daughter."

The Marquis saw, with tender sorrow, the turn Emily's mind had taken; for to oppose her in her present delicate state, it was plain, would endanger, perhaps shorten, her life. Yet, as a man, he calculated at a higher rate than his retired, his gentle wife, the advantages they mutually inherited; and felt that to partake them, was, from the hour of their birth, the right of his children. One bold struggle with Sir Edward Arden would fix their fate. Could Emily be won from a fear and delicacy so erroneous, the moment her father knew she had confirmed the rights of her husband, and meant to pass her life with him, that very pride, which had disgracefully torn them asunder, would act for them, and urge him to assist the process which should establish their marriage. The Duke too, though not a tender parent, had never been an unkind or ungenerous one. To deprive him of natural ties, and the hope, always so dear to those declining in life, of seeing posterity around him, was painful to the Marquis. Yet all these rational considerations faded from his mind, whenever he discussed this point with Emily; and the single one, that she might die, while her father and he were struggling how to reconcile their modes of making her great and happy, rendered him unable to oppose a fancy, he daily became more certain was not new to her thoughts, but the long cherished object of them.

Many concurring circumstances could alone enable Emily to execute the extraordinary project of vanishing for ever from her father's eyes; while a very simple event would render it totally abortive—his suddenly returning to Frescati; which appeared to both the lovers equally probable, and obliged the fearful Emily to resolve on sounding the two persons she had, in her own mind, fixed on as confidants and auxiliaries. The first of these was her own woman. Mrs. Connor had waited on Lady Emily, ere she married Sir Edward Arden; had affectionately watched her in the sickness that laid her early in the grave, and, from that moment, had sole charge of the heiress of Bellarney: till ripened youth allowed Emily to feel her power of acting for herself. From that moment the servitude of Connor was of her own choice. Not being, however, intitled to rank among Miss Arden's friends, and quite unable to live without some share of her society and regard, she had preferred attending on her lady, to the kind offer made by her of independence and her own way. These humble friends are among the peculiar blessings the Irish may boast; as if the high polish of cultivated minds left their hearts* so very smooth a surface, that every object slid over them; while, in those more rough, there remained an adhesive power, which fixed whatever it once attracted. Natures of this cast have too often a generous defect in their coarse, but strong perceptions of the injuries offered to those they love, which to the sufferer magnifies the evils, reflexion would otherwise diminish. Let no one say they are proof against this insensible operation of mind on mind. The wise would be wise, indeed, were they not liable to be biassed by the weak; but it requires a great effort to silence the voice of kindness, even if you think the speaker not wholly competent to his subject. Connor had all this secret and insensible influence over her lady; and a horror of the lofty character of Sir Edward Arden, which made her give the most chilling interpretation to his words, the most irritating one to his actions. She was among those to whom he gave the "imperial" (as she termed it) command, to call the wife of the Marquis of Lenox, Miss Arden. He had not thought it proper, or necessary, to assign his reason for this; and, had he commanded her to lay down her own existence, she could not have been more determined never to comply; till the gentle Emily, with tears, requested her father might be obeyed. From that moment, Mrs. Connor persisted in it, he would be the death of that angel his daughter; hourly bewailing the day he had ever set foot in Bellarney, and carried away its heiress to become a martyr to his whims, and know only sickness and sorrow. If any thing had been wanting to complete her detestation of Sir Edward, he would have supplied it, when he refused to see the "dear jewel," his grand-daughter, on the sad day of her birth. All the erroneous opinions of a woman, really worthy, were, however, from the danger of Emily, lost and swallowed up in her fears. No mother could be more watchfully tender; and, perhaps, but for even her unrefined attention, Sir Edward Arden's daughter had never survived her sickness at Frescati. As her lady amended, by slow degrees Connor discharged her mind of all its chagrins, which sunk into the already wounded soul of Emily, and produced the deepest horror of her father.

How dangerous is it for parents, in any station, to make over the care of their children, from an early age, to others. Of the tie, so necessary to both as they advance into life, nothing then remains, even in minds well turned, but a sense of mutual duty. The melting look that cherished an infant virtue, the tear that cured an infant fault, has never been rivetted on the fond remembrance of the child. The sweet endearments, the soft concessions, which made every fault forgotten, the gay delights of unfolding nature, live not in the doating recollection of the parent. But when children have fortunes and rights in life, independent of their parents, it becomes peculiarly necessary for those parents to fix that influence, by early and unremitting kindness, which even the most insensible will lament the want of, whenever the younger party is entitled to judge and act.

Little did the Marquis suspect the great influence of Connor with Emily, or that she was meditating to commit to her sole charge the second dear treasure of her life. But the person she thought it most important to embark in her views, she knew, as yet, only from the friendly sensibility with which he soothed her sorrows; while, with exquisite professional skill, he perhaps saved her life.

Dr. Dalton had, to oblige Sir Edward, broken through the rule he had laid down, when he took up his abode in Rome, never to practise, but for the benefit of those unable to reward him, except with "true prayers, which reach heaven's gate ere sunrise."* This gentleman was beyond the middle of life, easy in his own fortune, and married to a lady of a still ampler one. His taste for the fine arts made him abandon his own country, to fix his residence in the centre of the ancient world; whose venerable reliques formed his only pleasure. A man of this character could not but be courted by strangers; and Sir Edward Arden had made on him so favourable an impression, that he took pleasure in being his *cicerone*. Such a friend, with medical knowledge, was a treasure to the afflicted father, in the desperate contingence that followed Emily's arrival at Frescati. Her bitter grief, her exquisite loveliness, the disposition she shewed to be grateful for his generous exertions to continue that existence she valued not, had interested Dr. Dalton's feelings; and urged him to improve the predilection, by bringing his lady to wait on her. But in the melancholy and humbled situation of Emily, the deep dejection of her mind, and the weakness of her health, the good doctor wondered not at her shrinking even from kindness: and when he found his medical assistance no longer necessary, he had no choice, but, sighing, to retire from the interesting widow. Sir Edward had, however, obtained his promise, ere he left Rome, that, if summoned to Frescati, he would still have the kindness to attend on his daughter.

The present situation of Emily rather inclined her to shun Dr. Dalton's presence; and her loveliness was never more obvious. For herself, therefore, she could not summon the person she most desired to see. The infant Emily was a cherub in beauty, and in the full glow of health; and to trouble a man of independence, with making a visit to two of her servants who were ill, seemed too great a liberty: yet rendering their poverty an excuse to his benevolent mind, she risqued entreating a visit at Frescati.

Dr. Dalton obeyed the summons, and congratulated his fair patient on having recovered a higher degree of health, than he thought she ever did or could possess. Her beautiful child delighted him; and he assured her he could not any longer contend with the impatience of his wife to see both. Emily smiled, but declined not the compliment. The doctor returned, however, from visiting the servants, with an air of gravity; and not moving from a window remotely situated, enquired if she had ever had the small-pox. Emily replied, it was a disputed point between Connor and her grandmother; but the former could be called, and give him her reasons for thinking she had had it. "A simple proceeding will spare a long detail," said the kind physician. "Even if *you* have had this disorder, your little angel has not; and she must not remain here a moment. Your two servants have taken the small-pox, and no human care can prevent its running like wild-fire among your Italian domestics. I shall, therefore, wave Mrs. Dalton's waiting on you, madam, and fulfil my promise to Sir Edward, by insisting on your company to Rome. My house is pleasantly situated,—the gardens are large,—your babe will be safe, if it has not already received the infection, and anxiously attended if it has. This is a contingence when ceremony must be given up, and the old-fashioned thing, called prudence, only govern us."

A thousand thoughts fluttered at the heart of Emily, and varied her complexion every moment. Could she have guessed the danger, she might have previously apprized the Marquis; but to go without his knowledge, was impossible. To keep her darling in the reach of infection, and the dread of death, she could not answer to herself. To the kind urgency of her medical friend, she replied, some very particular concerns rendered it impracticable for her so suddenly to quit Frescati; but the babe, dearer to her than life, she would tear from her own arms and commit to his care, as a pledge that she would follow to-morrow. Dr. Dalton ordered a horse to be made ready for himself; and Connor, with the infant Emily, drove immediately off in his carriage.

For a time, the tender mother felt as if stunned. She ran from room to room seeking the babe she knew she could not find; and half fancying she should never see it more. A new and pleasing idea then took total possession of her mind; and she past the interval, ere she could greet the Marquis, in collecting and packing all her valuables; appreciating each jewel, as she enfolded it, with a miser's eye. That done, she measured the room for hours, dreading some accident had happened to her dear nocturnal visitant; though her watch assured her it was yet too early for his appearance;—not but he might safely have ventured; for the nature of the malady which had seized the sick servants, threw the deepest dismay over those yet in health, insomuch that each fancied himself walking about the house in a dying state; nor failed to conclude that the memorable music of the marble Faun, had been a solemn warning of the approaching mortality in the family.

When Emily apprized the Marquis of the danger that had obliged her to part with her child, she soon saw his parental anxiety equalled her own. A moment, however, impressed him with a conviction, that this removal would involve them both in much inconvenience. Dr. Dalton, he perceived, was, by this hasty confidence, rendered of necessity a party in all their future prospects and fluctuating plans.

"What, my dearest," cried he, impatiently pacing the chamber, "could induce you so suddenly to impose restraint on yourself and me? If you will not consent to my appearing, how can you reside at Dr. Dalton's house? What will you do there?"—"Die, perhaps," returned Emily: "I would not, my love, be understood literally; yet to be thought dead is my only chance for passing my life with you: and without the aid of a character, as respectable in itself, and as highly estimated by my father, as Dr. Dalton's, vainly should I attempt an imposition of that kind."—"How improbable then is it that you should persuade such a man to sanction so strange a fraud, and one, many occurrences in life may betray!"—"I know not any, save choice, that can betray us, my Lord," sighed Emily; "and I will rather die in reality, than ever again endure the severe controul of my father. I have well digested my plan, in which I do not ask your aid; grant only your concurrence; and this, if I am indeed dear to you, I may claim. The circumstances I am in, are very interesting and peculiar; I am a wife, a mother; if robbed by an inhuman father of the first title, the last would only double my misery. In human life, the least must yield to the greater duty. Reason, nature, law, make me yours for ever: nor can even the power of a parent break the tie he hallowed. A mind so generous and dispassionate, as Dr. Dalton's, will surely see, that, in thus disappearing from society, I rather seek to guard from another bloody contention, two fiery spirits, who claim each so dear a right in me, that, to one or the other, I should be every moment in danger of falling a victim, than to indulge a bold and romantic passion."—"Emily," solemnly repeated the Marquis, "I am yours—for ever yours; the miseries I have caused you to endure, entitle you to judge for both. Greatly have I erred; may I alone err! Use the power I so fully give you, more wisely than I have used mine."

Morning carried away the Marquis, no more to haunt the beloved shades of Frescati. Noon set down Emily at the house of her friend; who welcomed her with the happy news, that her babe appeared to have escaped the infection. Mrs. Dalton took the mother to her bosom, with as kind a greeting as she had given the infant; and, conducting her to an elegant apartment, entreated her to be there entirely at home.

The first few hours were spent by all parties in those ingratiating attentions, that insensibly remove the impression of novelty from a scene, or acquaintance. As evening came on, Emily began to be painfully sensible of the task she had taken on herself, when she engaged to interest absolute strangers in her fate, and her feelings, while she had unwarily deprived her heart of its dearest adviser, support and consolation. Her tears flowed in silence; and Mrs. Dalton, moved by her extreme youth, and her deep mourning, found so natural a grief but too infectious.

Dr. Dalton sought to divert the thoughts of both ladies from sorrowful ideas, by interesting them in the account he gave of a young Englishman, who had, without a regular introduction, applied to him for advice, and won him to regard. He expressed great impatience for the morning, when the stranger had promised him a more full knowledge of his situation, both in fortune and feelings; which his dignity of mien, and intelligent countenance, made matter of great curiosity. A vague kind of agitation seized on Emily; she faintly enquired if the stranger was pale, and had been wounded? Dr. Dalton assented; dwelling anew on his air of distinction, "that noble kind of physiognomy which an enlightened mind alone can give even to correct beauty." The flutter of Sir Edward's daughter increased; and Dr. Dalton wistfully surveyed her fair cheeks, on which, in spite of the efforts of her reason, glowed the tender alarms of her heart; while her ingenuous eyes, ever ready to convey its meaning, escaped those of her observing friend, only by seeking the ground. "You are, perhaps, Madam," said the doctor, after a pause, "already acquainted with this interesting stranger?" Emily shook her head, sighed, but trusted not her lips with a word. He again paused; then continued his discourse. "It is, I dare say, impossible to be much with you, and think of any thing distinct from yourself. I can no otherwise account for the singular idea that haunts me, of a striking resemblance between my unknown visitor and Sir Edward Arden. Yet, the youth's complexion is not so dark, and his hair a bright auburn: it is the form of his face—a certain keen turn in his black eyes—something in the tone of his voice—but, above all, the lofty grace of his manner, that seemed to give the very man to my mind."

Emily clasped her hands in silence at the imprudence of the Marquis, whom she recognized in every particular Dr. Dalton dwelt on, but remained determinately silent: and her tears might well be imputed to painful recollections, that had no reference to the stranger. He would have vanished from the mind of Dr. Dalton, had not a billet been brought, half an hour after, to Emily.—"Proceed and prosper, my beloved: I could not resist my racking desire to see this friend, on whom you have made me dependant; and find in his countenance that prepossessing benignity his voice confirms. Act on his feelings with your best speed, that you may become wholly his, who knows not how to live a day without you. All my objections to your proposed deception vanished the moment I saw you no longer. Early in the morning, I will send for your answer: would we were, till then, with the Dryads* at Frescati."

The surprize Dr. Dalton and his lady felt at finding their lovely guest, whom they supposed to be without one friend or connexion in Rome, was already greeted by a correspondent, increased greatly on perceiving Emily's agitation. When her eye glanced on the superscription, hardly could her trembling fingers break the seal—her overflowing eyes connect the words—or her perturbed mind conceive their purport. Yet, her native ingenuousness told her in a moment, that the smallest reserve, the least hesitation, might give her new friends a humiliating impression of her conduct. She therefore folded the billet, and, with a dignified tenderness kissing it first, put it into her bosom, offering an immediate explanation of the mystery it implied.

So touching, though simple, was her little history, that it hardly needed the graces her drooping youth, exquisite beauty, and tearful sensibility, gave it to her hearers. The forms of life at once were swallowed up in its feelings. Already were Dr. Dalton and his lady embarked in her fate, joyed in her joys, suffered in her sufferings; glowed with her indignation at the recital of Sir Edward's harshness, and shrunk finally with her horror, when she told them it had been his cruel hand that had struck at the life of her husband. They vowed to renounce, hate, abhor, the tyrant father; while, to the fair, unfortunate daughter, they promised unalterable friendship, paternal affection.

At this crisis in Emily's narrative, the nurse brought in the babe for the evening blessing of the tender mother; who intuitively knew how to heighten every generous sensibility she had excited, by taking it, and dismissing the woman. This simple effect of a delicate tenderness awakened the most lively sympathy for the Marquis, of whose prolonged existence she was about to speak. Enlightened by a word, as to the visitor of the evening, Dr. Dalton deeply regretted not knowing the truth before he withdrew. It was needless for Emily to plead the cause of her beloved: his pale and anxious countenance was yet before the eyes of Dr. Dalton, and had already so prepossessed him, that the worthy man declared it would have been impossible for any human being, so painfully circumstanced, to have avoided his error; though few would have made so ample an atonement for it. Far from approving Sir Edward Arden's conduct, he applauded that of his daughter, and should receive the husband with the same cordiality he had the wife; nor would he hesitate to assist in any measure proposed for perpetuating the union of a pair so formed for each other. The tears of apprehension were yet undried on the cheeks of Emily, when those of transport washed them away:—her beauty assumed almost a celestial charm, when lighted up by gratitude.

The warm heart of Dr. Dalton made him now grieve, he knew not where to find the Marquis; for then would he have hastened to add him to the little party: "so should no one heart in it be ill at ease."—Alas! good man! had he been twenty years younger, well would he have guessed that he need not look far for a lover so anxious; who past half the night in wandering near the house that contained his treasure. It is possible Emily could have quickened her friend's perception, but that she had a task to execute, which admitted not an abrupt avowal that the Marquis yet existed. In the exhausted state of her spirits, it was a great effort to communicate to Connor, the secret history of the midnight musician at Frescati.—The ungovernable joy it caused in her humble friend, was almost more than Emily could support: yet was she obliged to make a further exertion, that she might talk down to rationality the delighted creature. Even at last Emily was reduced to keep her for that night in her own apartment, lest, in the intoxication of the moment, the important secret of the disguise of the Marquis should circulate through a train of servants, who did now know he was in existence.

With all her sensibility thus afloat, it was impossible for Emily to find repose. If a momentary slumber came over her, she seemed to hear the well-known strains of her nocturnal harmonist, and starting abruptly up, paused—listened—sighed at being undeceived, and wished herself again at Frescati.

The morning at length came, and with it the messenger for Emily's letter.—The joyful summons bade the Marquis assume any name but his own, and be a welcome visitor to Dr. Dalton.—Mr. Irwin was in a moment announced; and received by that gentleman as a friend long known, and newly recovered. The melting sensibility so many concurring feelings and kindnesses must necessarily call forth in the refined, and generous soul of the Marquis, made him, in the eyes of all the party, the most charming, and interesting of human beings.

A very short time gave Emily so unlimited an influence over the mind of Dr. Dalton, that, whatever her opinion might be on any subject, he had a singular facility in persuading himself it had been first his own.—He therefore soon found it meritorious to assist the Marquis to run away with his own wife. Sir Edward might then discover at leisure how to reconcile himself to the re-union; as well as how to annul the ceremony of the marriage in Sicily. Having thus far carried the point of embarking the Doctor in her cause, Emily chose a moment when she was alone with him, to dwell upon the horrors that had almost precipitated her into a premature grave at Frescati; and seeing the strong impression the description made on the worthy man, she represented how probable it was that some dreadful catastrophe might again attend the meeting of her father, and husband.—By slow degrees she reached the meditated point; and spoke of her being supposed dead as the only sure way of avoiding the dreadful contingency.—Would Dr. Dalton but sanction the belief, that she had taken the malady now raging among her servants at Frescati, it would be no disgrace to have it reported that even his skill could not prolong her life. On the fidelity of her woman she could depend; and in Rome the interment of protestants was even more than private—absolutely secret.—A corpse might be substituted; and if Sir Edward chose to see it, in a disorder like the smallpox, a parent would vainly seek to identify a child. As, however, it was her fixed intention to leave not only her daughter, but all her fortune, and personal effects behind, Sir Edward would not have a doubt that he had thus lost her.—Escaping by this plan at once from his power, and the horrors that tormented her when she thought of his meeting her husband, they might, without incurring the disgrace of an elopement, steal unobserved away, and, in some obscure but happy home, pass those years, which heaven might please to give her father.

Dr. Dalton listened, in mute astonishment, to this well-arranged, extravagant plan. He saw, at once, it would involve his character, perhaps endanger his safety, were it ever to be known; yet observing Emily's apprehensive heart quivered on her lips, he loved her too affectionately to reject it utterly, or treat it with ridicule. The utmost power he had over himself, when she was concerned, was to point out the perpetual danger she would be exposed to by her interesting loveliness, and the youth of the Marquis. The confidence she had in her own prudence, and the full reliance she placed in the honour of her husband, made her treat these objections lightly. The inconveniences, which, as he hinted, he might bring on himself, Emily more fully considered and answered. It had been Sir Edward's intention, when he left Frescati, she assured the Doctor, to set out for England immediately on his return: and when he found himself charged with the sole care of her child, the journey would rather be hastened than retarded. Should, therefore, any unforeseen occurrence (though that appeared to her impossible) betray to Sir Edward that she was yet in existence, it must be when he was far from Rome and Dr. Dalton: for whose honour and safety she felt herself deeply concerned. Her warmth had an effect in her favour, she did not foresee: a strange apprehension that she thought him selfish, if not timid, crossed Dr. Dalton's mind; and to avoid incurring her contempt, he risqued deserving that of her father. He therefore dropped all opposition to her plan. This doubtful success was more than Emily had dared to promise herself; and seeing the Marquis approach, she left the gentlemen together. The conversation had been so singular, that Dr. Dalton communicated it as news to the Marquis; but found himself obliged to re-consider the proposal more seriously, when he learned that the husband, whom Emily, with sweet feminine affection, almost implicitly obeyed, had not been able to remove from her mind this cherished project. The manly character of the Marquis, however, gave it another complexion. He could not agree with Dr. Dalton, in seeing the fraud in so serious a light. It rather appeared to him a means of chastening the heart of a fond, though mistaken, father, from the pride and prejudice that had already destroyed his own peace, as well as the happiness of the two persons most dear to him. He could certainly claim Emily, in despite of her father, would she allow him to assert his influence; but as the bare idea of a struggle between persons almost equally dear, half killed her, he foresaw the return of Sir Edward would, even against her choice, subject her to his will. The plan in question did not necessarily lead to ill consequences: quite the contrary, since, in the grief of supposing his daughter for ever lost, Sir Edward would be obliged more candidly to review his own conduct towards her. Perhaps he might then take the infant he now loathed to his bosom; and cherishing there all its native elevation, gradually expunge thence the only littleness it ever knew. A friend, as kind as Dr. Dalton, would find a generous pleasure in aiding the workings of an ingenuous nature; and might easily guide, towards his daughter, the sorrowful heart of a mistaken but affectionate parent. On his own part, every influence, both of reason and tenderness, should be employed to bring back, to the wonted habits of filial affection and duty, the beloved creature who was willing, for her husband, to become an impoverished wanderer. A temporary alienation, thus managed, might reunite the whole family in an affection, the more tender and lasting, as it would be free from human prejudice, and refined by human suffering. The character of Dr. Dalton would be, he added, as it ever ought, always in his own keeping: since it would pain alike the two he obliged, were he to incur a censure, even from himself, to serve either. The Doctor would always, therefore, be at liberty not only to avow the deception, but his own motive for joining in it; which, perhaps, as nearly concerned the happiness of Sir Edward, as that of his children. Further to engage the Doctor's sympathy, the Marquis ventured to entrust him with the tender secret of his wife's present state; and nothing hitherto urged was half so influential. The fragile form of Emily had, even in the care of Dr. Dalton, almost sunk into a premature grave; nor did he think it possible she should, in the same perilous situation, survive, if terror of mind were again to accompany those sufferings, no kindness could save her from. The tender husband, on hearing this, applauded himself for having implicitly indulged a creature, whose fate might so easily become precarious. Reasoning was, with him, out of the question; and feeling alone determined the future. Emily had, in the interim, called in a powerful coadjutor in Mrs. Dalton; and the league was too strong for the Doctor to resist; though still his conscience secretly revolted at consenting to sanction a fraud of any kind, or from any motive.

News arrived the next morning from Frescati, that one servant was dead, and several more had sickened, with the small-pox. All communication with that part of Sir Edward's family was therefore entirely prohibited, and the Marquis began to make arrangements for the flight of Emily; who now thought it prudent to impart her views to her humble friend Connor: and well she knew how hard would be the task of reconciling her to them.—How to the gross of soul can delicate minds explain that acute sensibility, which, when once awakened, binds heart to heart by a power discriminating as reason, yet impulsive as sensation,—or, when once wounded, throws each in a moment to the utmost limit of creation?—It knows not how to qualify—descends not to contention—disdains to be soothed—given to dignify existence, even though it entails sadness on those who have it—a good never valued, because never understood, by those who have it not.—No human eloquence could have persuaded Connor, a being born to ride in her own coach need ever know misery; or a daughter inheriting a fortune independant of her father need shrink from a power it was at her option to acknowledge.—How great then was the poor woman's astonishment, when told that Emily, instead of maintaining her own pleasure against Sir Edward, was determined to fly from him; and not only to fly, but to leave her behind. "So, after all her services, all her love, her dear young lady chose to live without her!" In vain did Emily represent that she was obliged to leave her child to her father, and how could she trust the treasure to any other woman's care? All the power a rational affection can exercise over a weak one, Emily often tried before she could influence Connor; who, though she had learnt to hate Sir Edward Arden's lofty spirit, knew not how to respect it: and always urged her lady to consider only herself and child.—Wearied out at last by the tender importunity, and nervous agitations of Emily, she reluctantly took solemn charge of the child: consenting to confirm the account of the mother's death to Sir Edward, and for her sake endure what she termed "all his humours."

The Marquis had never been long enough in Rome to be generally known, yet he was too much distinguished by nature, as well as rank, to venture to appear in the day: and the humiliation of stealing to his friends and wife made him, when once Emily was fully resolved on her project, eager for its execution. Dr. Dalton purchased a travelling carriage; and his lady secretly made every necessary preparation for the travellers.

Emily now secluded herself in her own apartment.—The alarm of her having taken the small-pox, was circulated through the whole family.—Her infant remained shut up in a remote part of the mansion; and the domestics, save Mrs. Connor, were prohibited access to the chamber of the visitor.—Dr. Dalton, and his lady, with that favourite humble friend, were all who entered it: and the servants had too great a horror of a malady already so fatal at Frescati, to be tempted to break through the strict injunction. Convinced even when the Marquis, as well as herself, had gathered together all the limited wealth they could, so circumstanced, command, they would be poorly provided for the uncertain future, Emily carefully collected her jewels, and other valuables, to secrete them among the few common habiliments she chose to allow herself.—The yet untarnished bridal vestments she, with a sigh, saw packed to remain behind; that no visible deficiency in her effects might awaken a doubt of her death in the mind of her father.—Within her jewel-case she enclosed a letter in her own hand, signifying that all it once contained she had herself appropriated; nor was any human being to be charged with purloining aught.—This done, she locked the empty casket, and affixed on it her own seal, with a written address to her daughter: whom she exhorted not to break that seal till she should be eighteen.—There was something so melancholy in these indispensable arrangements, each of which produced a new lamentation from Connor, that poor Emily felt ready to sink under the task she had imposed on herself.—Yet she had only to recollect her increasing size, and fancy she saw the indignant eye of her father flash upon her, to return with fresh vigour to her painful employments. Dr. Dalton saw her pale cheeks, and high irritation, with great alarm; and, dissatisfied as he was with her plan, often fairly wished her gone, lest she should die in reality.

On the appointed night all was ordered within the house to favour the departure of the lovers; and the Marquis, an hour before break of day, came in the chaise to the door.—At sight of her little one, Emily sunk half fainting in the arms of Connor: yet when her friends again proposed staying, her resolution instantaneously returned.—She saw in imagination the husband of her heart stretched lifeless at her feet; and the voice of her father sounded fearfully in her ears. "Farewell, farewell then awhile, my infant blessing!" cried she, folding the unconscious smiler to her bosom:—"for thy father, for thy father only, would I for one hour abandon thee!—But it will be thy happy fate to soften the heart of mine:—when he looks in thy innocent face, he will not see aught of the wretch now hanging fondly over thee, but rather the likeness of the nephew once so dear, so inexpressibly dear to him:—to you he will strive to atone for his past severity to both of us; nor will bitterness mingle in the love you may bear each other."—Dr. Dalton saw nature too highly wrought in a creature so delicate, and gave a sign to the Marquis; who rather bore than led her to the carriage, which rapidly carried them from the dearest ties both of nature and choice.

It was soon circulated through Rome that the daughter of Sir Edward Arden was dead of the small-pox: she had never been seen there, and of course this was the news only of a day. The ladies spoke the following one of her infant daughter, as the heiress of two great families; and on the third both mother and child were forgotten.

Dr. Dalton, who had only consented to countenance, not promised to support the fraud, chose to absent himself from home, that he might avoid all embarrassing enquiries; and with his lady went on a tour among their friends. Hardly had they quitted Rome ere Sir Edward Arden arrived there, and having, when he set out for Naples, left his daughter in the charge of Dr. Dalton, chose his house as the most proper one to alight at. A strange and painful feeling seized him at suddenly seeing a servant of Emily's, who vanished.—That he was in black, did not surprise Sir Edward, as the family yet wore it for the Marquis. He continued alone for a while, and then was informed of the absence of his friends: the regret he was expressing he no longer remembered, when he perceived Connor enter the room; who, throwing open a mantle of black crape, shewed him the fairest sleeping cherub that ever graced mortality.—It was the first moment Sir Edward could be said to behold the interesting offspring of an unhappy love.—Ah! how forcibly did nature assert her rights over him!—He eagerly snatched the miniature of his Emily, and looked wildly around for herself.—"Ay, prize that jewel," cried the incautious Connor: "it is the only one you can now call your own."—A horrible sense of unexpected calamity weighed down the father: he turned, disgusted, and afflicted, from the savage who thus announced the completion of his misfortunes; still fondly clasping his darling babe, his infant Emily—alas! now his only Emily.

His valet aided his recovery; and having in the interim learnt the ingenious fabrication of the death of the Marchioness, imparted it to his master; adding that the family at Frescati were still far from well.—There was nothing in a recital and catastrophe so simple, to rouse suspicion, or lead to enquiry.—Sir Edward relied on the tale, and wept—alas! he could only weep:—in Emily the Marquis died to him again; and it was his hard fate to blend the horrors of the past, with the misery of the present loss.

A packet from the Duke of Aberdeen, which had been lying for some weeks at Rome, was now delivered to Sir Edward. Hardly had he power to break the seal: for what could it contain likely to interest his feelings? The whole universe could not, to him, supply a woe, like either of those he must for life bewail. The letter proved to be in answer to that he had sent, recounting the outrage offered to Emily by the Marquis, whose prior marriage, and supposed suicide, formed its whole subject. The Duke of Aberdeen, never rigid, but always coarse and worldly, began his epistle with reprobating Sir Edward's interference between the young people, when once they were united: nor did he less censure the listening to an idle, and, as far as he was empowered to judge, unsupported assertion of a worthless wanton, that the Marquis had married her. Had he, in reality, twenty such extra wives, it would not be possible for any of their claims to interfere with those of a lady of Miss Arden's consequence in life, regularly, and with the approbation of the parents on both sides, espoused to the Marquis of Lenox. As such, he was impatient to greet her: and she might rely on his ever regarding her child, or children, as entitled to all he could bestow. Nor was this strange interference, on the part of Sir Edward, his only or his greatest oversight. The frantic passion that had induced him to dispossess his daughter of the name and title of her husband, was more likely to render the legitimacy of her child disputable, than the improbable assertions of those light ladies, whom the Marquis might be weak enough to prefer to her. In fine, he exhorted Sir Edward immediately to restore

Miss Arden to her rank as wife to the Marquis of Lenox; and if she was sufficiently recovered to undertake the journey, to hasten with her to England; where she and her daughter would be fully acknowledged, and all their rights legally established. The Duke concluded with observing, that he could have pardoned a fond girl of Emily's age, for quarrelling with her husband about giving away her diamonds and carriages; but for her father to expatiate on such baubles, was unworthy both his experience and sex. He desired she might be told, a more magnificent set of jewels were preparing for her; and he requested her to forget those, which it would be an impropriety for her now to appear in, were it possible to recover them. As to the Marquis, he did not pretend to judge of his past conduct; but he supposed he would, in the end, prove no worse than other people's sons; and when he had run about the world for a year or two, and spent all the money he could get, he would return to Emily in his penitentials; who, if she was as sensible and gentle as she appeared to be, might live better then with him than she ever yet had.

The letter dropped from the hands of Sir Edward! A new light broke upon the deep gloom of his soul, which seemed shot from heaven to make his sorrows supportable. "The Duke then thought his son alive!—Ah! why, if he was not so?"—Well he remembered, the idea could never have been gathered from the letter of his, that this epistle answered. To avoid owning, or denying, the deed that for ever clung to his conscience, he had simply enclosed the testimonial of the Neapolitan monks, which even detailed the interment of the Marquis. Yet not by one word did the father refer to that affecting record.

Oh! how did Sir Edward wish that the heart, so powerfully bounding in his bosom, could have borne him instantaneously to England! for to doubt was to die.—Again he read the letter; again assured himself that no father would so have written, who was not convinced of his son's existence. Another pointed conclusion followed; the Marquis was admitted to be gaily wandering with some woman;—who could it be but Emily Fitzallen? Ought then the father of his wife to lament she was in the grave? With a head crowded with conjectures, a heart overflowing with variety of passions, poor Sir Edward cast his eyes around, and felt himself alone in the world;—without one being to counsel with, one friend to comfort him. Suddenly he recollected Cardinal Albertini; and, at the same moment, that the truth, whatever it was, must rest in his bosom: since, though monks might fabricate a tale to deceive other persons, they would not venture an imposition on one of their own body. Wild with impatience, Sir Edward demanded his carriage; ranged like a madman through the house and garden till it was ready, creating new fear and astonishment in Connor, and the domestics; then rapidly threw himself into it, and bade the postillions drive to the villa, where the Cardinal usually passed the summer. Hardly allowing a moment for the greeting of friendship, the agitated Sir Edward gave that prelate the letter of the Duke; and, as he slowly perused it, watched, in silent agony, its effect on him. The Cardinal read, and reread, remaining long thoughtful; till Sir Edward, worn out with expectation, snatched his hand, and almost inarticulately cried, "lives he or not?" The acuteness of misery was in his voice, the horrors of frenzy in his eye. "I know not," gravely, though kindly, replied the Cardinal, "whether I ought to own, that even when I, in compliance with your nephew's wishes, sent you the attested account of his death, the true record, lodged in the College, informed me he was recovering." The start Sir Edward Arden gave, the glare of melancholy joy that shot over his careworn countenance, shocked the pious prelate.—Spreading wide his hands, and wildly surveying them—"they were not then dipt in his vital blood?" groaned he; "this heart is not blackened with the eternal consciousness of involuntary guilt? this brain, this bursting brain, may discharge, in tears, some of its anguish; and in those tears I may yet find virtue,—consolation! Now may I venture to visit the grave of my Emily, nor fear even her ashes will shrink, as she herself did, from the murderer of her husband. I am now then only miserable;—for this mitigation of suffering, let me, oh! God! bow to thee!—only, only, miserable!"—The alarm and astonishment with which the Cardinal heard Sir Edward impute to himself the guilt of shortening his nephew's days, gave way to that of learning the fair, unfortunate young Marchioness, was really in her grave: for he doubted not but that grief had destroyed her. He reproached himself for having complied with the wishes of the wounded Marquis, conveyed through the monks, in ascertaining his death to his family: yet, as not one word, in either account transmitted, threw a shadow of guilt on Sir Edward, it was impossible to foresee of how much consequence to his peace, the disclosure of the truth would be. In all Sir Edward had at first imparted, the Cardinal had seen only an injured, aggrieved parent's feelings; he thence concluded, that time, and time alone, could allay the keen sorrows separately preying on the hearts of all parties: and he was impatiently watching for the moment of general reconciliation. That moment, it was now obvious, would never come. Most severely did he censure himself for veiling the truth, even from benevolent motives.

In the uncontroulable restlessness of a wounded mind, Sir Edward was now eager to fly to Frescati; whither his venerable friend insisted on accompanying him. In the way thither, the latter first learned the malady yet among the servants, to which the young lady was concluded a victim. It was some relief to the Cardinal, to find that a natural, and not a mental calamity, had thus early subjected Emily to the stroke of mortality.

Alas! what a state is his, who feels a deep sense of unkindness to an object still exquisitely dear, though for ever vanished! The tear that would have melted the beloved heart, then drops like caustic on your own; the groan, re-echoing affection would have impatiently replied to, then rings unanswerable on your ear; and the deep solitude of the soul, even amidst all the distracting tumults of an ever busy, ever fluctuating world, becomes an awful punishment, even before the final audit.

Sir Edward now stood on the threshold of his villa at Frescati: the sad moment was still present to his mind, when he came there to receive the lovely, unfortunate Emily, ere yet she was conscious of the misery he had brought upon her youth. Again she threw herself into his paternal arms, as certain of pity, protection, fondness; his secret soul told him she found not these poor alleviations of irremediable calamity. Again she seemed, in the agony of conjugal love, to spring from those arms, as though a single word had snapt the weaker chord of nature: and starting—he felt himself childless.—He vainly wept; vainly he smote his bosom; blending all the misery of a late repentance, with the keen pangs of parental anguish.

The Cardinal interrogated the servants, who were visible sufferers by the malady, which was said to have deprived Emily of life; and from them he gathered such particulars, as he hoped would lighten the affliction of the father. They all agreed that she had recovered health and bloom before she left Frescati; and even her melancholy had considerably abated; that she removed to guard her child from infection, and not as fearing it herself. To this information, the Cardinal added his own just remark, that, by going to Dr. Dalton's, she had taken the best chance for life; since, if skill or kindness could have prolonged hers, she would not have died beneath his roof.

"He talks to me, who never had a child," sighed poor Sir Edward to himself;—his was gone, for ever gone; repentance, sympathy, sorrow, no more could soften, soothe, conciliate Emily. The mansion he was once so fond of, now appeared a dungeon to him. Her works, her musical instruments, her drawings, yet scattered about in all the apartments, gave various forms to the unceasing sentiment of sorrow. The Cardinal, lest he should sink into stupor, ventured the hazardous experiment of recalling his nephew to his mind, as one who must yet more lament for Emily.—"Ah! yes, he must indeed lament her," sighed the father; "for he had purchased, by a crime, the sad pre-eminence in suffering." Well now could Sir Edward calculate the excess of that passion, which stamped with horror the hours of bridal felicity. His generous heart recovered its spring, and bade him again receive the solitary sufferer to his affection; so might they lighten to each other a loss, no time could repair. But how was he to trace this husband, more miserable than himself? how make him sensible of his absolute forgiveness, his anxious sympathy, his eternal regret?—One link of the many that once bound them together, alone remained;—it was the little orphan Emily. Motherless before she had known the cherishing warmth of a parental embrace; surely the father could not forget the tie that bound the grandfather?— Yes, the Marquis would one day assert his right in the darling child; and thus, most certainly, should he discover him. But so fearful was Sir Edward become of losing her, by the strong desire his nephew might have to make her wholly his own, that he hardly would trust her out of his sight. As Emily predicted, her daughter soon gained that indulgence, her father had denied to herself.

In turning over his papers at Frescati, Sir Edward laid his hand on the will, he had so wrung his daughter's heart, and his own, to obtain. It was, at last, of no use, if the marriage was not contested; and only a new cause of eternal chagrin. In observance of the rational advice of the Duke, the Lenox arms were again painted on the carriage of his grand-daughter; and she was committed, as the heiress of both families, to the strict charge of Mrs. Connor, to whom Sir Edward assigned a liberal stipend, and the sole authority over the establishment of Lady Emily Lenox. He was not without a secret hope that the Marquis, even then, kept a strict watch on his conduct; which thus, indirectly, was calculated to convince him that the afflicted father was tenderly disposed to a union of sorrows and interests. Cardinal Albertini insisted on his residing with him, as Dr. Dalton was absent; for whose return Sir Edward indeed waited, to inform himself of such particulars respecting Emily, as he deigned not to enquire of servants: after which,—if in the interim the Marquis did not appear,—it was his full intention to set out once more for Naples, there to seek the treasure he had learned, by suffering, duly to value. But long might Sir Edward have waited for Dr. Dalton, who left Rome with a fixed determination, never to re-visit it while the father staid: for whom his regard had entirely ceased. He answered to Sir Edward's letter, by a cold condolence on his great *loss*, but entered no farther on the interesting subject: and spoke of his own return as an indifferent matter, wholly uncertain. Sir Edward, piqued and chagrined at such an alteration of conduct in a man he esteemed, and who had conferred a great obligation on him, remitted not proper attentions, but hastily removed Lady Emily, and her suite, to the purified mansion at Frescati; after which he eagerly set out for Naples.

Dr. Dalton now returned home, and was not long in visiting Frescati: where he learned, with a deep shock and surprize, the rational conduct and manly grief of Sir Edward Arden; the just consequence he had given his infant grand-daughter, and the boundless fondness he expressed for her.—Connor, engrossed by the importance and honour of her new situation, which gave her the full command of all her vanished lady's rights in life, could not find as much leisure, as formerly, to lament that premeditated delusion, Dr. Dalton every moment more heavily reproached himself for having become a party in. From whatever cause Sir Edward had again absented himself, not to meet him became a relief to the worthy man, as he flattered himself daily with the arrival of letters from the dear fugitives; whose home he should then know, and could urge them to an immediate disclosure of their re-union, which, it was very obvious, could have no ill consequence to any party.

Day after day, week after week, however, elapsed, without bringing one line from either the Marquis or Emily. Vague fears, and alarms, often came across their kind friends; who now made every enquiry on the road, that could be made without naming the parties: but so many travellers had passed since the fugitives, that no account could be gathered of them. Dr. Dalton too well remembered that Emily had packed up valuables with their common baggage: and the painful possibility that her anxiety might lead the postillions to suspect this, and expose them to fall thus into the hands of banditti, haunted him for ever. Yet it was possible the lovers had, from motives not to be guessed, changed their route; nay, even taken shipping. Whenever the idea that they ungenerously meant to ensure his silence, by leaving him in eternal ignorance of their retirement, crossed his mind, he hastily rejected it, however horrible the fear that sprung up in its place.

And where then were these lovers, so anxiously dwelt on by the few to whom they were known? Alas! in a very public and humble spot, where they were passed, and repassed, by a variety of travellers, without exciting in a single one an emotion of curiosity. Such is commonly the case with persons who travel in a leisurely manner, and unattended by a suite of servants: who, in reality, attract attention much more than those they wait on. The morning soon broke on the Marquis and Emily, after they left Rome, and gave to their glad eyes each other, now most truly wedded, since without any equal claim or feeling, to clash with a mutual, a fond affection. The hand of Sir Edward Arden can never more be lifted against the life of the Marquis, thought Emily; and she gladly compounded for all the drawbacks attending this certainty. Never can my uncle again tear his daughter from me, thought the Marquis, and turned, with contempt, from all he had resigned for her sake. Incapable of personal fear, a secret one that Sir Edward was even now seeking means to annul the marriage of his daughter, had always poisoned the pleasure of being forgiven and beloved by Emily to her husband. In the idea she was dead (for well he knew Sir Edward would soon learn *he* was not so) it was possible he might sacrifice his resentments to the good of that child, his pursued indignation would render illegitimate. Thus might a few years, either by the death or marriage of Miss Fitzallen, and the united forgiveness of their parents, render his appearance, with Emily in his hand, the wish of all parties. Occupied with thoughts like these, and a sweet sense of happiness, unknown to each till the hour of their flight, the fugitives passed unobserved. Emily had never changed her deep mourning; and the Marquis, to avoid observation, assumed it. They affected no consequence, but spoke of themselves as having attended a young lady in a consumption to Naples, whence, having buried her, they were now returning to their own country. Conscious of the value of their baggage, and afraid of others suspecting it, Emily affected severe economy in her travelling expences; and found it a sure way of being overlooked. Whether the spirits or constitution of Emily had suffered more than either could bear, or heaven frowned on her flight from her father, cannot be determined: but, four days after she left Rome, she was obliged, however unwillingly, to own to the Marquis, that she was too ill to proceed.—A few hours convinced her, that it would not then be her fate to give brother or sister to the dear babe she had left behind. Too late did her husband regret acceding to a plan, his opposition, if determinate, would certainly have ended: nor knew he how to procure her advice, or the least domestic comfort.—She bore her situation very patiently, and making the best of it, declared herself in a few days able to pursue her journey, the fatigue of which she supported better than her lord expected. They beguiled the time till they reached the foot of that stupendous natural barrier, the Alps, which they must necessarily pass in the way to Switzerland. In the visionary world lovers form for themselves, happiness and Switzerland have become almost synonymous terms.*— The Marquis, and Emily, might well think them so.—Still was the hour fresh in the memory of each, when they romantically crossed each other near Lausanne.—The days that followed were the brightest in the lives of either. Though their hands had long been united, and their beings blended, time had not yet taken any thing from the charms they then found in each other.—To Switzerland it had therefore been their choice to retire. They meant to quit the traveller's usual track, and seek some sequestered scene, where all the agitations they had struggled so long with, might subside into the sweet transports of confiding love, and mutual sensibility. Dreams as aërial and delusive as these were absolutely necessary to render endurable, to those highly born, and delicately bred, the odious inconveniences of Italian inns:* where even the most distinguished travellers vainly demand the necessary comforts, for which they are exorbitantly charged.—The Marquis, and Emily, with all their natural and acquired graces, found it impossible to inspire that deference in these sordid wretches, which they only pay to the courier that precedes, the horses that draw, and the servants that follow their guests.

The little inn had nothing to keep the lovers within doors: but nature invited them abroad in a manner not to be resisted.—Over the deep and woody glen the house was seated in, impended an enormous mountain; on whose aged head hung tresses of snow, that threatened to inter the hamlet, with every blast that blew:—beyond, and around, far as the eye could reach, his numerous, and ancient brethren, of different heights, and hideous aspects, with grotesque yet chilling beauty, gave elevation to the mind, while they compressed the nerves. It was a solemn heavenly solitude, where the children of fancy must delight to pause.—Emily wandered through the wilds the whole day, and playfully made the Marquis, touching his flute, give voice to the echoes of the mountains.—Their vile supper had been waiting till quite spoiled, yet exercise and pleasure gave it a relish. The chamber, like many they had been obliged to tolerate, disgusted them both—it appeared close and humid, if not noxious—they hastened in the morning to breakfast under an arbour in the little garden, where the Marquis gently remonstrated with the host for giving them so unpleasant a room.—The man turned to his wife, and chid her for not having had the bed-cloaths washed, or the room aired.—The following altercation too plainly proved that a young person had only the day before been taken out that chamber, who had died in it, of the small-pox.—A dreadful faintness, and nausea, seized Emily—excruciating head-achs followed, with other symptoms, which convinced her that she had received the loathsome infection.—To attempt, while this was a doubt, to cross the Alps, would have been madness: yet to remain in this miserable unlucky inn, appeared no less detestable, than hazardous. It was a lone house; and every traveller either way, must stop there. The increasing illness of Emily, soon, however, rendered it impossible for her to venture over the mountains.

In these contingencies men know all the value of that foresight, and firmness, even-handed nature bestows on rational women, to compensate for the personal courage she has not granted to them. Emily soon obtained from her penitent landlady the best accommodation her poor house afforded; and having ordered her baggage to her chamber, calmly retired thither, as to her tomb: having engaged the two daughters of the host to nurse, and attend upon her.—In the fond apprehensiveness of a mother, Emily had, from the moment she became one, endeavoured to inform herself on every malady that might affect the welfare of her babe; happily, therefore, she had some judgment in her own case. She entreated the Marquis, if she should lose, as it was too probable she might, the power of enforcing her directions, carefully to guard her from all mistaken kindness; and that she might not fall a victim to an ignorant nurse, or village practitioner, she obliged him to commit to paper what it would be vain to hope he could, thus circumstanced, remember; requesting him to abide by her judgment, whatever the consequence.

The Marquis on his knees swore implicit obedience: and having received, and recorded her injunctions, took the keys of her trunks, and medicine chest, preparing on his part to fulfil the sad but tender duty of watching by her sick bed, who had so often, and so unremittingly, watched over his. In a few days the delicate skin of Emily was covered by the eruption. In a few more it became confluent. Her beautiful eyes were sealed up; and hardly dared her agonized husband hope ever again to see them open. Delirium followed; and only the voice of the Marquis, which still she knew, which still she heard, in whispers as fond as those in the days of bridal felicity, could have saved her from the grave: but never did she speak that he was not impatient to answer—never did she extend a feverish hand his did not fondly receive, and cherish—never breathe a sigh, his tender heart did not fearfully echo!

Three weeks elapsed in this miserable manner before the wretched Lenox could promise himself the restoration of Emily; and, oh! what a ravage had that short time made in her beauty!— The Emily his boyish heart worshipped, it was plain he never more would behold.—Those fine features, that skin more "smooth than monumental alabaster,"* no more would charm his sight; but the pure, the elevated, the generous soul, to which in ripened manhood his own was inviolably plighted, still survived the wreck of human beauty, and diffused over the ruin celestial sweetness. A piety, and patience, so exemplary marked the days of Emily's suffering, that never, never, was she more adored, than during her convalescence; the only pleasure she found in recovered vision was to gaze on him, more dear than aught on earth; and had not the appearance of her arms told her what that of her face must be, she might have thought its loveliness improved, so animated were the looks of her husband at seeing only recovered life in it.

During this severe trial to the Marquis, he had a thousand times lamented being out of the reach of Dr. Dalton; on whose professional skill he had great reliance: but never once could he resolve to write to him. Ah! how could he be certain that the ingenious tale of Emily's death, fabricated to veil her flight, would not be a sad certainty before his letters could reach Rome?—Nor would he afflict a faithful friend in telling him they were overtaken by a calamity when out of his reach, he could so materially have lessened had they remained within it.

Emily, though very weak, was now able to leave her chamber; nor could her husband any longer conceal from her the cruel change made in her features, to all eyes but his own:—the conviction shocked her very sensibly; and she anxiously sought to learn from him his real sentiments and feelings on so trying an occasion.—He frankly owned, that, had he not been the daily, hourly, witness of her sufferings, he might have been struck with the change; but when he expected every moment to lose the gem, he heeded not the casket that contained it: and since he still had his Emily, he should delight through his whole life to convince her that sense, and self, were weak ties compared with those sorrow, and sensibility, had formed between them.—A certain noble reliance Emily ever had on the few she could love, made her, when thus generously assured of her influence, disdain to mourn such perishing advantages as mere feature, and complexion, and by exerting the charms of her mind, as well as the softness of her temper, she daily made a large compensation to the husband who adored her.

Ere she attempted the severe passage of the Alps, Emily thought it right to try the milder atmosphere of the valley; and whenever she could induce the Marquis to hunt, or course, for the benefit of his health, she would lean on the arm of her young nurse Beatrice, and creep to a shady seat where a streamlet fell near the roadside: this was yet the extent of Emily's walk; and having with great fatigue one fine morning reached it, she was resting, when an equipage, magnificently appointed, drove by towards the inn she had quitted.—A loud laugh told her that the company had been tempted by the beauty of the spot to alight, nor could she possibly escape their eyes.—To complete her distress, she perceived Miss Fitzallen leaning on the arm of Count Montalvo.—Yet her astonishment surpassed her confusion when she saw the Count, after pointing his glass towards her, drop it carelessly; while the lady, glancing her quick eye from a face she no longer knew, to a habit which only attracted her attention as being English, turned alike away, as having regarded an absolute stranger.—Altered as Emily supposed herself, it had never occurred to her, till this moment, that she should be wholly unknown to her acquaintance: yet the painful chill of this conviction was lost in the happy idea that followed it.—How did she rejoice, when the Marquis returned, at the singular good luck which had caused him to be absent.—Nay, their having been detained at this poor inn became a subject of congratulation, since otherwise this worthless pair, who were set out to make, as their servants had published, the tour of Switzerland, would infallibly have disturbed their repose, before they could have breathed in their chosen asylum.

The Marquis in wrath knew not now, he cried, where to look for a peaceful retreat—"Say not so, my love, for I can point out a safe and pleasant one," cried Emily; "let us avail ourselves of my misfortune, and since my features are altered past recollection, let us at least escape for ever the woman who yet might find means to embitter our fate.—There is a spot where we may learn from day to day, and year to year, without a single enquiry, or one confidant, all that interests our feelings: my cruel malady, to my deeper thought, seems sent by heaven to ascertain our peace.—No eye shall henceforward know Sir Edward Arden's daughter, save yours—no heart acknowledge her—those native wilds I without you detested, with you I shall find paradise; nor will Bellarney appear to you a chearless scene.—The mansion will be wholly deserted during the infancy of our Emily, for my father never since he lost my mother set foot in it voluntarily.—At the bottom of the hill it is seated on, a wild romantic river winds to the sea;—on its banks are many cabins beautifully situated: some one will surely bear improving. There, untitled and unknown, may we fix our home, and wait the course of time, contented tenants to our own sweet Emily."

The glow of mind the Marchioness ever threw over her projects, the heart of her husband had been used to catch: if they must bury themselves, no place was indeed so eligible. He well knew she might appear as a stranger, even on her own domains; and he had never set foot on the shore of Ireland. Bellarney had not only the advantage of being the spot where they could, without difficulty, learn all they wanted to know, but the only one where they were sure of never being sought for. Above all, it was the residence Emily preferred; and to make her happy, was so entirely the wish of her husband, that he would hardly, to his own heart, admit it to be a duty. How, how could he ever merit, or return, the sacrifices she had made for him? For him she had quitted for ever her father; nay, for him awhile left even her child! for him, without a murmur, lost her beauty! for him resigned a splendid fortune, and a favourite home. When he discovered how inherent the love of that home was, well could he calculate the value she set on those goods, of which this was the least: well, too, could he estimate his own consequence with her; since he was the only equivalent she desired. Nor did she desire in vain. The refined and generous nature of the Marquis rendered her, in a love that never swerved, a faith till death unbroken, the return, the sole return, the tender Emily would have accepted.

Whenever they were out of Italy, to write to Dr. Dalton the Marquis thought would be absolutely necessary: but this did not seem a wise step to Emily. She found such a sense of safety in having wholly escaped, and had so strong an idea that to keep up, in a retired spot in Ireland, a correspondence in Italy, would sooner or later betray them, that she persuaded him to with-hold the promised information; in the belief that the reasons she urged, would always make their peace with a true friend. It, however, occurred to Emily, that the alteration of her features might one day make it difficult to identify herself, even among her domestics. She, therefore, thought it a prudent precaution to take Beatrice with them, as a witness, at any future period, that it was, at this very time and place, she was so changed by the cruel malady. Nor would this step lead to any discovery, as the young Italian spoke no language but her own; nor could know more of them than they were pleased to impart. Beatrice had attached herself greatly to Emily; and, as the prospect of seeing the world is always pleasant at sixteen, she gladly consented to abandon her parents, and her native mountains, with the travellers.

And now what became of poor Sir Edward Arden; when, on arriving at Naples, he found every thorn, yet rankling at his heart, sharpened, by learning, from the monks who had preserved his nephew, how generously that young man screened him from the odium of the duel, and how tenderly he had ever mentioned him? Yet, by their account, the Marquis was very unfit for a journey when he left Naples; nor was there a clue by which he might afterwards be traced. If, as was probable, the news of Emily's death had reached him, while in a weak state of mind and body, it was but too likely that the heart-broken husband should, as the priests surmised, have entombed himself at La Trappe,* or some other monastery. Again was the disappointed heart of Sir Edward Arden without a resting-place:—after a thousand times visiting the scene of his guilty fury,—a thousand times sprinkling, with his tears, the sod where the beloved victim fell,—he found no alternative but once more to return to Rome, and entreat Cardinal Albertini to use his influence, in exploring the Carthusian, and other monasteries, where it might be likely his melancholy nephew had taken refuge. On reaching Rome, a new shock awaited him;—the worthy Dr. Dalton had expired suddenly of an apoplexy; and Mrs. Dalton had left that city for Montpelier,* from whence the Doctor married her. At Frescati, he, however, found his grand-daughter well, and daily improving in strength and beauty. Letters from the Duke were again lying at Rome for him, which he now tore open with agonized impatience. He found only a condolence on the death of the Marchioness, and a very severe censure of her husband, as the supposed cause, by previous unkindness towards her. Again the Duke exhorted Sir Edward to lose no more time in seeking a young libertine, they should both see too soon, whenever he appeared, unless there was a great change in his conduct; and, for his satisfaction, enclosed the only letter he had received from the Marquis. It consisted of a few hasty lines, recommending his adored Emily, and her babe, should it survive the misery it was now sharing with its hapless mother, to the tender care of his father. He further entreated him to reconcile the misjudging Sir Edward Arden to himself; and finally implored all three to pity, and forget for ever, the unfortunate Lenox. Alas! how did this billet, which had no effect on the father's heart, make that of the uncle bleed! The date, no less than the uneven writing, and incoherent diction, proved that it was sent while the young man was still fluctuating between life and death: yet, though writhing under the wound, no mention was made of it in the whole letter.

From the arrival of this billet, till his banker notified to the Duke that his son had at Naples drawn for some thousands, through the medium of the bank in Genoa, that nobleman added he had heard no more of him; nor did he suppose he should, till he wanted money again. The letter concluded with another exhortation to Sir Edward, to bring Lady Emily without delay, to England, and explain, at large, the obscure business of the prior marriage; that, by the sudden and decisive steps they should jointly take, the rights of the heiress of Bellarney might descend, without disgrace or diminution, to her daughter.

But of heirships, bankers, and bills, Sir Edward thought not;—his bleeding heart demanded still his nephew: nor could he resolve to quit Italy while there was one monastery unexplored, once chance unstudied, by which he might be found. Cardinal Albertini exerted all his influence to relieve the mind of his friend; and priests were dispatched to enquire, in every possible direction, for the suffering and melancholy fugitive.

Connor, who now found that the Marquis was known to be alive, laboured with the interesting intelligence that Emily was with him; but she stood in too much awe of Sir Edward and Dr. Dalton, to impart it to the first, without the concurrence of the latter: when the news of the sudden death of that worthy friend, made her the sole depositary of the important secret. Doubtful whether she might not for ever lose the love and confidence of her lady, if she avowed the truth without her consent, and always apprehending the severity of Sir Edward, Connor, after many struggles with her conscience, resolved to maintain her promised silence. Nor was it possible for her to guess in what part of the world the Marquis and his lady had sought refuge; or whether, indeed, they still inhabited it: for Dr. Dalton had often discussed with her his various and melancholy conjectures on their long silence; and left a mind, so weak and superstitious, rather disposed to conclude them both murdered, than thus deliberately dumb.

The journey to England, by land, with so young a child, appeared in all respects hazardous to Sir Edward. He, therefore, resolved rather to endure the tediousness of a passage by sea; and having engaged a vessel at Leghorn, provided with suitable comforts and accommodations, he took a kind leave of the venerable Cardinal; and setting out for that port, embarked with the little Lady Emily for England.

The amiable young man, Sir Edward so vainly sought, was now travelling peacefully, and pleasantly, with the beloved of his heart, through such high roads in France as were least frequented by the English, for the port of Havre:* from which, as one of mere business, they thought it most safe to cross the Channel. Having there procured a vessel to themselves, they landed in Sussex; and crossing England to Holyhead,* without stopping in any large town, they were soon and safely set on shore in Ireland. Here Emily breathed freely; and indulging herself with only a few days of rest, she guided the Marquis through that wild and beautiful country, to the seat of her maternal ancestors,—her own Bellarney. It was the close of a summer evening, when they arrived at the well-known spot; doubly pleasant to its owner, since gilt not only by the sun, but the rich beams of early remembrance. In dear luxurious silence Emily paused upon its

"Deep'ning glooms, gay lawns, and airy summits,"*

while her lord imbibed from her a sense of pleasure, the active soul of man is not so exquisitely alive to, as the more passive, but not less enlivened, nature of woman. That sex, destined in a manner to become stationary in the world, is by wise heaven endued with such tastes, as shall, well considered, make pleasures of their duties. It is theirs to reign at home,—with varying elegance to improve the spot on which they are to dwell, and by bountifully dispensing around the blessings they inherit, or obtain, find as perfect a delight, as moving in the enlarged circle of power or politics, can give the man they are to share existence with. Who has not known the vague, but boundless joy, of re-treading the spot recollection first marks in the mind? Those hours and places, when the soul knew not sorrow, the happiest delight to look back to, the most miserable recall with a suspension of suffering: the roses that then bloomed before our eyes, the tree that then lent us its shade, will have, for fond fancy, a charm, the richest scenery must ever want, when the heart sickens with oppressive knowledge, or the eyes are dimmed with continual weeping. This spot of our birth, this little country of the heart, so dear, so inexpressively dear to universal remembrance, might well affect the tender soul of Emily; since, though to the vulgar sense impoverished, she had brought back to the estate she dared no longer appropriate, as her own,—her own for life, the only treasure she ever sighed for,—the beloved Marquis of Lenox.

The little rural inn the pair now put up at, the heiress of Bellarney had been too great a person ever to be permitted to enter; yet she recalled the comely face of the landlady to her mind, as one of the auditors at the chapel of the mansion, where Lady Bellarney had always ordered regular service. An enquiry, made by Emily, into the cause of her mourning gown, brought out a simple, but touching eulogium on herself, that made the fine eyes of the Marquis swim in tears of tenderness: for how could the good woman guess at her hearers? All the tenants of the estate had, it seems, made it their choice, alike "to mourn for the young, the lovely lady of Bellarney, cut off so in her bloom as it were."

Hardly could luxury have invented a more refined enjoyment, than Emily and her lord found in the voluntary privation of her inherited rights. They passed whole days in wandering through the park, the woods, the green solitudes of Bellarney; while Emily marked to her delighted Edward, each fairy walk, by the little incident that impressed it for ever on her own memory. And often, when the gay idea glowed full upon her soul, she would turn to him with sweet exultation, and cry, now, now only was it enjoyment:—for only now had she been accompanied by him, who made the happiness he so fondly shared.

In these long rambles, they met many rustics, Emily was ready to greet with kind remembrance; but not one who recognized her. She became thus assured that she should not risque discovery, did she venture to shew the Marquis the gardens and mansion of Bellarney. So little of the fortress remained, that it was hardly entitled to the name of a castle, though it was termed so. Many and various had been its modifications, through a long line of noble possessors; insomuch that it was now only an irregular, grand, and venerable dwelling. The towers, long since converted into turrets, were half embosomed in the rich woods, that were the pride of the country. On the east and north, those woods had grown to an almost savage wildness and grandeur; but, on the south and west, were gracefully broken with light plantations* and variegated shrubberies, to the bottom of the knoll, on which the building stood. The sea almost flowed up to the hill, and bathed the green oaks with every tide; while a little creek, with beautiful indenture, formed a secure harbour for the vessels of the family, and a new object of beauty from the house.

The gardens were chiefly on the south side, when the descent was, at length, abruptly checked, by a projection of rocks, crowned with fox-glove and wild plants, which fancifully impended over a mountain torrent, the natives called a river,—wholly unnavigable from its rude course and stony bed, which often threw up crags, resembling curled and half-burnt volumes of enormous size; between, and over which, the pure waters rushed and foamed, with ever beautiful variety; till taking suddenly a bold sweep, the stream smoothed to polished crystal, ere it discharged itself into the sea. Here, through a tuft of willows and poplars, peeped the white cabin of a ferryman, who led not a life of idleness; for across the river was the nearest way to the next market-town. At some little distance, nearer the sea, appeared the yard of a boat-builder, enriching the scene with the busy charm of human labour and ingenuity. The land beyond rose with a verdure, rarely seen so close to the beach; and a quarter of a mile further, half sheltered by woods, was seated the house of the boat-builder; for that was above the rank of a cabin. Before it, for many a mile, with graceful undulation, wandered the high road; while the smooth and beautiful sands offered a cool and delightful ride in calm weather; and the rich and wild woods, that every-where fringed the swelling shore, promised safety when the winds of winter should rage. Such was the near prospect from the mansion of Bellarney: while the sea, with bold expansion, and all its grand varieties of surface, supplied, to the reflecting mind, images yet more impressive.

To cross this well known ferry, and drink tea at the boat-builder's house, had once been the extent of Emily's wishes; and lucky seemed the hour when Lady Bellarney would allow her the satisfaction of gathering, in those more remote woods, worse strawberries than she found at home. The novelty that formed the pleasure, was for ever vanished; but the sweet remembrance of it still lived at her heart, and made this ferry, and this dwelling more pleasant to her eyes and to her soul, than any other. The name of poor Kerry, who used to inhabit the house, was on her lips, when, checking herself, she asked the attending gardener to whom it belonged, and who lived there? "God knows," cried the man, "who it will belong to now; but the little Lady, they say, is to have all: and as to *living*,—I know a poor honest fellow who is almost starving there. Jack Crosby was head-man to poor Mr. Kerry, when he was killed by the fall of a piece of timber in the yard, and his widow found that he was worse than nothing. What does Jack do but take to the business, because he was *ingenus*; and now the bailiffs, they say, will take to Jack, unless he is *ingenus* enough to keep out of their way. We used to have such fine boats, and vessels, on the stocks there, it was a pleasure to look at them. Now you see there is hardly any timber to work upon; and the little there is, our steward says he is not paid for. Had our poor young lady not gone beyond seas, she might, please God, have lived; and she had a kind heart: so things would have gone otherwise at Bellarney. Now I suppose all our fine oaks, that are the pride of this county, and the next to it, will be felled, to float off in cash to England,* like all the rest of our neighbours' woods; for nobody will live at Bellarney till little Madam is a lady grown, they say, but servants."

While the gardener was thus simply engaging the thoughts of Emily and the Marquis, the eyes of the latter were eagerly contemplating the beauty of the prospect, from the brow they stood on. The near scene attracted him as being at once wild and domestic, retired and busy: nor was the yard of the boat-builder the least striking feature in the beautiful whole. They now descended with the gardener (whom Emily could alike have guided had she dared) through woodwalks, to the bottom of the hill; where, standing on the brink of the river, the Marquis raised his eyes to the scene they had left, and, on comparison, found that he beheld hardly less to his taste.

The elevated and irregular rocks they lately stood on, impended now over their heads, and shook the wildly streaming garlands of summer above them, with an interesting charm, confined scenery alone can supply: while the river, which the eye traced, with many a rude fall, along a deep glen, softening its roar as it approached, expanded at their feet into grandeur; and, through its translucent waters, gave to the eye the rocky inequalities of its bed. An aged ferryman, on seeing them waiting to pass, rushed so hastily from his cabin to convey them, that he spared not a moment to cover his venerable locks; which, while he pushed off with his pole, fantastically caught the wind, and the beams of the setting sun, as, dipping his golden orb into the sea, he threw his long radiations even to the shore.—Again was Emily going to hail the well-remembered old ferryman, and again she checked herself.

Having crossed the romantic stream, the Marquis, and his beloved, wandered slowly towards the boat-builder's house; ever and anon turning to survey the beautiful scenery of Bellarney, and then, with new wonder, gazing on the ever-fluctuating waves of liquid gold.

"Oh! well my Emily knows how to chuse her home," fondly whispered the Marquis, pressing the arm that, with such sweet content, hung within his; "poor as she is, she has yet the power of stretching forth her beneficent hand, to save the industrious and unfortunate tenant of that little mansion, her taste and her tenderness will so exquisitely embellish." The full heart of Emily allowed of no other reply, than returning the affectionate pressure.

And this *was* the happy home of the Marquis of Lenox and his Emily.

To the poor young man who had rashly embarked without a capital in his master's business, Mr. and Mrs. Irwin seemed dropped from heaven. They paid his little debts, allowed him to remain in the family, and employed his ingenuity to repair and beautify the little mansion. Emily, knowing the ready channel to every elegant accommodation, by applying, as Mrs. Irwin, to the tradesmen in Dublin she used to employ at Bellarney, soon obtained such furniture, as united simplicity and taste at a very moderate expence. The refinement of her mind made her sparing in all she provided for herself: a harp, and a spinning wheel, formed almost the whole of her exclusive possessions. For the Marquis, Crosby fitted up a large and retired parlour as a study; where soon were arranged such a collection of books, as secured the mind from stagnation; with a telescope, and whatever else might assist the study of astronomy, a science for which the Marquis had ever shewn a decided taste.

Poor Crosby was not convinced, by his own failure, that boat-building might be an unprofitable employment. He became urgent with the Marquis to make a fortune, by purchasing the stock, and leaving him the active part of the business. This, on reflexion, appeared to the fugitives a measure of prudence; since nothing but an ostensible occupation could prevent them from soon becoming objects of curiosity in the country: and it was more dangerous to be supposed rich than poor. The lease of the whole was, therefore, made over to Mr. and Mrs. Irwin, and the timber-yard once more abounded in the oaks of Bellarney. Crosby, proud to deserve the trust of his master, shewed at once such capacity, ingenuity, and industry, that the Marquis found, in improving that young man's little knowledge in the mathematics, amusement, and in learning from him mechanics, exercise: as well as that in both instances he felt himself relieved from the lassitude a liberal mind must always feel, when conscious it is become a cold blank in that circle of society it was meant to animate.

Such was the humble fate, such the simple pleasures, such the active pursuits of the Marquis of Lenox, on the day that made him two-and-twenty; which he celebrated with his Emily, in the bowers of Bellarney, where, as mere tenants of the estate, they had almost sole possession.—Life had much earlier opened upon him than on most men, and sorrow prematurely ripened reflexion.—Of all that fortune in the insolence of abundance once offered to him, able only to grasp a single good, his sense of its value was quickened by the perpetual fear of losing it, so many trials had occasioned.—Emily had long been all to him, and if she could have wanted a charm, the situation he soon saw her in would have made his wishes wholly concentre in herself, save the fond one he now and then sent towards his daughter.—The hearts of both were however awakened to their other ties, when, on the steward's tendering the lease to Mr. Irwin to sign, Emily heard her daughter termed Emily Lenox, the lady of Bellarney.—Her sense of her father's cruelty and injustice, in depriving her of a name his pride thus capriciously invested her child with, revived with all its force; and in the bitterness of recollected sorrow, she secretly applauded her own resolution in quitting him for ever.—To the Marquis on the contrary the name of Emily Lenox was a dear acknowledgment of his right in the little angel, and a sure proof that no steps had been taken to annul the marriage, by which he yet hoped one day to claim all his rights, as well as his daughter. This only subject on which the pair did not think alike, was, however, by delicacy of mind, entirely sunk between them, and they lived wholly isolated from society, (save of the poor and grateful rustics, whom they liberally assisted) like the first pair in paradise, when they had only God to look up to.

Ah! what cannot an active and intelligent mind do when once it resolutely adopts, and pursues, an idea? Never did Emily appear so interesting as while regulating her little household, and preparing, without one querulous word, for the hour that was to give her both a care, and a pleasure, in another dear babe.—The Marquis had now become almost as diligent, and expert as Crosby himself in boat-building; and promised Emily, on recovering, a most gallant little vessel to sail about the coast in: an indulgence she much desired.— The mornings were thus, by mutual consent, passed separately by the married lovers, save when Emily, fearing it was too hot, or too cold, would risque alternately either danger herself, to walk to the river-side, and see whether the Marquis was taking proper care of himself; or he, finding a new moss, shell, or plant, hastened home to amuse with the simple diversification of objects the elegant pencil of Emily.—The evenings were beguiled now in music, and now in deep contemplation of those unnumbered worlds hanging in majestic silence over the heads devoutly raised to view them; while a thousand rich and solemn thoughts, chastened from the little cares, or hopes, of mortality, the beings who dared to look for happiness beyond it.

Nor was winter without its peculiar pleasures.—The stormy ocean had its sublimity, the cheerful fire-side its indulgence.—Never did the hands of Emily look so white as when employed on the spinning wheel—never did her air seem so graceful as when she was tuning the harp:—if the Marquis issued from his study impatient to share with her the delight of a favourite passage in a favourite author, never would Emily recollect it; for the voice, and the taste, ever made it new to her heart, melodious to her ear.

To fill up every thought, and moment, a son was born to the Marquis, and his Emily. A lovelier never fond parents contended to embrace: sighing, yet rejoicing, they named the babe Edward.

Nor was the young stranger a joy to the parents alone. Beatrice, who had found a vague disappointment in quitting a solitude at the foot of the Alps, for even a more sequestered situation in Ireland, was invested with the office of nurse, under Emily, and found a strange kind of pride and fondness suddenly awakened; with a certain consequence peculiar to those new in office. Crosby saw her thus intrusted, with some regret that he was not a woman to contest for the employ with her; if, indeed, he could have contested any thing with the lively little Italian, whom he had vainly tried to teach English (totally unconscious of the brogue that rendered it impossible), till he had learned another much more universal language of her—that of the eyes. Nor was Jack so bad a linguist but that Beatrice understood, and approved him.—She suddenly ceased to lament Italy;—forgot "her father's dear little dwelling at the foot of the Alps," and became of importance to herself. The Marquis, and Emily, saw with pleasure the love that made the happiness of their own lives, thus extending through their little household.—A cabin near the timber-yard was beautified by Crosby, and furnished by his bountiful employers; who gave him all the profit of boat-building, though he was to appearance only a servant: to Beatrice they allotted the timber as a portion. Crosby soon carried his bride to his own little home; but as Beatrice could neither live without her mistress, nor the little Edward, the latter passed his life pretty nearly in being carried from the house to the cabin, and from the cabin to the house.

Few young creatures born to wealth had ever reflected so deeply on human life as Emily. She was persuaded that happiness was a good we often tread under our feet, while we look for it in the clouds;—that natural affections, early cherished, and innocently indulged, bring with them natural duties, and busy pursuits, which guard the heart from a coldness and languor, that, if it does not produce vice, engenders discontent—the worm that never dies;—the voluptuary cannot long find pleasure unless he restricts his appetites;—the man of reason must bound his wishes to obtain that chaste felicity which alone can be lasting. Thus did Emily think—thus did she live—the happiest of the happy.*

It seemed as if heaven, to compensate for the beauty it had taken from her, gave Emily a superior power of bestowing it.—Her little Edward was soon so strikingly handsome that she pronounced him the very image of his father; while that fond father saw in his darling boy the most marked resemblance of his own mother, the beautiful Duchess of Aberdeen.

The pleasure-bark was now built, and gaily ornamented. With her child, Beatrice, the Marquis, and Crosby, Emily spent a great part of her time on the sea, of which she grew very fond. Her husband soon found that it is only to the indolent of body, and listless of mind, life stagnates.—When the affections have full play in the heart, and generous sensibilities call us frequently out of ourselves, to assist others, while the general duties of existence make incidental claims on our time, the year rounds almost before we know it—in such happiness has each day escaped us. Another lovely boy came, to record the progress of time. The fond parents baptized him Vincent; and while his hair, fair, and playful as Emily's own, curled over his rosy cheeks, his mother, with soft and voluntary error, would sighing press him to her bosom, and call him Emily; in dear remembrance of the sister he resembled.

Not thus, alas! did Sir Edward Arden's years pass on. Obliged to leave Italy without being able to trace the retreat of his nephew, a hope had sprung up in his heart, that the Marquis had only outtravelled him, and he should find the unfortunate beloved young man in London.—When, on the contrary, he was told that the Duke had never heard more of him than the letter he had transmitted to Rome, a deep though silent remorse seized on Sir Edward that made society insupportable.—The guilty are often oppressed with the sense of being haunted by the dead; perhaps the delicate mind hardly feels less, that is haunted by the living.—To know there exists a being to whom you are odious, whom you in a manner annihilate, yet whom your heart demands incessantly, and languishes to soothe, and satisfy, is a refined, and exquisite affliction beyond all complaint—beyond all comfort.

The Duke of Aberdeen, astonished ever at what he called the

strange flights, and lofty fancies of Sir Edward, always composedly looked to his banker for news of his son; and, when year after year passed without a demand for money in his name, coolly concluded he had, in some Italian intrigue, got a stab with a stiletto, and been secretly interred, either to conceal his condition, or because he was not known.—Lady Emily was now his heiress, of whom he became dotingly fond.—The sweet child was not less, though more rationally, endeared to her maternal grandfather; who, to protect her, and form her infant mind, constantly resided at a seat on Windsor Forest. Here, day after day, year after year, did Sir Edward image to himself his nephew appearing in all shapes and forms; still seeking, by boundless love to the early orphan, to win her father to avow himself, if within reach of his own family.—Sometimes he supposed that the Marquis, who had once desired a commission, had, in disgust to his own country, served in a foreign one: yet this he hardly thought possible without his being discovered:—sometimes, that he had sailed for the Indies, and there married:—much oftener, that he was now almost his neighbour, though determined to be ever, to the man who would have murdered him, invisible.—Thus were his days filled up with anxious surmises,—his nights with melancholy personifications; nor had he any probable termination for either but his life.

Crosby was in such habits of intimacy with all the domestics at Bellarney, that the happiness of the young Emily, in being so beloved by both her grandfathers, was well known to her parents.—A third boy being born to them, they now no longer hoped for another daughter. In caressing her sons the tender mother often felt a sigh, and sometimes a tear, follow the silent blessing she morning and evening breathed for her girl; although she was unable to add the kiss that the boys contended for.

It is a happiness in our nature that the common tie of offspring in some respects circumscribes, while in others it dilates, our views. Even well-informed parents, anxious to fulfil their duties, have always much to learn; and sweet is the study that has such a motive. The Marquis missed no more the bustle, or the pleasures of the gay world, but was as busy at five and twenty in acquiring the kind of knowledge which should enable him to lighten the dear delightful task of Emily, in instructing their boys, as if he had reached his grand climacteric.*

The mother had a quicker source of information in her own heart. She had been herself in early youth the victim, in turn, of each turbulent temper connected with her, and always concluded this was because no maternal influence had been used to soften the bolder character of man. To her boys therefore in infancy she supposed herself as important as their father would afterwards become. In her progress through life it had struck her that equanimity of character is rarely attained after the season of childhood is past: but, while the unripened mind, yet feeble and unpoised, is now putting forth, and now drawing in its uncertain powers, as passion, or caprice induces; the wise, and well-governed soul of a mother has a full command over it, through the medium of the affections, ere example can operate; and all the regulated virtues, so important to society, may be implanted, and confirmed with our growth into rational habit, till they rather assume the form of our pleasures than our duties. So, when the tyrant passions press with destructive fury to the heart, they find it firmly guarded by temper, and by conscience; who set limits to their ravages: and thus in the soul of her son, to his last hour, may live endeared the image of the mother, who loves him so wisely, and rules his infancy so well.

Thus to employ the hours that fly so fast, and never can return, was now the first object of Emily's life; and that, in giving this important bias, she might be assured just modes of thinking regulated her own decisions, she began with a deep examination of herself, and a severe consideration of all she meant to inculcate. Justly is it said, that,

"——but to wish more virtue, is to gain."*

Emily's own nature, at once refined and elevated by the softening sense of her duties, blending with the matron dignity of her mind, formed, even in youth, so rare a character, as rendered her to her husband the object of a love so devoted, tender, and true, that to both ever blessed was the day when they withdrew from all other ties; since in no other way could their souls have ripened to such corrected knowledge, such simplicity of manners, such hallowed endearment.

As the three lovely boys grew (for Emily, after an interval of four years, gave up the hope of ever being blest with another daughter), the tender mother saw she had indeed judged rightly in thinking herself the best tutor of their early days. Edward, the elder, had, with strong intellect, enchanting beauty, and grace, but impetuous passions, and that intuitive pride which marked the Arden family.

When his mother had fully impressed Edward with reverence for her understanding, and a due feeling of her boundless tenderness, she would, by occasionally yielding to him, with an air of coldness and compassion, make him painfully sensible of his own childish weakness, and violence of temper,—thus checking the gratification he would have found in indulging his passions, by making him know he was too unimportant to act on those of any one around him,—the desire of recovering his usual influence taught him to subdue his temper. Vincent and Alleyne, though there was only a year between any of their ages, had, neither in mind nor body, a proportion of vigour like their elder brother. With exquisite flexibility, and a cherub sweetness, these little charmers would climb the knees of either parent, and press their rosy lips on the ready cheek, whenever they had erred; while the melting heart, so addressed, sanctified, by a silent blessing, the little fault, thus touchingly atoned.

Whole hours would these two little creatures stand at their mother's side, each claiming, as his own, the white hand nearest to him; and fixing on her, with sweet and silent seriousness, their beautiful eyes, imbibe her admonitions to love and respect their elder brother, as the immediate representative of his father, and, even in infancy, their protector. Edward, to deserve this pre-eminence, became in turn the organ of her will: often was he obliged to yield to his brothers the indulgence he most desired, and practise the hardest, therefore the first of human virtues, self-denial. By the magic of mind, the Marquis saw, with dear delight, the purest harmony, thus breathed early into the tenacious bosoms of mere babes, and owned his Emily wanted not yet his assistance. To give strength and freedom to their limbs, a thousand sports were invented by Crosby, whose employment it became at those hours to guide and guard them.

Resting on the arm of her lord, the happy Emily often stood to contemplate, in their plays, the graceful children; who owed to a voluntary seclusion, advantages, which high rank, and unlimited fortune, far from giving, would infallibly have robbed them of; since a thousand real or imaginary claims on the time of the parents, must then have driven out of their presence the darlings, in whose improvement they were most interested, to whose failings they were most sensible.

When reflecting minds once seek in their children an exercise of their powers, it is astonishing to how great a degree those powers can be engrossed by them: and oh! how sweet is the hallowed approbation of themselves, parents so employed must ever feel! To become the organ through which the divinity speaks wisdom and virtue to those little beings, who would otherwise owe to us only that coarse and common existence, which is almost as often a curse as a blessing, is indeed, an employment worthy man; and the only one calculated to fill his whole heart: for all his other pursuits have no positive end, however great his attainments.

The three boys had just arrived at the turbulent ages of eight, seven, and six years, when an unexpected blessing was added to the family, in an infant daughter.—She became another happy means of impressing Emily's lessons to her boys; and they soon vied with each other in tenderness to the little stranger.

On rising in the morning, it was the custom of Emily to fly to her chamber window, where a telescope had been fixed, through which she could not only discern her sons in the care of Crosby, playing in his ground, but their individual employments. In his cabin, Beatrice always superintended the breakfast they earned and relished, by activity. Pleasant to the eyes of a fond mother, ever was the column of smoke that ascended from the happy cot.—One morning, the Marquis having rested very ill, Emily forbore to steal from his side till a much later hour than common, lest she should break his slumbers: as usual, she immediately resorted to the telescope. The sun was high, and the column of smoke that announced the children's first meal, had now subsided.—The landscape, freshened by a shower that spangled the leaves of the trees, revived the soul through the eyes. The tide was full in the river, and the two younger boys were poised at each end of a plank, in Crosby's yard, to which the elder now and then gave motion, and at intervals, threw himself into an attitude of grace Praxiteles* might have borrowed. Beatrice, with the infant Mira in her arms, stood carefully by to guard them. Touched by this sweet assemblage of interesting objects, Emily stole to the bed-side of her husband, to share it with him by description: but he was still asleep, and she indulged, in silence, the soft and affectionate emotion.—Again she returned to gaze through the telescope, when an object, unseen before, astonished her faculties—arrested her attention—"Can it be?"—"yes!"—it was a small vessel moored in the creek of the castle, where none but those of the family ever had harbour.—Its gay streamers seemed all hoisted, as in joy, and playfully dipt in the full tide.—To the entranced Emily it appeared to be the very one that bore her from Scotland, home again, when she had been so cruelly overlooked by the Marquis.— Time stood still while imagination acted; and hardly could sight satisfy her that she was in the room with her beloved, now a tried and faithful husband; or that the graceful creatures she beheld employed in chasing each other on the sands, were all his, no less than her own—the sacred treasures of their blended existence.—Self, however, almost instantaneously gave way to a new, a complicated feeling.—That vessel could no more bring home Emily Arden.—Ah! whom then had it brought?—Perhaps her daughter.—Sweet was the revulsion of soul that followed this idea.—Panting, speechless, she tottered to the bed, and waked the Marquis by the tears and kisses with which she covered his hand.—He felt something extraordinary must have happened.—She pointed to the window, and sinking on her knees, prayed heaven to bless with happiness the surprise of the moment.—The Marquis, in turn, remained in deep silence at the telescope.—The sashes thrown up in almost every room of the castle,—the sailors busily employed in landing baggage,—the air of hurry in the country people, bespoke surprise and pleasure.—In a moment he saw, though he could not stop, Crosby, who leaped into the ferry-boat with his youngest son in his arms; while the two elder joyfully sprang after him: and Beatrice could hardly still the cries of the little Mira, who wanted to be of the party.—A strange impulsive conviction that their little ones were thus unconsciously rushing into the presence of the only persons to whom they themselves could be dear, gave a suffocating throb to the hearts of both parents, that made them fall into each other's arms, as though their all were for ever snatched from them.—The arrival of Beatrice ended their doubt—the vessel in sight, had indeed, on a sudden, and without any notice, brought over the little Lady of Bellarney, with both her grandfathers. All the tenants were flocking to see them; and the whole neighbourhood, she added, was in a joyful confusion.

But who could be in such a confusion as the pair to whom Beatrice never turned her eyes?—Taken thus by surprise, the Marquis and Emily had no longer recollection enough to consider the present, much less to ponder on the past, or regulate the future.—It was their utmost effort to endure the mysterious throbs of nature, now so powerfully drawn back to those, to whom they owed their being, and now so fondly impelled towards those to whom they had given it!—Oh! moments of rare and exquisite enjoyment—when reason becomes almost visionary, sensation almost sublimed!

Neither father nor mother could have told how the interesting interval passed ere the ferryman re-landed their precious boys; who, far outstripping Crosby, flew panting into the arms of Emily.—As soon as they had regained breath, all with one voice exclaimed, that they had seen the little Lady of Bellarney, and she was *so* good, and *so* pretty—and she had given them these,—shewing in their hats, roses of pink and white ribbon, in honour of the May-day. The parents, all eye, as they had been before all ear, now gazed on their own living roses, these garlands so sweetly embellished; when Edward, well recollecting that it was his duty to shew his mother's lessons had not been lost on him, plucked the knot from his hat, and for a kiss gave it to Mira.—Emily, more than recompensed the dear self denying boy, in the embrace she bestowed on him.—The Marquis at length found voice to ask faintly, "if they saw no one—no creature else."—"Oh! yes," they cried, "they saw a great Duke so portly—but very good-natured notwithstanding; and there was a pale, thin, grave old gentleman, who laid his hand on Edward's head, and bade them come, and their parents with them, to Lady Emily's feast tomorrow."

Was ever pleasure like the pleasure with which Emily and her lord recognised, in the innocent detail of their children, each a parent, and felt that they themselves had thus, by representation, stood once more in the presence of those who thought them long since inhabitants of another world?—The boys, who had vainly waited to know whether they were to accept the kind old gentleman's invitation, now impatiently cried out, "and shall we not go to the feast, mamma, and see the heiress?"—"Yes, my precious children," sighed

Emily, folding them to her heart, with a smile of significant tenderness to their father, "you shall see the heiress—and go to the castle to-morrow."

At Bellarney all was rejoicing, hurry, and delight, while those for whom the feast should have been preparing, silent, agitated, and thoughtful, remained shut up at home.—The Marquis, still fixed to have, in this instance, no will but Emily's, sought through her ingenuous eyes to explore the meaning of her soul.—It had always been her intention to absent herself, with her whole family, on the first intimation of the two fathers coming to Bellarney; but thus taken unawares, she found that plan more likely to excite suspicion, than remaining on the spot. Her sons, the Duke, and Sir Edward, had already seen, nor was it possible, little creatures so gifted by nature, so polished by care, should escape a strict observation. And then her Emily—her dear first-born, the child of many sorrows—the lovely memorial of a thousand, thousand, affecting remembrances—could her mother fly her?—Ah no! the heart that gave her being, made such a powerful claim in the bosom of Emily, that even the fear of Sir Edward gave way to the wish of once more embracing her daughter.

Thoughts like these made rest that night almost unknown to Emily, and her lord. A slumber in the morning was necessary to enable them to undergo the probable agitations of the day. Again was the sun high when Emily threw up her chamber window, and looked through the telescope.

What a prospect awaited her there!—Crosby had, in honour of the heiress, cleared out the little pleasure-bark of his master, and gaily decked it with all its streamers: he was putting it from shore when Emily looked: while holding the rudder, or rather leaning on it with infantine majesty, stood her young Edward. Above among the shrouds playfully hung the two agile Cupids, his little brothers. On the deck sat Lady Emily, unpacking a little basket of fruit, to hand to the children:—while, oh! yet more impressive, by her were two gentlemen, in mute contemplation of the lovely sea-boys.—In that small space, and the room she stood in, was comprehended, to Emily's eyes, the whole world.—Sir Edward, she saw, though time had a little bent him, still preserved the grace of his fine person; and the "pale cast of thought"* in his cheeks, took not even yet from the fire and intelligence of his black eyes; which, eagerly scanning the unknown charmers, every moment turned to consult those of the Duke.—That nobleman was not so unchanged;—coarse and worldly in his ideas, a voluptuary in all his pleasures, he was grown older than his years;—his face appeared swoln, and red;—his figure corpulent, and gouty.

Again did Emily awaken her lord—but to how great a trial!—In the glow, as he yet was, of youth, and ever alive to the most pungent feelings—from a dead sleep he rushed into a rapid torrent of tumultuous emotions.—Emily, in whom maternal fear was the most powerful of impulses, in a moment implored him to let her again look if the young ones had been taken from their hazardous situation in the shrouds; and her husband resigned to her the telescope: the cherubs were still swaying about, regardless of Crosby; and Emily forgot even her father; till, having seen them leap safely into the arms of their guardian, she eagerly turned towards the Marquis—but he was no longer by her side:—the assemblage of affecting objects, that had so suddenly greeted his eyes, had been too trying to his heart; and he had plunged into the thick woods that spread so beautifully above the beach. He remained some hours there, striving to master his highly-wrought sensibility, and unconscious of that lapse of time, which cruelly distressed his wife.—Alas! he was alike unconscious that the fever of his brain was passing into his blood. When he returned, his wild and heavy eyes, inflamed cheeks, frequent shiverings, and continual thirst, at once announced malady; and Emily soon sadly convinced herself that his pulse was beating even faster than his heart: this he considered as the effect of agitation merely; but she thought otherwise, and she was right: the fever in a few hours rose to an almost desperate height, and the doctor sent for, ordered every process that could reduce it; strictly enjoining that the chamber of the patient should be kept quiet, and his mind entirely calm:—the first Emily could accomplish by shutting out every creature save herself; but how, how could she compose the mind, when in that the malady originated? On the contrary, the Marquis soon became delirious—fancifully imagined now her father by him, now his own; and sometimes imploring from both a blessing on himself, and sometimes in the most moving manner bestowing one on his children, he would enjoin Emily to shut them all from that moment out, and allow him to expire in peace in her arms.

A thousand times did the agonized wife meditate sending for both their fathers, in the hope of giving even a temporary relief to the mind of the Marquis: but yet, the miserable state she found herself in, and the dangerous one she witnessed, made it an effort almost beyond human strength to venture the important disclosure.—Nay, might she not by mistaken tenderness surround the bed of her husband with those whose importunate affection might aggravate the disease, and accelerate his death?—The injunctions of the physician were at each visit repeated; and silence, with peace, the only chance, he insisted, that she had for saving her beloved.

Shut up in a sick chamber, watching with unclosed eyes every painful breath the Marquis drew, did Emily pass the days when all the country assembled to the festivities at Bellarney.

Crosby, with Beatrice, attired in their best, conducted, according to Sir Edward's invitation, the three sweet boys to the castle; who, little innocents, were yet too young to share their mother's tears, or judge of her cause for them. Emily had, alas! no longer leisure to think of either parents, or children. Her husband occupied her wholly.

Sir Edward Arden had with much reluctance resolved to visit Bellarney, on the letters of the steward having alarmed him, and the Duke, with the idea that the heirs at law were agitating, as a question, their grand-daughter's right to possession.—The sight of a place where he once knew perfect felicity with Lady Emily, could not but reduce the spirits of Sir Edward; and the more immediate impression of her lovely child, who still seemed to embellish the scene, from which he thought her for ever vanished, would have wholly dejected him, but for a vague and exquisite pleasure he suddenly felt on seeing the three little strangers; in the elder of whom he could not be persuaded that he did not trace a strong likeness to the Duchess of Aberdeen, though the Duke was not struck with it.—He became impatient to see their parents, and naturally expected them at the feast.

When the children, however, appeared, Sir Edward forgot he had wished to see their parents, in the mysterious delight which melted his nature, and almost brought back the long-forgotten flows of youthful sensibility.—He enquired their degree—admired Edward with a fond distinction—spoke of offering to take, educate, and promote him, and wondered why Crosby shook his head, as implying that his father would not give him so great an advantage; since he seemed to be of a rank to make the offer flattering.

In the little plays of the younger party, invented to amuse Lady Emily, she was commanded to sing, and instantly complied: commanding in her turn Edward to do the same.—The child paused a moment—said he did not know a song—but having whispered with his brothers, they began a little Italian trio their fond mother had amused herself with teaching them during the summer days they sailed about with her: when their father, softly touching his flute, would fill up each little pause, and regulate the time.—It was only a trifle, but one that spoke refinement,—feeling,—fancy.—Sir Edward started—he thought his sense deceived him—to hear three wild lovely Irish children breathe, in the nicest harmony, a delicate piece of music, and in another language—it was absolute enchantment!—He called them to him, and eagerly demanded who had taught them? They all, with one voice, cried, "their mother!"—"Their mother!— and who could that mother be, so exquisitely accomplished?"— Again he thoughtfully traced the lineaments of Edward, who, with the intuitive skill of childhood, found himself a favourite, and adhered to his grandfather's side.—Again Sir Edward pondered on the possibility of his being the son of the Marquis, although, alas! not of his daughter.—Yet to suppose his nephew should fix on Ireland to conceal himself in, and, above all, the neighbourhood of Bellarney, seemed too extravagant an idea to be admitted. The Duke thought it so, and dismissed it with a cool air, as one of the many romantic visions he had often seen poor Sir Edward troubled with.

The three boys early in the evening took leave of the party at Bellarney—but never during the whole night did they quit Sir Edward:—every look, every motion, recurred to his memory; and, above all, their sweet little musical performance. He longed for the morning, that he again might see them; and the little Lady Emily, not less fond of her new companions, caught her grandfather going to take his early walk, and conjured him "to bring home the little Irwins."

On descending the hill, Sir Edward perceived those he sought catching the pure breath of the morning on the sands: he then turned towards the poor home their parents inhabited. Nothing could be more improbable than that the only son of the Duke of Aberdeen should have chosen such a dwelling, or become for subsistence a boat-builder.—Yet he determined to see its master, and end all his doubts.—At the ferry the three delighted cherubs awaited him; and, while Edward readily agreed to be his guide to their house, the two younger ones playfully ran races before them.

In the distressed state of Emily's mind, she could only charge Crosby to take the tenderest care of the children, without permitting them to approach the spot where their little innocent sports might disturb their suffering father. On suddenly hearing their voices close to the door, she felt offended at Crosby's neglect, and abruptly appeared there.—To her astonishment, surrounded with her children, she fixed her eyes on her own father. Unable to speak, she lifted a finger to quiet the two younger boys, and waving to the eldest to come to her, bent her trembling knees with reverence to Sir Edward, and, hastily tottering into the parlour, fainted away.

Sir Edward, seeing in the mother of these interesting children, a person quite a stranger to him, and, as her retiring curtsy shewed, willing still to be so, had in politeness no choice but to return. Crosby met him by the ferry, and informed him of the sudden and desperate attack of Mr. Irwin, which had thrown his wife into despair, and the whole neighbourhood into a consternation.—Sir Edward pardoned to an unhappy wife a want of civil regard, and bade Crosby hasten to offer her in his name any accommodation Bellarney could afford the sufferer; and to entreat that he might have charge there of the sweet boys till her domestic anxieties should be lessened.

The agitated Emily had hardly recovered breath when Crosby arrived; and fearing another abrupt visit from her father might render her as much an invalid as the Marquis, she acceded to the invitation: only desiring Crosby would bring her children to her once a day.

A thousand dismal thoughts filled up the tedious nights Emily watched by the bed of the Marquis.—It seemed to her as if again the presence of her father were to annihilate her happiness: and bitterly did she regret the not having quitted the country with her young ones, the moment she saw the vessel moored at Bellarney.— The morning after she had thus parted with her children, she heard their little voices with that of Crosby, and flying down to bless them, clasped suddenly in her arms her Emily—her own dear little Emily—

who had asked to join the boys in the walk.—A gush of tears sweetly maternal fell from the cheeks of the elder Emily on those of the other; who, fair as herself at the same age, soft and endearing, wept readily with her.—The mother now withdrew her arms, but it was only in fond admiration to survey the well-known features, formed and improved by growth;—to mark the turn of her graceful person;—to delight in her gentle manners—her air of sensibility.—The boys, so very dear, suddenly found themselves almost overlooked by their mother; but each caught a hand, their sister, smiling through her tears, readily held out to them.—Edward told his mother, "Lady Emily *would* come to see her, and offer to nurse papa; for she could do it very well, as she often nursed her grandfather."—"And does thy tender heart act thus early, my little angel?" cried the fond mother, again caressing her.—The young Emily kissed in soft silence the arms that enfolded her, and wondered why the pressure was so sweetly endearing,—so unlike Connor's.

In the precarious state of the Marquis, Emily dared not allow him the exquisite indulgence of seeing his daughter; who, something surprized, though highly delighted, with her mother's tearful fondness, asked why she wept. Emily, in a faltering voice, uttered, though mysteriously, the simple truth, in saying the lovely stranger recalled to her mind a precious daughter she had long lost.—"And it is so long since I lost my mamma," returned the engaging child, "that I have quite forgot her; but I should like to be called your Emily, and have all these dear little boys for brothers."—The full heart of the mother allowed not one syllable in answer.

Lady Emily returned home, eager to tell the endearing reception she had met with; and Sir Edward Arden, actuated by an unconquerable curiosity, or rather an unconscious interest in the fate of the Irwin family, now interrogated the steward concerning them. He soon learned that they had long excited the same feeling in all around them; but, either from choice, or chance, were no more known, than on the first day of their arrival: that they certainly came from abroad, as they brought only a foreign maid-servant with them, who did not speak English;—that they never mentioned any relations, nor were known, in many years, to write or to receive a letter. The employment of boat-building, the steward added, Mr. Irwin pursued for his own amusement, the support of Crosby and the accommodation of the poor fishermen, to whom on all other occasions he and his wife were beneficent beyond what their own bounded expences would make probable;—that when they wanted money, Mr. Irwin drew for it, through the medium of himself; and he had made enquiry of the Dublin banker, but found he had no other knowledge of the strangers than that his trust gave him.

A pair so nobly-minded and exquisitely accomplished, standing thus alone in creation, must, Sir Edward thought, have some extraordinary reason for their conduct.—The time of their settling in Ireland, was very nearly that, when the Marquis disappeared. To behold Mr. Irwin, though but for a moment, would have ended all his suspence—yet how was he to press a visit, when he had seen the mistress of the house, without her thinking it necessary to invite him in?—He tried to busy himself in the affairs of the estate; but only found rest from the trouble of his own soul, when surrounded by all the dear, the playful children, who now brought him better accounts of their suffering father.

Sir Edward, however, was not the only surprized or inquisitive person in the family.—Mrs. Connor, infirm and old, had lost her hearing; but her sight was still good, and it told her that the babe, Beatrice brought in her arms one morning to the castle, was the very image of Lady Emily, when her lovely mother was carried, at Rome, into the chaise by the Marquis. After puzzling herself for a day or two, and then every one else, with enquiries, that brought no conviction, poor Connor resolved to encounter Sir Edward's wrath, and discharge her conscience of the treasured secret.

How great was Sir Edward's astonishment—how extreme his indignation at the long silence, the late confession of the poor woman! His Emily alive!—with the Marquis!—both hating—both shunning him alike—What a perpetual source of bitterness and sorrow! Far from supposing the doting old woman right in turning his eyes to this secluded pair, he became assured by this information, that he had no interest in them: for the wife he had seen, and she was not his Emily.—Thus to have approached a felicity that melted in his grasp, aggravated all his past griefs, and disappointments, to poor Sir Edward Arden.

Connor, as decided in her opinions as Sir Edward himself, refused to credit any eyes but her own; and having astonished the

Duke with her story, obtained his leave to go immediately and "see these Irwins."

Emily had waited impatiently, till the Marquis was enough recovered to be removed to a camp-bed she had prepared for him in the study, as the largest and coolest room in the house. She had hardly seen him in this comfortable situation, when a most unusual sound, the approach of a carriage, caused her to hasten into the parlour, and shut the intermediate door. Emily perceived it to be the coach of the Duke. Perturbed as her mind must be, she could not forbear smiling, to find it had brought poor Connor only; who had been growing so great a person while she had herself been shrinking to a little one.

Connor immediately perceived she greeted a stranger; and Emily, at the same moment, discovered that she was not in danger of being known by her voice; which she had always feared would betray her. Mrs. Connor was not too condescending, and seemed to doubt whether she should, by sitting down, authorize this obscure person's doing so in her company. Cold thanks for her civilities to Lady Emily, with an invitation to Bellarney, terminated the visit: and Connor ascended her splendid conveyance in the full conviction, that it was not here the fugitives would be found; nor did she fail to regret risquing the dislocation of her bones, by the execrable road she had rumbled through to no purpose.

And here would have ended all enquiry, had only the Duke of Aberdeen and Mrs. Connor been concerned; but here it did not end with Sir Edward, in whose soul every powerful feeling was again afloat.—Hope, pleasure, passion, throbbed there with all the energy of youth. Oh! might he be blest enough to find the two so long loved, so long lamented—to find them surrounded with such a beautiful race of children—at once to multiply treasures so unhoped—it was a happiness too exquisite to trust his imagination with—a thousand times he execrated the fidelity of the old crone, and the connivance of Dr. Dalton. Had a word been dropt by either, he could instantly have followed, and should certainly have traced the beloved fugitives, who would not then have known long years of comparative poverty; nor he of unremitting remorse. In going over the past, it suddenly glanced across his mind, that his Emily was said to die of the small-pox; and the mother of these interesting boys was certainly much marked by it. It had then been his daughter he had greeted—she shrunk from him!—Ah! why, if she knew him not?—The sweet persuasion played before his eyes, in all the forms eager affection could give it, till the morning, when Connor annihilated that fond belief, by assuring him, that the story of the small-pox had been wholly a fiction, as her lady left Rome with the Marquis, in all the bloom of youth and beauty; and that Mrs. Irwin was not in the least like her, "for she had seen that person with her own eyes."

Again was Sir Edward in despair; yet he wandered down to the ferry; and crossing the river, threw himself on a rustic seat near it, to meditate on the least impolite means of gaining a view of the sick Mr. Irwin.—Beatrice saw him from her cabin, and approached with Mira in her arms, to invite him to repose there as a safer place. Her foreign accent struck him—he availed himself of the lucky chance that had brought her in his way, and spoke to her in Italian. Her native language she delighted in, and he soon brought her to inform him where she had first met with Mr. and Mrs. Irwin,—"Gracious! where should she meet with them, but at her father's?"—"But where might her father be?"—"Did he speak Italian, and not know her father's, at the foot of the Alps?" She described, and Sir Edward remembered well, the inn—presumptions grew strong—hope again throbbed in wild pulsations at his heart.—As if to amuse the child he had taken in his arms, he drew from his bosom a miniature of his daughter, set in the back of her mother's picture.—Beatrice looked sharply at it, and crossing herself, cried—"Santa Maria! kiss it, Miss—it is your own mamma's."—Sir Edward trembled, and could hardly avoid dropping the babe—"Yet, no it is not your mamma's either—but it was hers before that cruel small-pox so altered her.—Ah! when she stept out of the chaise at our door, she was as like it as two peas—but we must think it a mercy she ever left the house alive."

And now what a torrent of emotions convulsed the bosom of Sir Edward!—It was more than happiness obtained—it was happiness recovered—it was a fullness of satisfaction, that made him exult in so resigning the life he felt in a manner fleeting from him.—Beatrice ran for water, and offered him salts—he feebly and silently arose—pressed her hand, and tottered towards the retreat, where he was, as by resurrection, to find his long-lost son and daughter.

The weather was still so warm, and the Marquis so sensible of the additional oppression, that not only the door of the room, but that of the house, had been set open, to circulate the air. The poor Emily, worn out with intense fatigue and fearful tenderness, having disposed all things for the Marquis to take a little repose, sat down in the adjoining parlour, and resting her head on her hand, fell into a languid slumber herself. There was a desolation in her appearance, an utter disregard of self, that, when the effect of true sensibility, affects the heart beyond the most delicate attire.—Her fair hair, which still remained in all its beauty, had almost escaped from the cap that was meant to confine it.—Her wrapping-gown shewed the unaltered grace of her form; and on her left arm, which hung down as she slept, were three small moles, that would as fully have identified her to her father, as all the charms she had lost.

Fancy carried the weary sleeper to Frescati—dreaming she was in the cool shade by the fountain, she suddenly found the marble Faun was breathing forth strains as sweet as those of the Marquis.— While listening with entranced delight, by a strange extravagance, common to the disturbed slumbers of the unhappy, she thought the statue leaped from its pedestal, and came towards her—she faintly struggled—half groaned—opened her eyes, and—fixed them on her father.—Yes! it was Sir Edward himself, hanging passionately over her—his wan countenance expressing the tenderest emotions, and a full conviction of the truth. She clasped her hands piteously, but had neither power nor time to utter one word, for her cry had awakened the Marquis, who called to her in a voice of agony, to come and let him see her.—That voice, that well-known voice, more dear than any thing on earth to Sir Edward, seemed to arise from the grave— he rushed impetuously to the inner room—made but one step from the door to the bed, and falling on it, faltered out—"Now let me die, since I have seen thy face, because thou art yet alive."

Already Emily felt all the softness of a daughter, blending with that of a wife;—already was she at the feet of Sir Edward;—and conjuring the Marquis to support himself under a trial, to which he was so unequal, she took a hand of each,—uniting them with kisses and tears, she pressed them to her bosom. Oh! what an embrace was that which her father gave her!—it seemed to inter for ever all remembrance of suffering and of sorrow.—To the Marquis he was even more tender, for to him he struggled to subdue his feelings—never had he seen that much loved face since he left it convulsed in death in the convent garden. Still was it pale, but no longer lived there the traces of misery. Affection, gratitude, a thousand complicated softnesses wandered through each feature. Sir Edward sunk on his knees by the side of his nephew, and the tears that he then dropt, sealed in heaven, and on earth, his pardon.

These are the pure and elevating points of being, when even the passions, sublimed by virtue, seem to partake of immortality. Precious white-winged moments! which, soaring out of the dark wreck of human existence, still hover over, and illumine it with celestial glory, even as it sinks into eternity!

A silence so exquisite followed the transport, that it seemed as if the happy three lived by looking:—it was interrupted by the lovely head of Edward shewing itself at the door. On seeing his father awake, he crept softly to the bed-side, and kneeling, kissed his hand. Sir Edward fondly pressed the tender boy to his bosom, energetically repeating "my own!"—The astonished child turned to his mother, who bade him honour, in the kind stranger, her father. Crosby, who was within hearing, caught the news, and was ordered to convey it to the Duke. Fleeter than the wind, with all the train of lovely boys, ran Crosby towards Bellarney: but, unable to controul his own transport, he lost the merit, perhaps the reward, of first imparting the discovery. The ferrymen, the fishermen, the gardeners, the grooms, all had caught the news from the eager messenger; and twenty voices at once proclaimed to the Duke, that Sir Edward had found the Marquis of Lenox, and the Lady of Bellarney!

Crosby, again as rapidly on the wing to return, meeting Lady Emily, caught her up, and, still accompanied by her brothers, bore her in triumph over the ferry.—At sight of his daughter, the Marquis indeed revived:—a thousand, thousand times, he kissed, and blest her.—To see her encircled in the arms of her mother, appeared to the father the summit of human felicity.—The tender little Emily fondly clasped by turns her lovely brothers; while their rosy cheeks were doubly suffused, thus to be caressed by the heiress, whom they had never dared to treat with the least familiarity.

Hardly crediting the extravagant tale, came more slowly the Duke of Aberdeen; and, not without some displeasure, greeted his son:—examined with indelicate attention the altered face of

Emily:—acknowledged the race of lovely children; and immediately assured Lady Emily, that, should there be twenty more, he would never love one as well as he did her.—He then with contempt surveyed the humble home love alone could have embellished, and remained astonished at its having been the choice of his only son, and Sir Edward Arden's only daughter, to pass the best years of their lives in this dismal dwelling, when the sumptuous one of Bellarney was quite unoccupied.

To the blind of body, human art can sometimes give perception: to the blind of soul, it never yet was given. The Marquis and Emily therefore attempted not to explain the motives of their conduct to the Duke; and it is possible Sir Edward Arden would not have been better understood, had he told that nobleman why he requested the Marquis to remove neither bush, nor stone, table, nor chair, from this blessed little home, when the lovers should quit it for Bellarney: since "where he had first found the happiness he had vainly sought for many years, he was determined henceforward to live, and to die; chastening thus in his own soul its pride, and its passions, and preparing it for the better world he must be now fast approaching: till, on that very bed where now lay his beloved son, and in the dear arms of those who encircled it, he should breathe his last."—The Duke shrugged his shoulders at this flight:—that two young people might fancy an Arcadia* of their own making, he thought among the strange possibilities of life; but for Sir Edward, in his old age, to turn a grey-headed shepherd, and solicit the reversion of this delectable possession, appeared to him curious enough!—too much so for discussion.

Bold in character, impetuous of soul, the Irish find pleasure always transport, anger fury. The romantic story of the Lady of Bellarney, interred alive on her own estate, circulated rapidly, and caused a commotion of joy in the country. All ranks and descriptions of people waited impatiently to hail the resurrection of the married lovers: and as only Crosby and his wife knew even the outline of their history, they, and their cabin, soon grew into great notoriety.—Feasts and visitations occupied the Duke, and the dwellers at the castle, whither all the world resorted.—To Sir Edward, and his daughter, that world was comprised in the sick chamber of the Marquis: which the father would no more leave than the wife. In the fond jealousy of an equal affection, they contended who should most anxiously attend on him; yet sweet was it to Sir Edward to see that it was Emily his nephew would ever have—Emily he always looked for, with eyes full of tenderness, and gratitude.—When sighing over the ruin of her beauty himself, how could a fond father fail to adore the husband who found it all in her heart?

It was at length safe to remove the Marquis, and at Bellarney he now took possession, with the rightful Lady. The next Sunday, service was ordered in the chapel of that mansion; where the lovers prepared to offer up their grateful effusions for the protection of that God, who thus, the storms of life overblown, assembled themselves, their parents, and their children, in their happy home.—Had the little chapel been a cathedral, it would have been filled.—Emily, simply attired, with her fair locks, so long hid, once more flowing over her graceful shoulders, was led to the seat she had always occupied by the Duke of Aberdeen. The Marquis, yet feeble and interesting, followed; holding, in his right hand, his elder daughter; and, in the other, his son Edward. His uncle, in speechless exultation, came behind, with the younger boys; who gazed, now on him, and now on each other, as if they knew not yet how they had gained this sudden grandeur. Beatrice, though a Catholic, shared, with the faithful Crosby, the happiness of that day; and truer prayers never ascended to heaven than those offered up in the chapel of Bellarney.

The return of Emily with her lord, and her children, terminated the enquiries of the heirs to her estates; and she resided there a while to make arrangements on her own domains, ere she could accompany the Duke to visit his.—The parade of being presented at court, and all the vain shews of life, Emily never delighted in, and now retired from; as wholly incompatible with the great duties of a wife, and a mother. Yet she already found how difficult it would be, in re-assuming her rank, to act up to her own sense of right, in watching over her young ones; and once to withdraw from that important employ, was to make vain the labour of her life.—She felt nevertheless that the Duke had a right to claim his son for a while, and it was a point of respect, for her to follow with her family.

In Scotland new festivities succeeded; and, to the happy children, life seemed all holiday.—Their parents found it not wholly so. The Duke had discussed with the Marquis his strange indifference to the business, and the honours of the great world: urging so strongly his appearance in London that he knew not how to refuse.—Emily would not influence him, but decided for herself; and entreated she might stay with her family.

If it was a trial to the Marquis to quit for a short time the dear domestic circle in which for ten years he had wholly moved, what must it be to his wife to see him depart?—He who must ever be, to her, happiness or misery, was now associated with a libertine father, and going to be impressed with a high sense of his own advantages: even if his heart should stand the test, and remain wholly uncorrupted, and unalienated, how could she be sure that ambition would not seize on him? She had learnt to dread those dangerous enchantments,—power, and politics.—Yet must she boldly venture all: for never can we call the blessing our own, we are in daily fear of losing.—One only good did she solicit her lord to add to that he would bring back in himself:—a wise and well-governed mind, to take from them both the charge of their sons' actual tuition.—Crosby was still to continue the inventor, the guardian, of their sports.

It is much more difficult to change our tastes than to fix them; and this it is makes right habits of such importance in youth.—Circumstances had early guided the heart of the Marquis of Lenox to true and tender feelings; busy and pleasant duties. Thus the delights he could not share with Emily, and his children, faded before the recollection of those he daily lost in his painful, but necessary, absence from them. Nor was it in the house, or circle, of his father, he could ever become indifferent to the virtuous, or rational happiness his own afforded. An expensive establishment formed of persons who cared not whether the prodigal master lived, or died,—a luxurious table, no faithful, or scientific friends surrounded,—a licentious arrangement with some painted nymph of St James's Street, who came into, and went out of, the house, with the fashion, was not likely to win to the corrupt modes of polite life a man, who saw he could always maintain there his natural consequence, while in his purer conduct, and simpler manners, he must ever rank higher in the scale of society.—The trial was over.—The Duke gladly escaped the observing eye of his son, and Emily found herself again in the arms of the husband she adored; who vowed never more to undergo the penance of living without her, and the dear young ones now contending for the "envied kiss."*

Sir Edward Arden had not been insensible to the danger that might arise to his daughter's happiness from the Duke having full power to act on his son, yet he applauded in his heart the magnanimity of mind, and sacred consciousness of desert, which induced Emily to risque the trial. By remaining with her, and her children, he at once gave her due protection, and the Marquis boundless freedom.—How fully did he share the delight of that re-union, which made the endeared circle his own for life!

And now the Marquis prepared to conduct his whole family to Bellarney, where they purposed chiefly to reside. It was an unexpected gratification to find the Duke meant to be for a time of their party. The fond mother naturally imputed the distinction to his partiality for her Emily, as it was with much reluctance he had resigned her to the Marchioness, who would not allow any other woman to form the mind of her daughter. Had the Marquis considered his father's character, he might have better understood the cause of the compliment: for he alone knew, that the Duke on leaving town had dismissed a worthless extravagant mistress; whose place he secretly meditated to fill with the innocent wife of Crosby.—To the son, Beatrice had only appeared a worthy good girl, devoted to his Emily, and tender of his children—it remained for the father to discover that she had expressive black eyes, a smart figure, and a little Italian coquetry, with which she often contrived to keep Crosby on the fret; though hardly to himself would he own that he was jealous.—From the moment the Duke first saw Beatrice, he had taken this idea into his head; and in consequence made her occasional presents, so suited to her wants, or her wishes, that she had not the prudence strictly to scrutinize his motive for offering them.—The tender billets with which they were accompanied, he always had the address to write in Italian, thus making poor Crosby bear his own sentence, without being able to decipher one word of it.* With this base and selfish intention did the Duke accompany a pure and virtuous pair, rejoicing in the ripening age of their young ones, to whom they had promised a last gala on the day which should make Emily eleven years old.

However happy the return of the day, that memorable one which actually called the child into existence, was too deeply impressed on the mind of the Marchioness not to make her mingle seriousness with endearment, when she gave the blessing, and embrace of the morning.—The gravity, however, was soon forgotten, and the gay innocents engrossed every thought of the happy elders.

In sitting down to dinner, Emily cast her smiling eyes over the table, and saw it encircled with every being in creation that interested her heart.—On her right hand sat the father of the Marquis—on her left, her own: opposite to her, the husband so beloved, and on his right hand Emily, the lady of the day.—The dear boys made their claim; and even Mira was for once allowed a place, while Beatrice entreated to attend on the least of her ladies. During the dessert Sir Edward called on the three boys for their sweet Italian trio; and the pleased Marquis had ordered his flute, to guide their little voices justly, and fill up each pause, when Crosby coming hastily in, spoke in a low voice to the Marchioness:—a deadly paleness came over her—she struggled to speak—could not utter a word, but reaching out her hand, at once silenced the children and summoned their father. No sooner however did his arms enfold her, than with a groan, as if her soul were separating from her body, she sunk into a swoon.—The whole astonished circle environed her in a moment.—The Marquis was too intent on her recovery, to enquire what had caused her fainting: but Sir Edward angrily turned to Crosby, who stood like a culprit though unconscious of a fault, and commanded him to repeat whatever he had said to his lady—"Lord, Sir," cried he, "it could not be what I said that struck my lady for death, as it were. I wish I had let the poor dying creature die outright, rather than see such a frightful consternation on Lady Emily's birth-day.—I only came to humour a sick body the house-keeper took in from pure compassion; just to enquire of my lady if she pleased we should let her have an old coffer, she says is in the belfry—Lord knows she may be light-headed, and I should not wonder if there is no old coffer there at all.—It is not likely a poor vagabond should have any trunk in our house."—A tale so wholly trifling, and uninteresting, engrossed not any ear. The Duke, and Sir Edward, imputed the attack to the powerful scent of a melon that had stood very near Emily. The anxious soul of the Marquis told him she had never so yielded to mere constitutional weakness, and that the groan she gave could have no common cause.—When life returned, Emily indulged a gush of tears so profuse, and so bitter, that all around her remained in dismayed silence.—Her husband, pressing her yet more tenderly in his arms, ventured to draw aside the handkerchief from her eyes; but saw such an expression of agony, and terror, that eagerly he hid her face on his bosom.—As soon as she could muster strength, she arose, and leaning through feebleness, as well as fondness, on the arm of the Marquis, waved from her both their fathers; while, with a sweet maternal grace, she invited towards her, the whole affrighted race of little ones, who gladly flew to clasp her knees, and those of their father.—"Come to me, my precious babes," sighed she, striving to encircle them all—"It is yours early to embark in the sorrows of your parents—Oh! Edward, the hour is come—the fearful heavy hour of renewed persecution—the avenging fiend yet haunts us, and our innocent children. The visitation comes too in the moment of security.—But my mind has now claims upon its fortitude that will enable it to meet my fate.—Feel not thus fearfully my pulse, my father—*that* may fluctuate, but my mind is steady.—Poor Crosby! he knew not what he asked for! I, only I, could tell, that the coffer demanded is the property of Emily Fitzallen; and no human being, save herself, could have known such a trust remained in this house."—"You shall not see her, Emily," cried Sir Edward fiercely:—"Pardon me, my father," meekly returned the Marchioness, "if a greater duty than the one due to you makes me break through that.—Encompassed thus by my children, protected by my husband—sanctioned by our parents, and supported by my God, I feel it becomes not me to falter, and I will know now—even now, the end of all my miseries."—The meek and matron dignity of his daughter silenced, and awed, Sir Edward:—to the Marquis she clung, that no transport of his might interfere with her purpose; and having desired Crosby would guide them all to the stranger, Emily and her lord led the whole family through long galleries, to a remote apartment adjoining the nurseries.

At the electrifying sound of Emily Fitzallen's name, imagination had presented her to the whole group, in the very form in which they last beheld her—gay, glowing, beautiful, imperious, savagely exulting in her power over the unfortunate, and appearing only to torment. The daughter of Sir Edward felt she was now come with the same invincible malignity, to wrest from her, if possible, a title doubly endeared, and hallowed, by its importance to her children. But what a revulsion of soul did the whole family experience, when they suddenly surveyed a miserable object, in whom they were hardly able to trace the vindictive beauty, who had poisoned the promised happiness of their former years. Almost without power to move, ghastly, and livid, as if already in the grave; a surgical and bloody bandage encircling her temples, lay the living spectre of Emily Fitzallen—opening her hollow eyes, upon which seemed to hang the films of death, they wandered, without recollection, over the whole company, who remained silent and horror-struck.

The gentle and generous Marchioness felt all sense of her own sufferings evaporate from her mind, on thus beholding the companion of her childhood, the misery of her youth, the victim of the world!—by some incomprehensible means thus brought back to the roof that first sheltered her, and the circle she had injured, to repent, as it should seem, and die. The expiring wretch, having tried to clear her dim sight, demanded of the servant nursing her, who all these persons were.—"This, infamous woman," cried the Marquis, in a voice almost inarticulate through passion, and pressing the hand of Emily to his heart, "is my wife; and all these little ones our children."—Her deep-sunk eyes glared yet more horribly—she turned appalled from him she had so basely injured, and seemed as though she would, if possible, have ceased to hear.—"Oh! dear mamma," cried the young Emily, who stood nearest to the bed, "pray send for another doctor; I am afraid this poor woman will bleed to death, and you will not let any one die on my birth-day surely."—"You are then another Emily Arden," cried the expiring wretch, abruptly turning to gaze on the tender child, who shrunk from her: "you have her every feature—and would *you* save my life? poor child!—I came here only to disgrace you—but who stands by your side?"—"Her mother," answered the Marchioness firmly, "who, though changed in features, has still a heart ready to forgive the penitent—a hand ready to assist the wretched. A just and powerful God has, by some strange ordination, brought you, at this awful hour, and in this fearful situation, to the very house, nay to the very chamber, where you first knew recollection; to awaken in your own breast, compunction for your sins—in ours, compassion for your sufferings. I bless the power he has given me of forgiving you, as only by that means, could you implore his pardon."—"And can you, even you, breathe thus a blessing on me," groaned the wretch, in a hollow tone, "cut off, as I am, in the moment of a new sin meditated against your little one? for

I knew not you yet existed.—An hour ago, to steal into the grave unknown, as I too surely must unlamented, was all I wished;—for could I hope such angelic goodness was to be found on earth? How I have injured you both, needs not be told—how God has avenged you, I would have you see;" she lifted a gown that was lightly laid over her neck and arms, and shewed the skin, once so exquisitely white and delicate, now frightfully discoloured with bruises, and black with mortification. This, and the bloody bandage on her forehead, marked, too plainly, the premature death that had overtaken her. Emily, sickening, turned to weep in the arms of her husband, who, even yet, could hardly deign a look towards the wretch who had destroyed his early happiness; nor would he have endured to stay, had he not felt his presence a support to his trembling wife.

"I shall not have life, nor perhaps intellect," resumed, after a pause, the dying Miss Fitzallen, "to relate my whole story—nor need I shock the pure beings, who thus deign to speak comfort to my soul, with a repetition of all my errors:—that they have not been as fatal as I supposed, alleviates a little my sufferings:—to the weak, yet bountiful Lady Bellarney, I owe my first fault.—She encouraged me to be vain of my natural advantages: yet every hour told me I must never rank with her grand-daughter. Envy thus became my first sin, and malice soon grew out of it.—I began to over-rate my own understanding, when I found myself able to play on the weaker one of my benefactress, and overbear the meek nature of Miss Arden: till, in the insolence of limited power, I invented a diabolical amusement, in practising on the temper, and undermining the comfort, of the rich heiress others supposed I was born to yield to.—As my reflexion ripened, I became yet more alive to the importance of those external goods I fancied Miss Arden's only advantages over me. While conscious of boundless influence with Lady Bellarney, and assured I was to be her heiress, I suffered not my evil views to go further: but when at her death I found a youth of servility had been lost, I became yet more desperate in my projects—yet more inveterate towards Miss Arden. I knew she had sought her cousin—I knew he had slighted her;—to rob her of this plighted and admired lover, and cross Sir Edward Arden's views, became the first object of my heart. I thus launched into life an unprincipled adventurer; resolved on vengeance, wealth, and rank, if human art, or any sacrifice, could attain them;—to fortify my resolution, I ran over, in my brain, the many of my sex, whom the same boldness had exalted to the highest situation. I traced the steps of Miss Arden,—understood the delicate motive of her disguise, and instantly availed myself of the hint. In the one I assumed, I was not actuated by love for the Marquis.—A handsome Italian friend of his, however, soon won my heart; yet would I marry Sir Edward's nephew, and him only.—My sex was guessed at by all around me, but those two who were most likely to suspect it.— Signor Gheraldi, to satisfy his doubts, ordered some men to attack me, when he was my companion; and without attempting to draw my sword, I fainted away.—My fears, on recovering, for his safety, shewed him he was not only master of my secret, but my heart; and he urged me to quit the Marquis. Finding I was fixed on some project that concerned him, not all my protestations could convince Gheraldi love was not my inducement. At a moment when I had almost resolved to give up the Marquis, fortuitous circumstances made him in my power for ever. Hardly had we pledged the fatal vow, when the news of Sir Edward's sudden return agitated and perplexed me. In a week he had been most welcome.—Hoping he would not yet arrive, I resolved to assume the habit of my sex, and hardly had dressed myself, ere Gheraldi, in a transport of jealousy, rushed in, determined to tear me from the Marquis for ever. My refusal, and the flutter so complicated a situation must cause, confirmed him in his purpose; he solemnly vowed reluctance or delay would cost the lover who induced it, his life: two trusty villains being now in waiting either to escort me and my baggage to the bark, ready to put to sea; or, if the Marquis should cross the threshold while I was deliberating, to strike their stilettos into his heart, and lay him a corpse at my feet.—As the least of two horrible evils, and not at that moment the act of my choice, I yielded to my frantic lover, and embarked for Baia,* where Gheraldi had a beautiful villa. The savage looks of my conductors chilled my blood; but all other fears soon gave way to that of the earthquake. I saw I had, by a strangeness in my fate, owed my life to my jealous lover; nor could hope the Marquis survived the wreck of Messina. Yet, even at that moment, I exulted in the triumph I should have over Sir Edward and his daughter, in the certificate I treasured in my bosom, which I had taken care should be ample and unquestionable. Arrived at the villa, Gheraldi bade me be mistress alike over that and his heart: but alas! I soon found what it was to throw myself wholly into the power of a man I so little knew. I saw him the victim, by turns, of every passion, yet uniformly jealous, revengeful, and implacable: no kindness could soothe, no protestation satisfy him. By a singularity in my fortune, the only man I ever really loved, was the only one I could not persuade of my tenderness.—Even the solitude and secresy Gheraldi kept me in, could not convince him I was wholly his own. He saw lovers and letters in every look; plots and elopements in every gesture. The veriest wretch who ever bathed in tears the chain of matrimony, was not more completely enslaved than that high spirit which had broken all the laws of religion and morality, only to remain free. Every extravagance of every passion, he nevertheless expected me to impute, as he did, to love; and if he deigned to offer this excuse, I was neither permitted to revert to the past, nor to guard against the future. Yet, thus circumstanced, I found I was not forgotten. More than one lover discovered means to offer me liberty; and perhaps only my own fears prevented my escaping the tyrant: but I had not, for some time, raised a cup to my lips without the idea that it might be poisoned; or dropt into a slumber, I did not expect to be roused from by the stab of a dagger; and that my next breath would be my last. In those beautiful eyes, where I had looked away the quiet of my life, I now saw only a mean and sinister expression. My tenderness changed to horror and disgust. To have been discovered in attempting to escape, would have ensured my death; for no human eloquence would have convinced my tyrant, it was his own vile temper that reduced me to the necessity. That temper, however, gave me a sudden release. A fit of passion, at a gaming-table, left the beautiful Gheraldi a dead man, and Count Montalvo hastened to protect and conduct me to Naples. I had many rich presents from my tyrant, his brother did not dispute with me, and I insisted on inhabiting a hired hotel at Villa Reale. To my astonishment, I there learnt that the Marquis of Lenox not only survived the earthquake, but was to be married in great splendour to Miss Arden. The step I took, I will not dwell upon. When I afterwards knew the Marquis in my power, by the interesting situation of his wife, I used that power most basely. But the love of evil is as apt to grow into habit as the love of good; and even when I thought the parents dead, I meditated to disgrace their innocent child.

"From the moment I had reigned, by the weak indulgence of my benefactress, in Bellarney, I had set my heart on possessing it. The many palaces I have dwelt in since, never had the same charm; and making it my object to amass wealth enough for the purchase, I knew I could condition with the heirs at law, ere I supplied them the proofs that might bastardize the grand-daughter of Sir Edward Arden, who, thus circumstanced, must evacuate the estate.

"I will not detail scenes of vice and extravagance, painful to remembrance; yet, keeping my object ever in view, I had secured wealth enough to hint a year ago my intention, and my power of purchasing, to the heirs of Emily Arden. I was courted, immediately, to visit Ireland, and assured of all I wished here. I set out with immense property; and resolving to land on the estate I already appropriated, engaged a vessel to myself and servants. It is only four days ago that the vessel cast anchor in sight of this well-known mansion; and while the sailors were getting a boat out to land me, I stood on the deck, surveying, with delight, the remembered scenes of many a childish pleasure. Through my mind passed the painful recollection, that I had quitted this spot an insulted beggar. It gave place to the haughty consciousness, that I now returned in the bloom of life and of beauty—with wealth enough to command my wishes, and power to expel, with contempt, the young heiress of Bellarney.—Alas! even in this moment of full-blown arrogance and guilt, the hand of heaven impended invisibly over me, and a single stroke laid me once more on the threshold of that mansion, as very a beggar, and a wretch, as I left it!

"Accustomed to command, and unused to the common concerns, or meaner interests of life, it had never occurred to me, that, in chusing to have a vessel to myself, I should be totally in the power of those I hired. My valet and two female servants had been about me for years; nor had I a doubt of their attachment: but how little can we depend on any tie virtue forms not? These wretches, apprized of the value of my baggage, in which, besides other riches, I had brought the magnificent jewels I wrested from the Marquis at Naples, with many more equally valuable, leagued together at once to plunder me. When the boat was declared to be ready, I saw with surprize, it was empty; and ordered my baggage to be put in, ere I would descend. What was my astonishment and rage, to hear all my servants declare, every thing on board was their own, save a small portmanteau with a little raiment! The master, four sailors, and a boy, were, probably by confederacy, standing near me. Incensed at a fraud so gross, I forgot my danger, and threatened, not only my base domestics with punishment, but the crew. This imprudent passion, perhaps, first determined them on brutality: but with a torrent of oaths, they swore to throw me overboard; and finding my resistance violent, they beat and bruised me as you have seen, nor could all my efforts prevent their lifting me, at last, over the side of the vessel. In lowering after me the little portmanteau, either by accident or design, they let it fall, and with so good an aim, that it struck me this mortal blow on the temple. I sunk into the bottom of the boat, nor ever recovered recollection till I opened my eyes in the very chamber in which they first opened. The villains landed me, I was told, at a fisherman's cabin below, inhabited only by a woman and some children, then hastily rowed off, to fetch, as they told her, assistance, but in reality, never to return. The charity of your steward induced him to order me to be brought up to Bellarney, where a surgeon was summoned, who dressed my fractured head, and applied emollients to this mortifying flesh.

"When loneliness, and misery, obliged me to ponder upon the awful and extraordinary incident that thus concludes my worldly career, my nature, hard as it has long been, felt it: but I had neither power, nor will, to make a right use of the infliction. Pride survives every other passion. It was some relief to find I knew not one of the surrounding servants; nor did they recollect me. I might therefore steal into the grave unknown; as, too surely, I should otherwise be unpitied. The surgeon, yesterday morning, tenderly hinted to me that I could not survive; and requested to be informed who I was, and what friends of mine he should address.—I answered, with a bitter sullenness, that I never knew who I was myself,—never belonged to any human being,—nor had one friend in the whole world:—all I requested was to be left to die.

"When the joy of the servants, in the evening, announced the return of the family, I shrunk into myself, but ventured not an enquiry. In my lonely ruminations I called to mind a coffer Lady Bellarney once told me contained her account of my birth; but which I had never demanded, as she herself had often related the story to me.

That no memorial of me might remain, I asked for it, as a thing without value; meaning to destroy only the writing.—Ah! how could I foresee the blessed consequence of this request?—I knew not that the Marquis, and his Emily, lived at all: still less could suppose they lived at Bellarney:—lived to commiserate a dying sinner, to whom heaven, at their intercession, may yet, perhaps, extend its mercy. With an almost purifying power, the meltings of humanity rushed even now into my guilty heart, when that ministering angel so sweetly said it was yet possible she might forgive me."

The wretched woman now made an effort to raise her hands to heaven, and those around her, but sunk back as helpless:—an awful example that human charms, and powers, even in their extent, may fail to accomplish the views of the wicked in this life;—the hardest nature be unable to resist the horrors of that which is to come.

The pious and gentle Emily, drawing the Marquis after her, and every little innocent intuitively following the blessed example, knelt round the bed of the penitent sinner; where she offered up prayers so fervent, and benignant, that no eye could with-hold those drops, which, while they prove the weakness of our nature, sanctify it.—Then pressing the hand of the Marquis to her heart, she made him a party in the solemn forgiveness she audibly pronounced. Sir Edward, hanging over his angel daughter, answered her imploring eye by an imperfect Amen.

The Duke of Aberdeen, who had been a surprized spectator of this memorable scene, only because he felt it impossible to retreat, now approached Emily; and, being seconded by her father, would have led her out of the room; when, throwing the door suddenly open, Crosby appeared, with another man, carrying the coffer demanded, covered with dust, and cobwebs.—The languid sufferer, lost in more momentous considerations, bade them take it away again; but recollecting herself,—"no," cried she,—"open it.—I ought to have no pride if I am truly penitent:—let then all who thus witness the manner of my death, know too the extraordinary manner of my birth."—Crosby, who was burning with impatience to see what this coffer could possibly contain, had brought a hammer in his hand, and struck off at once the old lock. A written packet lay on the top, which he handed to the lady, while he hastily drew forth the faded, but valuable, garments of a woman; which would have engrossed the attention of all the servants, had not the fall of the Duke, in a kind of fit, obliged them to raise and recover him. Sir Edward Arden, too, abruptly wrung the hand, and threw himself faintly on the shoulder, of the Marquis; which made Emily utterly regardless of the servants, who were unfolding for her notice a rich, and remarkable Indian shawl. Her father again glancing his eye fearfully on it, as hastily turned away. "Put it out of my sight," cried he, in a low, shocked voice, to his nephew: "that shawl unfolds a tale, my son, best understood by the Duke, and myself.—By the mysterious ordination of heaven, I am deeply involved in the guilt of that creature—and now can account for the severe visitation on me, and mine.*—Wretched libertine!" added he, gazing contemptuously on the yet insensible Duke—"is the hour then come for thee to feel?"—Grasping the Marquis yet closer, he whispered, "Let your father be taken out of the room:—that wretch is his daughter—his own child—by Miss Archer.—Oh! Lenox, she is your sister:—and even earthquakes, in the wonder-working hand of heaven, can, to individuals, become mercy!"

Sir Edward now eagerly led his daughter away; and the Marquis accompanied his father. The dying sufferer requested the chaplain to satisfy all around, by reading aloud a letter, inscribed—"To be opened by my god-daughter, Emily Fitzallen, whenever she reaches woman's estate."

"Our days being all numbered, I may never live, my dear girl, to see you the good, and accomplished, woman, I hope you will be. As, however, rich, or poor, we all like to know who we belong to, I will give you what account I can of your parentage; though that, God knows, is not much.

"After the untimely death of my poor dear daughter, I found myself very sad, and lonely, at Bellarney: so all my kindred made it a point to have me a-visiting among them. Poor Emily Arden was so little a baby, that I was of no use to her, nor her company for me. I staid a while at Sir Arthur Gore's seat*; where you, I remember, so admired, and drew, the rocks. Poor child! you little knew how dear they had cost you.

"Lady Gore had many good qualities, but was a woeful manager of children. Four such rude boys, as her's, I never met with in my whole life. They were always in some mischief, or other:—now scouring the country on unbroken horses:—now floating out to sea in little skimming pleasure-boats:—for my part, I thought they would all be, sooner or later, brought home with broken bones, or drowned carcases: but children, and fools, they say, are the care of providence; and, when I think how these young tigers became the means of saving your little life, I cannot but think so.

"One windy October there came, on a sudden, such a tempest as I never saw. I really thought the crazy old house of Kirkalty* would have been blown about our ears; while the sea rolled on mountains high, and lashed the shore with fearful roarings:—but all the storm without, was nothing to that we had within doors, as soon as Lady Gore found her ungovernable boys had put off at early tide with an old fisherman they paid handsomely. All night, and all day, the tempest raged; and my poor cousin's grief would have melted a heart of stone. We all gave the boys up for lost, though we did not tell her so; and the fisherman's wife made as bad an outcry in the kitchen, at Kirkalty, as ever we had in the parlour. At noon, next day, the wind fell, and the sky cleared; but no sign of the boat could we espy; though we looked, and looked, as long as there was a blink of light. At midnight, lo! the tide brought in the boat; and the voices of the boys resounded, as usual, through the house, and now almost killed their poor mother with joy. Such chafing, as we had, of their chilled limbs;—such cramming of their empty stomach's; for they had had a starving, and a perilous, time of it, you may easily imagine. Arthur, who had the most feeling, and sense, of the four, staid at home all next day; and kept looking, and looking at me, as if he had something on his mind. Lady Gore, between anger and joy, fell sick, and took to her chamber. Well, in the evening, Master Arthur taps at mine, and muttered something of a secret, if I would hear him with patience: and such a surprizing secret did it prove, that I thought the boy was romancing; which, to say truth, they all could to perfection.

"It seems the storm had driven them very far out to sea; and the two men said if the boat had been either bigger, or heavier, they should never have weathered it. They were all employed in emptying the water, that every moment broke over their heads:—thus they passed the night. At peep of day the men found they were driving fast to St. Peter's Nose,* a famous, and dangerous rock. Again they gladly got out to sea; for, if it had been dark half an hour longer, the men swore they could never have escaped the rock. About noon, fortunately, the weather changed; and now they were as glad to get to St. Peter's Nose, as they before were to shun it. As they neared, they saw a wreck stuck fast, and ready every moment to go to pieces: they hailed her, but not a soul answered; and, after going round, as doubting what they should do, they boarded her. She proved, by their account, a poor little vessel, with a cabin they could hardly stand up in. Having removed the dead lights, they saw that every thing had been rummaged, and all the chests and lockers were wide open, and mostly empty; so they agreed the poor men had taken for safety to the boat, and were all returning to their own, when the cry of a baby amazed them:—they at last looked into a bed, where they saw a woman in a dying state, with a young child in her arms:—she seemed like one newly lain in:—mighty weak, and quite speechless. Nothing but cold water had they to give her, but they hoped she would revive with that, and tell them who she was, and how she came to be left in this melancholy way; though that, they guessed, was only because she could not bear moving, as all her cloaths were lying by her, and the baby very well drest:—how they managed the poor soul I cannot tell:—whether they killed her with their cold water, or she was dying before:—but die she did, in half an hour, and without power to utter a word; but clasping you, my poor child, for you was this unfortunate baby, to her bosom to the very last. The fisherman, God forgive him, wanted to leave you behind, but the boys would not consent to that, bad as they were. You must have been rarely nursed among them all the rest of the day; however, as they came home, they dropt you at the fisherman's cabin, till they had consulted what should be done with you. I must confess I was studying, while Master Arthur told me this story, which of his companions (for my cousins were too young for me to impute such a fault to them) had set him on to get his child taken care of by me; but I could not fix on any body, and all four boys told exactly one tale: so in the morning I walked with them down to the fisherman's cabin, and there first saw you; as thriving a little lass as I ever set my eyes on. The man told the same story with the boys; but I was so uneasy at their having left the poor woman, that I offered the men money, if they would fetch her, and the empty trunks, in hopes either the directions, or some letters, might inform me of your parentage; but they returned with the melancholy news that there was no sign of the wreck now:—so your wretched mother (though, I doubt, she was an ill one, or God, and man, would not so have forsaken her) had found, in the interim, a watery grave. My anxiety made the fisherman's wife come, and bargain to let me have the poor woman's cloaths, which, it seems, her husband had bundled up for himself, while the boys were staring at you, if I would give her more than their value. I was willing to have them on any terms; and, must say, when I saw them, I found the unhappy creature must have been above the common degree:—all I got I have had packed up with this letter, not that I could hope such mere trifles would ever lead you to any discovery, but only I thought it might be a melancholy satisfaction one day to you to have all I could save for you.

"A few days after, we heard that the bodies of several sailors, and one woman, had been washed ashore, and buried at a village some miles on: most likely those who took to the boat, and left your poor mother to expire alone.

"I would not leave a poor babe to perish, or depend on the charity of school-boys; so I sent you privately, with one of my own maids, to Bellarney, and forbade her ever saying how I came by you. I told my inquisitive little cousins you was dead.—When, some months after, I returned, I found you a brave girl, and much stouter than Emily Arden, who doated on you. I then had you christened by my own name, and have always loved you both alike. May you deserve that love, is the prayer of your unfailing friend,

"E. Bellarney."

The spectators satisfied, though not by this letter informed, joined in solemn prayers for the departing spirit.

To the only person it could inform, the chaplain afterwards conveyed it. Sir Edward Arden, however, wanted not this simple proof of the parentage of Emily Fitzallen, which the shawl had at once ascertained. Rich, and very remarkable in pattern, it had been among the costly presents of Governor Selwyn to his bride; who, when Duchess of Aberdeen, bestowed it on Miss Archer. Well did Sir Edward remember seeing it wrapped round her, to conceal her enlarged figure, as she feebly tottered through the garden, to a bark that became her tomb.

Softened by this recollection, to a full forgiveness of the wretched woman's guilty daughter, Sir Edward now returned to her chamber, lest the agitation they had all been in, might have added to the horrors of her mind: but he no sooner cast his eyes on her, than he saw that human joy, or sorrow, would never more affect her. Delirium and stupefaction had come rapidly on, from the moment they retired; and only the glorious benignity, and firmness of Emily's mind, had given the erring wretch the poor chance of a death-bed repentance and pardon.

But if Sir Edward thus accused himself, how did the Duke settle with his own conscience; since it was plain the shawl explained the painful truth, no less to him than to his brother. The frank and liberal soul of the latter induced him to seek the father of this miserable woman; and disdaining to conceal his own share in the well-meant plan, the Duke had no sooner perused the authentic memorial of the old Countess, than Sir Edward avowed the share he had taken in the removal of Miss Archer, and the wounding reproaches his own soul had long made him, when he found the unhappy woman had been by some strange means lost. A generous or feeling mind, would have silenced the man who thus imputed to himself a sin, white in comparison with the one that led to it; but the Duke was incapable of so delicate a sensation; and relieved from the sense of his past fault, by viewing Sir Edward's through the magnifying medium of his own representation, he made the Marquis painfully sensible of the difference between his father and his uncle. The *eclaircissement*, however, put the Duke on good terms again with himself; and had any other person in the house been able to be at ease, he would not have found himself otherwise.

To recover a little from the horror of these exhausting scenes, Emily, and her Lord, with their race of little ones, wandered to a rustic seat, on a brow commanding the river, and the boat builder's house. There, with endeared remembrance, they reviewed their past lives, and the happy years they had spent in that sweet sequestered home: then worshipped the heaven which hallowed, even from the hour it had taken place, their marriage, by the affinity of the Marquis and the other Emily: thus leaving not a doubt of the legitimacy of their children. Without a care but for those around them, the married lovers, as evening closed, wandered home; when the Marchioness anxiously enquired if the wretched woman had yet recovered her senses. The surgeon ventured to inform her he never hoped it, and rather thought it a miracle that they had remained at all.

They found Sir Edward traversing the saloon; still exquisitely alive to the pang of the moment; and always picturing to himself Miss Archer trepanned by his emissary, and both consigning themselves to a watery grave. The Duke, on the contrary, was sitting, coolly answering his letters from London;—regretting the purgatory he was enduring, and assuring his friends that he should hasten to join them at some public meetings now approaching. On supper being announced, Sir Edward retired, on the plea of indisposition. The Marquis and his Lady sat down to table, but the Duke alone could enjoy the splendid entertainment Emily had almost forgot having ordered in honour of the birth-day of her daughter. Her grandfather, however, made a voluptuous meal; and the lovers hastened, as soon as they decently could, to the bed-side of Sir Edward; whom they found so nervous, that both insisted on sitting by him.

The Duke, now necessarily alone, and obliged to reflect, used all his customary address to veil from a heart always selfish, and by his vicious intercourse with the world, now almost callous, an uneasy sense of error the refined Sir Edward had left there. Ingenious in palliating his own faults, he soon almost fancied his brother the only culpable person, and himself the most aggrieved one. What had Sir Edward Arden to do with his little gallantries?—he should have taken good care both of the mother and the child, without any sentimental interference. As to this girl, it was not very likely she should recover; but if she did, he would give her a handsome annuity. Above all, he would get out of the dungeon of Bellarney, the moment he could make his little arrangement with Beatrice. Under this agreeable impression, the Duke fell into as sound a sleep as if the wretched being he had called into existence, and who was now dying within a hundred yards of him, had never been born at all.

But though the extraordinary events of the day had not acted very sensibly on the heart of the Duke, they had seized on his constitution; and the blood had strangely ebbed and flowed in his veins, without his observing it. Repletion was at such a moment dangerous, and his profound sleep very far from a wholesome one. Suddenly he dreamt that Miss Archer, wrapt in the shawl so lately displayed before his eyes, and holding in her hand her daughter, changed to a negro blackness, stood at his bed-side. The shock of seeing them was doubled, when the mother, in a voice of thunder, told him they were come to claim their own; and gashing, with a single stroke, his bosom, they joined to pluck forth his heart, yet spouting with blood, and quivering with life. The exquisite torture of mind and body waked him; or rather, perhaps, corporeal agony caused the mental delusion: for he felt the gout had flown into his stomach, and the rack of pain was insupportable. From the chamber of Sir Edward, whom they had soothed into a sweet slumber, Emily and her lord were hastily summoned to that of one, who never was to sleep more. Short but intolerable was the torture of the Duke; attended with a delirium which realized his dream, and presented the tremendous phantom of Miss Archer for ever to his eyes.—At the very hour, nay, almost at the very moment, under the same roof, expired the Duke of Aberdeen, and his guilty, but unfortunate daughter—an awful warning to all the survivors.

Miss Fitzallen was, by the orders of Emily, privately interred at the feet of Lady Bellarney, and the secret of her affinity to the Marquis never circulated.

The remains of the Duke were sent to Scotland, to join those of his ancestors.

Sir Edward Arden, purified from his only fault, and eminent for his many virtues, by the temperance of his habits, and the unremitting cares and tenderness of his children and grand-children, had the peculiar happiness to reach a very late period of life, without suffering, in any great degree, its infirmities.

Virtue and sweetness, personified in Emily, formed the centre of a wide circle—their mingled beams diffusing a glowing happiness over her own immediate family—a warm interest towards her friends,—and an affecting benevolence among her dependants; while supplying, in her regulated mind, now an example to her father and husband, and now to her children, she had the rare felicity of seeing not one of the many was ever tempted, through the course of her long life, to diverge from the sphere of so dear an attraction.

NOTES

PAGE

1 *epigraph*: Source not found. Hereafter, quotations that could not be identified will not be noted.

1 *an Irish family of that name, lineally distinguished for birth, and for many generations very highly allied*: Throughout, Lee uses names that seem to signify real people, but there is rarely any meaningful correspondence between her characters and people of the titles she uses. The Irish Barony of Arden was created in 1770, for instance, with Catharine, wife of John Perceval, 2nd Earl of Egmont (Ireland). The Barony passed to her male heirs, but this would obviously have occurred long after this Sir Edward Arden lived, so to speak; he could have been born no later than the 1720s, and obviously the branch of the Irish family that produced him would have lived even earlier. Elsewhere, I will note the real figures who bear titles given by Lee where there really was an individual bearing the name or title Lee provides; I typically will not note, however, where no such title exists as given by Lee, or where the title makes no sense.

1 *the expelled house of Stuart*: The rule of the Stuart family ended in 1688 with the deposition of James II (of England) and VII (of Scotland). Jacobites—supporters of the house of Stuart—attempted to reinstate Stuart rule under the son of James II and VII, James Francis Edward Stuart—James III and VIII, as he styled himself, or the Old Pretender, as he was otherwise called. Major attempts were made to reinstate James in 1715, under the leadership of James Francis Edward Stuart, who had been living in exile in France, and in 1745, under the leadership of Charles Edward Stuart—Bonnie Prince Charlie, Charles III, to his supporters, or the Young Pretender to those who rejected the Stuarts' claim to the throne. This rebellion was finally unsuccessful, marking the end of realistic hopes for the return to power of the House of Stuart.

2 *a desperate scheme; the event of which the courtiers prognosticated*: The scheme is the Jacobite rebellion of 1745; the courtiers correctly predicted its failure.

2 *after the battle of Culloden*: Under Bonnie Prince Charlie, the Jacobite army got as far as Derby, England, but then retreated to Scotland; they were pursued to Culloden, where they suffered a bloody defeat from government forces on 16 April 1746.

2 *whose innocent little hand took, from that stained with the blood of his father, a commission*: Prince William Augustus, Duke of Cumberland (1721-1765), the youngest son of King George II; the Duke led the government army at the Battle of Culloden. At the hands of the man responsible for his father's death, the young Sir Edward thus gains a commission in the army against which his father fought.

2 *he perpetuated in his letters to his son, since published*: Lee refers to the posthumously published letters of Philip Dormer Stanhope, 4th Earl of Chesterfield (1694-1773) to his illegitimate son, Philip Stanhope (1732-1768). These letters were written from 1737 on and meant only for Philip's eyes, but in 1774, Philip's widow, Eugenia Stanhope, had them published. Their worldly precepts include advice that Philip learn good breeding by fraternizing with married women of fashion. Chesterfield was an anti-Jacobite, supplying the government with information from Paris about the Jacobite plot of 1715. In addition to being raised in part by his father's military enemy, he is educated by an enemy of his father's cause as well.

2 *the Countess of Yarmouth*: Amalie Sophie Wallmoden (1704-1765), mistress of George II, who created this title for her in 1740; the title lapsed at her death.

3 *chicken gloves*: According to H. A. Dillon, F. S. A., these became popular in the mid-eighteenth century and were "eagerly adopted by exquisites of both sexes, who occasionally slept in them to 'bleach the hands' properly." He refers to a shopbill in 1778 that explains,

> The singular name and character of these gloves induced some to think they were made from the skins of chickens; but on the contrary, they are made of a thin, strong leather, which is dressed with almonds and spermaceti, and from the softening, balmy nature of these gloves, they soften, clear, smooth, and make white the hands and arms. And why the German ladies gave them the name of chicken gloves, is from their innocent, effectual quality. (Dillon II: 192)

3 *a dice-box*: A vessel from which dice are cast, here signifying gambling.

5 *that India was a soil rich in wealth ... where a young woman, with merely a tolerable person and reputable introduction, seldom failed to make her fortune*: India was seen as a land where Britons could go to make a fortune through involvement in the East India Company, which in effect ruled much of southern, eastern, and western India at this time. British women were generally scarce in India, so travelling there was seen as a way in which a woman unable to find a husband—or a husband with money—could go to improve her fortunes, by marriage to

a "nabob," a word which to the British signified British men who had amassed wealth in India.

6   *the Alley*: Exchange, or 'Change Alley, the center of the English stock exchange during the eighteenth century; "the Alley" here signifies the stock market in general.

6   *coquets*: In the second edition, this reads "coquettes."

7   *this was fugitive*: In the second edition, the term "fugitive" is replaced with "fleeting."

7   *relict*: Widow.

7   *The fame of possessing a large fortune is almost equal to the possession of it, if the feelings are not nice*: In these next scenes, Mrs. Selwyn picks up fairly directly on knowledge she might have gleaned from Daniel Defoe's Moll Flanders (1722). This particular scene resembles one in which Moll helps a friend get a captain as a husband; she thereafter has rumors spread that she herself has a fortune—leading, unfortunately, to marriage with a man who turns out to be her brother (97-110); it also resembles a later scene in which Moll goes to Lancashire and marries Jemy, who also pretends to have a fortune, spending the little he has to use his supposed wealth as bait, as Moll herself is doing. See Appendix B, pp. 223-229, for the first of these scenes.

7   *weeds*: Mourning clothes.

7   *But Mrs. Selwyn now knew the world in all its ways; and had no time to lose in fixing some man of rank and fortune, yet unversed in them*: Another apparent allusion to Moll Flanders. After Moll has been seduced and virtually abandoned by her first lover, the unnamed "elder brother," and widowed by Robert, her first lover's younger brother, she says, "I had been trick'd once by *that* Cheat call'd, LOVE, but the Game was over; I was resolv'd now to be Married, or Nothing, and to be well Married, or not at all" (*Moll Flanders* [London: W. Chetwood and T. Edling, 1722], 67). She does not however follow through on her determination; she marries a "gentleman draper" who has little wealth, and who spends the wealth she brings him.

7   *the young Duke of Aberdeen*: The Duke of Aberdeen at this date was George Gordon, Earl of Aberdeen (and also Lord Haddo, Methlick, Tarves, and Kelie, Viscount of Formartine); he lived from 1722-1801.

8   *mauvaise honte*: Shyness, bashfulness.

8   *Circassian slave*: Women from Circassia, North Caucasus were supposed to be particularly beautiful and desirable as concubines. In 1733, François-Marie Arouet de Voltaire (1694-1778) wrote, in his *Letters Concerning the English Nation*,

The *Circassians* are poor, and their Daughters are beautiful, and indeed 'tis in them they chiefly trade. They furnish with Beauties, the Seraglios of the *Turkish* Sultan, of the *Persian* Sophy, and of all those who are wealthy enough to purchase and maintain such precious Merchandize. These Maidens are very honourably and virtuously instructed to fondle and caress Men; are taught Dances of a very polite and effeminate kind; and how to heighten by the most voluptuous Artifices, the Pleasures of their disdainful Masters for whom they are design'd. (*Letters Concerning the English Nation*. London: Davis, 1733 [75]).

8   *a Mahometan paradise*: According to Islam, men are met in Paradise with beautiful, pure, available maidens.

9   *in learning that Mrs. Selwyn had nothing to give him but her heart and hand, the Duke felt a transport so great, that all the factitious part of her conduct and character was at once forgotten*: Lee once again apparently refers to *Moll Flanders*, to a scene in which Moll suggests to a suitor that she has no money, so that when she turns out after marriage to have *some*, he is relieved. This is, once again, the scene in which she unfortunately marries her brother. For this scene, see Appendix B, pp. 223-229.

9   *spleen*: Here, spleen refers to emotions supposedly situated in the physical organ itself; the emotions intended in this case are spite, ill temper, or resentment.

10   "Showed" is added in the second edition.

10   *ennui*: Boredom (French).

10   *estates of the Bellarney family*: There was no Countess of Bellarney; the closest we come to the name at all is Blarney Castle, in County Cork, Ireland, which Cormac Macarthy was required to surrender to Queen Elizabeth I in 1602. His stalling tactics became called "Blarney," conveying the meaning the word currently has: talk with no substance, sometimes with the implication that the nonsense is meant to charm or beguile from the truth.

10   *the Castle*: Presumably Dublin Castle, which at this time was the seat of English administration of Ireland.

14   *dismissing*: "Dismissing" is replaced by the word "expelling" in the second edition.

14   *éclaircissement*: French, meaning explanation—here, however, meaning discovery as well.

17   "Her" is added in the second edition.

17   *Marquis of Lenox*: There was at this time a *Duke* of Lenox: Charles Lenox (or Lennox), the grandson of Charles II and his mistress Louise de Kérouaille. He was born on February 22, 1735, inherited the title

at his father's death in 1750, and died in 1806. He had no legitimate children so the title passed to his nephew, Charles Len(n)ox (1764-1819). The Marquis's dates align him with this Lenox, but the titles they hold are different.

19 *Emily Fitzallen, for this upstart was Lady Bellarney's god-daughter*: Emily Fitzallen is not just Lady Bellarney's name and that of her goddaughter; it is also the name of the countess's daughter, Emily Arden's mother.

20 *surprize the sister of this lady by an unexpected visit*: Crossing the channel from Ireland to England or Scotland to attend a party would be difficult, even if their starting point were on the east coast of Ireland, which it presumably is not, if Bellarney is associated with Blarney, in County Cork.

21 *dominos*: Dominos were masquerade costumes involving loose cloaks, sometimes with hoods, and with masks covering the upper face. A domino in this case refers to a person wearing this costume.

21 *the gentle Emily knew not the revolting spirit that man often thinks virtue*: Women were not supposed to recognize that they were in love without some shock to their modesty, and they were certainly not supposed to love before they knew that they were loved by the man in question. See Ruth Bernard Yeazell, *Fictions of Modesty* (Chicago: University of Chicago Press, 1984), 41-42. Emily Arden is a little more excusable than she might otherwise be, because she is tractable in this love: her father has authorized it.

24 *resent, regret,/Conceal, disdain, do all things but forget*: Alexander Pope (1688-1744), "Eloisa to Abelard" (1717), lines 199-200.

28 *the grand tour*: The Grand Tour, a tour of Europe, was considered requisite to finishing the education of well-born British men, especially those who expected any political position, as the son of a duke naturally would; his rationale for making the tour is, thus, utterly correct. See below, note to p. 83, for a characterization of the Grand Tour as instead more harmful than beneficial.

29 *the high style of life his daughter's birth demanded, and her fortune accustomed her to*: Typically, any property to which a woman had rights would pass to her husband on their marriage, unless marriage settlements or a will made this more conventional conveyance of property invalid. Clearly, Emily Arden has inherited property passed down from her mother, which would have come to her via that Emily's father, the Earl. Emily Arden's grandmother equally clearly has property of her own, no doubt directed to her by marriage settlements drawn up before she and the Earl married.

31 *she might be an intruder in the mansion of her fathers*: Lee is mistaken

NOTES

here: Bellarney is Emily's *maternal* ancestral mansion; it is the home of her mother and grandmother. Lee calls Bellarney Emily's paternal home again later, but towards the end of the novel corrects herself, calling Bellarney Emily Arden's maternal home.

34 *infatuated*: In the sense of being prepossessed by some madness or mad idea.

37 *adorned for a birth-night*: The birth-night of King George III, the 4th of June, which Sir Edward imagines Emily celebrating, as many subjects did.

37 *cot*: Cottage.

37 *an earthly immortality*: There are multiple sources for this term, from John Calvin's *The Institution of Christian Religion* (1561) on; it may have entered common parlance by Lee's time.

39 *Port Patrick*: Also Portpatrick, a town in the far southwest of Scotland, and a main landing point for ferries from (Northern) Ireland until the late nineteenth century.

40 *opened a vein in his arm*: Allowing blood to flow from the body in this fashion—"bleeding"—was thought to relieve a variety of ailments.

46 *Orpheus*: A musician, poet, and seer from Greek mythology who is said to have invented or perfected the lyre, a strummed string instrument from Greek antiquity.

47 *Antipodes*: Here, meaning the opposite ends of the earth.

47 *Cicerone*: Guide to art collections in museums and galleries and to historical and archeological sites who provides pertinent antiquarian and archeological information.

47 *Messina*: City on the northeast side of Sicily.

47 *the Lipari isles*: Lipari is the largest in the Aeolian Islands, an archipelago of volcanic islands slightly to the northwest of Messina.

50 *the deep revenge she had so bitterly vowed on Sir Edward and his daughter*: While cross-dressing to follow a lover occurs in various works of literature of this time, it is worth noting here the similarity of the incident with Hypolito/Emily Fitzallen with an incident in another of Lee's novels, *Life of a Lover*, in which we learn of "an English lady's elopement, in men's clothes, with the [libertine] Marquis Louvigny" (III: 196); unfortunately, the novel's male protagonist, Lord Westbury, mistakenly believes that this Miss Rivers is the woman he loves, Cecilia Rivers, the novel's protagonist; it is in fact the immoral Eliza Rivers, who has intercepted letters between Lord Westbury and Cecilia to prevent the happy union of these two lovers but who has done so without any interest in gaining Lord Westbury for her own.

51 *Palazzata*: The Abbé Lazzaro Spallanzani describes the Palazzata and its situation thus: "the curvature of the harbour was . . . embellished, for the extent of more than a mile, with a continued range of superb palaces, three stories in height, usually called the *Palazzata*, inhabited by merchants and other persons of opulence, which formed a kind of superb amphitheatre." *Travels in the Two Sicilies, and Some Parts of the Apennines*. 4 vols. London: G. G. and J. Robinson, 1798. (4: 153-154).

51 *repeated, as he gazed, the verses of Homer*: He most likely recites lines from Book XII of Homer's *Odyssey* (c. 700 B.C.) about the Strait of Messina, formed by Scylla on the mainland side and Charybdis on Sicily. Odysseus must navigate this strait with as little damage as possible, so he follows Circe's directions to stick closer to Scylla and to avoid Charybdis; the body count is six men rather than all his crew. These lines have little to do with love but are particularly pertinent given the situation that follows. For these lines, see Appendix B, pp. 252-256.

52 *As quickly returning, it bore away a train of bruised and helpless wretches*: For similar accounts of the great earthquake of 1783 that destroyed much of Messina and Calabria, see Appendix C.

55 *Embassador*: This spelling remained accepted into the early nineteenth century in England. The actual ambassador at this time was Sir William Hamilton (1730-1803), who served as British envoy to Naples from 1764 to 1800.

57 *strand*: Beach.

59 *When all his toils were past,/Still to return, and die at home at last*: A misquotation or alteration of Oliver Goldsmith (c. 1730-1774), "The Deserted Village" (1770), lines 95-96: "I still had hopes, my long vexations past,/Here to return—and die at home at last."

60 *knight-errantry*: Chivalrousness.

60 *"Milor Anglois"*: French for "English lord." In modern French, "Anglois" would be "Anglais." The new orthography is sometimes called the "orthographe de Voltaire," as Voltaire was influential in bringing about the shift. It became obligatory in France in 1835.

61 *"the cunning'st pattern of excelling nature"*: Shakespeare, *Othello*, 5.2.; Othello's speech comes right before he smothers his wife Desdemona based on jealousy from the misapprehension that she has been unfaithful to him.

67 *al fresco*: Outdoors.

67 *divertissement*: Entertainment.

69 *"A thousand innocent shames/In angel whiteness bore away those blushes"*: Shakespeare, *Much Ado About Nothing*, 4.1.159-60.

76 "*He withers at his heart; and looks as wan,*/[...] *The loss of reason, and conclude in rage*": These lines are a slight misquotation of "Palamon and Arcite," Book I, lines 528-529, 534-535, and 539-542, by John Dryden (1631-1700). This work, based on Chaucer's "The Knight's Tale" from *Canterbury Tales*, was originally published in Dryden's *Fables, Ancient and Modern* (1700). For Lee's "Nor, mix'd in mirth, in youthful pleasure shares," Dryden writes, ". . . in youthful pleasures shares"; for Lee's "Uncomb'd his locks, and careless his attire,/Unlike the trim of love, or gay desire," Dryden writes, "Uncomb'd his locks, and squalid his attire,/Unlike the trim of love, and gay desire."

77 *the Corso*: Probably the Strada del Toledo. Hester Thrale Piozzi writes that "The Strada del Toledo is one continual crowd—nothing can exceed the confusion to a walker," given the number of carriages drawn by horses "tear[ing] along with inconceivable rapidity"; her comments on the beauty of the horses there suggest the importance of Emily Fitzallen's showing herself in a carriage drawn by horses as beautiful as those Sir Edward has gotten his daughter. Piozzi writes,

> Horses are particularly handsome in this town, . . . very beautiful and spirited; the cream-coloured creatures . . . shine like satin: here are some, too, of a shining silver white, wonderfully elegant, and the ladies upon the Corso exhibit a variety scarcely credible in the colour of their cattle [horses] which draw them" (Hester Thrale Piozzi, *Observations and Reflections made in the Course of a Journey through France, Italy, and Germany*, London: Strahan and Cadell, 1789; reprint, Ann Arbor: University of Michigan Press, 1967, 231-232).

77 *Gorgon*: The Gorgon is a female monster from Greek mythology with sharp fangs, and poisonous snakes for hair; anyone who looked at a Gorgon supposedly turned to stone.

79 *gallantries*: Sexual affairs, more typically applied to men's affairs.

79 *the Queen*: The queen of Naples at this time was Maria Carolina of Austria (1752-1814), who became queen on her 1768 marriage to Ferdinand IV of Naples (1751-1825); Ferdinand assumed the throne in 1759. Maria Carolina's better known sister was Marie Antoinette.

80 *debt of honour*: A debt incurred from gambling.

80 "*For never should'st thou lie by Portia's side,/With an unquiet soul*": Shakespeare, *Merchant of Venice*, 3.2.308-309; the lines usually appear thus: "for never shall you lie by Portia's side/With an unquiet soul."

83 *the gay travellers who wander from England, to disseminate the bad habits of their own country, and bring home those of all they visit*: Although the Grand Tour was meant to provide men with knowledge of foreign governments and societies so that they could best rule their own country,

all too often, the Grand Tour devolved into the form that Lee here describes. See also my previous note on the Grand Tour (note to p. 28).

85 *convent*: Here, "convent" means "monastery," as it frequently does in the eighteenth century. That it is a monastery, a religious order of men only, becomes clear below (152).

85 *satisfy his mind as to the predicament the laws of that country would place him in*: The Marquis hopes that English laws will not recognize the validity of this marriage performed in Italy. A key issue here is that both Emilys as well as the Marquis are still under age, and according to English law after Lord Hardwicke's 1753 Marriage Act, which regularized the forms of marriage that were legal, a marriage uniting an underage pair without formalities including the permission of the parents would not be valid. A marriage officiated over by a Catholic priest in England would also not be valid in England. A marriage performed and legal in another country, however, would be recognized as valid in Great Britain.

93 *Frescati*: Also spelled Frascati, this town 20 kilometers southeast of Rome contained, in the second half of the eighteenth century, a palace of the Cardinal Henry Stuart Duke of York, last legitimate descendent of the house of Stuart (1725-1807) and brother to "Bonnie Prince Charlie."

94 *Civitá Vecchia*: A port town on the Mediterranean to the west-northwest of Rome.

104 *The bark that had conveyed the Marchioness to Civitá Vecchia*: It is perhaps noteworthy that Sir Edward takes the same route to Sicily taken by Rosalie and Montalbert in Charlotte Smith's 1795 *Montalbert*. See introduction (xxxix-xl) for more on these two novels' overlaps.

107 *Faun*: A rural deity from Italian mythology that is primarily human from the waist up and goat from the waist down. Originally, a faun was a man with a goat's ears and tail, but later, fauns were depicted as all goat below the waist. They became linked with satyrs, who were known for drunkenness and the lustful pursuit of nymphs.

109 *cloaths*: Here bedclothes, rather than clothing.

110 *This is no mortal visitation, nor no sound/That the earth owes*: A variation from Shakespeare's *The Tempest*: "This is no mortal business, nor no sound/that the earth owes" (1.2.410-411); in these lines, Ferdinand, the son of the King of Naples, hears the spirit Ariel singing.

111 *"might create a soul under the ribs of death"*: From *Comus* (1634) by John Milton (1608-1674), ll. 561-562.

122 *poorly*: "Poorly" appears in both the first and second editions, but Lee may mean "purely."

125 *their hearts*: The first edition reads "the heart", but the erratum at the end of the volume says "for 'the heart' read 'their hearts'"; the second edition, however, reads: "as if the high polish of cultivation gave hearts so very smooth a surface" (351-352).

126 *"true prayers, which reach heaven's gate ere sunrise"*: Source not found. The quotation is omitted in the second edition.

131 *Dryads*: Deities of the woods.

146 *happiness and Switzerland have become almost synonymous terms*: Probably a reference to *Julie, ou La Nouvelle Héloïse* (1764) by Jean-Jacques Rousseau (1712-1778).

147 *the odious inconveniences of Italian inns*: British travelers consistently complained about the lack of cleanliness not only of Italian inns but of rented homes as well. On the accommodations Italy had to offer, for instance, Hester Thrale Piozzi wrote, "our inn [in Bologna] is not a good one ... the place we are housed in is full of bugs, and every odious vermin: no wonder, surely, where such oven-like porticoes catch and retain the heat as if constructed on set purpose so to do."

148 *"smooth than monumental alabaster"*: Shakespeare, *Midsummer Night's Dream*, 5.2.5.

152 *La Trappe*: Monastery of the Order of Cistercians. Monks of the Reformed Order of Cistercians, formed in 1908, are also commonly referred to as Trappists. While monks of this order currently maintain perpetual silence, except where necessary, Cistercians in the eighteenth century maintained only night silence.

152 *Montpelier*: City about six miles inland and slightly west of the midpoint on the French Mediterranean.

154 *the port of Havre*: Havre is presented here as a port from which tourists, in distinction to other freight, did not travel to or from. Britons travelling to the continent were more likely to cross to Calais.

154 *Holyhead*: Holyhead is in the northwest of Wales and is a common point of departure from that country to Ireland, typically to Dublin.

154 *Deep'ning glooms, gay lawns, and airy summits*: From *Tancred and Sigismunda* (1745), III.i, by James Thomson (1700-1748).

156 *plantation*: Wooded area.

157 *Now I suppose all our fine oaks, that are the pride of this county, and the next to it, will be felled, to float off in cash to England*: Lee alludes here to absentee landlords, who live off the produce of the estates which they do not inhabit and which they rarely visit; Maria Edgeworth explores the type and the problem in her *The Absentee* (1812).

162 *Thus did Emily think—thus did she live—the happiest of the happy*: This

sentiment might usefully be compared to one shared by Cecilia Rivers, the protagonist of Lee's *Life of a Lover*; there, she says,

> Happy indeed are the great, if only in having so glorious an incentive to goodness, as the flattering conviction of its influence over others! But oh, how far more good and happy are the poor! who without such an incitement, live and die to God only, and their own consciences: as their dwellings for their children, their hearts seem just large enough to contain the virtues, nor have room for the train of vain and troublesome wishes, which bring more pain than pleasure with them. (V: 86)

163 *Grand climacteric*: "a year of life, often reckoned as the 63rd, supposed to be especially critical" (*OED*); here, the height of maturity and knowledge of life.

164 *but to wish more virtue, is to gain*: Alexander Pope, Epistle IV, "Essay on Man," line 326.

166 *Praxiteles*: One of the most celebrated Greek sculptors, Praxiteles lived in the 4th century B.C. and is best known for his Aphrodite of Cnidus, a copy of which is located in the Vatican.

169 *"pale cast of thought"*: Shakespeare, *Hamlet*, from Hamlet's well-known soliloquy that starts, "To be, or not to be" (3.1.85).

180 *Arcadia*: Arcadia was a region of ancient Greece in the Peloponnesus that in British literary tradition, especially with the romance by Sir Philip Sidney (1554-1586), *The Countess of Pembroke's Arcadia* (published posthumously in 1590 and in various revised forms thereafter) came to signify a peaceful, simple pastoral locale, typically peopled by shepherds and shepherdesses.

182 *"envied kiss"*: Thomas Gray (1716-1771), "Elegy Written in a Country Church-Yard" (1751), line 24.

183 *without being able to decipher one word of it*: Charlotte Smith, in her *Montalbert*, also has two characters, both named Rosalie, courted in Italian under the uncomprehending eyes of their English families. See the introduction, pp. xxxix-xl, for more on the parallels between Smith's and Lee's novels, as well as Appendix B on Smith's treatment of the 1783 earthquake in Sicily and Calabria.

188 *Baia*: Baia is a town six kilometers west of Pozzuoli on the west side of the Bay of Pozzuoli, in the Gulf of Naples; in the late Republic, it contained villas of the wealthy and powerful, purportedly including a summer residence of Julius Caesar's, and was known for the dissipation of its denizens.

193 *now can account for the severe visitation on me, and mine*: Lee perhaps alludes here to one of the ostensible morals of *The Castle of Otranto*

(1764), by Horace Walpole (1717-1797). This work, commonly considered to be the first Gothic novel, offers the moral thus: *"the sins of the fathers are visited on their children to the third and fourth generation."* (vi). My source is the first edition (London: Lownds), to which Walpole did not originally claim authorship.

193 *Sir Arthur Gore's seat*: Sir Arthur Gore, 3rd Baronet and 1st Earl of Arran of the Arran Islands, County Galway, (1703-1773), created Earl in 1762; although less likely, Lee could refer here to Sir Arthur's eldest son, Sir Arthur Saunders Gore, 4th Baronet and 2nd Earl of Arran of the Arran Islands (1734-1809). The family seat is Castle Gore, located in County Mayo, on the north end of Lough Conn; this locale is not consonant with the subsequent story of Emily Fitzallen's discovery, which has to occur on the coast. Even were Lee referring to his estate in the Arran Islands, her geography would be a far stretch; it would mean that Emily Fitzallen's mother had drifted from Scotland to the west of Ireland.

194 *Kirkalty*: Not found. Perhaps Lee means Kirkcaldy, but that is a town on the north of the Firth of Forth, on the east of Scotland. This location, like Castle Gore, makes no sense in terms of the tale the elder Emily Fitzallen is here recounting.

194 *St. Peter's Nose*: An imaginary location.

Appendix A: Contemporary Reviews of *The Two Emilys* and Biographical Sketches of Sophia Lee

Although Sophia Lee may have been "one of the best-known novelists of her day," that reputation came from the popularity of her *The Recess* (1783-1785).[1] *The Two Emilys*, which constituted the second volume of the five-volume *The Canterbury Tales*, which Sophia Lee wrote in collaboration with her sister Harriet,[2] was only very slightly noticed in contemporary publications. The only two substantial reviews of *The Two Emilys* when it first appeared were published in *The Monthly Review* and *The Critical Review*, the latter of which is primarily a plot summary; all other sources referring to the novel simply announce its appearance or praise it in one line, for instance in the mention of the novel in the *Monthly Magazine and British Register*, which, in a list of multiple works, says merely that "A second volume has appeared of Miss Lee's 'Canterbury Tales,' which, like the first, are lively, elegant, and ingenious."[3] In this appendix, I provide those parts of the articles in *The Monthly Review* and *The Critical Review* that are not summaries of or excerpts from the novel. Following those reviews, I provide biographical notices and obituaries on Sophia Lee printed during her life and obituaries printed shortly after her death.

The Critical Review ns 23 (1798): 204-209.

Canterbury Tales. Volume the Second. By Sophia Lee. 8vo. 7s. Boards. Robinsons. 1798.

WHEN we noticed the preceding volume of these tales,[4] we object-

---

[1] James R. Foster, "The Abbé Prevost and the English Novel" *PMLA* 42.2 (1927): 455.
[2] Harriet Lee wrote most of the stories in the five-volume set; in addition to *The Two Emilys*, Sophia Lee contributed the introduction to the first volume and a story in the third volume (1799), "The Clergyman's Tale" (195-521). *The Two Emilys* first appeared as "The Young Lady's Tale: The Two Emilys"; even though the story is novel length, as part of this larger work it is referred to in quotation marks. I italicize it in my own use because it also appeared as a freestanding novel (1798, 1827), as it is in this edition.
[3] *Monthly Magazine and British Register* 5 (1798): 509.
[4] See Crit Rev. New Arr. Vol. XXII. p. 170. [Note in original.] This review can be found at <http://www2.shu.ac.uk/corvey/cw3/ContribPage.cfm?Contrib=109>.

ed to the circumstance from which they derive their title: we thought that they would have appeared better without the Introduction. The present volume has furnished another reason for that opinion; it is occupied by one tale, which seems too long for a young lady to relate to her fellow-travellers.

The two volumes are not the work of the same lady, the second being written by the well-known authoress of the Recess, and of the Chapter of Accidents, one of the best of our modern comedies. The present tale will not diminish the reputation of this lady. Many of its events are strange, and, we may say, improbable; but they are calculated to excite a strong interest; and those readers who begin the story of the two Emilys will not, in all probability, desist till they finish it.

[Following is a lengthy summary of the tale.]

Such is the history of the two Emilys, which, faulty as its plan certainly is, will be read with pleasure and emotion. The style is frequently inaccurate, and also affected. We often find sentences rendered obscure by omissions of connecting words.

> 'The grand enthusiasm of her nature blending the hallowed charm of another world with the wild visions of this, [which] the nursery leaves on every mind, at times almost led her to believe [that] her prayers were heard, and [that] heaven granted to her sorrowful soul this visionary intercourse with him, [whom] it no longer permitted her to behold.' p. 304.[1]

Lenox, in his narrative to Emily after his recovery, says, 'on the ground were scattered flowers, which, as perishing, she had cast from her bosom. I gathered them up as devout pilgrims do holy reliques, and thrusting them into mine, bade them thus return to Emily.' This is a conceit fit only for the love sonnet of one whose imagination is warmer than his heart. We do not admire the passage respecting sculpture: the deathy [sic] appearance of a statue, to us at least, affords no delight. A turnpike road is described as wandering in graceful undulation. But no passage in the work struck us as being worse worded than the description of a scene near the Alps.

---

[1] The words in brackets in this quoted passage are added by the reviewer. Lee's passage appears in this edition on p. 108 the other lengthy passage quoted in this essay, below, can be found in this edition on p. 147.

'Over the deep and woody glen the house was seated in, impended an enormous mountain, on whose aged head hung tresses of snow, that threatened to inter the hamlet with every blast that blew:—beyond and around, far as the eye could reach, his numerous and ancient brethren, of different heights and hideous aspects, with grotesque yet chilling beauty, gave elevation to the mind, while they compressed the nerves.'

A burlesque writer could scarcely have crowded a sentence with more incongruities, or concluded it with a worse antithesis.

We have pointed out the faults of this tale with some minuteness, because any production of miss Lee merits attention. We cannot think the present performance equal to her Recess; but it is certainly the offspring of genius.

The Monthly Review ns 27 (1798): 416-419.

ART. VIII. *Canterbury Tales.* Volume II. By Sophia Lee. 8vo. pp. 564. 7s. Boards. Robinsons. 1798.

THE first volume of this work, from the pen of Miss *Harriet* Lee, was noticed in our Review for April last; and we then expressed a favourable opinion of the inventive powers of the fair writer, with which we would associate a similar judgment on this production of her sister. The story of the two Emilys, occupying the whole of this volume, abounds with a great variety of incidents, with many striking and affecting scenes, and is not without a considerable mixture of that distress and horror which are congenial to the present fashionable taste. The texture of the fable, however, is wild and romantic; little attention is paid to probability; and although manners are well described, and many observations are interspersed which seem to evince a knowledge of the human heart, yet we cannot compliment Miss S. Lee on the truth and consistency of her characters. The Duke of Aberdeen, on his entrance into life, gives no indication of that cold, selfish, unfeeling temper, and that turn for low debauchery, which disgrace him in his latter years; and which seem scarcely reconcileable with the *energetic* sense and strong passions which are ascribed to him. The diabolical malice and revenge of Emily Fitzallen are such as, we hope, never existed: the disguises which she assumes, in order to impose on the Marquis of Lenox, are scarcely within the verge of possibility; and though her marriage with that Nobleman doubtless surprises the reader, the astonishment may arise as much from the gross violation of probability, as from the skill and art of the writer.

We know not whether we can approve of that practice, among our Novelists, which is now very common, of killing their heroes and heroines, and bringing them again to life. In the history of John Buncle,[1] one of his many wives not only dies but is buried; yet she contrives to make her appearance again, and is introduced to her former husband as the wife of his friend. The revival of the Marquis of Lenox, after his duel, appears to us not less extraordinary.

The great defect of this novel, however, is that the perplexity, which in every tale is necessary in a certain degree to interest and agitate the passions of the reader, is occasioned not by those events which may happen in the ordinary course of human affairs, but by artificial concealments, the indulgence of absurd and unaccountable prejudices, and the wanton assumption of false characters. At the same time, in justice to the fair writer, we must observe that no objection can be made to the moral tendency of her work; that the prevailing sentiments are virtuous and pious; and that Emily Arden and her husband, the Marquis of Lenox, are bright examples of excellence in domestic life, and are rewarded with its never-failing concomitant, true happiness.—The language may be considered by some as rather too florid, and is not always correct.

We shall lay before our readers the following extract, which will enable them to judge of the descriptive powers of the author; and it will recall to their memory a calamitous event, which not many years since made a deep impression on every feeling and reflecting mind, and can never be contemplated but with sentiments of terror, mixed with reverential awe.

[The review incorporates the scene following the Marquis's marriage in Messina ending in the Marquis's recovery, watched over by a hidden Sir Edward. The scene draws on the earthquake that

---

[1] *The Life of John Buncle, Esq.* (1756-1766), by Thomas Avery (ca. 1690-1788).

struck Sicily and Calabria in 1783, reports of which can be found in Appendix C. The scene in question appears on pp. 51-52].

From the termination of this tale being designated only as the end of the *second volume*, we are induced to suppose that a prosecution of this joint undertaking is intended.

Biographical Sketches and Obituary Notices in Journals

In biographical sketches of Sophia Lee in late eighteenth-century journals and in obituaries in 1824 and 1825, Lee's father, John Lee, occasionally figures large. In one case—the obituary notice in *Blackwood's Edinburgh Magazine*—only about one-third is about Sophia Lee. Because my focus is Lee as an author, rather than her father and his celebrity (or notoriety), I include here only the information on Sophia Lee, noting, as above, where I have cut extraneous material.[1]

"Biographical Sketch of Miss Lee," *The Monthly Mirror* 4 (1797): 7-11

SOPHIA LEE is one of the four daughters of Mr. John Lee, a comedian of celebrity, and sufficiently powerful in talents to be, at one time, the formidable rival of the late master of the scene, Mr. Garrick. Mrs. Lee died while Miss Lee and her sisters were young [...]

When [John Lee] died, he left one son, who was engaged with a manufacturer at Manchester, and four daughters. The girls, each happily possessing a good understanding, which their parents had taken care to improve by a proper education, and by an instructive example (their father being himself a literary man, and their mother by no means deficient in intelligence) finding themselves cast upon the world, without any other help than their own exertions could administer, set up a school at Bath; in which pursuit, from their ex-

---

[1] I have omitted one piece because it is too long to include: "Mrs. Sophia Lee," *The Annual Biography and Obituary, for the Year 1825*. Vol. 9. London: Longman, Hurst, Rees, Orme, Brown, and Green, 1825. 127-135. I have likewise omitted an obituary that appeared in the *Literary Chronicle*, because it is primarily about her father rather than Lee herself, and because it erroneously attributes a novel, *Ormond*, to her. The full text can be found at <http://www2.shu.ac.uk/corvey/cw3/ContribPage.cfm?Contrib=242>.

cellent and unimpeachable character, their unwearied assiduity and sedulous attention, they have eminently succeeded; having been enabled, by the profits of their industry, to erect a handsome, spacious, and airy mansion, called Belvidere House, and, to this day, are at the head of a great and reputable school; it being allowed, by all who have had children under their tuition, that they have left their place of education with better manners, better morals, and more general knowledge, than was to be acquired in most seminaries of learning throughout the kingdom.

As soon as Sophia Lee felt herself on *terra firma*, and that the project of keeping a school was likely to answer, she gave way to her literary propensities, and employed the luxury of her leisure in the exercise of her pen. She wrote a work, rather voluminous, which has been in the writer's hands, but has never yet seen the light from the press. She afterwards wrote her play, called *The Chapter of Accidents*, which was first offered to Mr. Harris, who advised her to change it into an opera; she then wrote songs to it, but Mr. Harris made the best excuse he could for not bringing it out. That the excuse did not appear satisfactory to our author, was evident from the preface she wrote and published with the first edition of her play. The real fact was, Mr. Harris had in his hands, at the time, a play written by Mr. Macklin, and founded on the *Pere de famille* of Diderot, from which the character of the Governor, in Miss Lee's comedy, was taken; and the manager, not entirely approving either the plan of Macklin, or that of Miss Lee, chose not to embarrass himself with an argument of controversy with the former, as Macklin had long since publicly boasted, "that he could manage a quarrel better than any man."

To return to our heroine—Miss Lee took her opera-comedy from Covent-Garden theatre, and sent it, anonymously, to the late Mr. Colman, who shewed it to a friend, whose advice happening to coincide with the opinion of Mr. Colman, that there was too much comic point and substance, as well as force in the scenes, to suffer the piece to remain in its shape of a comic opera, it was recommended to Miss Lee to omit the songs. She readily followed the advice, and the comedy succeeded eminently. The theatre reaped great advantage of it, but the author very little: her whole emolument did not amount to 120l. from the playhouse, the evenings of her nights of its representation accidentally falling on the close of most sultry days, when the public were driven to Vauxhall Gardens, the parks, and other walks, to gasp for breath in the open air, while the skies rained down their favours partially to the manager, especially towards the close of the season. [...]

The Chapter of Accidents came out on the fifth of August 1780, and was performed fourteen times the first season, and still more the second. Though the theatre yielded our heroine but a scanty and inadequate profit, the press proved a better friend to her. The price given by the booksellers for a play that was well received the first night of representation, had been generally 100l. for some years previous to the representation of the *Clandestine Marriage*, the conjoint work of Mr. Garrick and Mr. Colman; and they received 200l. for the copy-right of that comedy. This broke into the general and established rule, and dramatic authors just got as much as they could persuade the bookseller they applied to for the purchase of their piece to give them, between the years 1767 and 1780. The consequence was, various prices having been given for dramatic pieces by the booksellers, sometimes 150l. sometimes 200l. sometimes 250l. and in one case (that of Mr. Kelly's *Clementina*) 300l. the trade had so frequently burnt their fingers, that they became panic-struck, and would scarcely treat at all for a dramatic copy-right, when the *Chapter of Accidents* came to market. The price offered by a reputable bookseller to a friend of the author, was so contemptibly below the value, that he advised her to print it on her own account; the advice was taken, and several large impressions have been sold off, much to her advantage, and in proof that the trade might have ventured to have bid for the copy handsomely with safety. To the first edition, Miss Lee prefixed "a preface explaining its treatment from the different managers." But she has withdrawn that preface from the later editions of a play which still holds its place in the theatre, and is represented every winter and summer in town and country, with great popularity and success, although, by death, and other accidents in life's varying chapter, the cast of it on the London stage has been weakened.

In 1782, Miss Lee published the first volume of The RECESS; *or, a Tale of other Times*: which no sooner saw the light than it was read with avidity; and the irresistible command over the tender passions which the work possessed, acknowledged, bowed to, and admired.

A second and third volume of the RECESS were published (with a new edition of the first) in 1785, and other editions of the first volume in the next year.

The *Hermit's Tale* was published by our author in the year 1787, which was a beautiful and affecting poetical *morceau*.

The tragedy of *Almeyda*, which had been written some few years, was not presented to the theatre till the season 1795-6. It was produced in the spring of 1796, and the heroine of the play was supported by the aid of the distinguished talents of Mrs. Siddons. The public received the tragedy with the loudest applause, and it produced very crowded audiences for four nights representation, when it was unaccountably stopped in its career. So unusual and injurious a circumstance to the author, both in point of profit and reputation, naturally alarmed her and her friends; the latter conceiving that it could not be intended by the theatre, to depart so entirely from all precedent and practice with respect to any author, whose play had been favourably received, and had not been acted to an indifferent house, undertook to wait on the principal proprietor, and enquire to what cause they were to ascribe the sudden cessation of the representation of *Almeyda*. They were received by that gentleman with great cordiality and friendly attention; an explanatory conversation took place, and the result was a declaration, on the part of the proprietor, that he thought Miss Lee had been very unhandsomely treated by the theatre, and a promise that the tragedy of *Almeyda* should be performed on the last night of the season, which was then near its close, and that it should be acted the remainder of its run in the course of the ensuing season. The promise, in the first instance, was duly performed; the tragedy was acted on the last night of the Drury Lane company's performing that season; the receipt of the house was 400*l*. and upwards, and it has never been performed since.

It is the province of the writer of the present memoir, to state the fact; he leaves it to others to account for it; he will only remark, that he does not believe a similar instance of such conduct of a theatre to an author of established reputation, is to be found in the history of the English stage.

Having followed our heroine through all her literary productions, and their history, the reader may be assured that no anonymous publication is to be considered as having come from the pen of Sophia Lee. The works that are mentioned in this biographical sketch, are all that she has published. If she has written more, they have not yet been in the press.

In private life, Miss Lee has walked most evenly; commencing her career, from her infancy, with a dutiful obedience to her parents, and an attentive compliance with all their desires, accompanied with an affectionate regard for her brothers[1] and sisters, she early endeared herself to the circle of her acquaintance; as she matured in life, she displayed that degree of good understanding and valuable talent, which have so well enabled her, with the joint industry and exertions of her sisters, to establish that reputable and successful seminary of education, over which she at present presides at Bath, and the literary uses to which she has put her understanding and talents in the hours of leisure and relaxation, from the severer duties of her school, notwithstanding they have been attended with some mortifications, have built her a reputation in the world of letters equally enviable and honourable. May Miss Lee's example and success, and the circumstances above stated, teach all other females, who are left unprovided for, how preferable personal diligence and professional employment are to the precarious honour and profit of writing for a theatre, or of any other visionary scheme of life.

"Lee, Miss Sophia." *Literary Memoirs of Living Authors of Great Britain*. London: Faulder, 1798. 2 vols. I: 360-361.

A Daughter of Mr. John Lee, [...] she has, for some time, in connection with her sister, [...] kept a Boarding School for young ladies at Bath, and may boast of a very honourable distinction, acquired by her publications. Her first literary production, which reached the press, was "The Chapter of Accidents," a comedy, very favourable [sic] received at the Haymarket, and printed in 1780. She next wrote "The Recess; or, a Tale of other Times," a novel, in three duodecimo volumes, of which the first appeared in 1783, and it was completed in 1786 [sic]. This performance attracted a considerable degree of attention. It consists of the adventures of two imaginary daughters of Mary Queen of Scots and the Duke of Norfolk. It engaged the

---

[1] Miss Lee has only one brother living at present. [Note in original.]

warm patronage of Mr. Sheridan, and is a most ingenious and affecting novel, discovering in the author much acqu[a]intance with the human heart, a copious fund of imagination, great powers of description, and strong marks of genius. Miss Lee next wrote "A Hermit's Tale," an elegant poem, published in a quarto pamphlet, in 1787; and, since that time, she has only produced "Almeyda, Queen of Granada," a tragedy, performed at Drury Lane in 1796.[1] The last of these pieces possesses, in our opinion, many excellent and beautiful parts. If the circumstance of its having been withdrawn from the stage, when supported by the exquisite powers of Mrs. Siddons, while so many wretched puppet-show exhibitions, entitled Comedies, are heard with attention and applause be solely owing to the *public*, it is a melancholy mark, indeed, of the precipitation of our national taste.

"The Late Miss Sophia Lee," Blackwood's Edinburgh Magazine 15 (1824): 476.

IN the obituary, our readers will, we are persuaded, see with regret the name of SOPHIA LEE, author of 'The Chapter of Accidents,' 'Recess,' &c. Those amongst them who recollect the great success of these works, as well as their striking and original merit, will wonder that a writer, who, at an early age, could thus secure the admiration of the public, should have had self-command enough not to devote her after-life to that which was evidently both to her taste and talent; but the correct judgment and singular prudence of Miss Lee early induced her to prefer a permanent situation and active duties to the dazzling, but precarious, reputation of a popular author. Together with her sisters, one of whom had also a literary talent, she established a seminary at Bath for the education of young ladies; and her name, like that of Mrs. Hannah More, in a similar situation at Bristol, gave a distinction to it which it is to be wished was always as well deserved in every establishment of this kind. At intervals, however, she found relaxation in the indulgence of her genius; and among her later productions, the tragedy of "Almeyda, Queen of Granada," and the "Canterbury Tales," in which she associated her-

---

[1] This publication must have been published or in press before the second volume of *The Canterbury Tales* appeared.

self as a writer with her sister, are most admired; and these, with the "Life of a Lover," and a ballad called the "Hermit's Tale," were all the works she ever published.

On the 13th of March, she closed a long and meritorious life with pious resignation, preserving almost to the last those strong intellectual powers, and the tenderness of heart, which rendered her valuable to the public, and deeply regretted, not only by her relatives, but by all to whom she was personally known.

Appendix B: Literary Correspondences

Daniel Defoe, *Moll Flanders*. London: Chetwood and Edling, 1722, pp. 76-84, 88-98.

[Moll Flanders, the eponymous female protagonist of Daniel Defoe's 1722 novel, has a colorful life including love, bigamy, theft, and even incest. After she is first seduced by a man she claims to love (though she is equally taken by the money he gives her), she is sacrificed in marriage to her lover's younger brother, who is kind enough, but whom she cannot love as she does the man she believes has betrayed her. Hereafter, she claims to eschew *"that Cheat*, called LOVE, [and] resolv'd [thereafter] to be Married, or Nothing, and to be well Married, or not at all" (67). Nonetheless, she writes as though she is fond enough of each of the men she marries . . . if she can be considered to marry, given that at a certain point, her husband simply leaves, making all her subsequent marriages bigamous. Her fondness for the men with whom she becomes involved, however, set her quite apart from Miss Arden, who marries Governor Selwyn and then the Duke to make her fortune.

The experiences of Moll's on which Lee draws in her treatment of Miss Arden's marital scheming can best be understood with some background information. Moll was born in Newgate prison to a mother who was subsequently transported for theft. She is raised by a good woman in Colchester, at first by the charity of the parish and then by sewing and earning her keep; when the woman dies, she is adopted by a genteel family, and it is here that she is seduced by one brother—the elder of the two—but is assiduously courted by the other. Once the younger brother starts pursuing Moll, the elder tells her she can do nothing better than marry the younger, whom we know only as Robin, or Robert. The family at first objects to this match, because Moll has no money, one of the sisters even saying that it is really only money that makes a woman marriageable. Robin loves her and insists on the marriage. It is when he dies five years later that she vows not to be cheated by love but only to marry for interest. She marries a man she refers to as a "gentleman-draper" who runs through the money she has from her marriage to

[Robin—about £1,200—and shortly thereafter he is arrested for debt. He tells Moll that he intends to escape and disappear, and that she is free to marry again. Now in London, she meets a widow who invites her to her home, advising Moll that in this neighborhood, Moll may be able to meet a ship's captain and marry him.]

THIS Knowledge I soon learnt by Experience, (*viz.*) That the State of things was altered, as to Matrimony, and that I was not to expect at *London*, what I had found in the Country; that marriages were here the Consequences of politick Schemes, for forming Interests, and carrying on Business, and that LOVE had no Share, or but very little in the Matter.

THAT, as my Sister in Law, at *Colchester*, had said; Beauty, Wit, Manners, Sence, good Humour, good Behaviour, Education, Vertue, Piety, or any other Qualification, whether of Body or Mind, had no power to recomend [*sic*]: That Money only made a Woman agreeable [...] for a Wife, no Deformity would shock the Fancy, no ill Qualities, the Judgement; the Money was the thing; the Portion was neither crooked, or Monstrous, but the Money was always agreeable, whatever the Wife was. [...]

BESIDES this, I observ'd that the Men made no scruple to set themselves out, and to go a Fortune Hunting, *as they call it*, when they had really no Fortune themselves to Demand it, or Merit to deserve it; and That they carry'd it so high, that a Woman was scarce allow'd to enquire after the Character, or Estate of the Person that pretended to her. [...] (76-77)

[Moll especially learns this to be true from the experience of a neighbor, who makes inquiries about the character and property of a man who is courting her, only to find that her doing so causes him to decamp. Moll advises this woman to tell others that she was the one who ended the relationship, and that she did so on the basis of hearing that the man had no money, and, perhaps worse, that he had a wife in the West Indies. The man finds himself turned out from homes where he might court other women and ultimately returns to the first woman, who then confronts him with the rumors she had spread. As a result, the man brought her proofs that he had money and he was then incapable of asking her about her own financial status; as Moll puts it,]

This young Lady [...] made his obtaining her be TO HIM the most difficult thing in the World; and this she did [...] by a just Policy, turning the Tables upon him, and playing back upon him his own Game; for as he pretended by a kind of lofty Carriage, to place himself above the occasion of a Character, and to make enquiring into his Character a kind of affront to him; she broke with him upon that Subject; and at the same time that she made him submit to all possible enquiry after his Affairs, she apparently shut the Door against his looking into her own. (83-84)

[Moll then finds she must play a similar and similarly perilous game.]

BUT I come now to my own Case, in which there was at this time no little Nicety. The Circumstances I was in, made the offer of a good Husband, the most necessary Thing in the World to me; but I found soon that to be made Cheap, and Easy, was not the way: It soon began to be found that the Widow had no Fortune, and to say this, was to say all that was Ill of me; for I began to be dropt in all the Discourses of Matrimony: being well Bred, Handsome, Witty, Modest and agreeable; all which I had allowed to my Character, whether justly, or no, is not to the Purpose; I say, all these would not do without the Dross, which was now become more valuable than Virtue itself. In short, *the Widow*, they said, *had no Money*.

I resolv'd therefore, as to the State of my present Circumstances; that it was absolutely Necessary to change my Station, and make a new Appearance in some other Place where I was not known, and even to pass by another Name if I found Occasion.

I Communicated my Thoughts to my intimate Friend the Captain's Lady; who I had so faithfully serv'd in her Case with the Captain; and who was as ready to serve me in the same kind as I could desire: I made no Scruple to lay my Circumstances open to her, my Stock was but low, for I had made but about 540 *l.* at the Close of my last Affair, and I had wasted some of that; However, I had about 460 *l.* left, a great many very rich Cloaths, a gold Watch, and some Jewels, tho' of no extraordinary value, and about 30 or 40 *l.* left in Linnen not dispos'd of.

MY Dear and faithful Friend, the Captain's Wife [...] was so sensible of the Service I had done her in the Affair above, that [...] at last she made this unhappy Proposal to me (*viz.*) that as we had observ'd, *as above*; how the Men made no scruple to set themselves out as Persons meriting a Woman of Fortune, when they had really no Fortune of their own; it was but just to deal with them in their own way and if it was possible, to Deceive the Deceiver.

THE Captain's Lady, in short put this Project into my Head, and told me if I would be rul'd by her I should certainly get a Husband of Fortune, without leaving him any room to Reproach me with want of my own; I told her as I had Reason to do, That I would give up myself wholly to her Directions, and that I would have neither Tongue to speak, or Feet to step, in that Affair, but as she should direct me; depending that she would Extricate me out of every Difficulty she brought me into, which she said she would Answer for.

THE first step she put me upon, was to call her Cousin, and go to a Relations House of hers in the Country, where she directed me; and where she brought her Husband to visit me, and calling me Cousin, she work'd Matters so about, that her Husband and she together Invited me most passionately to come to Town and be with them, for they now liv'd in a quite different Place from where they were before. In the next Place she tells her Husband, that I had at least 1500 *l*. Fortune, and that after some of my Relations I was like to have a great deal more.

IT was enough to tell her Husband this, there needed nothing on my Side; I was but to sit still and wait the Event, for it presently went all over the Neighbourhood that the young Widow at Captain ———'s was a Fortune, that she had at least 1500 *l*. and perhaps a great deal more, and *that the Captain said so*; and if the Captain was ask'd at any time about me, he made no scruple to affirm it, tho' he knew not one Word of the Matter, other than that his Wife had told him so; and in this he thought no Harm, for he really believ'd it to be so, because he had it from his Wife; so slender a Foundation will those Fellows build upon, if they do but think there is a Fortune in the Game: With the Reputation of this Fortune, I presently found myself bless'd with admirers enough, and that I had my Choice of Men, as scarce as they said they were, *which by the way confirms what I was saying before*: This being my Case, I who had a subtile Game to play, had nothing now, to do but to single out from them all, the properest Man that might be for my Purpose; *that is to say*, the Man who was most likely to depend upon the *hear say* of a Fortune, and not enquire too far into the particulars; and unless I did this, *I did nothing*, for my Case would not bare [sic] much Enquiry.

I Pick'd out my Man without much difficulty, by the judgement I made of his way of Courting me; I had let him run on with his Protestations and Oaths that he lov'd me above all the World; that if I would make him happy, that was enough; all which I knew was upon Supposition, nay, it was upon a full Satisfaction, that I was very Rich, tho' I never told him a Word of it myself.

THIS was my Man, but I was to try him to the bottom, and indeed in that consisted my Safety; for if he baulk'd, I knew I was undone, as surely as he was undone if he took me; and if I did not make some scruple about his Fortune, it was the way to lead him to raise some about mine; and first therefore, I pretended on all occasions to doubt his Sincerity, and told him, perhaps he only courted me for my Fortune; he stop'd my Mouth in that part, with the Thunder of his Protestations, *as above*, but still I pretended to doubt.

ONE Morning he pulls off his Diamond Ring, and writes upon the Glass of the Sash in my Chamber this Line,

You I Love, and you alone.

I read it, and ask'd him to lend me his Ring, with which I wrote under it thus,

And so in Love says every one.

He takes his Ring again, and writes another Line thus,

Virtue alone is an Estate.

I borrow'd it again, and I wrote under it,

But Money's Vertue; Gold is Fate.

He colour'd as red as Fire to see me turn so quick upon him, and in a kind of a Rage told me he would Conquer me, and writes again thus,

I scorn your Gold, and yet I Love.

I ventur'd all upon the last cast of Poetry, as you'll see, for I wrote boldly under his last,

I'm poor: Let's see how kind you'll prove.

This was a sad Truth to me, whether he believ'd me or no I cou'd not tell; I supposed then that he did not. However he flew to me, took me in his Arms, and kissing me very eagerly, and with the greatest Passion imaginable he held me fast till he call'd for a Pen and Ink, and then *told me* he could not wait the tedious writing on the Glass, but pulling out a piece of Paper, he began and wrote again,

Be mine, with all your Poverty.

I took his Pen and follow'd him immediately thus,

Yet secretly you hope I lie.

HE told me that was unkind, because it was not just, and that I put him upon contradicting me, which did not consist with good Manners, any more than with his Affection; and therefore since I had insensibly drawn him into this poetical scribble, he beg'd I would not oblige him to break it off, so he writes again,

Let Love alone be our Debate.

I wrote again,

She Loves enough, that does not hate.

This he took for a favour, and so laid down the Cudgels, that is to say the Pen; I say he took it for a favour, and a mighty one it was, if he had known all: However he took it as I meant it, that is, to let him think I was inclin'd to go on with him, as indeed I had all the Reason in the World to do, for he was the best humoured merry sort of a Fellow that I ever met with; and I often reflected on my self, how doubly criminal it was to deceive such a Man; but that Necessity, which press'd me to a Settlement suitable to my Condition, was my Authority for it, and certainly his Affection to me, and the Goodness of his Temper, however they might argue against using him ill, yet they strongly argued to me, that he would better take the Disappointment, than some fiery tempered Wretch, who might have nothing to recommend him but those Passions which would serve only to make a Woman miserable all her days.

BESIDES, tho' I had jested with him, as he suppos'd it, so often about my Poverty, yet, when he found it to be true, he had foreclosed all manner of objection, seeing whether he was in jest or in earnest, he had declar'd he took me without any regard to my Portion, and whether I was in jest or in earnest, I had declar'd my self to be very Poor, so that *in a word*, I had him fast both ways; and tho' he might say afterwards he was cheated, yet he could never say that I had cheated him. (88-94)

WHEN we were married I was shrewdly put to it to bring him that little Stock I had, and to let him see it was no more; but there was a necessity for it, so I took my opportunity one Day when we were alone, to enter into a short Dialogue with him about it; MY DEAR, said I, we have been married a Fortnight; is it not time to let you know whether you have got a Wife with something, or with nothing; your own time for that, my DEAR, *says he*, I am satisfied that I have got the Wife I love, I have not troubled you much, *says he*, with my enquiry after it. [...]

THE less you have, *my* DEAR, *says he,* the worse for us both; but I hope your Affliction you speak of, is not caus'd for fear I should be unkind to you, for want of a Portion. No, No, if you have nothing tell me plainly, and at once; I may perhaps tell the Captain he has cheated me, but I can never say you have cheated me, for did you not give it under your Hand that you were Poor, and so I ought to expect you to be. (96-97)

[Over the course of the next few days, she bring him about £340 pounds, gold worth £100 pounds, and linen worth £60.]

And now, MY DEAR, *says I to him*, I am very sorry to tell you, that there is all, and that I have given you my whole Fortune. [...]

HE was so oblig'd by the Manner, and so pleas'd with the Sum, for he had been in a terrible fright least [*sic*] it had been nothing at all, that he accepted it very thankfully: And thus I got over the Fraud of *passing for a Fortune without Money*, and cheating a Man into Marrying me on pretence of a Fortune. (98)

[Moll has a similar, but more complex, experience later, in which she allows someone to represent her as having a fortune, not realizing that this same woman is representing Jemmy, the man who woos Moll, as likewise having a fortune he does not have. They wed, only to find that they have involved themselves in a double cheat.]

Hannah Cowley, *The Belle's Stratagem*. 1780. London: T. Cadell, 1782.

[Most of the action in *The Two Emilys* stems from the masquerade which Emily Arden feels she must practice in order to gain the love of the man both their fathers have chosen to be her husband—her cousin, the Marquis of Lenox. Just as the Marquis fears his intended will be too countrified for him, Hannah Cowley's Doricourt, in *The*

Belle's Stratagem, feels his intended, Letitia Hardy, will be too little urbane for him; here, however, the fear is that she will be too insipidly English, rather than continental. Both works play with the ostensibly inadequately urbane nature of their female protagonists, Lee's work by having Emily Arden get the Marquis to fall in love with her while she is dressed like a rustic, and Cowley's by having Letitia pretend to be a hoyden ignoramus, utterly lacking in gentility and wit, while also presenting herself to him as she really is—albeit with her identity as masked as Emily Arden's is when the Marquis first falls in love with her. There are differences in their treatments of what nationality a woman must be to be worth a well-born man's love, but their treatment of masquerade makes their similarity meaningful and a comparison is helpful for understanding *The Two Emilys*.

This play has two main plot lines; the one I have excerpted here as a useful parallel for understanding Sophia Lee's *Two Emilys* primarily concerns Doricourt and Letitia Hardy. Also involved are Letitia's father, Hardy; the Hardys' cousin, Mrs. Racket; Doricourt's friend and confidant, Saville; a male gossipmonger, Flutter; and another male character of Doricourt, and Saville and the Hardys' class, Villers. For the sake of brevity, I have cut out anything not immediately pertinent to *The Two Emilys*, but there are of course subtleties of correspondence and difference between the two works that can best be understood by reading the play in its entirety.

Doricourt has returned from his travels abroad and met with his intended, whom he has not seen for many years, and signed marriage settlements. In the first scene with which we are concerned (1.3), Doricourt discusses his response to his bride-to-be with his friend, Saville.]

> *Saville*: When do you expect Miss Hardy?
>
> *Doricourt*: Oh, the hour of expectation is past. She is arrived, and I this morning had the honour of an interview at Pleadwell's. The writings were ready; and, in obedience to the will of Mr. Hardy, we met to sign and seal.
>
> *Saville*: Has the event answered? Did your heart leap, or sink, when you beheld your Mistress?
>
> *Doricourt*: Faith, neither one nor t'other; shes [*sic*] a fine girl, as far as mere flesh and blood goes.—But—
>
> *Saville*: But what?

Doricourt: Why, she's *only* a fine girl; complexion, shape, and features; nothing more.
Saville: Is not that enough?
Doricourt: No! she should have spirit! fire! *l'air enjoué!* that something, that nothing, which every body feels, and which no body can describe, in the resistless charmers of Italy and France. [...] *English* beauty! 'Tis insipidity; it wants zest, it wants poignancy. [...]
Saville: And has Miss Hardy nothing of this?
Doricourt: If she has, she was pleased to keep it to herself. I was in the room half an hour before I could catch the colour of her eyes; and every attempt to draw her into conversation occasioned so cruel an embarrassment, that I was reduced to the necessity of news, French fleets, and Spanish captures, with her father. [...]

[In the next scene (1.4), various people discuss the match and Letitia gives her impression of her intended.]

Letitia: Men are all dissemblers! flatterers! deceivers! Have I not heard a thousand times of my air, my eyes, my shape—all made for victory! and to-day, when I bent my whole heart on one poor conquest, I have proved that all those imputed charms amount to nothing;—for Doricourt saw them unmov'd.—A husband of fifteen months could not have examin'd me with more cutting indifference. [...] There's the sting! The blooming boy, who left his image in my young heart, is at four and twenty improv'd in every grace that fix'd him there. It is the same face that my memory, and my dreams, constantly painted to me; but its graces are finished, and every beauty heightened. How mortifying, to feel myself at the same moment his slave, and an object of perfect indifference to him!

[Her father enters, and she shares her impression and response to Doricourt with him.]

Letitia: [...] A plan has struck me, if you will not oppose it, which flatters me with brilliant success. [...] It may seem a little paradoxical; but, as he does not like me enough, I want him to like me still less, and will at our next interview endeavour to heighten his indifference into dislike [...] because 'tis much easier to convert a sentiment into its opposite, than to transform indifference into tender passion.

[The next pertinent scene (3.1) reveal Letitia's plan in action. We start with a conversation among Doricourt, Letitia, and Mrs. Racket.]

Letitia: You have been a great Traveller, Sir, I hear?

Doricourt: Yes, Madam.

Letitia. Then I wish you'd tell us about the fine sights you saw when you went over-sea.—I have read in a book, that there are some countries where the Men and Women are all Horses.—Did you see any of them?

Mrs. Racket: Mr. Doricourt is not prepared, my dear, for these enquiries; he is reflecting on the importance of the question, and will answer you—when he can.

Letitia: When he can! Why, [he] ... stands gaping like mumchance.

Mrs. Racket: Have a little discretion.

Letitia: Hold your tongue!—Sure I may say what I please before I am married, if I can't afterwards.—D'ye think a body does not know how to talk to a Sweetheart. He is not the first I have had.

Doricourt: Indeed!

Letitia: Oh, Lud! He speaks!—Why, if you must know—there was the Curate at home:—when Papa was a-hunting, he used to come a suitoring, and make speeches to me out of books.—No body knows what a *mort* of fine things he used to say to me;—and call me Venis, and Jubah, and Dinah!

Doricourt: And pray, fair Lady, how did you answer him?

Letitia: Why, I used to say, Look you, Mr. Curate, don't think to come over me with your flim-flams; for a better Man than ever trod in your shoes, is coming over-sea to marry me;—but, ifags! I begin to think I was out.—Parson Dobbins was the sprightfuller man of the two.

Doricourt: Surely this cannot be Miss Hardy!

Letitia: Laws! why, don't you know me! You saw me to-day—but I was daunted before my Father, and the Lawyer, and all them, and did not care to speak out:—so, may be, you thought I couldn't;—but I can talk as fast as any body, when I know folks a little:—and now I have shewn my parts, I hope you'll like me better.

Enter Hardy.

Hardy: I foresee this won't do!—Mr. Doricourt, may be you take my Daughter for a Fool; but your [sic] are mistaken: she's a sensible Girl as any in England.

Doricourt: I am convinced she has a very uncommon understanding, Sir. [...]

Letitia: [...]. Laws! Papa, how can you think he can take me for a fool! when every body knows I beat the Potecary at Conundrums last Christmas-time? and did'nt [sic] I make a string of names, all in riddles, for the Lady's Diary?—There was a little River, and a great House; that was Newcastle.—There was what a Lamb says, and three Letters; that was *Ba*, and *k-e-r*, ker, Baker.—There was—

Hardy: Don't stand ba-a-ing there. You'll make me mad in a moment!—I tell you, Sir, that for all that, she's dev'lish sensible.

Doricourt: Sir, I give all possible credit to your assertions.

Letitia: Laws! Papa, do come along. If you stand watching, how can my Sweetheart break his mind, and tell me how he admires me?

Doricourt. That would be difficult, indeed, Madam.

Hardy: I tell you, Letty, I'll have no more of this.—I see well enough—

Letitia: Laws! don't snub me before my Husband—that is to be.—You'll teach him to snub me too,—and I believe, by his looks, he'd like to begin now.—So, let us go, Cousin; you may tell the Gentleman what a genus I have—how I can cut Watch-papers, and work Cat-gut; make Quadrille-baskets with Pins, and take Profiles in Shade. [...]

[In the next passage (4.1), our characters meet at a masquerade. Doricourt sees Letitia in masquerade but doesn't know it is she. He watches her.]

Doricourt (*during the Minuet*): She dances divinely.—(*When ended*) Somebody must know her! Let us enquire who she is. [...] Ha! Saville! Did you see a Lady dance just now?

Saville: No.

Doricourt: Very odd. No body knows her.

Saville: Where is Miss Hardy?

Doricourt: Cutting Watch-papers, and making Conundrums, I suppose.

Saville: What do you mean?

Doricourt: Faith, I hardly know. She's not here, however. [...]
Saville: Your indifference seems increas'd.
Doricourt: Quite the reverse; 'tis advanced thirty-two degrees towards hatred. [...] Do you know the creature's almost an Ideot? [...] What the devil shall I do with her? Egad! I think I'll feign myself mad—and then Hardy will propose to cancel the engagements. [...]
Saville exits.
As [*Doricourt*] *stands in a musing posture,* Letitia *enters, and sings.* [...]
Doricourt: By Heaven, the same sweet creature! [...] [*Addressing her*] You, the most charming being in the world, awake me to admiration. Did you come from the Stars?
Letitia: Yes, and I shall reascend in a moment.
Doricourt: Pray shew me your face before you go.
Letitia: Beware of imprudent curiosity; it lost Paradise.
Doricourt: Eve's curiosity was rais'd by the Devil;—'tis an Angel tempts mine.—So your allusion is not in point.
Letitia: But *why* would you see my face?
Doricourt: To fall in love with it.
Letitia: And what then?
Doricourt: Why, then—Aye, curse it! there's the rub. [*Aside.*]
Letitia: Your Mistress will be angry;—but, perhaps, you have no Mistress?
Doricourt: Yes, yes; and a sweet one it is! [...] Pho! don't talk about *her*; but shew me your face.
Letitia: My vanity forbids it;—'twould frighten you.
Doricourt: Impossible! Your Shape is graceful, your Air bewitching, your Bosom transparent, and your Chin would tempt me to kiss it, if I did not see a pouting red Lip above it, that demands—
Letitia: You grow too free.
Doricourt: Shew me your face then—only half a glance.
Letitia: Not for worlds. [...]
[*She exits; he follows. They appear together shortly thereafter.*]
Doricourt: By Heavens! I never was charm'd till now.—English beauty—French vivacity—wit—elegance. Your name, my Angel!—tell me your name, though you persist in concealing your face.
Letitia: My name has a spell in it.
Doricourt: I thought so; it must be *Charming*.
Letitia: But if reveal'd, the charm is broke.

Doricourt: I'll answer for its force. [...] The name your Father gave ye!

Letitia: That can't be worth knowing, 'tis so transient a thing.

Doricourt: How, transient?

Letitia: Heav'n forbid my name should be *lasting* till I am married.

Doricourt: Married! The chains of Matrimony are too heavy and vulgar for such a spirit as yours.—The flowery wreaths of Cupid are the only bands you should wear.

Letitia: They are the lightest, I believe: but 'tis possible to wear those of Marriage gracefully.—Throw 'em loosely round, and twist 'em in a True-Lover's Knot for the Bosom.

Doricourt: An Angel! But what will you be when a Wife?

Letitia: A Woman.—If my Husband should prove a Churl, a Fool, or a Tyrant, I'd break his heart, ruin his fortune, elope with the first pretty Fellow that ask'd me—and return the contempt of the world with scorn, whilst my feelings prey'd upon my life.

Doricourt: Amazing! [*Aside.*] What if you lov'd him, and he were worthy of your love?

Letitia: Why, then I'd be any thing—and all!—Grave, gay, capricious—the soul of whim, the spirit of variety—live with him in the eye of fashion, or in the shade of retirement—change my country, my sex,—feast with him in an Esquimaux hut, or a Persian pavilion—join him in the victorious war-dance on the borders of Lake Ontario, or sleep to the soft breathings of the flute in the cinnamon groves of Ceylon—dig with him in the mines of Golconda, or enter the dangerous precincts of the Mogul's Seraglo [*sic*]—cheat him of his wishes, and overturn his empire to restore the Husband of my Heart to the blessings of Liberty and Love. [...] Though Cupid must give the bait that tempts me to the snare, 'tis Hymen must spread the net to catch me.

Doricourt: 'Tis in vain to assume airs of coldness—Fate has ordain'd you mine.

Letitia: How do you know?

Doricourt: I feel it *here*. I never met with a Woman so perfectly to my taste; and I won't believe it form'd you so, on purpose to tantalize me.

Letitia: This moment is worth my whole existence. [*Aside.*]

Doricourt: Come, shew me your face, and rivet my chains.

Letitia: To-morrow you shall be satisfied. [...]

Doricourt: Where then shall I wait on you to-morrow?—Where see you?

Letitia: You shall see me in an hour when you least expect me. [...]

[Hardy has entered to hear the last of their interaction. Letitia exits.]

Doricourt: [...] What, and is this really serious?—am I in love?—Pho! it can't be—O Flutter! Do you know that charming Creature?

Enter Flutter.

Flutter: What charming Creature? I pass'd a thousand.

Doricourt: She went out at that door, as you enter'd.

Flutter: Oh, yes;—I know her very well.

Doricourt: Do you, my dear Fellow? Who?

Flutter: She's kept by Lord George Jennett [...] Colonel Gorget had her first;—then Mr. Loveill;—then—I forget exactly how many; and at last she's Lord George's. [...]

Hardy: Now's the time, I see, to clear up the whole. Mr. Doricourt!—I say—Flutter was mistaken; I know who you are in love with.

Doricourt: A strange *rencontre*! Who?

Hardy: My Lettie.

Doricourt: Oh! I understand your rebuke;—'tis too soon, sir, to assume the Father-in-law.

Hardy: Zounds! what do you mean by that? I tell you that the Lady you admire, is Letitia Hardy.

Doricourt: I am glad *you* are so well satisfied with the state of my heart.—I wish *I* was. [He exits]

Hardy: [...] I'll plot *with* Lettie now. [...]

[In the next pertinent scene (5.1), Hardy and Villers discuss Doricourt's refusal to recognize the masked beauty as his intended.]

Villers: WHIMSICAL enough! Dying for her, and hates her; believes her a Fool, and a Woman of brilliant Understanding!

Hardy: As true as you are alive;—but when I went up to him last night, at the Pantheon, out of downright good-nature to explain things—my Gentleman whips round upon his heel, and snapt me as short as if I had been a beggar-woman with six children, and he Overseer of the Parish. [...]

Enter Letitia.

Hardy: [...] I ha'n't slept to-night, for thinking of plots to plague Doricourt . . . I wish to goodness you could contrive something.

Villers: Contrive to plague him! Nothing so easy. Don't undeceive him, Madam, 'till he is your husband. Marry him whilst he possesses the sentiments you labour'd to give him of Miss Hardy—and when you are his Wife—[...]

Letitia: Oh, Heavens! I see the whole—that's the very thing. My dear Mr. Villers, you are the divinest Man.

[In the next scene (5.2), we see Doricourt's plans to act mad in action.]

Saville: [...] 'tis Flutter himself. Tip him a scene of the Mad-man, and see how it takes.

Doricourt: I will—a good way to send it about town. Shall it be of the melancholy kind, or the raving?

Saville: Rant!—rant!—Here he comes. [...] Oh, Mr. Flutter, what a melancholy sight!—I little thought to have seen my poor friend reduced to this.

Flutter: Mercy defend me! What's he mad?

Saville: You see how it is. A cursed Italian Lady—Jealousy—gave him a drug; and every full of the moon—

Doricourt: Moon! Who dares talk of the Moon? The patroness of genius—the rectifier of wits—the—Oh! here she is!—I feel her—she tugs at my brain—she has it—she has it—Oh! [...]

[Flutter is convinced, and a bit later (5.3), a group of characters discuss the news Flutter has spread.]

Saville: Madam, I am sorry to say, that I have just been a melancholy witness of his ravings: he was in the height of a paroxysm.

Mrs. Racket. Oh, there can be no doubt of it. Flutter told us the whole history. Some Italian Princess gave him a drug, in a box of sweetmeats, sent to him by her own page; and it renders him lunatic every month. Poor Miss Hardy! I never felt so much on any occasion in my life.

Saville: To soften your concern, I will inform you, Madam, that Miss Hardy is less to be pitied than you imagine.

Mrs. Racket: Why so, Sir?

Saville: 'Tis rather a delicate subject—but he did not love Miss Hardy.

Mrs. Racket: He did love Miss Hardy, Sir, and would have been the happiest of men.

Saville: Pardon me, Madam; his heart was not only free from that Lady's chains, but absolutely captivated by another.

Mrs. Racket: No, Sir—no. It was Miss Hardy who captivated him. She met him last night at the Masquerade, and charmed him in disguise.—He professed the most violent passion for her; and a plan was laid, this evening, to cheat him into happiness.

Saville: Ha! ha! ha! [...] Why, Madam, he is at present in his perfect senses; but he'll lose 'em in ten minutes, through joy.—The madness was only a feint, to avoid marrying Miss Hardy, ha! ha! ha!—I'll carry him the intelligence directly. (*Going.*)

Mrs. Racket: Not for worlds. I owe him revenge, now, for what he has made us suffer. You must promise not to divulge a syllable I have told you; and when Doricourt is summoned to Mr. Hardy's, prevail on him to come—madness, and all. [...] I am going home; so I'll set you down at his lodgings, and acquaint you, by the way, with our whole scheme. [...]

[In the next scene (5.4), Saville tells Doricourt that Hardy is dying and that Doricourt should go to Hardy's deathbed, feign madness, and get Hardy's commands that he not marry Letitia. They go to Hardy's in the following scene (V.v); Doricourt then emerges from Hardy's bedroom, having been convinced that Hardy is on his deathbed, and having married Letitia to grant Hardy's dying wish.]

Villers: [...] how shocking a thing it is for a Man to be forced to marry one Woman, whilst his heart is devoted to another.

Mrs. Racket: Well, now 'tis over, I confess to you, Mr. Doricourt, I think 'twas a most ridiculous piece of Quixotism,[1] to give up the happiness of a whole life to a Man who perhaps has but a few moments to be sensible of the sacrifice. [...]

---

[1] Misguided chivalry.

Doricourt: To Felicity I bid adieu—but I will endeavour to be content. Where is my—I must speak it—where is my *Wife*?

Enter Letitia, *masked, led by* Saville.

Saville: Mr. Doricourt, this Lady was pressing to be introduced to you.

Doricourt: Oh! (*Starting*).

Letitia: I told you last night, you shou'd see me at a time when you least expected me—and I have kept my promise.

Villers: Whoever you are, Madam, you could not have arrived at a happier moment.—Mr. Doricourt is just married.

Letitia: Married! Impossible! 'Tis but a few hours since he swore to me eternal Love: I believ'd him, gave him up my Virgin heart—and now!—Ungrateful Sex!

Doricourt: Your Virgin heart! No, Lady—my fate, thank Heaven! yet wants that torture. Nothing but the conviction that you was [sic] another's, could have made me think one moment of Marriage, to have saved the lives of half Mankind. But this visit, Madam, is as barbarous as unexpected. It is now my duty to forget you, which, spite of your situation, I found difficult enough.

Letitia: My situation!—What situation?

Doricourt: I must apologise for explaining it in this company—but, Madam, I am not ignorant, that you are the companion of Lord George Jennet—and this is the only circumstance that can give me peace.

Letitia:—a Companion! Ridiculous pretence! No, Sir, know, to your confusion, that my heart, my honour, my name is unspotted as her's you have married; my birth equal to your own, my fortune large—That, and my person, might have been your's.—But, Sir, farewell! (*Going*).

Doricourt: Oh, stay a moment—Rascal! is she not—

Flutter: Who, she? O Lard! [sic] no—'Twas quite a different person that I meant.—I never saw that Lady before.

Doricourt: Then, never shalt thou see her more. (*Shakes* Flutter.) [...] you have snatch'd from me joy, felicity, and life. [...]

Hardy *bursts in.*

Hardy: This is too much. You are now the Husband of my Daughter; and how dare you shew all this passion about another Woman?

Doricourt: Alive again!

Hardy: Alive! aye, and merry. Here, wipe off the flour from my face. I was never in better health and spirits in my life.—I foresaw t'would do—. Why, my illness was only a fetch, Man! to make you marry Letty.

Doricourt: It was! Base and ungenerous! Well, Sir, you shall be gratified. The possession of my heart was no object either with You, or your Daughter. My fortune and name was all you desired, and these—I leave ye. My native England I shall quit, nor ever behold you more. But, Lady, that in my exile I may have one consolation, grant me the favour you denied last night;—let me behold all that mask conceals, that your whole image may be impress'd on my heart, and chear my distant solitary hours.

Letitia: This is the most awful moment of my life. Oh, Doricourt, the slight action of taking off my Mask, stamps me the most blest or miserable of Women!

Doricourt: What can this mean? Reveal your face, I conjure you.

Letitia: Behold it.

Doricourt: Rapture! Transport! Heaven! [...]

Letitia: [...] This little stratagem arose from my disappointment, in not having made the impression on you I wish'd. The timidity of the English character threw a veil over me, you could not penetrate. You have forced me to emerge in some measure from my natural reserve, and to throw off the veil that hid me.

Doricourt: I am yet in a state of intoxication—I cannot answer you.—Speak on, sweet Angel!

Letitia: You see I *can* be any thing; chuse then my character—your Taste shall fix it. Shall I be an *English* Wife?—or, breaking from the bonds of Nature and Education, step forth to the world in all the captivating glare of Foreign Manners?

Doricourt: You shall be nothing but yourself—nothing can be captivating that you are not. I will not wrong your penetration, by pretending that you won my heart at the first interview; but you have now my whole soul—your person, your face, your mind, I would not exchange for those of any other Woman breathing. [...] My charming Bride! It was a strange perversion of Taste, that led me to consider the delicate timidity of your deportment, as the mark of an uninform'd mind, or inelegant manners. I feel now it is to that innate modesty, *English* Husbands owe a felicity the Married Men of other nations are strangers to: it is a sacred veil to your own charms; it is the surest bulwark to your Husband's honour; and cursed be the hour—should it ever arrive—in which *British* Ladies shall sacrifice to *foreign Graces* the Grace of modesty!

FINIS.

Charlotte Smith, *Montalbert*, London: Booker, 1795. 3 vols., II: 167-195; III: 275-281.

[This novel involves the fortunes and misfortunes of its protagonist, Rosalie, and her relationship with the man she loves and secretly marries, Montalbert. He is Italian, and a Catholic, and he knows that his mother, Signora Belcastro, will disapprove of his marriage to Rosalie, an Englishwoman who has been raised Protestant, although she later learns that she is the illegitimate daughter of a Catholic woman, Mrs. Vyvian, hence Catholic by birth herself. They marry in England (in a Catholic ceremony which is thus not, as it turns out, valid in England, although Rosalie is uncertain on this point) but Montalbert must return to his mother in Naples, who has been sick. Montalbert is wholly financially dependent on his mother, so wants to keep the marriage secret until he can figure out how to break the news to her without her casting him off—or until she dies, rendering such an issue moot. He decides to hide Rosalie at a villa belonging to a friend of his, Count Alozzi, near Messina. Of a jealous nature, however, he becomes suspicious of his friend, but he must return to Naples lest his mother become suspicious of his own absences. He returns briefly to see Rosalie in time for the birth of their son but then goes back to Naples for a few weeks, after which time he intends to make another visit to Rosalie. They are separated by the same earthquake recounted in *The Two Emilys*; we first read of Rosalie's experiences in that earthquake and then of Montalbert's, as he searches for his wife and child. The first passage occurs nearly exactly midway through the novel, in the middle of the second of its three volumes.]

In Sicily there is no winter such as is felt in the more northern countries, and now, in the month of February, spring every where appeared in the rich vales that stretch towards the sea from the base of Etna. His towering and majestic summit alone presented the image of eternal frost, and formed a singular but magnificent contrast to the vivid and luxuriant vegetation of the lower world. [...]

When [Rosalie] reflected how entirely she was secluded from all knowledge of what passed [in England], she felt her tenderness and solicitude return for Mrs. Vyvian, and would have given half a world, had she possessed it, to have known how that beloved parent bore her absence, and what was the state of her health. Even the passionate fondness she felt for her child most forcibly recalled that affection which she owed her mother ...... "Just so, (said she, as she studied with delight, in the features of her little boy, the resemblance of Montalbert), just so, perhaps, my poor mother, as soon as she dared indulge herself with a sight of me, endeavoured to make out, in my unfortunate lineaments, the likeness of my unhappy father. [...] Dear, unhappy parents!—never shall your daughter see either of you perhaps again—never shall she know the blessing of being acknowledged by a father; of being pressed to the conscious heart of a mother proud to own her!" [...]

She remembered for how many misfortunes such a husband as Montalbert ought to console her, and tried, though in vain, to call in a train of more cheerful ideas [... but Rosalie's] spirits became more and more depressed. A thousand vague apprehensions beset her for the health of her child; she now never quitted him a moment, and watched him incessantly with a vigilance which fed itself with imaginary terrors.

This state of mind had continued some time with no other relief than what the hope of Montalbert's speedy return afforded, when, sitting in a lower apartment with her infant in her arms, Rosalie was surprised by a singular motion in the floor, which seemed to rise under her feet; she started up, and saw, with horror and amazement, the walls of the room breaking in several directions, while the dust and lime threatened to choke her, and so obscured the air, that she could hardly distinguish Zulietta, who ran from another room, and seizing her by the hand, drew her with all the strength she could exert through a door which opened under an arch into the garden. Zulietta spoke not; she was, indeed, unable to speak.

Rosalie, to whom the tremendous idea of an earthquake now occurred, followed as quickly as she was able, clasping her boy to her breast.[1] They were soon about fifty yards from the house, the ground heaving and rolling beneath them like the waves of the sea, and beyond them breaking into yawning gulphs, which threatened to prevent their flight; Rosalie then looked round, and saw, instead of the house she had just left, a cloud of impenetrable smoke, which prevented her knowing whether any of it remained above the convulsed earth that had entirely swallowed part of the shattered walls. No language could describe the terror and confusion that overwhelmed this little group of fugitives; for no other fearful spectacle can impress on the human mind ideas of such complicated horrors as now surrounded them. They heard the crash of the building they had just left, as it half sunk into a deep chasm; before them, and even under their feet, the ground continued to break; the trees were torn from their roots, and falling in every direction around them; and vapours of sulphur and burning bitumen seemed to rise in pestilential clouds, which impeded the sight and the respiration.

Rosalie called faintly, and with a sickening heart, as conscious of its inutility, on the name of Montalbert. Alas! Montalbert was afar off, and could not succour her. To the mercy of Heaven, who seemed thus to summon her and her infant away, she committed him and herself; and laying herself on the ground, with her child in her arms, and Zulietta kneeling by her, she resigned herself to that fate which appeared to be inevitable.

Flight was vain—all human help was vain, but nature still resisted dissolution, and she could not help thinking with agony of the state of Montalbert's mind, when the loss of his wife and child should be known to him. Another thought darted into her mind, and brought with it a more severe pang than any she had yet felt: Montalbert proposed about this time to return; within a few days she had began [sic] to expect him, in consequence of his last letters. It was possible—alas! it was even probable, that he was already

---

[1] When the ruins came to be cleared away, says Sir William Hamilton, the bodies of the men who had perished were universally found in the attitude of resistance; the women in that of prayer, unless it was those who had children with them, in which case they were observed to have taken such postures as were likely to shelter and protect them. [Smith's note.]

at Messina, and he too might have perished: he might at this moment expire amid the suffocating ruins—crushed by their weight, or stifled by subterraneous fires. The image was too horrible; she started up, as if it were possible for her feeble arms to save him; she looked wildly round her—all was ruin and desolation, but the earth no longer trembled as it had done, and a faint hope of safety arose almost insensibly in her heart. She spoke to Zulietta, who seemed petrified and motionless; she conjured her to rise and assist her—yet whither to go she knew not, nor what were her intentions, or her prospects of safety.

While Rosalie yet spoke incoherently, almost unconscious that she spoke at all, a second shock, though less violent than the first, again deprived her of the little presence of mind she had collected—and, again prostrate on the ground, she commended her soul to Heaven!

In a few moments, however, this new convulsion ceased, and the possibility that Montalbert might be returning, might be seeking her in distracted apprehension, restored to her the power of exertion. The hope that she might once see her husband, served as a persuasion that she should see, and she advanced heedless of any danger she might incur by it towards the ruins of the house, where it was probable he would seek for her; but between her and those ruins was a deep and impassable chasm, which had been formed during the last shock.

Zulietta, from her abrupt and wild manner, had conceived an idea that her mistress meant, in the despair occasioned by terror and grief, to throw herself into this gulph. Impressed with this fear, she seized her by the arm, and making use of such arguments as the moment allowed, she drew her away, and they walked together, as hastily as they had strength, through the garden and up a rising ground beyond it, which was terminated by a deep wood, which had been less affected than the lower ground, though one or two of the trees were fallen and some half uprooted. Unable to go farther, Rosalie sat down on one of their trunks, and Zulietta placed herself near her. [...]

"Zulietta, (said she, in a mournful and broken voice)—Zulietta! what will become of my child? [....] Could I but save my child! (exclaimed Rosalie, little encouraged by her companion).—Could I but know whether Montalbert lives!—O Montalbert! where are you—if you exist?"—

A shriek from Zulietta interrupted this soliloquy. She started from the tree where they sat, and fled to some distance; Rosalie involuntarily followed her, looking back towards the dark wood. "I saw some person move among the trees, (cried Zulietta, in answer to the lady's eager inquiries), I am sure I did—banditti are coming to murder us." (II: 167-176)

Rosalie was convinced that at least this time the fears of her woman were but too well grounded; the voices of two men talking together were distinctly heard, and, on turning round, they saw a light glimmer among the trees. As these persons, whoever they were, followed the path they had taken, and were advancing quickly towards them, escape or concealment became impossible; half dead with fear, and almost unconscious of what she did, Rosalie now stopped, determined to await the event.

The men approached, and, as soon as the light they held made the figures before them visible, one of them uttered an exclamation of surprize, and eagerly advanced towards Rosalie—it was Count Alozzi, who, with one of his servants, had come in search of her. Without, however, staying to tell her what circumstance had brought him thus from Agrigentum,[1] or how he knew that she had escaped with her child from the destruction that had overwhelmed the house, he entreated her to suffer him to conduct her to a place of security, which he hoped, he said, to find not far off. [...]

[T]hey reached a house, which, with two or three others, were [sic] situated among olive grounds, and which, Alozzi said, belonged to his estate. These buildings had received but little injury, yet the inhabitants of them, still doubting whether they might remain under their roofs, were so terrified and dejected by what had passed, and the dread of that which was to come, that the presence of Alozzi seemed to make no impression upon them. They coldly and silently acquiesced in affording the accommodation he asked, for the lady he brought with him, and set before the party such food as they happened to have. Zulietta, recovering some degree of courage, pressed

---

[1] Agrigentum, on the southwestern coast of Sicily, is best known as the site of the first major battle, in 261 B.C.E., of the Punic War; its fall led to the beginning of Roman rule of Sicily.

Rosalie to eat, and Alozzi watched her with eager and anxious solicitude, which, when she observed, she imputed to his solicitude, or sorrow for the fate of his friend, which she still fancied he knew.

Fatigue, however, both of mind and body, and the care necessary to herself for the sake of her child, overcame for a while her excessive anxiety for Montalbert, of whom Alozzi again and again repeated he knew nothing; at length Rosalie consented to retire with Zulietta to a bed, or rather mattress, which the wife of one of the tenants of Alozzi prepared for her, where her child appearing to be in health and in present safety, sleep lent a while its friendly assistance to relieve her spirits, and recruit her strength, after such sufferings and such scenes as those of the preceding day.

Her repose was broken and disturbed, for she fancied she heard Montalbert call her, and that the buildings were about to crush her and her infant. In the morning, however, she was refreshed and relieved, even by this partial and interrupted forgetfulness, and able to receive the visit of the Count [....] "It is impossible (said he gravely) to tell what Montalbert would have done, were he here; but, for myself, I own it appears to me that there is only one part to take. It is but too probable that another shock will be felt before many days are over. Here I have no longer a house to receive me, for that I inhabited at Messina is, I know, destroyed, though I was not near it yesterday when the earthquake happened, but about a mile from the town on my way home. The villa, which you did me the honour to inhabit, has shared the same fate. I approached it; I saw part of it buried in the earth, and the rest is by this time probably reduced to ashes. What then can I do but quit this devoted country, and return to Naples?— There I have a home, I have friends.—If you, Madam, will put yourself under my protection, I will defend you with my life, and consider myself highly honoured by so precious a charge." (II: 184-187)

[Alozzi and Zulietta return to the estate Rosalie has lately inhabited "to see if any thing useful to his late guests could yet be saved; which, though improbable was not impossible."]

When they were gone Rosalie went out with her baby in her arms, and seated herself on an open piece of ground, about a hundred yards from the house, which commanded from between the stems of a few straggling olive trees an extensive view of the city of Messina and the country round it. It presented a strange contrast of beauty and destruction. Those parts of the country that had not been convulsed or inverted were adorned with the blossoms of the almond, waving over fields of various coloured lupines and lentiscus; hedges of myrtles divided the enclosures, and among them the pomegranate was coming into flower; the stock doves in innumerable flocks were returning to feed among them, or fluttering amidst the purple and white blossoms of the caper trees: but within half a mile of this profusion of what is most soothing to the imagination, black and hideous gulphs, from whence pestilential vapours seemed to issue, defaced the lovely landscape. The beautiful town of Messina seemed more than half destroyed, and now Rosalie saw not far from her many groups of sufferers, who, frantic from the loss of their friends, their children, or their substance, were wandering about the fields without any hope but of passing the next night as they had done part of the preceding one, under the canopy of Heaven, gazing with tearless eyes on the melancholy spot where all their hopes were buried. From the sight of misery, which she could not relieve, her sick heart recoiled; she walked slowly back to the house, and attempted but in vain to form some resolution as to her future plans; but such was her situation, and so entirely did she feel herself dependent on the Count, that this was hardly possible ...... Again, in a convulsive sigh, she repeated the name of Montalbert—again implored the mercy of Heaven for him and her child, on whose little face, as it was pressed to her bosom, her tears fell in showers!

She turned her fearful eyes on the people among whom she was left. Many were now in the house whom she had not seen before, and some among them gave her but too forcibly the idea of those banditti, of whom Zulietta had expressed so many fears the evening before as they passed through the woods. Some of them were men of large stature, in a kind of uniform, and she fancied that they passed through the room where she was on purpose to observe her. A new species of terror assailed her in consequence of this remark, yet she endeavoured to reason herself out of it, and to suppose that where Count Alozzi had left her she must be in security.

The people, who appeared to belong to the house, brought her some slender meal, which she eat [sic] mechanically [....] Many new faces entered the house, and she understood, from such conversation as she heard and put together, that they were come to obtain an asylum for the night. One of them was a lovely Sicilian girl, of sixteen or seventeen, who wept grievously, as Rosalie comprehended, for the loss of her sister and her sister's children. The beauty of the little Montalbert, as he lay sleeping in his mother's arms, seemed to interest and affect this young person; she spoke to Rosalie, and was approaching to caress the child, when an old woman who was with her said something in a sharp and severe accent, and drew her hastily out of the room.

This circumstance, and indeed every remark she now made, increased the impatience and uneasiness with which she waited for the return of Alozzi. Night was at hand; the parties in the house were contriving how to pass it most at their ease, but nobody seemed to attend to her; on the contrary, she believed that a disposition to shun her was evident in the women, while the looks of the men gave her infinitely more alarm, and she sometimes resolved, rather than pass the night among them, to set out alone, and seek the protection of Alozzi.

On this she had almost determined, and, trembling and faint, left the house with an intention of discovering how far such an attempt might be safer than to remain where she was. She had proceeded only about a hundred yards, when a new convulsion of the earth threw her down, and her senses entirely forsook her; nor did she recover her recollection till she found herself on board a small vessel at sea, her child lying by her, and a woman, whom she had never seen before, watching her. As soon as she appeared to be sensible Alozzi came to her, endeavouring to sooth and console her. He told her, that another shock of an earthquake had compelled all who could leave Sicily to depart; that he had before engaged a bark; that they were now far on their way to Naples with a fair wind, and that they should be there in a few hours.

The shock she had received, the terror and confusion with which she was yet impressed, were such as left Rosalie little sensation but that ever predominant one of love and anxiety for her infant boy, whom she clasped with more fondness than ever to her breast, and, amidst the terrors that on every side surrounded her, found in his preservation something for which to be grateful to Heaven. (II: 189-195)

[Alozzi takes Rosalie to his house in Naples; there, recalling Montalbert's jealousy of Alozzi, she becomes suspicious of him and decides to seek other protection. She writes to Signora Belcastro, Montalbert's mother, hoping that in light of this disaster, she will forgive Montalbert for having married Rosalie. She tells Signora Belcastro that she is Montalbert's wife and that both she and Montalbert's son are in need of proper protection. Rosalie is kidnapped by ruffians and taken to a castle in Squillace, a town on the east coast of Calabria; if one sees Italy as a boot, this town would fall between the toes and the ball of the foot. She is ultimately rescued by an Englishman, Walsingham, who takes her back to England where, after a series of misunderstandings, Rosalie is finally reunited with Montalbert. Towards the end of the novel's three volumes, Montalbert recounts his experiences searching for Rosalie in Messina.]

The frequent absences, which our fear of my mother's displeasure had obliged me to submit to, became daily more insupportable, and I was forming schemes of retired happiness when I had thrown off this cruel restraint, and dared to be poor and independent. Judge then how horrible were my feelings, when, awaking from this dream of felicity, I found Messina in ruins, and the country for many miles around it convulsed by an earthquake, which had, two days before we made the coast, buried half its inhabitants.

I cannot tell you what were my sensations after I had with much difficulty landed, for I have never since been able to define them; nor do I know from whence sprang the resolution with which I explored the place where the villa of Alozzi had stood, of which no other vestige remained than some pieces of black and half-burnt ruins: yet I looked with tearless eyes into the dark chasms in which it was sunk, though I thought they but too surely contained all I had loved—my Rosalie and her child!

The first evening that I arrived at this melancholy spot, where I had so lately left the lovely treasures of my heart in apparent safety, there were none near it—I was undisturbed in my gloomy contemplation, and remained lingering about the place, till my servant, who had followed me at a distance according to my direction, came to me at night fall, and led me to a cottage not far off, inhabited by a woman and her daughter, who had lost the rest of their family. Of these my servant made some inquiries, as they were tenants of Count Alozzi. He heard that the Count was seen after the first great shock, and had hired a vessel to take himself and some of his dependants to Naples; but whether he escaped the second, or whether he was drowned with many others on the sudden reflux of the sea, these women had no means of knowing.—Here then was a glimpse, and but a glimpse of hope, that my wife and child might exist; but, on farther inquiry the next evening, I thought even this faint hope vanished. [...] All my thoughts were bent on trying to recover from the ruins of his villa the sad remains of my lost family; and with this dreary sort of satisfaction I occupied my mind, repairing the next day to the place, where I found three or four stout peasants already at work.

I inquired of them by whom they were employed?—they answered, in no very mild manner, by themselves, and for their own purposes and profit. I saw that they feared I was disposed, if not authorized, to impede their designs; but by the most infallible of all arguments, (for I emptied my purse), and soon satisfied them that they should not be interrupted in the possession of whatever valuable effects they might recover, since my sole purpose was to search for the mangled relics of a wife and child. I offered them more money if they would procure farther assistance to expedite this search, and, explaining to them who I was, promised farther reward if they could procure me any certain intelligence of Count Alozzi. They agreed that he had been seen after the first violent concussion of the earth; but all believed, or affected to believe, he perished in the second.

It was now nine days since the fatal catastrophe, three of which I stood by the yawning cavern that had swallowed the villa of Alozzi. Little was discovered by the men who went down among the ruins; they were, indeed, more intent on their own purposes than on mine. On the evening of the third day I went down myself, and I thought that by the remains of wainscoting, or furniture, I should be led to the ruins of that part of the house Rosalie had inhabited. Desperate, I tore away, at some risk to myself, the door cases, broken or scorched pieces of building, and at length found the room where Rosalie usually sat. I could clearly distinguish that there were no remains of human bodies in it; two only had been found, and they were known to be servants; but another day's search satisfied that no more persons were buried in these ruins, yet even this circumstance afforded no proof, that those my sickening soul inquired after were living.

With an anxious and hopeless heart I left the peasants busily employed in labour, which had already amply repaid them, and now sat [*sic*] out to wander over the country, asking questions of the unhappy persons who were yet scattered about it, though their answers only irritated my misery, or confirmed my despair. Most of them were too much occupied by the wants and woes of their own condition, to give much attention to me. After some days were thus vainly wasted, I crossed over to the other side of the island, and went among such relations and friends of Alozzi as had escaped any immediate share of the misfortune by being at a distance from that part where its violence had fallen. Among them I learned that Alozzi had quitted Agrigentum four or five days before the earthquake, and had gone, as they believed, to Messina, where they had no doubt of his having perished, as they had never heard of him since. There was hardly one of those families who had not some relation or friend to lament; and I only quitted one house of mourning to enter another.

To me, all appeared equally desolate and wretched; the image of my lost happiness continually haunted me, and I returned more unhappy than ever to the place where once stood the villa of Alozzi.

By this time some peasants who had been dispersed, had come back to that neighbourhood also; among them I met two or three Sbirri,[1] who were, I thought, likely persons to have seen Alozzi, if he had indeed escaped, for they were daring and active, and were probably busy wherever pay or plunder were likely to be had from the rich that survived the earthquake. I entered into conversation with them, and heard that they had passed the night, after the first violent shock, at a house belonging to the Count, where they had seen him with a lady and her child, and a Neapolitan servant. That they knew the lady was an Heretic from the woman of the house, who, as well as those to whom she had given shelter during the horrors of that night, had expressed their fears of remaining under the same roof with a person of that description, and that some of the women had actually left it, lest she should draw Divine vengeance on the house. (III: 275-281)

---

[1] Cops—*i.e.*, slang for police.

[Hereafter, we learn of Montalbert's tracing Alozzi, who admits he does not know where Rosalie is, and of Montalbert's then managing to trace Rosalie to England. Ironically, Rosalie's situation worsens not directly because of the earthquake but because of Italian misbehavior; were Alozzi more forthright with Rosalie and innocent of Montalbert's suspicions, he would have let her seek the aid of other Englishmen in Naples and thus not have driven her to her ill-conceived plan to write to Montalbert's mother, Signora Belcastro. Signora Belcastro, were she not the implacable heartless stereotype of Italian mother disseminated by such novels as Ann Radcliffe's *The Italian*, would not have had her kidnapped. Were Montalbert not the stereotypical jealous, passionate, and impulsive Italian man, he would not misconstrue Rosalie's actions of leaving Italy under Walsingham's protection; he would not then have their child wrested from her as the infamous woman he believes she is, resulting in Rosalie's nearly deadly illness and wanderings of intellect, and he would not challenge Walsingham to a duel, which nearly results in Walsingham's death. Ultimately, Montalbert casts off his mother, but Walsingham, having recovered, intercedes and gets Signora Belcastro at least to will her estate to Rosalie and Montalbert's child. Rosalie and Montalbert live on the bounty of Rosalie's father, who has been in India, not having known he had a daughter, but who has returned with great wealth and has discovered his daughter on her apparent deathbed and saved both her and her family from penury.]

Alexander Pope, *The Odyssey of Homer*. London: Bernard Lintot, 1725-26. 2 vols.

The passage of the Odyssey (ca. 700 B.C.E.) the Marquis calls to mind is from Book XII. The version of *The Odyssey* the Marquis read may have been in Greek; if in English, it was probably the translation (1725-26) by Alexander Pope (1688-1744). In this passage, we first read Circe's advice to Odysseus on how to navigate the dangerous straits between Scylla and Charybdis, the former being on the mainland of Calabria and the other being across the strait on the northeastern tip of Sicily closest to Calabria.

APPENDIX B: LITERARY CORRESPONDENCES

Here *Scylla* bellows from her dire abodes,
Tremendous pest! abhorr'd by man and Gods!
Hideous her voice, and with less terrors roar
The whelps of Lions in the midnight hour.
Twelve feet deform'd and foul the fiend dispreads;
Six horrid necks she rears, and six terrific heads;
Her jaws grin dreadful with three rows of teeth;
Jaggy they stand, the gaping den of death:
Her parts obscene the raging billows hide;
Her bosom terribly o'erlooks the tide.
When stung with hunger she embroils the flood,
The sea-dog and the dolphin are her food;
She makes the huge Leviathan her prey,
And all the monsters of the wat'ry way;
The swiftest racer of the azure plain
Here fills her sails and spreads her oars in vain;
Fell *Scylla* rises, in her fury roars,
At once six mouths expands, at once six men devours.

Close by, a rock of less enormous height
Breaks the wild waves, and forms a dang'rous streight;
Full on its crown a fig's green branches rise,
And shoot a leafy forest to the skies,
Beneath, *Charybdis* holds her boisterous reign
'Midst roaring whirlpools, and absorbs the main;
Thrice in her gulphs the boiling seas subside,
Thrice in dire thunders she refunds the tide.
Oh if thy vessel plow the direful waves,
When seas retreating roar within her caves,
Ye perish all! tho' he who rules the main
Lend his strong aid, his aid he lends in vain.
Ah, shun the horrid gulf! by *Scylla* fly,
'Tis better six to lose, than all to die... (XII: 107-138)

[Odysseus and his crew leave Circe; Odysseus then narrates their voyage through Scylla and Charybdis.]

Now thro' the rocks, appal'd with deep dismay,

We bend our course, and stem the desp'rate way;
Dire *Scylla* there a scene of horror forms,
And here *Charybdis* fills the deep with storms.
When the tide rushes from her rumbling caves
The rough rock roars; tumultuous boil the waves;
They toss, they foam, a wild confusion raise,
Like waters bubbling o'er the fiery blaze;
Eternal mists obscure th'aereal plain,
And high above the rock she spouts the main;
When in her gulphs the rushing sea subsides,
She dreins the ocean with the refluent tides:
The rock rebellows with a thund'ring sound;
Deep, wond'rous deep, below appears the ground.

Struck with despair, with trembling hearts we view'd
The yawning dungeon, and the tumbling flood;
When lo! fierce *Scylla* stoop'd to seize her prey,
Stretch'd her dire jaws, and swept six men away.
Chiefs of renown! loud echoing shrieks arise;
I turn, and view them quivering in the skies;
They call, and aid with out-stretch'd arms implore:
In vain they call! those arms are stretch'd no more.
As from some rock that overhangs the flood,
The silent fisher casts th'insidious food,
With fraudful care he waits the finny prize,
And sudden lifts it quivering to the skies:
So the foul monster lifts her prey on high,
So pant the wretches struggling in the skie;
In the wide dungeon she devours her food,
And the flesh trembles while she churns the blood.
Worn as I am with griefs, with care decay'd,
Never, I never, scene so dire survey'd!
My shivering blood congeal'd forgot to flow;
Aghast I stood, a monument of woe! ... (XII: 277-311)

[They go to the Island of Trinaria where the shipmates slay the Oxen of the Son; as a result, they become caught in a storm which only Odysseus survives; he travels on to

APPENDIX B: LITERARY CORRESPONDENCES 255

the Island of Calypso. The following relates the storm and Odysseus's passing again through Scylla and Charybdis and his then arriving at Calypso.]

Now heaven gave signs of wrath; along the ground
Crept the raw hides, and with a bellowing sound
Roar'd the dead limbs; the burning entrails groan'd
Six guilty days my wretched mates employ
In impious feasting, and unhallowed joy;
The sev'nth arose, and now the Sire of Gods
Rein'd the rough storms, and calm'd the tossing floods:
With speed the bark we climb; the spacious sails
Loos'd from the yards invite th'impelling gales.
Past sight of shore, along the surge we bound,
And all above is sky, and ocean all around!
When lo! a murky cloud the Thunderer forms
Full o'er our heads, and blackens heav'n with storms.
Night dwells o'er all the deep: and now out flies
The gloomy west, and whistles in the skies.
The mountain billows roar! the furious blast
Howls o'er the shroud, and rends it from the mast:
The mast gives way, and, crackling as it bends,
Tears up the deck; then all at once descends:
The pilot by the tumbling ruin slain,
Dash'd from the helm, falls headlong in the main.
Then *Jove* in anger bids his thunders roll,
And forky lightnings flash from pole to pole;
Fierce at our heads his deadly bolt he aims,
Red with uncommon wrath, and wrapt in flames:
Full on the bark it fell; now high, now low,
Toss'd and retoss'd, it reel'd beneath the blow;
At once into the main the crew it shook:
Sulphurous odors rose, and smould'ring smoke.
Like fowl that haunt the floods, they sink, they rise,
Now lost, now seen, with shrieks and dreadful cries;
And strive to gain the bark; but *Jove* denies.
Firm at the helm I stand, when fierce the main
Rush'd with dire noise, and dash'd the sides in twain;

Again impetuous drove the furious blast,
Snapt the strong helm, and bore to sea the mast.
Firm to the mast with cords the helm I bind,
And ride aloft, to Providence resign'd,
Thro' tumbling billows, and a war of wind.

Now sunk the West, and now a southern breeze,
More dreadful than the tempest, lash'd the seas;
For on the rocks it bore where *Scylla* raves,
And dire *Charybdis* rolls her thund'ring waves.
All night I drove; and at the dawn of day
Fast by the rocks beheld the desp'rate way:
Just when the sea within her gulphs subsides,
And in the roaring whirlpools rush the tides.
Swift from the float I vaulted with a bound,
The lofty fig-tree seized, and clung around.
So to the beam the Bat tenacious clings,
And pendent round it clasps his leathern wings.
High in the air the tree its boughs display'd,
And o'er the dungeon cast a dreadful shade.
All unsustain'd between the wave and sky,
Beneath my feet the whirling billows fly.
What time the Judge forsakes the noisy bar
To take repast, and stills the wordy war,
Charybdis rumbling from her inmost caves,
The mast refunded on her refluent waves.
Swift from the tree, the floating mass to gain,
Sudden I dropt amidst the flashing main;
Once more undaunted on the ruin rode,
And oar'd with labouring arms along the flood.
Unseen I pass'd by *Scylla's* dire abodes.
So Jove decreed (dread Sire of men and Gods).
Then nine long days I plow'd the calmer seas,
Heav'd by the surge and wafted by the breeze.
Weary and wet th'*Ogygian* shores I gain,
When the tenth sun descended to the main.
There in Calypso's ever-fragrant bow'rs,
Refresh'd I lay, and Joy beguiled the hours. (XII: 464-534).

Appendix C: Accounts of the 1783 Calabrian-Sicilian Earthquake[1]

Although modern readers may associate southern Italy with volcanoes—Vesuvius and Etna, among others—the region also has an extensive history of destructive and deadly earthquakes, centering on the Messina straits, and including both Sicily and Calabria (the southernmost part of mainland Italy, or the "toe" of the boot that Italy resembles). One of the worst of these occurred in a sequence that lasted from 1783 to 1785, bringing with it a death toll of more than 30,000.[2] Frequent and devastating tsunamis accompanied these earthquakes, leading to additional deaths and destruction.

The earthquake about which Lee writes appears to be the first in the sequence that started on 5 February 1783. The largest shock hit that day, around noon, with an approximate measurement of 7 on the Richter scale, with an epicenter on the mainland;[3] another hit shortly after midnight that night with an approximate measurement of 6.5, with an epicenter in the Messina straits; another of the same magnitude hit on the 7th, with an epicenter in Calabria; and

---

[1] Because of the frequent republication of 18th- and 19th-century sources on the earthquake to which I refer in this appendix, I depart from the format of the rest of this book by listing the works I cite at the end of this appendix rather than giving bibliographic information in footnotes. Notes would otherwise have been overburdened. Furthermore, because I have not always had access to the first version of essays to which I refer or which I quote, I have marked the particular version I cite with an asterisk.

[2] Estimates vary; as Jacques et al. note, among contemporary observers, Déodat Gratet de Dolomieu and Sir William Hamilton say the death toll was at least 40,000 (504). Hamilton questions the report given out by the secretary of state's office in Naples that 32,367 died from the earthquake and aftershocks alone (rather than from those events plus the tsunamis), asserting that if one "includ[es] strangers, the number of lives lost must have been considerably greater, 40,000 at least may be allowed [...] without any exaggeration" (171-172). Others, however, including Giovanni Vivenzio, put the toll in the low- to mid-30,000s (Jacques et al. 504). J. Barlow provides a different number given out by the secretary of state's office—33,567—but suggests the number is higher, especially since the one given does not include those who later perished from "want, diseases, anguish, and every species of subsequent distress" (4: 173).

[3] The Richter scale had not been established at this time, but contemporary accounts of the destruction and the shift in the earth have enabled recent geophysicists to approximate the intensity of the shocks.

other strong shocks hit on the 1st and 28th of March of that year. As a result of the first shock, "more than 380 villages[, mostly on the Calabrian mainland,] were damaged, 180 were almost totally ruined and [...] fatalities exceeded 25,000" (Graziani, Maramai, and Tinti 1055). So strong was this shock that "more than 200 lakes formed as a consequence of stream damming" (Graziani, Maramai, and Tinti 1055); "people in fields were [also] thrown down [and] trees swung so hard that the tips of their branches touched the ground[;] many were uprooted [and] others had their trunks broken near the base" (Jacques et al. 504). While the shock that occurred during the following night was not as strong, it was more destructive to Messina and also to Scilla, on the mainland, towards which the Marquis of Lenox is looking when the earthquake occurs that prevents the consummation of his marriage to Emily Fitzallen. This earthquake was particularly devastating because, as Graziani, Maramai, and Tinti explain, it caused "a huge rockfall [...] at Scilla, that fell into the sea generating a disastrous tsunami" (1055) that produced "6-9 m[eter] high waves" (Monaco and Tortorici 170).[1] In fact, however, a tsunami accompanied or preceded the first main shock as well, hitting the eleven miles of the Sicilian coast from Messina to Torre de Faro, the northeasternmost point of Sicily, and the point closest to Scilla.[2]

These earthquakes, tsunamis, and their destruction were widely covered, not only in the weeks and months immediately after the first shock but well into the nineteenth century. One of the first and most influential of these reports was sent to the Royal Society of London by volcano enthusiast Sir William Hamilton, whose proximity to the scene as ambassador to the Kingdom of Naples enabled him to provide a first-hand account of the devastation he witnessed in his visit to the areas hardest hit. His position and the highly respect-

---

[1] As Jacques et al. point out, there is in fact disagreement about the cause of this tsunami; they note that M. Baratta, an early twentieth-century earth scientist, and Dolomieu, the only contemporary earth scientist to view the destruction (and for whom Dolomite is named), "disagree on whether the wave was a mere consequence of the rockslide or a small, earthquake-generated tsunami" (502). Jacques et al. fall on the side of those who believe that the shock itself caused both the rockfall and the tsunami (511).

[2] Graziani, Maramai, and Tinti note reports that the sea was troubled for the four hours before the earthquake (1056). Count Francesco Ippolito's account corroborates this movement (see below, pp. 260-261).

ed venue in which his report was first published—the *Philosophical Transactions of the Royal London Society*—no doubt contributed to his report's being particularly widely reprinted, excerpted, and disseminated.[1] Other ostensibly first-hand accounts appear to have been influential as well, given that the information they provide is repeated in various publications. Two appear in publications that post-date the publication of *The Two Emilys* but may have been published earlier. One of these, "Phenomena of the Great Earthquake of 1783 in Calabria and Sicily, From the Journal of a Traveller," acknowledges its debt to Giovanni Vivenzio, whose 1783 and 1788 works on the earthquakes are highly enough respected to serve even today as sources to geophysicists and geophysical historians studying the event; another essay, "Some Account of the Earthquake in Calabria, in the Year 1783, in a Letter from a Gentleman on his Travels Through Calabria, in 1786" provides so much of the same material that it may have been penned by the same traveler or have shared Vivenzio as a source. The information they provide no doubt appeared in other publications to which Lee may have had access, and because the reports these two articles in particular give quite usefully parallel Lee's description of the event and its aftermath, I provide excerpts from them here.

Lee's narration of the event shares numerous elements with other reports on the earthquake. First, it shares its description of the cosmological precursors to and geophysical effects of the earthquake. Lee's passage reads thus:

> The blue strait, hardly dimpled by a breeze, was half covered with gaudy galleys, and the boats of fishermen; the fires of the lighthouse were reflected in glowing undulations on the waves; heavy black clouds, tinged with a dun red, seemed to seek support on the rocky mountains on Calabria; and the winds, after a wild concussion, subsided at once into a horrible kind of stillness. The rowers, whose laborious and lively exertions animate the sea they people, now made vain, though more vigorous efforts, to take shelter in the harbour. Suddenly the atmosphere became murky and oppressive; the clouds, yet more swoln [sic] and dense, sunk so low, they almost blended with the waters. Not a bird ventured

---

[1] See the works cited at the end of this appendix for its early publication history.

to wing the heavy and unwholesome air; and the exhausted rowers could not catch breath enough to express, by a single cry, the agonizing fear that caused cold dews to burst from every pore. A tremendous sense of impending evil seemed to suspend all vital motion in the crowd late so busy around the Marquis. [...] This intuitive sense of the approaching convulsion was, however, only momentary. A tremendous shock followed. (51-52)

Lee's description to some extent agrees with the information given in "From the Journal of a Traveller," which states,

The morning had been lowering and foggy, and at noon, the sun emitted through the mist a light feeble and pale as moonshine. There was an oppressive sense of languor and exhaustion. At length about noon, and while all nature appeared to pause for the issue, a rattling noise was heard, which seemed to come over from Calabria. It came gradually nearer, and, as it approached, the sea swelled up in higher surges. Thus awfully and slowly did the convulsion roll over from Calabria, heaving earth and sea in its appalling progress; and when it reached the shores of Messina, the harbour-mole,[1] which first encountered the shock, heaved like a billow, and the splendid Pazzalata[2] was in great part laid in ruins. ("Phenomena" 106)

Others highlight the rain that accompanied the earthquake. Sir William Hamilton notes, "I found it a general observation [...] that before a shock of an earthquake, the clouds seemed to be fixed and motionless, and that immediately after a heavy shower of rain, a shock quickly followed" (178).

Count Francesco Ippolito wrote to Sir William Hamilton with a similar description, going, however, into long-term cosmological changes before the earthquake:

this extraordinary catastrophe of our afflicted province was preceded by great and extraordinary frosts in the winter of 1782; by

---

[1] Breakwater.
[2] Several authors use this spelling, although the correct form is "Palazzata." As my note to the text of *The Two Emilys* explains, the Palazzata, according to the Abbé Lazzaro Spallanzani, was a "continued range of superb palaces . . . inhabited by merchants and other wealthy people" extending over a mile in length along the curvature of the Messina harbor (4: 153-154).

an extraordinary drought and insufferable heats in the spring of the same year; and by great, copious, and continued rains, which began in autumn, and continued to the end of January. These rains were accompanied by no thunder or lightning, nor were any winds hardly ever heard in these cities where they are used to blow very fresh during this time; but at the beginning of the earthquake they all seemed to break loose again together, accompanied with hail and rain. For a long time before the earth shook, the sea appeared considerably agitated, so as to frighten the fishermen from venturing upon it, without there being any visible winds to make it so. (vi-vii)

The article taken "From the Journal of a Traveller" offers a slightly different take, in fact contradicting other information in the article, quoted above, which suggests stillness rather than wind: "Besides the electric flashes peculiar to this climate, a dense and heavy fog covered the earth, and driving gales from the south-east or southwest (Scirocco o Libeccio) swept over all Calabria Ultra with increasing violence" ("Phenomena" 98). Another author states simply, "the usual remark of the stillness of the weather did not hold good; for the severest shocks were attended by the most violent showers of rain, and the sky never once cleared up during the whole continuance of this tremendous scene" ("On the Several Earthquakes" 142). As we see from the other passages I have included above, this assertion does not depart from the observations of most others; the main point of contention is when the downpours started.

Another point of contention was the temperature of the water. Lee writes that "the sea, in one moment, burst its bounds; and boiling, as it were, with subterraneous fires, rolled forward, with horrible roarings, a mountainous deluge" (52). Whether the sea was in fact hot is, however, questionable. Sir William Hamilton writes that the water of the second tsunami "was represented to have been boiling hot, and that many people had been scalded by its rising to a great height"[1] (172) and adds that "several fishermen assured me, that during the earthquake of the 5th of February at night,[2] the sand near

---

[1] He probably is referring to an account by the Vicar General, reported by Ippolito, that the water of the second tsunami "was so hot that it scalded several of those who were saved" (iii).

[2] This is actually the second shock, hitting shortly after midnight on February 6.

the sea was hot, and that they saw fire issue from the earth in many parts" (194). The "officer who commanded the Citadel," a structure in the harbor that survived the earthquake, also told Hamilton that "on the fatal 5th of February, and the three following days, the sea, about a quarter of a mile from that fortress, rose and boiled in a most extraordinary manner" (201). He received a similar account from a priest near Torre de Faro, who "at first said the water was hot; but as [Hamilton] was curious to come to the truth of this fact, which would have concluded much, [he] asked [the priest] if he was very sure of it? and being pressed, it came to be no more than the water having been warm as it usually is in summer" (202). An article that abstracts Hamilton's observations sums up Hamilton's views, if not the reports he had been given, by noting that the tsunami that hit Scilla shortly after the second shock "was at first rumour affirmed to have been formed of boiling water, but all who had been involved in and survived it, assured Sir Wm. H. they did not feel any symptom of heat in it; nor did fire issue from any cracks, as was reported" ("Abstract" 97). Graziani, Maramai, and Tinti, however, basing their report on Vivenzio, write that in the first tsunami, "the sea withdrew boiling" (1056).

In addition to these points of comparison between Lee's and others' accounts of the earthquake and tsunamis and their effects, there are also points of comparison between Lee's and others' accounts of remarkable escapes of some residents of Calabria and Sicily and the suffering of others. Lee's description of the Marquis's "hardly [...] escap[ing] the abyss he saw close over the miserable wretches, who, but a moment before, were standing beside him" (52) picks up on accounts of experiences of actual victims. Two cases were particularly widely reported. One is of "the prior of the carmelite monastery at Jerocarne, not far from Soriano," in Calabria. The accounts of a "Gentleman on his travels through Calabria" report that

> the earth shook, according to his account, dreadfully under his feet, moved to and fro like a ship, then burst open in several places near him, with a horrid noise, and then suddenly closed, like a trap laid under him, from which he was constantly and laboriously endeavouring to keep his feet.[...] All at once the earth opened again under his steps, and suddenly closing again, held fast his foot. In vain he repeated his efforts to rescue it, and was now in

the utmost despair from the horror of his situation, when a second shock came to his relief; the earth opened again under his feet, and he happily escaped. ("Some Account of the Earthquake" (1: 118).

Another more skeptical writer "heard this incident from individuals who knew the prior, and had seen the marks left by the crushing pressure on his foot, but [is] inclined to refer much of his marvellous tale to the excitement and terror of the moment, and [asserts] the injury to [the prior's] foot must have been trifling, as it permitted him to proceed homeward" ("Phenomena" 98).

The other widely repeated case is that of three paper makers of Soriano: Vicenzo Greco, Michaele Roviti, and Paolo Felia. One writer describes the situation thus:

> Greco and Felia fled for it, and were so fortunate as to escape the death that threatened them. Roviti, who had a gun with him, and being unwilling to throw it away, could not run so fast; a great chasm opened before his feet, and he was tumbled down into it. Another shock from the bowels of the earth cast him up again with so much force that he was flung into a deep bog. [...] The earth, still in perpetual agitation, threw him hither and thither in the bog; and he struggled a long time to free himself from it: but all in vain. At length his deliverance came in a new convulsive effort of the earth, which tossed him half dead on the brink of a fresh-opened gulph. He thus happily escaped; but never could find the least trace of his hat, or his jacket which he had hung across his shoulders; whereas he found his gun again a week afterwards on the bank of the river Caridi, which had entirely changed its bed. ("Some Account" 119)

A tale of suffering, in this case focusing in part on a survivor, is told by Hester Thrale Piozzi; I include this story here because it is indicative of stories retold in many accounts of the earthquake, and because Piozzi was a friend of Sophia Lee and her sister Harriet, so the Lees would certainly have known it; as with many of the articles I have mentioned thus far, this piece too was frequently republished, both in England and in America. Piozzi had gone to Naples and there met a woman who suffered losses in the earthquake at Messina; Piozzi acts as interlocutor to that woman in the following passage:

"You see that girl there," pointing to a child about seven or eight years old, who stood listening to the harpsichord: "she escaped! I cannot, for my soul, guess how, for we were not together at the time."—"Where were *you*, madam, at the moment of the fatal accident?"—"Who? *me?*" and her eyes lighted up with recollected terror: "I was in the nursery with my maid, employed in taking stains out of some Brussels lace upon a brazier;[1] two babies, neither of them four years old, playing in the room. The eldest boy, dear lad! had just left us, and was in his father's country-house. The day drew *so* dark all on a sudden, and the brazier—Oh, Lord Jesus! I felt the brazier slide from me, and saw it run down the long room on its three legs. The maid screamed, and I shut my eyes and knelt at a chair. We thought all over; but my husband came, and snatching me up, cried, *run, run*.—I know not how nor where, but all amongst falling houses it was, and the people shrieked so, and there was *such* a noise! My poor son! he was fifteen years old; he tried to hold me fast in the crowd. I remember kissing *him*: Dear lad, dear lad! I said. I could speak *just then*: but the throng at the gate! Oh! that gate! Thousands at once! ay, thousands! thousands at once; and my poor old confessor too! I knew him: I threw my arms about his aged neck. *Padre mio!* said I—*Padre mio!* Down he dropt, a great stone struck his shoulder; I saw it coming, and my boy pulled me: he saved my life, dear, dear lad! But the crash of the gate, the screams of the people, the heat—Oh such a heat! I felt no more on't though; I saw no more on't; I waked in bed, this girl by me, and her father giving me cordials. We were on shipboard, they told me, coming to Naples to my brother's house here; and do you think I'll ever go back *there* again? No, no; that's a curst place; I lost my son in it. *Never, never* will I see it more! All my friends try to persuade me, but the sight of it would do my business. If my poor boy were alive indeed! but *he!* ah, poor dear lad! he loved his mother; he held *me* fast—No, no, I'll never see that place again: God has cursed it *now*; I am sure he has." (248-249)

In addition to tales of sufferers on land, there are accounts of sufferers in the water—victims of the tsunamis accompanying the earthquake and its first aftershock especially. In *The Two Emilys*, Lee

---

[1] A receptacle for holding burning charcoal, generally either for heating a room or, if covered with a grill, for cooking.

has Sir Edward witness such a scene looking towards Sicily; other reports focus more particularly on Scilla, which had the most dramatic loss of lives due to the tsunami accompanying the first aftershock. Sir William Hamilton reports that over two thousand people were immediately affected by this tsunami. He explains,

> The Prince of Scilla having remarked, that during the first horrid shock (which happened about noon the 5th of February) part of a rock near Scilla had been detached into the sea, and fearing that the rock of Scilla, on which his castle and town is situated, might also be detached, thought it safer to prepare boats, and retire to a little port or beach surrounded by rocks at the foot of the rock [with many of his subjects]. (203)

That night, of course, a large section of the cliff fell into the sea, preceding a devastating tsunami that, according to Hamilton, drew 2,473 people, including the Prince, into the sea (203).

The account of the same story derived "From the Journal of a Traveller," is particularly fully and graphically articulated, although it provides a much lower death toll and suggests that the Prince went unwillingly to the beach. That author writes,

> When the concussion of the fifth of February frightened them out of their houses, they fled with their cattle and portable property to this low level on the shore; forgetting in their panic how often during former earthquakes the sea had rolled over it like a deluge, and swept away the unfortunate fugitives. And such was their own melancholy fate on the night of the fifth. Twelve hours after the first shock, and soon after midnight, the inhabitants of Scilla, exhausted with the terrors and exertions of the day, had fallen asleep amidst their fishing nets, some on the damp soil, and others in their boats, when the earth rocked, and a huge mass of cliff was torn with dreadful uproar from the contiguous Mount Jaci. The people were roused from their slumber by the loud convulsion; night and darkness increased their dismay, and an universal scream of horror raised their panic to the highest pitch. With beating hearts and fervent prayers for succour, the appalled multitude waited some moments in dread suspense, when suddenly a rising murmur in the sea indicated some terrible commotion in its waters. The awful sound approached, and in an instant the raging element, rising 30 palms above the level of the plain, rolled

foaming over it, and swept away the multitude. Then retreating, it left the plain entirely, but soon rushed back again with greater violence, bringing with it some of the people and animals it had carried away; then rising higher than before, it reached the roofs of the houses, threw men and animals into trees, and upon the roofs, destroyed several buildings, and by thus rapidly retreating and returning several times, brought back many of the inhabitants alive, and carried off others who a moment before had rejoiced in their escape. The water reached the roof of the house in which I lodged at Scilla, and swept away my hostess and her child. She caught hold of a plank and clung to it with one arm, clasping her child of four years old with the other. The returning wave threw them on the beach, where they remained almost senseless until the following morning, when her husband found them struggling in the mud, a considerable distance from his house. The number of people drowned on the beach and in the boats was 1431, according to Vivenzio; and amongst them perished the aged and infirm Prince of Scilla. [... A]fter long persuasion, [...] he was induced to accompany a number of his vassals to the beach. Stepping into a fishing boat, he remained there until midnight, when the wave rolled in, and swept away him and his companions. This terrible convulsion covered the sea with dead, like a field of battle, when the strife is done. Along the shores of Calabria, across to Sicily, and along the coast of that island as far as Catania, the surface was strewed with corpses, and the sea threw up its prey along the beach in heaps, of 10, 20, and 50 bodies.

This author explains that his details come from Vivenzio's descriptions of the event but asserts, "I heard many similar accounts from the inhabitants, some of whom had been thrown into trees and upon house roofs by the mountain wave" ("Phenomena" 104).

The mainland was particularly hard hit by the earthquake and tsunamis; there are conflicting accounts of how widely destroyed Messina was. The tsunamis were very destructive not only to Scilla but to Sicily from Torre de Faro to Messina, both before this shock—in the earliest of the tsunamis—and in this second one. Destruction was particularly felt by the buildings along the shore, most noteworthily the Palazzata. Jacques et al. explain that it was "to the surprise of many [... that] Messina [... was] relatively undamaged" by the first shock (503). Barbano, Azzaro, and Grasso, however, write that "the strong shocks occurring on February 5 and 6 [...] caused extensive collapses and severe damage in Messina, especially to the buildings close to the sea" (814), an account that accords with what one might expect given the tsunami that hit before, during, and/or after the first earthquake, in addition to the one that hit after the second major shock. Referring in part to Sir William Hamilton's report, Graziani, Maramai, and Tinti assert that the result of the tsunami from the first shock was that "sea water got over the quays in the harbour, inundating and destroying them; [in addition,] the Teatro Marittimo and nearby buildings along the shore were violently inundated" (1057). Barbano, Azzaro, and Grasso note, however, that "it is difficult to discriminate the damage scenario due to the February 5 and 6 earthquakes from the cumulative effects of the entire sequence" (814), and indeed, Hamilton only saw the destruction after both these and later earthquakes.

Nonetheless, there seems otherwise to be unanimous agreement with Spallanzani, who claims that the second shock was more destructive to Messina than the first; Monaco and Tortorici, for instance, claim that the tsunami following the second shock "destroyed all the villages placed along the Straits of Messina" (1). There is not, however, uniform agreement that this second shock, in Spallanzani's words, "completed the destruction of the remainder of the fabrics of Messina" (159). He writes,

> it may be asserted without hesitation, that dividing them [the city's buildings] into four parts, two were levelled with the ground; the third half laid in ruins, and the fourth greatly damaged. [...] Among the ruined edifices, the most considerable were the [...] Palazzata, [...] the royal palace; the palace of the senate, [the merchant's exchange,] the church and professional-house of the ex-jesuits; the archbishop's palace, with the basilica of San. [*sic*] Niccolo; the seminar of the clergy; [the court,] the church of the annunciation of the Theatines ... [and] the Carmelites, the priory of the Hierosolymitans, [and various other palaces of nobles and the wealthy]. (160-162).

When he viewed the city, he says,

> Excepting some of the wider and more frequented streets, the rest were all heaps of ruins. [...] Many of the houses were [...] destroyed and levelled with the ground, others [were] half thrown

down, and others [were] still standing, or rather hanging in the air, merely from the support afforded by the ruins around them. Those which had escaped this destruction appeared as if preserved by a miracle, torn and rent as they were. The cathedral was among the number of these fortunate edifices. (153-156)

Hamilton, however, who visited Sicily after the February and March earthquakes and tsunamis, presents a somewhat different view. He had been told that "Messina was no more," but on arriving, he saw a more intact city than Spallanzani's account suggests he would. Hamilton reports,

> All the beautiful front of [...] the Palazzata [...] had been in some parts totally ruined; in others less; and [...] there were cracks in the earth of the quay, a part of which had sunk above a foot below the level of the sea. [...] Many houses are still standing and some little damaged, even in the lower part of Messina; but in the upper and more elevated situations, the earthquakes seem to have had scarcely any effect. [... T]he convent of Santa Barbara, and that called the Noviziato de' Gesuiti, both on an elevated situation, have not a crack in them. (198)
> I found the citadel [at Torre de Faro] had not received any material damage. [...] The Lazaret has some cracks in it, like those on the quay. [...] The port has not received any damage from the earthquakes. (201)

Given these conflicting reports, it is hard to know what to conclude about the extent of the damage in Messina and Torre de Faro; only about 700 people died out of a population of 30,000, no doubt because much of the damage came in the second, third, and fourth shocks, and the populace had moved away from ill constructed buildings.[1] We can be certain, however, of the fascination with the earthquake among Britons (and Americans), given the number of publications on the event, including not only ostensible first-hand reports and news briefs but extending, in at least one case, to a poem, J. H. Wynne, Esq.'s, "The Changes of Nature, Occasioned by Reflections on the Late Earthquake at Messina."[2] And Lee was not

---

[1] Note, however, that according to "On the Several Earthquakes," the total dead in Sicily is "computed at [...] 4,000" (142-143).
[2] The poem appears in *The British Magazine and Review; or, Universal Miscellany*.

the only author recognizing the potential the event offered for functioning symbolically, as a rupture, and for forwarding a novel's plot; so too did Charlotte Smith, who includes it as a seminal episode in her *Montalbert*, from which I include an extract in Appendix B. I discuss it in my introduction as well (xxxix-xl).

I will end this appendix by noting the authors who saw the earthquakes and tsunamis as perhaps a sign of the Last Judgment.[1] In *The Two Emilys*, Lee writes that "columns of the Palazatta, and other surrounding buildings, fell with a crash, as if the universe were annihilated" (52). The article taken "From the Journal of a Traveller" also makes this connection, quoting a survivor as saying, "Suddenly we heard a noise like thunder rolling beneath us, which was immediately followed by such violent heavings of the ground that we were tossed about in every direction; and being unable to maintain a safe footing on the mountain-top, we fell down, clinging to the stems of trees, crying out, and praying in wild agony and fear. [... W]e thought the last day had arrived, and hearkened even for the voice of Him who is to judge mankind" ("Phenomena" 102). The article offering an abstract of Hamilton's report makes the same connection, suggesting that the earthquake should serve as a lesson to us all:

> We are sensible that it is not the fashion of this age to introduce Scripture into any comparison. But what impartial mind does not see a great conformity between these accounts and our Lord's prediction of events that were to precede [...] the general dissolution of this globe? [...] And is not the destruction of the cities of the plains, perhaps by the first earthquake after creation, [...] an exact counterpart of what happened in Calabria? [...] Innumerable are the earthquakes recorded in history, in a general and superficial way. It was reserved for this age to explore their causes, and trace their effects in detail. Let us be wise, and consider these things. ("Abstract" 98)

Although some may have felt it was too late to be thus wise—Christopher Cotter fits this pattern, as we see by his *A Solemn*

---

3 vols. London: Harrison & Co., 1782-1783. Vol. 2 (1783): 217. This publication has numerous brief news accounts of the earthquake as well.

[1] This was not the first natural disaster to evoke such a response; the 1755 Lisbon earthquake received copious coverage in such terms.

Warning to the Inhabitants of Great Britain: or, London to be Destroyed by an Earthquake in Less than Twenty-Nine Days!—Count Ippolito summed up a more hopeful view when he stated, "God grant that the pillars of the earth may be again fastened, and the equilibrium of both natural and moral things restored!" (vii).

Works Cited and Bibliography

"Abstract of Sir William Hamilton's Account of the Late Earthquakes." *The Boston Magazine* (January 1784): 95-98. [Not by Hamilton himself]

Barlow, J., Esq. *The History of England, from the Year 1765, to the Year 1795. Being a Continuation of the Histories of Mr. Hume and Dr. Smollett.* 5 vols. London: Parsons, 1795.

Cotter, Christopher. *A Solemn Warning to the Inhabitants of Great Britain: or London to Be Destroyed by an Earthquake in Less than Twenty-Nine Days! As Revealed in a Remarkable Vision to Mr. Christopher Cotter, of Vauxhall-Place, Lambeth, on Monday Night, April 13, 1795; and Communicated by him to Mr. G. Riebau.* London: n.p., 1795.

Graziani, L., A. Maramai, and S. Tinti, "A Revision of the 1783-1784 Calabria (Southern Italy) Tsunamis," *Natural Hazards and Earth System Sciences* 6 (2006): 1053-1060.

*Hamilton, Sir William. "An Account of the Earthquakes which Happened in Italy, from February to May 1783," *Philosophical Transactions of the Royal Society of London* 73 (1783): 169-208.
  Reprinted in:
    British Magazine and Review; or, Universal Miscellany. 3 vols. London: Harrison, 1782-83. 3: 179-198.
    The New Annual Register, or General Repository of History, Politics, and Literature for the Year 1783. London: Robinson, 1796. 121-142.
  Reprinted in stand-alone form:
    An Account of the Earthquakes in Calabria, Sicily, &c. as Communicated to the Royal Society (Colchester: Fenno, 1783).
  Shortened form:
    "Extracts from an Account of the Earthquakes which hap-

pened in Italy, from February to May 1783." *Annual Register, or, A View of the History, Politics, and Literature for the Year 1783*. London: Dodsley, 1785. 48-58.

*Ippolito, Count Francesco, "Translation of Count Francesco Ippolito's Letter to Sir William Hamilton, Knight of the Bath, F.R.S.; giving an Account of the Earthquake which happened in Calabria, March 28," *Philosophical Transactions of the Royal Society of London* 73 (1783): Appendix, i-vii.

    Reprinted in:

        The Annual Register, or, A View of the History, Politics, and Literature for the Year 1783. London: Dodsley, 1785. 58-62.

Jacques, E., C. Monaco, P. Tapponier, L. Tortorici, and T. Winter, "Faulting and Earthquake Triggering during the 1783 Calabria Seismic Sequence," *Geophysical Journal International* 147.3 (December 2001): 419-516.

Monaco, Carmelo, and Luigi Tortorici, "Active Faulting and Related Tsunami in Eastern Sicily and South-western Calabria." *Bollettino di Geofisica Teorica e Applicate* 48.2 (June 2007): 163-184.

"On the Several Earthquakes That Have Happened in Sicily and Calabria in Antient [sic] and Modern Times." *Selections from the Most Celebrated Literary Journals and Other Periodical Publications*. 2 vols. London: Debrett, 1798. I: 137-144.

"Phenomena of the Great Earthquake of 1783 in Calabria and Sicily, from the Journal of a Traveller." *Blackwood's Magazine* 26 (Dec. 1829): 879-894.

    Reprinted in:

        The Museum of Foreign Literature and Science 16 (Feb. 1830): 97-108.

    Reprinted with a different title:

        "The Great Earthquake of 1783, in Calabria and Sicily, from the Journal of a Traveller." *The Polar Star*. London: Flower, 1830. 393-399.

*Piozzi, Hester Thrale. *Observations and Reflections Made in the Course of a Journey through France, Italy, and Germany*. London: Strahan and Cadell, 1789. 2 vols. Reprint: Ann Arbor: University of Michigan Press, 1967.

    Extracts reprinted as:

        "Extracts from Mrs Piozzi's Observations, &c. in the

Course of a Journey through France, Italy, and Germany, Earthquake at Messina." *The Gentlemen and Ladies Town and Country Magazine* 1.11 (1789): 595-596.

"Affecting Picture of an Earthquake Scene." *The Ladies Magazine* 2 (March 1793): 187-188.

*"Some Account of the Earthquake in Calabria, in the Year 1783, in a Letter from a Gentleman on his Travels Through Calabria, in 1786." *Selections from the Most Celebrated Foreign Literary Journals and Other Periodical Publications*. 2 vols. London: J. Debrett, 1798. 1: 116-137.

Reprinted in:

The Philadelphia Magazine and Review 1.1 (1799): 11-14.

*Spallanzani, Abbé Lazzaro. *Travels in the Two Sicilies, and Some Parts of the Apennines*. 4 vols. London: G. G. and J. Robinson, 1798. 4: 151-174.

Reprinted in:

A General Collection of the Best and Most Interesting Voyages and Travels in All Parts of the World. Edited by John Pinkerton. 17 vols. London: Longman, Hurst, Rees, and Orme, and Cadell and Davies, 1808-14. Vol. 5 (1809): 259-262.

Vivenzio, Giovanni. *Istoria e Teoria dei Tremuoti in Generale ed in Particolare di Quelli della Calabria e di Messina del 1783* (Naples: Stamperia Regale, 1783).

—. *Istoria de' tremuoti avvenuti nella provincia di Calabria ulteriore e nella città di Messina nell'anno 1783* (Naples: Stamperia Regale, 1788).

BIBLIOGRAPHY

Sophia Lee: Biographical Notices and Obituaries

Alliston, April. Introduction. *The Recess* by Sophia Lee. Lexington: University of Kentucky Press, 2000. xxiii-xxxviii.

———. Lee, Sophia Priscilla. *Oxford Dictionary of National Biography*. 61 vols. New York: Oxford University Press, 2004. 33: 121.

Finan, Eileen. "Sophia Lee." *An Encyclopedia of British Women Writers*. Edited by Paul Schlueter and June Schlueter. New York: Garland, 1988. 288-290.

Kunitz, Stanley J. and Howard Haycraft. "Lee, Sophia." *British Authors before 1800*. New York: Wilson, 1952. 316-317.

"The Late Miss Sophia Lee." *Blackwood's Edinburgh Magazine* 15 (1824): 476.

L[ee], E[lizabeth]. "Lee, Sophia." *The Dictionary of National Biography*. Edited by Leslie Stephen and Sidney Lee. London: Smith, 1908-09. 22 vols. 11: 821.

"Lee, Miss Sophia." *Literary Memoirs of Living Authors of Great Britain*. London: Faulder, 1798. 2 vols. I: 360-361.

"Lee, Sophia." *Feminist Companion to Literature in English by Women*. Edited by Virginia Blain, Isobel Grundy, and Patricia Clements. New Haven: Yale University Press, 1990. 643-644.

"Miss Sophia Lee." *The Literary Chronicle* No. 253 (March 1824): 190.

Napier, Elizabeth R. "Harriet Lee; Sophia Lee." *British Novelists 1660-1800*, I. Edited by Martin C. Battestin. *Dictionary of Literary Biography*, BC Research, 1985. 39: 302-306

R[ogers], K[atharine]. "Lee, Sophia." *A Dictionary of British and American Women Writers*. Edited by Janet Todd. Totowa, NJ: Rowman & Allanheld, 1985. 194-195.

Shattuck, Joanne. "Lee, Sophia." *The Oxford Guide to British Women Writers*. New York: Oxford University Press, 1993. 257-258

"Sophia Lee." <http://www2.shu.ac.uk/corvey/cw3/AuthorPage.cfm?Author=SL2>.

Todd, Janet. "Lee, Sophia [... and] Lee, Harriet." *Dictionary of British Women Writers*. London: Routledge, 1989. 406-407.

"W." Biographical Sketch of Miss Lee. *The Monthly Mirror* 4 (1797): 7-11.

Biographical Work on Others Containing Information on Sophia and her Sisters:

Bloom, Edward A. and Lillian D. *The Piozzi Letters: Correspondence of Hester Lynch Piozzi, 1784-1821 (formerly Mrs. Thrale)*. 6 vols. Newark: University of Delaware Press, 1989-2002. Material on the Lees throughout.

Boaden, James. *Memoirs of Mrs. Siddons*. Philadelphia: H.C. Carey & I. Lea, and E. Littell, 1827. Pages specifically on Lee: 102-104.

Grant, Aline. *Ann Radcliffe*. Denver: Swallow, 1951. Pages specifically on Lee: 39-41.

Hett, Francis Paget, ed. *The Memoirs of Susan Sibbald (1783-1812)*. New York: Minton, Balch & Company, 1926. Pages specifically on the Lees: 32-83.

Original publication of *The Two Emilys* and reprints of it alone

Sophia Lee's *The Two Emilys* was originally published as "The Young Lady's Tale. The Two Emilys," which made up the entire second volume (1798) of the five volume *The Canterbury Tales*, which she wrote with her sister, Harriet Lee, and to which Sophia Lee also contributed the introduction, in volume one, and one other story, "The Clergyman's Tale. Pembroke," which appeared in volume three (1799, 195-521). Following is the publication history of the whole of the collection of tales, as well as the reprint history of Sophia Lee's two tales in particular. Given that the story was originally published as a story rather than a novel on its own, I place the title in quotation marks rather than in italics; however, I refer to it only by the second part of the name, "The Two Emilys." Editions published after Sophia Lee's death in 1824 sometimes list her name first, sometimes Harriet's. I have not had the opportunity to view most of these firsthand, so I list them as they appear in bibliographies to which I have had recourse instead.

Lee, Harriet, and Sophia Lee. *The Canterbury Tales*. 5 vols. London: G. G. and J. Robinson, 1797-1805.
    The second edition of volume 1 was published in 1799.
    The third edition of volume 1 was published in 1801.

The fourth edition of volume 1 was published in 1803-04.
The second edition of volume 2 was published in 1799.
The third edition of volume 2 was published in 1803-04.
The second edition of volume 3 was published in 1800.
The third edition of volume 3 was published in 1803-04.
The second edition of volume 4 was published in 1803-04.
The first and second editions of vol 5 were published in 1805.
A probably pirated version was published as:

Lee, Harriet, and Sophia Lee. *The Officer's Tale: and The Clergyman's Tale, or, History of William Cavendish and Henry Pembroke*. Dublin: Colbert, 1799.

Lee, Sophia, and Harriet Lee. *Canterbury Tales*. London: Colburn & Bentley, 1832. 2 vols. "Revised, corrected, and illustrated with a new preface, by Harriet Lee." "The Two Emilys" is in the first volume; "The Clergyman's Tale" is in volume two.

Lee, Sophia, and Harriet Lee. *Canterbury Tales*. Philadelphia: Carey, Lea and Blanchard. 1833. 2 vols. (The two volume "second series" was published in 1834). "Revised, corrected, and illustrated with a new preface, by Harriet Lee."

Lee, Sophia, and Harriet Lee. *Canterbury Tales*. London: Bentley, 1834-1837. 2 vols. (New printings were published in 1837-38, and in 1838-50). Revised, corrected, and illustrated with a new preface, by Harriet Lee." These volumes are volumes twelve and thirteen of the publisher's *Standard Novels* series. "The Two Emilys" is in the first of these; "The Clergyman's Tale" is in the second. In the third printing, quite oddly, volume one was published in 1850; volume two was ostensibly printed in 1838. Some bibliographies identify volume one as containing "The Two Emilys" and volume two "The Clergyman's Tale," but other information suggests that volume two no longer exists or perhaps was never published.

Lee, Harriet. *Canterbury Tales*. London: Bruce, 1842. While only Harriet is listed as author, this volume also contains Sophia's two tales. Bound along with them are three other works, all first published in 1842: Gilmore Simm, "The Yemassee"; "Beauchampe, or, The Kentucky Tragedy"; and R. J. Cleveland's "Voyages, Maritime Adventures, and Commercial Enterprises."

Lee, Harriet, and Sophia Lee. *Canterbury Tales*. New York: Mason, 1857.

3 vols. Volume three contains Sophia's tales. Mason also published separate collections of the two authors' tales; Harriet's makes up two volumes, Sophia's just one. The collection of Sophia's tales is listed below, under the heading of tales by her only.

Lee, Harriet, and Sophia Lee. *Canterbury Tales*. New York: Hurd & Houghton; Boston: Dutton, 1865. 3 vols. The third volume contains Sophia's tales.

Lee, Harriet, and Sophia Lee. *Canterbury Tales*. Boston: Houghton Mifflin, 1886. 2 vols.

Lee, Sophia, and Harriet Lee. *Canterbury Tales*. New York: AMS, 1978. 2 vols. Based on the 1832 edition published by Colburn and Bentley, the edition that is "revised, corrected, and illustrated with a new preface, by Harriet Lee."

Lee, Harriet, and Sophia Lee. *Canterbury Tales*. London: Pandora, 1989. This edition contains selections only; it includes "The Clergyman's Tale" but not "The Two Emilys." This publication includes the preface Harriet included in the edition Colburn and Bentley published in 1832, and that edition may be the source text.

Publication of Sophia Lee's Tales without Harriet's:

Lee, Sophia. *The Two Emily's*. Dublin: J. Moore, 1798.

Lee, Sophia. *The Canterbury Tales of the Late Sophia Lee: Consisting of* The Two Emilys, *and* Pembroke, or, The Clergyman's Tale. London: Longman, Rees, Orme, Brown and Green, 1826. 5th ed. 2 vols. Volume one contains *The Two Emilys*.

Lee, Sophia. *The Two Emilys, a Novel*. New Edition. 2 vols. London, 1827.

Lee, Sophia, and John Neal. *The Canterbury Tales*. London: J. Cunningham, 1842. Bound with Lee's work is Neal's "Logan, the Mingo Chief" and a translation from the German of A.F.E. Langbein's "The Bridegroom's Probation."

Lee, Sophia. *Canterbury Tales*. 1 vol. New York: Mason, 1857.

A translation of "The Two Emilys" and an adaptation of it as a play appeared thus:

von Stein, Charlotte, trans. and Friedrich Schiller. *Die Zwey Emilien, Drama in Vier Aufzügen*. Tübingen: Cotta, 1803; Augsburg:

Bürgeln, 1805. This work was reprinted in a collection of the author's work in New York and Hildesheim by Olms in 1998. This adaptation was translated into Dutch, thus: *De Twee Emilia's, of De Ontwerpen der Wraakzucht: tooneelspiel in 4 bedrijven*. Amsterdam: Mars, 1805.

Editions of Lee's other Works

The Chapter of Accidents, a Comedy in Five Acts. London: Cadell, 1780. The play went through five editions by 1792; it went through six editions by Lee's death and was published once thereafter. It was anthologized five times during Lee's life and once after. It was published in German in five editions.

The Recess; or, A Tale of Other Times. 3 vols. London: Cadell, 1783-85. This novel was republished with corrections into a fifth edition by 1804. It was republished about ten times thereafter, including April Alliston's edition of 2000. It was published as a condensation titled *The Recess, or A Tale of Past Times* in 1800 and 1820 and another titled *The Recess: A Tale of the Days of Queen Elizabeth* in 1840 and 1844. It was also published as an opera, *Elisabetta, Regina d'Inghilterra*, by Giacomo Rossini, in 1822, 1824, 1827, and 1832. It was published in French translations five times from 1786 to 1793, in German in 1788 and 1793, in Spanish in 1795 and in 1819, in Portuguese in 1806, and in Russian in 1794. More information on some of these printings can be found in Alliston's edition (363-364).

The Hermit's Tale. London: Cadell, 1787. This tale was also published in Dublin in 1787.

Almeyda, Queen of Granada. London: Cadell & Davies, 1796. This play was also published in Dublin in 1796.

Life of a Lover. 6 vols. London: G. & J. Robinson, 1804.

The Assignation. Performed at Drury Lane Theatre on 28 July 1807. Never published.

Secondary Material on Sophia Lee's Work

On *The Two Emilys*:

Shaffer, Julie. "Sophia Lee's 'The Two Emilys': When She Was Good,

She Was Very, Very Good ... or Was She?" *Women's Writing* 14.3 (December 2007): 399-418.

On *The Canterbury Tales*:

Guest, Harriet. Introduction to *The Canterbury Tales* by Harriet and Sophia Lee. London: Pandora, 1989. vii-xiii.

On *The Chapter of Accidents*:

Burroughs, Catherine B. "British Women Playwrights and the Staging of Female Sexual Initiation: Sophia Lee's *The Chapter of Accidents* (1780)." *European Romantic Review* 44 (2003): 7-16.

On *The Recess*:

Alliston, April. "*Corinne* and Female Transmission: Rewriting *La Princesse de Clèves* through the English Gothic." In *The Novel's Seductions: Staël's Corinne in Critical Inquiry*. Ed. Karyna Szmurlo. Lewisburg, PA: Bucknell University Press, 1999.
——. Introduction, Notes, and Chronology. *The Recess; or, A Tale of Other Times* by Sophia Lee. Lexington: University Press of Kentucky, 2000. ix-xliv.
——. "Of Haunted Highlands: Mapping a Geography of Gender in the Margins of Europe." *Cultural Interactions in the Romantic Age*. Edited by Gregory Maertz. Albany: State University of New York Press, 1998.
——. "The Values of a Literary Legacy: Retracing the Transmission of Value through Female Lines." *Yale Journal of Criticism* 4.1 (Oct. 1990): 109-127.
——. *Virtue's Faults: Correspondences in Eighteenth-Century British and French Women's Fiction*. Stanford: Stanford University Press, 1996.
Doody, Margaret Anne. "Deserts, Ruins and Troubled Waters: Female Dreams in Fiction and the Development of the Gothic Novel." *Genre* 10.4 (Winter 1977): 529-572.
Foster, James R. "The Abbé Prevost and the English Novel." *PMLA* 42.2 (June 1927): 443-464.

Gordon, Scott Paul. "Quixotic Perception in Sophia Lee's *The Recess*." *Eighteenth-Century Women: Studies in Their Lives, Work, and Culture* 4 (2006): 129-158.

Isaac, Megan Lynn. "Sophia Lee and the Gothic of Female Community." *Studies in the Novel* 28.2 (Summer 1996): 200-218.

Lewis, Jayne Elizabeth. "'Ev'ry Lost Relation': Historical Fictions and Sentimental Incidents in Sophia Lee's *The Recess*." *Eighteenth-Century Fiction* 7.2 (Jan. 1995): 165-184.

—. *Mary Queen of Scots: Romance and Nation*. New York: Routledge, 1998.

Nordius, Janina. "A Tale of Other Places: Sophia Lee's *The Recess* and Colonial Gothic." *Studies in the Novel* 34.2 (Summer 2002): 162-176.

Lobban-Viravong, Heather. "Bastard Heirs: The Dream of Legitimacy in Sophia Lee's *The Recess; or, A Tale of Other Times*." *Prose Studies* 29 (August 2007): 204-219.

Roberts, Bette B. "Sophia Lee's *The Recess* (1785): The Ambivalence of Female Gothicism." *Massachusetts Studies in English* 6.4 (1978): 68-82.

Robertson, Fiona. *Legitimate Histories: Scott, Gothic, and the Authorities of Fiction*. Oxford: Oxford University Press, 1994.

Stevens, Anne H. "Sophia Lee's Illegitimate History." *The Eighteenth-Century Novel* 3 (2003): 263-291.

Varma, Devendra P. Introduction. *The Recess; or, A Tale of Other Times* by Sophia Lee. New York: Arno, 1972. vii-xlviii.

Wright, Angela. "'To Live the Life of Hopeless Recollection': Mourning and Melancholia in Female Gothic, 1780-1800." *Gothic Studies* 6.1 (May 2004): 19-29.

Secondary Works on Masquerade and Cross Dressing

Castle, Terry. "The Culture of Travesty: Sexuality and Masquerade in Eighteenth-Century England." *Sexual Underworlds of the Enlightenment*. Edited by G. S. Rousseau and Roy Porter. Chapel Hill: University of North Carolina Press, 1988. 156-180.

—. *Masquerade and Civilization*. Stanford: Stanford University Press, 1986.

Craft-Fairchild, Catherine A. *Masquerade and Gender: Disguise and*

Female Identity in Eighteenth-Century Fictions by Women. University Park: Pennsylvania State University Press, 1992.

Dekker, Rudolf M. and Lotte C. Van De Pol. *The Tradition of Female Transvestism in Early Modern Europe*. New York: St. Martin's, 1989.

Friedli, Lynn. "'Passing Women': A Study in Gender Boundaries in the Eighteenth Century." *Sexual Underworlds of the Enlightenment*. Edited by G. S. Rousseau and Roy Porter. Chapel Hill: University of North Carolina Press, 1988. 234-260.

Shaffer, Julie. "Cross-Dressing and the Nature of Gender." *Presenting Gender: Changing Sex in Early Modern Europe*. Edited by Chris Mounsey. Lewisburg, PA: Bucknell University Press, 2001. 136-167.

Printed in the United States
150063LV00006B/1/P